Phantoms
of the Plains
Tales of West Texas Ghosts

Docia Schultz Williams

Republic of Texas Press

Library of Congress Cataloging-in-Publication Data

Williams, Docia Schultz.
   Phantoms of the plains : tales of West Texas ghosts / Docia
   Schultz Williams.
      p.   cm.
   Includes bibliographical references and index.
   ISBN 1-55622-397-8 (pbk.)
   1. Ghosts--Texas, West.   I. Title.
   BF1472.U6W553   1995
   133.1'09764'9--dc20   95-24493
                                          CIP

Republic of Texas Press is an imprint of Wordware Publishing, Inc.

Printed in the United States of America

ISBN 1-55622-397-8
10 9 8 7 6 5 4 3 2
9509

All inquiries for volume purchases of this book should be addressed to
Wordware Publishing, Inc., at 1506 Capital Avenue, Plano, Texas 75074.
Telephone inquiries may be made by calling:
(972) 423-0090

Contents

Chapter 4
Ghosts of the Great Big Bend

Chapter 5
Mysterious Ghost Lights

Chapter 6
Proprietary Phantoms in Public Places

Chapter 9
Strange Unexplained Things

Chapter 10
Four-Legged Phantoms

Chapter 11
Legends that Linger

Acknowledgements

Many people were extremely cooperative in sharing their own personal stories, or in giving me leads to good stories in their communities. Numerous newspaper editors and writers, educators, folklorists, librarians, and museum personnel supplied me with material. West Texas covers a much larger area than many states. It's also an area populated with a plethora of interesting, sometimes elusive spirits that have steadfastly refused to vacate the mesas, plains, and communities that they used to call "home." I could not have found them without a lot of help.

I especially want to thank the following individuals who were extremely helpful as they went the extra mile to assist me in the painstaking task of gathering material:

Dr. John O. West, Department of English, University of Texas, El Paso, who sent me some great stories from his personal files; Dr. Kenneth Davis, retired Professor of English, Texas Tech, who shared some great folklore stories with me; Mr. Ira Blanton, Department of English, Sul Ross University, for his stories from that part of the state; Mr. Quentin McGown, Director of Alumni, Texas Wesleyan University, Fort Worth. Terry Smith, of El Dorado Productions, Fort Worth, was very helpful in supplying information for several stories. Thanks to Mr. Tom Rountree, of Big Spring, for permitting me to use some of the writings of his late wife, Clarice.

Many librarians were extremely helpful in compiling and sending information to me. I wish to thank Anne Bell Pilgrim and Anne Holland, *Abilene Reporter News*; Evelyn Flynn, Fort Concho Museum, San Angelo; Gina Garza, *Big Spring Herald*; Wayne Daniel and Marta Estrada, Southwest Collection, El Paso Public Library; Virdie H. Egger, Hi-Plains Genealogical Society, Plainview; Barbara Hamby, Val Verde County Library, Del Rio; Harry Max Hill, Assistant Manager, Genealogy and Local History, Fort Worth Public Library; Catherine Marchak, reference librarian, City of Abilene; Gene Mathews, Kemp Public Library, Wichita Falls; Evelyn White, Tom Green County

vii

Library System, San Angelo; Fredonia Paschall, Southwest Collection, Texas Tech University, Lubbock; Vicki Stone, Fort Stockton Public Library; Cindy Hawkins, *Amarillo Globe News*; Anne Mead, Llano County Library System; and Kay Irby, Sales Director for the Abilene Convention and Visitors Bureau. I would also like to thank Helen Mathieson of Paint Rock and Pat Towler of Balmorhea for the material they sent me. Thanks also to Marsha Brown, a Fort Worth writer who supplied good stories and good leads and to Jim Lane of Fort Worth who took the time to take us to visit "Gussie's House."

A mere thank-you is not enough to Sam and Nancy Nesmith, who as historians, psychics, and good friends have shared their stories and insight into the realms of the supernatural with me.

To Polly Price, Polna Productions, San Antonio, producer of *Book Fare*, Paragon Cable Channel 19, who has been a constant source of encouragement and who has been so helpful in publicizing all of my works, thank you, Polly!

I appreciate the constant encouragement of Mary Elizabeth Sue Goldman, managing editor of Republic of Texas Press, and Joe Morse, for his assistance in promoting my work.

The assistance of many other individuals, whom I have named under *Sources*, who sent me material or granted personal interviews, is most gratefully acknowledged. Without them, I could not have completed this book.

Lastly, and mostly, to my husband, Roy D. Williams, who spent so much time with me, driving more than 3,000 miles over West Texas, taking photographs and conducting interviews, and spending countless hours at the computer preparing the final manuscript for publication, I am forever grateful!

Introduction

When I was a young woman in college, over forty years ago, my parents and I went on a summer vacation to Colorado. At that time the Jaycees in Colorado Springs presented a special program and barbecue for tourists at the Garden of the Gods which we attended. The grand finale of the Western musical program was the presentation of a film projected across the red rock walls depicting ghostly riders as the musicians played the haunting strains of "Ghost Riders in the Sky." I still love that old tune, now a Western classic, and I still get little shivers down my spine when I think of all the ghostly riders that still patrol the mountains, valleys, and plains of the Old West.

West Texas, with its rich heritage of pioneer settlers, cowboys, bands of Indians, soldiers who served at the cavalry posts, and Spanish speaking explorers who roamed the high plains, has its ghost stories. They are fascinating! Like the "Ghost Riders in the Sky," they are the haunting reminders of the glorious days when the West was won at the sacrifice of many lives. Spirits not quite done with what they set out to do keep returning, and I hope you'll agree their stories make good reading.

Prologue

There is so much of life, and death, and life after death, that we do not understand, nor can we pretend to comprehend. The Christian faith has taught us to believe in immortality, and that there is more, far more, after we leave our mortal shells on earth. Those who embrace this faith do not fear death because with it comes relief from trials and tribulations, earthly cares and worries, and physical infirmities and suffering.

But there are some souls that, for some reason known only to them, cannot lie down to the pleasant dreams of eternal peace. Some task was left undone, some gripping, all-consuming purpose was not realized, and so they still are with us in spirit form. The skeptics, the scientists, often say there absolutely are no such things as ghosts, or spirits. I am not writing to argue or disagree with them or to try and convince them there are such entities as ghosts. Frankly, I am fascinated with the subject. Having interviewed scores of people over the past five or six years in the course of writing three books, I believe that many people cannot all be wrong.

Only a very few people are actually gifted with psychic abilities. Some people consider this a gift. Others are not so sure! But whatever the definition, some few have been given the power to see, for a fleeting moment, an event that occurred a long time ago. They see figures dressed in garments from a long-past era; they suddenly find themselves standing in a room or setting very different from where they actually are. They become silent witnesses to traumatic scenes such as battles, Indian massacres, murders, fires, and storms. They become helpless bystanders at the re-enactments of events long past, and their inability to step in and stop the turn of events as they unfold before them is extremely frustrating to them.

Several such experiences have been a part of my friend Sam Nesmith's life. He explains that so much energy is expended at certain events that it must "imprint" on its surroundings, much as an image can be transferred onto film. When the time is right and the psyche is sufficiently sensitive, the event replays itself. Sam is extremely psychic, and that is why he has been witness to many events that happened a long time ago. Several stories in this book are experiences he has shared with me, since he spent his boyhood in West Texas.

I recently read an interesting article by William Deerfield that appeared in the November 1994 issue of *Guidepost Magazine*. Two different individuals had had very similar near-death experiences. Both men reported having been transported to an area strewn with litter, garbage and debris, derelict houses, and all sorts of cast-off and worn-out items left in a cluttered and unkempt field. They seemed to be surrounded by the very essence of ugliness. Then suddenly, they came out of this unsightly, unkempt area into a meadow green with grass and wildflowers. Their view took them to a distant hillside. There was a stream transversed by a little white bridge, and leading away from the crossing was a gently sloping hillside bathed in a glorious white light. In the midst of the light stood a figure, a man clothed in a robe of dazzling white, girded with a golden cord. His arms were spread wide in welcome and his face was wreathed in smiles. His hair and beard were dark, and his eyes shone with the essence of goodness and com-passion. His entire countenance radiated "perfect love."

Both men related that, just as they prepared to cross the glistening white bridge spanning the crystal waters of the stream, the figure bathed in the radiant light bade them to turn around and return in the direction from which they had come. Both of them believed the figure they had seen was Christ, and the grassy slopes on which He stood were the gateways to Heaven. Both reported they would never fear death because their brief glimpse into the glowing light of eternity had been so beautiful, filled with perfect peace and tranquility.

The ghosts, souls that you will read about in this book, are still seeking that place of light. Many are spirits that we can only hope will one day cease their wanderings and find their way into the hereafter of peace, love, and rest. They are, for a while at least, still earth-bound for various and sundry reasons which you will read about. Some are read-ily accepted by those who have felt their presence. Some are frightening and therefore unwelcome to their hosts. All are fascinating to read about and ponder, because they are a part of that "sweet mystery of life" that we all are witness to as we pass through the mortal portion of our lives.

Now, please don't call me to help you get rid of an unwelcome spirit! I am not a ghostbuster. However, I might be able to explain to you why they may be there, and possibly help you diagnose your situation if you think you are experiencing a haunting. There are many common denominators that indicate a place is haunted. There are unseen but frequently heard footsteps on stairways and in hallways, cold spots that suddenly turn warm rooms into frigid iceboxes, voices that are heard within walls and in closets, music that plays from unseen pianos and music boxes or radios, sudden gusts of wind blowing through a house on a still and windless day, doors and windows that are prone to opening and shutting by themselves, and lights that go on and off at will. All these happenings are very common in the realm of the supernatural. When ghosts become a part of a household they are seldom harmful, except in extreme situations. Most of them are prone to be both protective and benevolent. They DO want to be noticed!

In the extreme cases, when a spirit appears to be demonic or evil or becomes a source of "dark, negative energy," in the language of students of the paranormal, then a priest or clergyman may be called to perform an exorcism. This is done only in very rare cases, as most ministers do not care to become involved in such rituals. Some priests, however, will consent to "blessing" a house, which often puts the spirits to rest.

In this, my third in a series of books about Texas' ghostly citizens, I take you to far West Texas, where not only the deer and the antelope roam, but where the ghosts of former residents also have found good reason to remain "home on the range," haunting the mystical, magical land of the high mesas and rolling plains.

Docia Schultz Williams

Dedication

This book is dedicated to the memory of my beloved parents, John and Statira Schultz, whose great love for West Texas and interest in those things we refer to as "spirits" have always been a source of inspiration to me.

Phantoms of the Plains

Over broad and rolling prairies
'Cross the dry and dusty plains
Souls of men from days gone by
In phantom state remain.
On nights so still and lonely,
In the moon glow's yellow light,
Their earthbound spirits wander
In the stillness of the night.
On steep and rocky hillsides,
And on dusty plains they roam,
Those spirits that refuse to leave
The place they once called home.

Docia Williams

CHAPTER 1

GHOSTS AT THE OLD CAVALRY POSTS

It's a Mystery

I often wonder why there are so many stories connected with hauntings at the West Texas forts that were built to protect the early settlers from Indian depredations!

Life was terribly hard in those far-flung outposts, designed to protect the settlers as they steadily moved westward. The soldiers stationed at them often had to live in crude tent shelters while they struggled to build more permanent facilities. All the while they were doing this, they also rode patrols, fought Indians, planted gardens, and traveled long distances for supplies.

They suffered miserable weather conditions, too. The West Texas summers were blistering hot. Dry winds brought dust storms and dried up the streams. The gardens they planted died from lack of water. And then, when the winters came, the days were freezing cold. Often there was no wood for fires. Blizzards blew down from the Rocky Mountains, covering the rustic little forts with blankets of snow. Poor diets resulted in cases of scurvy, and many soldiers suffered from malnutrition. Many of the soldiers died from fighting Indians, from disease, from snakebites and numerous accidents. For the most part, these men were young, and they should have enjoyed many more good years. The army wives that followed their husbands suffered right along with the men. And many of them also died in childbirth or of disease and hardship.

According to reliable sources quoted in the individual stories, there are numerous accounts of ghosts and hauntings connected with the old West Texas forts. With such miserable surroundings and living conditions, it's a mystery to me why anybody, even in spirit form, would want to continue hanging around those lonely, desolate ruins out on the West Texas plains.

The Army Left, But the Spirits Remain

Fort Clark, near the town of Brackettville on Highway 90, west of Uvalde, was founded as a cavalry post in 1852. It had a long and colorful history, and the sturdy limestone buildings that formed the main section of the installation are now a part of the Fort Clark Springs Resort, a private retirement and recreation community.

Back in its beginnings, like so many other West Texas forts, this one was established here because of the plentiful water supply. There were natural springs here, called "Las Moras" for the mulberry trees that grew around it, and it was a favorite campground of the Comanches and the Mescalero and Lipan Apache tribes. It was an ideal place to locate a fort, as a plentiful supply of building stone was available, and there were also plenty of pecan and oak trees in the area.

Major Joseph H. LaMotte was in charge of establishing the fort. Companies C and E first encamped near the springs, and later the complete garrison was moved up the hill a short distance from the springs. By 1853 the soldiers' quarters were completed, and in 1854 three grass-covered officers' quarters were added. Finally, a stone hospital and a two-story storehouse were erected in 1855.

At first, all the supplies had to be brought in by wagon train from Corpus Christi, a thirty-day trip! Later on, supplies were brought in to Indianola (a seaport that is no longer on the Gulf Coast) and from there, transported by wagon to the fort by way of San Antonio, still about a thirty-day journey.

According to a pamphlet prepared by the Fort Clark Historical Society (copyright, 1985) of Kinney County, the Federal soldiers departed from the fort on March 19, 1862. The Second Texas Mounted Rifles moved in and stayed there until August of 1862. Then the fort served as a supply depot and a hospital for Confederate troops as well as civilians who lived in the surrounding area.

Although the post headquarters had been built in 1857, prior to the Civil War, most of the area referred to today as the Historic District was built between 1870 and 1875 after the Federal army returned. By 1874 the installation had quarters for 200 men and nine officer's dwellings. All of these were of stone. A second storehouse known as the "old commissary" and a granary capable of storing 3,000 bushels of grain was built in 1882. During the major construction period (1874) 104 civilian stone masons were employed! Most of the stone was quarried there on the fort property, but some was brought in by wagon from other locales. This was because the quarry at the fort did not provide the best quality of building stone.

Up until about 1881, when the last Indian depredations ceased, the fort was a very busy place. Lt. John L. Bullis, who later became a famous general, served as commander for the famous Seminole-Negro Indian Scouts who were stationed there. Later on, Colonel Ranald S.

Mackenzie's raiders were stationed at the fort. Their mission was to lead raids into Mexico punishing renegade Indians. During this era, Comanches came down from the north on their famous "Comanche moonlight" raids, raiding, killing, raping, taking horses and cattle, then escaping across the Rio Grande into Mexico where they continued to kill and plunder. The Lipan Apaches and Kickapoos from Mexico came over the border on raids, killing and stealing and causing general havoc. Outlaws fled from one side of the border to the other, and the pioneer settlers lived in a state of upheaval and general terror. Many abandoned their homes. On May 17, 1873, Mackenzie's men and Bullis' Seminole-Negro scouts led troops of the 4th U.S. Cavalry into Mexico on a punitive expedition against the Lipans. Finally, in 1878 a large peacetime army crossed the border and effectively stopped the Mexican-Indian hostilities forever.

During its heyday, the old fort was home to many famous military personalities, including General Wesley Merritt, Commander of the Philippine Expedition; General William R. Shafter, Commander of the Cuba Expedition; General George C. Marshall, U.S. Chief of Staff during World War II; General Jonathan M. Wainwright, hero of Bataan and Corregidor; and General George S. Patton Jr., famous for his daring exploits in North Africa, Sicily, and from France into Germany during World War II.

The last mounted Cavalry Division, the Second Cavalry, trained at Fort Clark until its 12,000 troops were deployed in February of 1944. During the war, there was also a German prisoner of war subcamp located on the 4,000-acre reservation.

Unlike many of the West Texas forts, whose careers were short-lived, Fort Clark lasted until June of 1944. In 1946 the property was sold to Brown and Root Company for salvage. Later it was used as a guest ranch. Finally, in 1971 it was purchased by a private corporation and developed into a recreational community. A large golf course, tree-shaded picnic areas, an amphitheater in the old rock quarry, and a beautiful swimming pool fed by the springs make the place a peaceful and idyllic spot for retirement. And, some of the old residents must have been reluctant to let go.

Many of the quarters along old Colony Row are large two-story two-family buildings, which were used by the officers stationed at the fort. My friend Barbara Niemann owns one of these, at Number 11. She moved back to San Antonio recently, and the house is presently being offered for sale. Much work was done to restore the old set of quarters, and it is a lovely and very spacious two-story duplex with a beautiful garden. During the time Barbara lived there, she experienced the presence of a benevolent, friendly spirit, whom she believes was a man, probably an old soldier who had once lived in the house. Perhaps he was an orderly, assigned to some officer's family, as was often the custom in early days. Barbara often awakened in the wee hours of the mornings to the strong aroma of fresh coffee brewing and bacon frying! The Niemanns did not drink coffee and made it only when they had houseguests. Especially around the kitchen area, Barbara felt someone was there many times. Once she heard a deep sigh, and of course, no one was there but her! For some reason, she refers to the spirit as "John," but really can't say why she chose that name for him. She also told me that often, Bucky, her big Doberman, would suddenly prick up his ears and look alertly around the room as if he had seen someone go by, but he never seemed disturbed or upset.

Barbara introduced me to Georgia and Pete Cook, who live a couple of doors down Colony Row at number 8-9. This is a very large one-story set of quarters. They quite freely admit to having a resident spirit, or maybe more than one. It is still quite active at times.

Pete Cook said the reason he decided to buy the house when it came up for sale was because it had once been in his family, when an aunt by marriage, Ollabelle Dahlstrom, had owned it. The house changed hands a couple of times, belonging first to Tully Pratt and then A.J. Foyt, the race car driver. When Foyt decided to sell, Pete was delighted, although Georgia did not at first share his enthusiasm. She was quite happy in her lovely home in Hunt, Texas, up in the Hill Country near Kerrville.

Georgia believes their live-in spirit might be Ollabelle Dahlstrom, rather than an early army wife who might have once lived there. Several times she has had cause to believe it's Ollabelle, but whether it is she, or another, Georgia definitely thinks the ghost is of the female gender.

Soon after the Cooks moved into the quarters, while Georgia was lying on the floor shoving boxes under a high four-poster tester bed in the guest room, someone grabbed her leg and tugged it hard. Thinking it was Pete or one of the relatives who was assisting them in getting settled, she said, "Oh stop that!" only to discover no one had been in the room with her when it happened.

Georgia told me that in the 1960s, Pete's cousin, Nina Dahlstrom, and several ladies in the family were there at the house spending the weekend. This must have been during the time Ollabelle owned the house. Well, Nina and her mother occupied the master bedroom. At the time, Nina's son Graham was just a baby, less than a year old. The infant was sleeping in a bassinet near the fireplace. During the night, Nina was awakened by a tug on her arm. Then she heard a baby crying. She got up to check on her little son and found that the baby was sound asleep. She went back to bed. Then, a little later on she was awakened by the sounds of a woman crying. She heard her say, "Help me! Help me! Help my baby!" and it was then she saw the apparition of a young woman with her arms outstretched to her, as if imploring her to come and help her. While the woman's appearance was rather misty, it was definitely a woman's figure. Of course, she woke up her mother when this very upsetting event took place.

The only explanation they had for this strange encounter with the spirit world was that perhaps a former resident of the house, an army wife who once lived there, might have had a very sick infant who needed help. Maybe her baby had died there before she could get help, and the coming of a small infant in the person of Nina's little son, Graham, had triggered the appearance.

Georgia said the Dahlstroms also told them of a time in the late 1960s when they entertained several couples at a weekend house party. One young couple from Houston occupied the family room, sleeping on couches that made into twin beds. Because it was a very cold night, they moved their beds up close to the fireplace. In the middle of the night, the young man's bed began to shake violently. In fact, it actually raised up off the floor, going up and down, shaking all the while. At first he thought his wife might be playing a joke on him, but then he glanced over and found she was asleep in her own bed. She was expecting a baby, and the young husband was so terrified that whatever it was would affect their unborn child, he insisted they leave early the next morning. Georgia said the couple absolutely refused to ever come back for another visit!

Since the Cooks moved in, they've had a lot of things happen that defy explanation. Pictures move about, and Georgia's jewelry often moves around, is missing a few days, and then appears on the dresser or back in the jewelry box where it is kept.

One of the strangest things that happened, soon after they moved in, concerned a bottle of brandy! Since Ollabelle liked to party, they believe this was in keeping with her character. It seems they had a couple of bottles of brandy on the bar, but neither had been opened. Yet, one day they found a brandy snifter on the bar with about a jigger of brandy left in the glass. There were no unsealed bottles of brandy anywhere in the house. Who poured the brandy, and from what? And plainly seen on the rim of the glass were little dainty lip prints, doll-sized prints as Pete described them. The next night someone, or something, again set out a brandy snifter on the bar and set the two unopened bottles of brandy on the bar beside it, removing them from the sideboard behind the bar. They have yet to find any plausible explanation.

Often Georgia and Pete smell bacon cooking, usually in the wee hours of the morning, when it is still dark. Just recently, Georgia woke up after Pete had already left for the day. When she came out to the kitchen to get some coffee, she saw some sausage patties that had been in the refrigerator had been cooked. Several of them were on a plate by the stove, and there was grease in the skillet where they had been prepared. Although she found it unusual, she figured Pete had been hungry, found the sausages in the refrigerator, and decided to cook them for breakfast. She went on and ate some of the cooked meat. When Pete came home later she told him she had eaten the sausage patties and they surely were delicious. He said, "But I didn't cook any sausage." In fact, Pete had seen the sausage there when he got up and thought how strange it was that Georgia had gotten up in the night and cooked sausage! To this day the Cooks can't figure out how that meat got cooked, unless, of course, it was their ghost!

The Cooks took me over to visit with Joy and Russell Williams, who live in the other side of Barbara Niemann's quarters, at number 10 Colony Row. The former Houston residents told us that they have often been awakened in the wee hours of the morning by the very strong smell of coffee brewing and bacon and eggs cooking. Usually this is around 4 a.m. (Just about the time the old army folks would have been getting up for the day!) Joy told me that there's a metal candleholder that hangs as a decorative fixture on the kitchen wall. Sometimes something pulls it off the wall and throws it on the floor. Most of the time the frame is bent and must be straightened out. Yet, the nail on which it hangs has always remained in place on the wall, indicating the piece was removed, and did not just fall off the wall.

Joy told me that soon after they purchased their retirement home, she spent some time alone in the house while Russell was winding up their affairs in Houston. One night she was awakened by their little dog, who sleeps on their bed. It was very agitated, growling and barking like something was there in the room with them. She reached over to nudge Russell and then realized he was not there. She said the dog has been visibly disturbed by something in the room several times.

On a recent visit to see the Cooks, we also walked over to Barbara Niemann's home, which is empty. The Cooks have the key in order to show it to prospective buyers for Barbara. As soon as we headed toward the kitchen at the rear of the quarters, we were assailed by the very strong aroma of bacon cooking! It absolutely permeated the room! The smell lasted only a few moments and then was not at all evident by the time we left. A later check with the Williams' next door revealed they hadn't cooked any bacon in quite some time, but they said it's just a "happening" that goes on all the time in both their quarters and in Barbara's old home.

The Cooks said a lot of other people along Colony Row have similar stories to tell. We just didn't have time to talk to all of them. I remarked to Georgia and Pete that the fort is such a tranquil retirement spot today that even the ghosts of the past hesitate to leave such a delightful place!

Of Course There are Phantoms at Fort Phantom Hill!

With a name like Fort Phantom Hill, you'd just naturally assume a ghost would figure in the story, wouldn't you? The old fort was established in 1851 as a part of the network of U.S. military posts stretching from the Red River to the Rio Grande. They were designed to protect wagon trains and settlers from depredations of the still-hostile Comanche and Apache tribes that roamed the canyons, caprock country, and plains of far West Texas.

The fort lasted only a few years. It was such a desolate, lonely place the army decided to abandon it in 1854. The troops had scarcely ridden out of the area before the roofs of all the fort's buildings were set afire, and the once bustling army post was quickly reduced to ashes. Only the stone walls of a few sturdy buildings and some of the tall chimneys survived the flames. Some people say that Indians slipped in and set the wooden shingles afire to make sure the army would not return. Others said the last commander of the fort ordered the roofs be put to the torch to assure no other soldiers would have to endure the loneliness of that God-forsaken area. Still another story credits an officer's wife for setting the fires, to "make a statement" about how she had hated being stationed there!

For whatever reason, the old fort, located about fourteen miles from present-day Abilene, did not last long. It was first referred to as "the Post of the Clear Fork of the Brazos." (There was nothing very clear about that part of the Brazos; the water was often brackish and muddy and not fit to drink at all.)

One story goes that one moonlit night a party of officers and men were encamped a short distance from the newly built station when one of the group spied a figure in white standing on the high hill overlooking their camp. It was probably an Indian wrapped in a white or light colored blanket. The soldier shouted, "A ghost! I see a ghost!" Another soldier said, "It's a phantom on the hill!" That's at least one version of how the place became known as Fort Phantom Hill.

Some people believed the fort was haunted by Indians because its location was on, or near, sacred Indian burial grounds.

Another story claims that in the early days of the frontier an innocent man was wrongfully hanged for horse theft near the hill. Before his execution the man vowed he would get revenge. Within a year everyone involved in the man's hanging died mysteriously.

According to former caretakers of the property, people living in those parts used to say there were ghosts in the area of the old fort ruins. A female apparition with long white hair supposedly walks the hill in the moonlight. And I heard a firsthand accounting of one episode concerning other-worldly inhabitants of the fort from a good friend of mine who used to live in Abilene who often visited the old fort in search of artifacts.

From day one, the fort was evidently a miserable station. The men had to build their quarters from stone and wood which had to be transported from some distance. The nearest rock quarry was two miles away, and the nearest stand of timber was about eight miles distant. Suitable drinking water had to be brought in by wagon from a distance of some four miles, and the fuel for heating the barracks necessitated an eight-mile haul. While the men were building the fort, they had to spend an entire winter sleeping in tents, since the "grand opening" of the fort took place in November!

What few supplies they had came in by wagon trains from Austin, and there was never enough of anything. Not even the little vegetable garden the men planted in 1852 could survive. There was no rainfall to speak of, and the tender plants soon withered and died beneath the scorching West Texas sun. The lack of fresh vegetables in their diet made scurvy a real threat to the health of the soldiers. At least one of them died of the malady. Finally, it got so bad that pickles packed in brine were added to the soldiers' rations to help prevent scurvy from wiping them out.

After the fort closed down in 1854 it stood vacant for a time. Then in 1858 the remains of the fort became a way station for the Southern Overland Mail line. At that time there were the ruins of forty or fifty buildings still in evidence. The powder magazine, which had been constructed of stone, had escaped the fires, and it had been taken over as the company store. The stables also were still usable.

A small community built up around the way station, and by 1880 around 500 people lived in the area. Most of them eked out a meager livelihood buying and selling buffalo hides. When the buffalo herds died out, so did the little settlement. There is a small cemetery just up the road from the fort ruins where many of the early settlers are buried.

My friend now lives in San Antonio, but as a boy, Sam Nesmith, a very psychic individual, grew up in Abilene, which isn't far from the fort. When he was in school, he used to go out to the site of the old fort and poke around the ruins looking for artifacts. Sometimes he went out alone, and sometimes several boys went out together. On the particular day he told me about, he had gone alone after school. He was about sixteen years old at the time, he recalls, since he was old enough to drive out to the fort. Sam has always been fascinated with military history (he is one of San Antonio's leading authorities on military history), and he liked to visit Fort Phantom Hill and think about what life must have been like when there was a lot of military activity there.

Ruins at Fort Phantom Hill

That particular afternoon Sam had been poking around the ruins of what had once been officers' quarters. Only a few walls and chimneys remained. It was about 5 p.m. and he knew he didn't have much daylight left. He stepped over what had once been the threshold of an officer's house, and suddenly he said the building started to "surround" him. He both saw and felt the building becoming what it had once been...the walls took shape, then there was once more a ceiling, windows, and doors. In the parlor he stood in he saw two men dressed in old-style officer's uniforms. He could just make out their figures in the fast fading twilight. The soldiers had been engaged in some sort of spirited conversation and stopped and looked long and hard at Sam when he entered the room. He had the distinct feeling that they had been planning something, maybe even something that was not quite legal, and heartily resented the interruption. He recalled one of the men was tall and thin. The other man, who had red hair, was short, only about five feet six inches tall, and Sam had the feeling his name might have been Philip. He had the most intense eyes Sam had ever seen, and they glowed like bright coals in the darkening room. He said both men looked at him as if they would like to kill him, and frightened, he began to back out of the room. Then, as suddenly as the apparitions had appeared, they were gone. He was once again standing in the pile of rubble and stone, with only a gaunt chimney remaining to show where the parlor had been.

Sam went home. Fast! He didn't mention his strange experience to his mother, since she did not quite understand the few previous psychic glimpses that her son had related to her. No one else in the family had the gift, and Sam was afraid she might laugh at him. He tried to put the memory of those burning, hate-filled eyes out of his mind as he did his homework and ate his supper.

Around seven or eight o'clock Sam began to feel very ill. He was violently nauseated. By midnight he had a raging fever up to 104 degrees. He had to be rushed to the hospital where he remained for about forty-eight hours, a very sick young man. Had medical care not been close at hand, he might have died. Yet, the physicians who examined and treated him could find absolutely no cause for his illness, other than it might have been an "unusual virus." They were otherwise unable to diagnose his problem. Sam says he has always felt that his mysterious visit into the "twilight zone" triggered his illness and was meant by the soldier-spirits as a warning sign that he was not welcome in their domain.

If you ask Sam Nesmith if he thinks Fort Phantom Hill is haunted, you will get a resounding, "Yes!"

In an article titled *Moonlight Becomes You*, by Linda Honea, that ran in the *Abilenean Magazine* (Vol. 4, No. 2, Summer of 1974) the writer stated the fort ruins, located on private property, consist of only three buildings. They are the store commissary, the guardhouse, and the old powder magazine. There are still twelve or so old chimneys left standing. Although it is located on private property, the remains of the fort are still open daily for visitors. The day of our visit there were lots of wildflowers, prickly pear in bloom, and mockingbirds singing. It was a place of peace and tranquility.

Although it is a pretty place by day, I don't think I would particularly want to visit Fort Phantom Hill at night. It would be a pretty eerie sight with the skeletal remains of the old chimneys silhouetted against the moonlit skies. And if a coyote were to howl, breaking the silence of the night with a mournful sound....

After all, what better place for a haunting to happen than at a place called Fort Phantom Hill?

Ghosts Still Occupy Fort Concho

At the confluence of the three Concho rivers, the U.S. Army established Fort Concho in 1867. The frontier post was on the southwest outskirts of what is today the city of San Angelo. Skilled German craftsmen from the small community of Fredericksburg came to construct the main buildings of stone, with their beams and rafters hewn of native pecan wood. Because the flat land would have prevented Indian raiding parties from coming in without detection, Fort Concho was never surrounded by walls.

At first, the fort consisted of just a cluster of tents. The troops, mostly black soldiers serving under white officers, were sent there to protect the stagecoaches and wagon trains from Indian raiders and outlaws. They also escorted the U.S. mail carriers, explored and mapped new territory, and built roads and telegraph lines. Many famous infantry and cavalry officers commanded the fort between 1867 and 1889. These included Colonel Ranald S. Mackenzie, Colonel William R. Shaftner, and Colonel Benjamin H. Grierson.

As the frontier moved farther west, the fort finally became obsolete. The soldiers were needed to protect settlers in New Mexico and Arizona as the frontier expanded. The colors were struck and the last company of the 16th Infantry moved out of the fort on June 20, 1889. The regimental band played "The Girl I Left Behind Me" in the sentimental farewell ceremonies.

A number of the former army installation's buildings have been restored. And some of them are reputed to be haunted!

Evelyn Flynn, librarian at the Fort Concho Museum, gave me a great deal of assistance in researching the haunting history of the fort. She sent me some interesting accounts of ghostly happenings there and shared some experiences with me. Although she dubbed visitor's guide Conrad McClure as the chief ghost expert, she said that most all of the staff members have felt presences in the library and museum at one time or another. One guide saw the hazy figure of a man, believed to be the spirit of a "ghost sergeant," in the museum shop, which is located in one of the old barracks. It appeared, then disappeared, right before his eyes! Another guide said she felt something, or someone, leaning hard on the back of her chair. Thinking it was another guide, she said, "Will you stop that!" But as she turned around to see who it was, the guide she thought had leaned on her chair was clear across the room and no one else was even close to her chair!

McClure says he has heard footsteps on the bare board floors of the former barracks, and he has seen lights go on and off in both the headquarters building and the court martial room.

There's also supposed to be a ghost that rides night watch around the parade grounds, and the ghost of a Sergeant Fletcher who used to live in barracks number 5 still makes appearances around his old hangout.

An article by Jeff Guinn in the *Fort Worth Star Telegram* dated Sunday, October 29, 1989, told about several ghostly encounters connected with the old fort:

> Joe Chavez, whose family lived in an officers' quarters when the city of San Angelo rented the structures from the 1930s to 1960s, says he woke up in his bedroom one night to see an army officer in full dress uniform staring at him from a corner. The ghost disappeared almost immediately. Chavez's memory of him has lasted a lifetime.
>
> In the mid '30s, a little girl named Dorothy Young came to play dolls with a friend in the attic of another officers' quarters. In broad daylight, the children heard a rhythmic tapping on the window. When they rushed to the window, they saw a transparent white shape floating outside. Dorothy's little friend died soon afterward of a mysterious illness. Throughout her long life, Dorothy proclaimed her ghost story to be true.

Officer's quarters number 7, built in 1876, has now been recycled into the fort offices and library and is probably the most haunted single area of the fort. Colonel Benjamin Grierson, commander of Fort Concho at the time, wrote to his wife saying the building contained a "double set of quarters for unmarried officers."

After the fort was abandoned, the building was used as a private residence for a time, then it was rented out. The late Mrs. Mary E. Rogers, who was born at Fort Concho, was interviewed by Mike Cox for an article that appeared in the *San Angelo Times* on May 3, 1968. Rogers recalled a murder that had taken place in about 1895 or '96 in the old building, which was then deserted. She said the house was often inhabited by vagrants and people just passing through. A man who made his living by trapping badgers, wolves, coyotes, and other small animals was shot to death. The evidence led the authorities to believe the killing might have taken place in a dispute over trapping rights. After the murder, the label "haunted house" was often attached to number 7. Although it was later remodeled and used as an apartment house, it was hard to rent, and nobody stayed there very long. Rumors of hauntings persisted, as strange lights and weird noises were often reported at night.

Quarters Number 7, Fort Concho

John Neilson, of the Fort Concho staff, interviewed Carlos Trevino, who lived in the building in the 1960s. An excerpt from this June 17, 1989 interview reveals:

Trevino: There was always something weird happening there. Small things but one time Robert Rodriguez was laying in bed and all of a sudden the fan fell on him and cut his nose all up. And that was weird.

Neilson: Supposedly there are rumors of ghosts and tales like that about number 7. Do you remember ever hearing anything about that or anything else strange?

Trevino: One time we were on the balcony and the door to the kitchen (I still get goosebumps thinking about it) was open. My parents were in the back bedroom. I saw a body come close the door to the balcony and I thought it was my dad. I got up to see what he was doing up so early in the morning as it was still dark, but there was nobody there. Right after it closed I had opened it... and there was nobody there. So I went real quick to dad's bedroom to see if he jumped in real quick, but my parents were asleep. I really tripped out on that!

For a long time the building was vacant. Finally, when interest in the fort as an historical site began to burgeon, the old set of quarters was restored and selected to house the offices and library of the Fort Concho Museum. Librarian Wayne Daniel says he has felt a presence there but feels it isn't threatening.

Some say the spirit of Fort Concho's first surgeon, Captain William M. Notson, who served there from January 1869 to July of 1872, still roams the area where the former post hospital stood. (This building is no longer standing.) Doubtless he saw much suffering and heartbreak during those times of privation and hardship.

The fort was just a collection of tents when the doctor first arrived. The first hospital consisted of three drafty tents heated by open fires. Later, the fort began to take form and a real hospital was finally built. However, medicine was in short supply. Often there was no chloroform to use in operations. It was a very discouraging post for the young doctor. It became even sadder when his own child, an infant boy, died in June of that first difficult year at the fort.

One of the museum guides, Conrad McClure, who has witnessed a lot of supernatural events at the fort, says he strongly senses Captain Notson's presence in the area (now a reconstruction) where his old hospital once stood.

And then there's the story of "Dead Ellis" that clung to the fort hospital for years. This was a hair-raising but humorous tale about a black private who was stationed at the fort back in the 1870s.

The soldier named Ellis had fallen ill while out on the prairies searching for Indians. He probably had a sunstroke. When he got back to the fort he reported to the hospital and almost immediately collapsed. In his unconscious state, he was pronounced dead by the medics.

His lifeless form was transported to the dead house, a small stone building behind the post hospital. There he was placed on a cooling table to be prepared for burial the following day. That evening some of his buddies came to pay their respects. They gathered in the anterooms outside of the dead room and, fortified with bottled spirits and strong coffee, prepared to keep watch through the night. Some of them sang spirituals to honor their dead friend.

About 11 p.m. they'd just finished harmonizing the old hymn "Are You Coming Home Tonight? Are You Coming Home to Jesus? Are You Coming Out of Darkness Into Light?" when one of the men heard sounds coming from the inner room where Ellis' body had been laid out on the cooling boards. The hymn must have been the signal for Ellis to revive because he suddenly sprang to life. A soldier shouted, "That man ain't dead. He's moving! He's getting up!" Mourners scattered in all directions, running through doors and jumping out of the windows. One man named Cox is said to have leaped out of a window, taking the shutter with him!

Ellis nearly killed himself for real as he jumped out of a window when he awoke and found himself on the cooling table, a most frightening experience.

A hospital orderly, roused by all the commotion, came to see what was going on. He found the now conscious "Dead Ellis" lying on the ground under the window from which he had jumped. He took him back into the hospital, where he was put to bed and treated. Within a few days he had fully recovered and returned to duty.

For years everybody called the soldier "Dead Ellis." He lived on for many more years, finally passing away in San Angelo in 1928.

With so many interesting tales attached to it, what a wonderful thing for all of us that Fort Concho has been preserved and restored so that generations to come can see and appreciate it!

Spirits at the Sutlery

Fort Stockton was founded in December of 1858, just a few years before the outbreak of the Civil War. It was named for Commodore Robert Field Stockton, a naval officer who distinguished himself in the Mexican War. The adobe post was built by about twenty soldiers from the First and Eighth Infantry. Today only a few of the old buildings remain in the town that grew up around the fort. At least one of the old buildings is said to be haunted.

The old sutlery, located at the corner of Nelson and Sherer streets today, was built by J.D. Holliday, the first fort provisioner. The rectangular building was located near an arroyo, or draw, and was sturdily built of two-foot thick adobe brick on a stone foundation. The first roof was of stripped sotol branches. From this building, supplies, plus a few luxuries such as tobacco, were sold to the troops stationed at the fort.

The building, which served both as a home and a place of business to Holliday, became a part of the fort on May 3, 1860. Soon after, in April of 1861, the installation was abandoned by the federal troops at the order of Brigadier General David E. Twiggs. The Confederates came for a time, but the fort did not flourish under their occupancy and was soon abandoned for the second time. The rebels put the wooden roofs of the buildings to the torch. Only the sutlery survived the fires set by the departing Confederates.

After the Civil War ended, the fort was re-established as a deterrent to the Indian massacres that were taking place all along the Trans-Pecos frontier when Colonel Edward Hatch and the Ninth Cavalry moved in. This time around the soldiers were mostly blacks and were known as the buffalo soldiers. This name was given to them by the Indians because their curly hair reminded them of the tightly coiled hair of the buffalo.

The old adobe house once more served as a sutlery, this time from 1872 to 1876 when a man named Joseph Friedlander ran the establishment. The Indian depredations were pretty well settled by 1874 when a survey of the military division of the Missouri stated that no Indians remained in the vicinity. By then the fort encompassed 960 acres plus a twenty-five-acre plot some three miles from the fort that was used as a garden. By 1879 the town around the fort, known first as St. Gall, had become a good-sized settlement of solid citizens, mostly German, Irish, and Mexican farmers and settlers. In 1881 they voted to change the town's name to Fort Stockton. The military finally abandoned the fort, for the third and last time, in 1886.

The old adobe house that once was a sutlery has had a colorful and somewhat turbulent history. That's why they say it is haunted!

After Friedlander closed down his sutlery, Aniseto Pina and his wife Matilde moved in. The kindly Matilde offered shelter to a woman named Annie Riggs and her four small sons after Annie divorced her hot-tempered outlaw husband, Barney Kemp Riggs, in late March of 1902. Barney had served time in prison, had killed several men, and was known to possess a violent disposition. Finally, after he had beaten Annie and burned their household goods, he threatened to throw kerosene on her and torch her. She fled with her children, and Matilde took her in. Barney came around looking for Annie on April 6, 1902. Her son-in-law, J.R. "Buck" Chadbourne, who was married to Annie's daughter by a previous marriage, was there at the Pinas' house, loading up Annie's belongings in his mule-drawn wagon. Riggs got into an argument with Chadbourne and threatened the younger man with a cane. Fearing the outlaw, Buck went for his gun and ended up shooting his mother-in-law's former husband. Shot in the chest, Barney staggered over to the arroyo beside the house, where he collapsed. He died the next day at the Koehler Hotel, cursing Chadbourne with his last breath.

A lot of people died in the house during the 1918 Spanish influenza epidemic, as the Pina home was used for a time as a hospital. A yellow quarantine flag flew over the place for weeks, and many unfortunate victims of the disease died at the former sutlery.

Other stories about the old house include rumors it was once used as a frontier courthouse, of sorts, back in the 1800s, and the guilty parties were hastily hanged somewhere back of the house.

The place stayed in the Pina family for a long while, then the Manuel Ramos family and some of their tenants occupied the place. Aniseto Pina's son-in-law, Pancho Robles, once had a blacksmith shop there, too. He was said to have been obsessed with witchcraft, which he practiced at night. He was considered a "brujo," or male witch, and

Old sutlery, Fort Stockton

studied books about the occult and devil worship. Then, from the 1930s into the 1950s, a man named George "Choche" Garcia lived there, and it was said he smoked and experimented with marijuana. He got into the habit of dressing all in black, wearing a big hat and a cape, and he went out at night to frighten people. Perhaps it is Choche who comes back to haunt the place because many people down through the years have claimed to have seen the figure of a man, dressed all in black, looking a bit Lincolnesque in his tall high-crowned hat and cape, just standing by the capped-off well beside the old house. No one seems to have seen his face, but the figure is very large and very real to those who claim to have seen him. The local Hispanics call him "El Bulto," which means shape or figure.

Some people seem to think the son of Aniseto Pino, Pancho, might be the spirit, because they recall there were no hauntings until after his death, around 1937. Some people say that he had a lot of gold coins buried in or around the house and his spirit comes back to guard them. Another version of who the black-clad spirit is came from an elderly resident of Fort Stockton who claims it is the ghost of Manuel Ramos. It could be just about anybody. But he's there, big, black, and bold, appearing to whom, and just when, he pleases. There have also been many reports over the years of flickering lights within the now vacant house, and some former residents said it was common to hear noises, like all the china breaking in the china cabinets at the house at night. A thorough search always failed to turn up anything broken or out of place. (These china-breaking noises, incidentally, are frequently mentioned in accounts of hauntings.)

For a lengthy dissertation about El Bulto, what he does and who he might possibly be, a fine accounting is given in Patrick Dearen's book *Castle Gap and the Pecos Frontier.*

According to Dearen, there have been many instances of calls to the Fort Stockton police department when sightings of the black-clad figure were made by local residents and passers-by of the old adobe. Even several police officers, dispatchers, and others connected with the department have observed the strange figure. There have been those who have suggested an exorcism be performed to put the strange spirit at rest, but so far as I know, none has ever taken place there.

There are many people in Fort Stockton who believe the place might still be haunted. Today, a very small part of the old fort itself remains. Three officer's houses and the guardhouse exist around a clearly defined parade ground. A building on the far side of the parade ground, on Spring Drive, is designated as the post hospital, but it's actually the Rollins-Sibley House, built in 1903 on the hospital's old foundations. The guardhouse is open and contains a jailer's quarters, a holding cell, and a solitary confinement cell, which is really a black dungeon. Frankly, that sounds like a dandy place for El Bulto to spend his off-duty hours!

The old sutler's house was designated a Texas historic landmark in 1966 by the Texas Historical Commission and was purchased by the Fort Stockton Historical Society in 1967. They have erected a fence around it to protect it from vandalism and have built a shed-like roof over it to protect it from the elements. No one lives there anymore. No one, that is, except "El Bulto."

The Chisos of Fort Leaton

Fort Leaton wasn't a cavalry post like most of the forts scattered over far West Texas. In fact, it wasn't even known as Fort Leaton until recent times. But there's a good story about the installation located four miles southwest of Presidio on what was the rugged San Antonio-Chihuahua Trail.

Fort Leaton had its beginnings as a post known as Presidio de San Jose, founded by a Spanish officer, Captain Alonso Rubin de Celis, in 1759. The Spanish kept a garrison at this presidio until 1767 when they decided to place their fort across the river, on the Mexican side. The abandoned and empty fort was pretty well vandalized by Indians in the area. Later on, about 1773, the Spanish again moved into San Jose and kept a fifty-man company there until the early 1800s. It was known then as El Fortin de San Jose.

According to a pamphlet distributed to visitors to Fort Leaton, a man named Ben Leaton bought the place in 1848, and it is for him the fort is named.

Leaton had made his living for years as a bounty hunter, collecting Indian scalps for the Mexican states of Sonora and Chihuahua. He evidently made a good living in this gruesome vocation, because he soon fixed up the place, making it into a fortified hacienda, no small task when one considers there were forty rooms arranged around a central courtyard, or plaza. Here he lived with his wife, Juana Pedraza, and their children. At his desert homestead he ran a profitable farming operation. He also traded with the Mescalero Apaches and Comanches that roamed the Rio Grande country, the very people he had once made a living by scalping! He was sometimes accused of encouraging the Indians to raid Mexican haciendas by trading with them for the stolen livestock. He was not very popular with either the U.S. or Mexican governments. But Leaton was friendly, generous, and hospitable to visitors. The soldiers who rode through the area were charmed by his affable disposition and lavish hospitality.

But Leaton's days were numbered. He bought the property in 1848 and died just three years later. His widow married a man named Edward Hall, a local customs agent and interpreter. They lived in the fortress from which Hall operated a small freighting business. Hall borrowed ten thousand dollars from John Burgess and went deeply into debt. Burgess, one of Leaton's old scalp-hunting buddies, decided to foreclose on Hall. A dispute ensued, and Hall was murdered, probably on Burgess' orders. The Burgess family then moved into the hacienda. Eleven years later, Bill Leaton, Hall's youngest stepson, murdered Burgess while he was on a business trip to Fort Davis. Young Leaton then fled to Chihuahua City, Mexico, where he later died in a shootout. Members of the Burgess family stayed on at the old former fort until 1926. Most of the Burgesses are buried just outside the fort in a rocky little cemetery.

There were evidently various owners and tenants at the place for a number of years. There was an interesting account in the October 1979 edition of *Texas Highways Magazine* about the fort that mentions it might be haunted. The writer, Elton Miles, author of *Tales of the Big Bend*, wrote:

To the Mexican Americans of the Big Bend the word "Chisos" today designates a savage, Indian-like bogy-man or spook. "Los Chisos" suggests an indescribable, supernatural menace with predatory Apache traits. Apparently the word is so thought of by Mexican children, for as a child Miss Delfina Franco of Presidio used "Los Chisos" in this sense, as did her playmates. While her mother, Mrs. Lucy Franco, had always understood Los Chisos to mean "Indians," the daughter says "Chisos means something like bogy-man."

A clear example of the more recently developed meaning was observed in 1946 by Mrs. Hope Tarwater at the picturesque adobe ruin of Fort Leaton, a few miles down the Rio Grade from Presidio. Mexican workers hired by her husband, Mark Tarwater, spoke of mysterious white turkeys they saw flying over the fort at night. When asked why they stopped sleeping on the porch and moved their cots into the field, they explained that evil spirits in the old fort had been turning their beds around.

One day Mrs. Tarwater was at Fort Leaton with two Mexican boys, 14-year-old Chapo Brito and his cousin. When she saw them walking toward town, she called in Spanish, "Chapo, where are you going?"

Chapo said, "My cousin has to go to the dentist. I am afraid to stay here alone. I don't like the ugly noises." His phrase, in Spanish, was "los ruidos feos."

As there were chores to do, Mrs. Tarwater reasoned, "I have to stay here by myself, and I don't mind."

Chapo replied, "But you don't see the Chisos! (no ve los chisos!) ...and away he went with his cousin to the dentist, confident that his gringa boss was immune to visitation by evil spirits that assail the Mexican's peace of mind. But to Chapo, "los chisos" were something he could see, though vaguely, and that he could most certainly hear.

We recently visited Fort Leaton, which now consists of twenty-five restored rooms and the corrals where the horses were stabled. Vivano Garcia, a most affable gentleman who is one of the Park Ranger guides, personally conducted our tour. I told him of my interest in ghost stories, and he volunteered that numerous visitors to the fort, some of whom claimed psychic powers, had mentioned feeling a presence in two rooms in particular. I asked him not to tell me which ones, and off we went to explore the vastness of the fort.

The rooms that have been restored are very large. The walls are at least two feet thick, and the ceilings are sixteen feet high. In one corner room, probably used for guest quarters, I suddenly felt cold and there was a prickly sensation on my arms. When I asked Mr. Garcia if this was one of the rooms, he said that it was. He added that he had heard one of the Burgesses had been shot by the sheriff in this room. We continued to walk about, visiting the salon, the huge master bedroom and adjacent nursery (Garcia also volunteered that Hall had been shot in the master bedroom), the dining room, and various family and guest quarters. Then we came to a room that was large and rather dark, with only a few high ventilation openings at the ceiling level. Garcia explained this room was where Leaton confined servants or anyone else he deemed were guilty of disobedience. Again, I felt cold, and a feeling of deep sadness came over me. I told Mr. Garcia I believed this was the other room that the psychics had identified. And I was right again!

The fort-like hacienda was built around a central courtyard. At one end is a roofed loggia with a dirt floor. Garcia explained that Leaton entertained his guests in the courtyard and loggia, and there was a special story told about two housewarmings Leaton had held there.

It seems soon after the building was completed, Leaton invited a large group of the Apache Indians in the area to come for a housewarming. There was much feasting, much dancing, and consumption of much firewater. As his guests reveled, Leaton finally retired to his quarters. When he awoke the next morning, he found the Apaches had

Inner courtyard, Fort Leaton

departed, having first pretty well trashed the place, and they had helped themselves to some of Leaton's prize horses as well.

Instead of riding after them immediately, Leaton decided to bide his time. About a year later he extended an invitation to a second house-warming party. Well, the tribe had such a fine time the first time around, they didn't hesitate to show up for this one! When the Indians arrived, they were told to stand close to one another in the loggia and wait for a surprise. When the unsuspecting Indians were all packed into the small space, Leaton had his men open fire on his startled houseguests. Not an Indian remained alive after the Leaton forces had finished their bloody task. This massacre must have been around 1849 or 1850, since Leaton built the place in 1848 and died in 1851.

Mr. Garcia told me that even now, local residents of the Presidio area consider Bill Leaton the epitome of evil; the personification of the devil himself! They refer to him as "un mal hombre." He told me that Leaton had once been paid $100 for an Indian brave's scalp, $50 for a squaw's scalp, and $25 for a child's scalp by the Chihuahuan government. Since most of the Mexican people living just south of the Rio Grande also had long, straight, black hair, it was rumored that Leaton had also killed and scalped Mexican citizens in order to claim the bounty from their own government!

Exterior walls, Fort Leaton

The unscrupulous trader had also paid the Indians for loot they had stolen from Mexican ranchers along the border, so double dealing seemed to be what the evil man knew best.

With so many evil deeds associated with the fort and with its builder, no wonder ghost tales still abound! Vivano Garcia said many local people claim the place is haunted and would not spend the night there for any amount of money!

The fort was finally abandoned, and the adobe rapidly deteriorated. During this period it was used occasionally as a shelter by transient families. It was largely a ruin when it was donated to the State of Texas in 1968. The original fort had contained forty rooms. Twenty-five of them have been restored, forming an interesting historical museum that sheds a real insight into early life along the Rio Grande frontier.

CHAPTER 2

HAUNTED HOSTELRIES AND EATING ESTABLISHMENTS

HAUNTED HOSTELRIES

Hotels, like houses, can haunted be,
By ghosts one can both hear and see.
In inns and little dining places
Spirits dwell in dark hidden spaces,
And in West Texas inns, those who've gone on
Still return in the hours before dawn.
In one, an owner, who still can't let go,
Of the hotel he built a long time ago,
While way up in Turkey, an old cowboy ghost
Still comes to rest in the room he liked most.
In Laredo, down on the Rio Grande
The Hamilton's haunted, so we understand.
These ghostly guests come again and again
And why they come, no one can explain.

Docia Williams

Ghosts at Fort Worth's Miss Molly's

It's said to be "where the West begins." At least, that's what any Fort Worth native will tell you!

The little town that began as a military encampment on the high bluffs along the Trinity River was established on June 6, 1849. It was just after the Mexican War when General Winfield Scott brought in forty-two men of Company F, Second Dragoons, to set up the camp which he named after General Williams Jenkins Worth, who saw distinguished service in the Mexican War.

The year after the small fort was organized, the Fort Worth-to-Yuma, Arizona, stage line was established. In 1860 the place, now a growing township, became the county seat of Tarrant County. After the Civil War, the economy really took off, as the settlement became a gathering place for the trail riders who drove their herds of cattle up the Chisholm Trail to the Kansas railheads. Between 1866 and 1890, more than four million cattle were driven north up the trail via Commerce Street, before fording the Trinity River into what is today called "North Side." (My paternal grandfather, William Schultz, was a drover on the very same Chisholm Trail!)

During the last half of the century the railroad came to Fort Worth, making the city a major shipping point for livestock. Then the meat packing industry came into the city's north side. Some prominent Fort Worth citizens built large holding pens, forming the stockyards that were to bring fame and fortune to their city. In 1902 two large packing companies located their plants in the stockyards area, and Fort Worth soon became the second largest livestock market in America. Within ten short years, sixteen million cattle passed through the stockyards. Now, that's a lot of beef, and probably how the city acquired its nickname, "Cowtown."

I've always had a special nostalgic feeling about Fort Worth. I grew up in the North Texas town of Garland, just northeast of Dallas. My father, John Schultz, was a district sales manager for Ralston Purina, and his home office and the big mill were located in Fort Worth. A graduate of Texas A&M University with a degree in Animal Husbandry, Dad was a fine livestock judge. Sometimes, back in the forties when I was a youngster, I'd be allowed to accompany him when he went to the Fort Worth Stock Show to judge some of the livestock events. I learned a lot about the fine points of judging cattle and horses from Dad, and unlike a lot of matrons my age, I do know a Hereford from a Brahman!

Fort Worth is a very Western city. A visit to the stockyard area, where some of the best steaks in the world are served up in the good restaurants that pepper that area, and a look around the antiques and Western-wear shops is a "must do" on any itinerary. It's a great city, rich in Western tradition, and it's home to numerous ghostly residents as well!

Our first encounter with a ghostly habitat in Fort Worth was at Miss Molly's, a great bed and breakfast inn that is situated right smack in the heart of the stockyard district.

Fort Worth in the late 1800s and early 1900s was the place where the cowboys came to have their last flings before taking off on the long dusty trail to Dodge City and Abilene, Kansas, via the route named for old Jessie Chisholm. These flings usually included a good soaking bath, a shave and a haircut, and a night of liquoring and gambling at one of the many saloons in the old settlement. And it was even better if it could be spent in the company of a pretty little girl-for-hire!

There were plenty of bawdy houses in Fort Worth in those days, and at least one of them has survived till now. This particular one isn't as old as some of those frequented by the trail riders. But it's similar in plan and right down in the stockyard area where the red light district used to be. Of course, it's taken on an entirely new purpose and is now a very respectable and attractive eight-room bed and breakfast inn called "Miss Molly's." Located at 109 West Exchange Avenue, it's just a hop, skip, and a jump from the famous coliseum where the world's first indoor rodeo was held in 1918.

Back in 1910 when the place first opened, it was a very proper boarding house for visitors, "drummers" (traveling salesmen), and cattle buyers who came to the stockyard area. Sometimes rodeo cowboys riding for either a fortune or a fall found their way up the steep staircase as well. The rooming house was arranged with nine rooms encircling a large central hall used as a parlor and reception area just as it is today. In the 1920s the place was managed by one Amelia Eimer, a very sedate and proper lady, who called her establishment "The Palace Rooms." Hers was a very successful and altogether respectable rooming house.

Then for a time another management took over and it became known as "The Oasis." It remained a short-term boarding house for Fort Worth visitors until the 1940s when the big packing companies moved into the stockyard area. Armour and Swift brought in many workers. There were a lot of cowboys who came to compete in the rodeo events, too. Then, the war years brought a lot of servicemen looking for a good time before shipping overseas, as well. The time was right for "Miss Josie" King to take over.

The former boarding house became a "sporting" or bawdy house, a bordello managed by Miss Josie that she called the "Gayette Hotel." Her "ladies" entertained their clients in any one of the nine available rooms. Many of the girls had regular clients, cowboys and businessmen who stopped by from time to time to pay their respects and play out their pent-up passions in the company of Miss Josie's pretty girls. And of course, the packing house workers always dropped a goodly portion of their weekly paychecks at the Gayette.

One such young man visited Miss Josie's weekly. He always requested the same young lady, who occupied room number 9. He became so enamored of her that he even proposed marriage. The young woman did not return his affections. In fact, his attentions and obvious sincerity had begun to disturb her so much, she finally decided to pick up stakes and move on. When the young man found she had left Miss Josie's with no message for him and no forwarding address, he was crushed. The madame, feeling pity for the love-struck youth, told him she had just what he needed, a beautiful new girl who would soon make him forget the young woman to whom he had become so attached. He was told which room to go to. Deciding there was nothing to lose, he knocked on the door. The young woman who opened the door to his knock was the absolute spitting image of his own mother in her youth! He was so stunned that he turned and fled down the stairs, never to return to Miss Josie's again! This true story was told years later by the very man who gave up the sporting life that night and later became a prominent minister and religious leader.

After Miss Josie's closed down, the place became an art gallery and the rooms were used by individual artists as studios. Today the former boardinghouse-bordello-art studio has entered still a new phase in its long and colorful history. Mark and Susan Hancock have made "Miss Molly's Bed and Breakfast Inn" a unique place in which to spend a night or two in the old stockyard section of Fort Worth. It's up a long flight of stairs, over the famous Star Cafe. If you can't climb, you can't come, but if you can possibly manage the stairs, the view at the top is well worth it! The Hancocks have done a superb job of restoring and decorating the former bawdy house, and their good taste is only surpassed by their warm and gracious hospitality.

I asked Mark how they arrived at the name of "Miss Molly's." He said that the lead cow on the cattle drives was often referred to as a "Molly." They just kind of liked that name and said since their place was located near the stockyards where a lot of "Mollys" started off on their long treks north, they thought it an appropriate one.

Each of the eight rooms has a theme reminiscent of the heyday of Miss Josie's bordello. And at least two of those rooms are haunted. Hancock told us about a night when a local journalist spent the night in the Cowboy Room, which is furnished, in Hancock's words, "Texas sparse" fashion, to resemble a bunk house. The writer awoke suddenly in the middle of the night to find a very attractive blonde young lady had suddenly materialized at his bedside. Although he admitted it wasn't too bad a way to be awakened, he did realize that his visitor was an apparition, and this was a trifle unsettling. Hancock could shed no light on who she might have been.

Miss Josie's bedroom at Miss Molly's Bed & Breakfast

The Cattlemen's Room, which is done up with a big oak double bed beneath mounted longhorns on the wall, a splendid accommodation for the cattle barons of that era, was the scene of another visit from the beyond. This time the occupant was an English gentleman who was traveling alone. In the night he awoke and saw, in the light coming in from the transom over the door, the figure of an elderly woman standing at the foot of his bed. She just stood and stared at him. She was attired in old-fashioned clothing and was wearing a sunbonnet and was an altogether proper-looking lady. Hancock thinks perhaps this specter might have been the spirit of Miss Amelia Eimer.

Hancock said once three ladies came up the stairs to tour the former bordello. One of the women, who was very psychic, said she felt the overwhelming presence of a female spirit in the kitchen adjacent to Miss Josie's former room. The kitchen is where the Hancocks make the coffee and serve up the delicious breakfast pastries that are daily offerings at the bed and breakfast. Mark is convinced that there are presences there, but he says they are friendly and nonthreatening.

Mark told us he encourages visitors to the stockyards to come upstairs to tour the establishment, to get a look at an authentically furnished rooming house of the early stockyard era. Visitors are shown around at no charge and seem to enjoy their visits very much. They are shown the various rooms, each of which has a special theme. All of them are furnished with antiques and beautiful handmade quilts. There are the Cowboy's Room, the Oilman's Room, the Railroader's Room, The Gunslinger's Room, and the Rodeo Room. As a tribute to the former proprietress of the "Palace," there's Miss Amelia's Room, primly decorated with a white iron double bedstead, lace curtains, immaculate linens, and a beautiful pastel quilt. My husband and I stayed in Miss Josie's, a flamboyantly elegant corner suite with an old-fashioned bathtub sitting up on claw feet, rich wall coverings, and a high-backed carved oak bed with a satin spread. It was a very appropriately furnished suite, named for the former madam.

For a comfortable, restful, and thoroughly enjoyable night, we heartily recommend a stop at Miss Molly's! A call to (817) 626-1522 will guarantee your reservation. But as to whether one of the resident ghosts will come to visit you, we can make no promises.

The Ghost of the Gage Hotel

Far West Texas is just about as large and lonely as the Western films depict it to be. And if you're driving down Highway 90 between Del Rio and Alpine, you'll notice that stopping-off spots are few and far between. So if you're looking for a good comfortable hotel room or just a delicious meal that'll stick to your ribs, as you're headed down that long stretch of highway you'll do no better than to slow down and take a breather at the old Gage Hotel in Marathon.

You'll probably be astounded to find such an attractive, beautifully appointed hostelry in a small community that's not much more than a wide place in the road. In 1882 Albion E. Shepherd, a former sea captain turned engineer for the Southern Pacific Railroad, named the fledgling community Marathon because it reminded him of the mountain wilderness terrain he had once seen in Marathon, Greece.

Alfred Gage was the first owner of the hotel, which he had designed by a renowned architect of that era, Henry Trost. It is now the only building in Texas that Trost designed as a hotel that still serves that purpose. A native of Vermont, Gage arrived in West Texas at the age of eighteen, ready to seek his fortune. He worked hard, first as a cowhand in the Panhandle, and later on he and his brothers organized the Alpine Cattle Company. Finally, Gage became a successful banker and businessman in San Antonio. He owned a 500,000-acre spread outside of Marathon, and it was for his convenience when visiting his property that he planned and built the Gage Hotel to serve as a combination home and ranch headquarters. He opened it to the public in 1927. Unfortunately, his time to enjoy the fine building built in the middle of a wilderness was short lived. He died the following year, in 1928.

According to a feature article in the March 1985 edition of *Texas Highways Magazine*, at the time of its construction the Gage Hotel was considered the most elegant building in Texas west of the Pecos.

Before driving out to Marathon, I had a good telephone visit with General Manager Bill Stephens. He manages the property for absentee owners J.P. and Mary Jan Bryan of Houston. It has been during Stephen's tenure at the Gage that extensive additions have been made on the property. A large section adjacent to the old brick building called "Los Portales" has brought the number of rooms up to thirty-seven. About 100 guests can be accommodated nightly, making it a fine stop for tour groups as well as individuals. The addition, which is covered with a shady porch featuring inviting benches for sitting and enjoying the West Texas breeze, is in a very traditional Chihuahuan desert style. Stephens said that 110,000 handmade adobe bricks went into the addition, as well as 40,000 dried sotol stalks, which have been used as cross beams. The vigas, or larger beams, are of ponderosa pine shipped in from New Mexico. Several beautiful patios and a fine Mexican tiled cross-shaped swimming pool form an oasis for guests to enjoy.

Front of Gage Hotel, Marathon

Of course, since I had heard it rumored the Gage was haunted, the conversation just naturally took a turn in that direction. When questioned, Stephens said a manager who worked there before him mentioned he had heard footsteps in a hallway, and there probably were guests who also heard, but just never mentioned, such sounds. Stephens cited one occurrence about three years ago that might lead one to believe there is a resident spirit at the old hotel. A young man employed as a dishwasher at the hotel was an excellent worker, willing to work late into the night doing extra chores, such as cleaning floors, polishing ashtrays and brass, and cleaning the fireplaces. He worked at whatever needed to be done, as he was very ambitious and liked to earn extra money for his family. Then, suddenly, he changed. He stopped working overtime. He wasn't very cheerful anymore. Instead of being willing to stay late and work extra hours, he'd up and leave before he'd even completed his regular chores. Such a sudden change in his personality and work habits was exceedingly strange, totally out of character for the young man.

Stephens said he was determined to get to the bottom of it. The young man finally broke down and told the manager that one evening when he had been in the basement level working into the wee hours, he suddenly felt a presence, a distinct feeling that someone was there in the room with him. He felt a hand upon his shoulder, and as he turned, he confronted the figure of Alfred Gage, which he recognized from the portrait hanging in the hotel. Gage's apparition looked straight at the startled worker and said, "I do not want you in my hotel any longer."

That's when the man quit staying late and working alone. Then came one night when he had to go down into the basement again. This was about two weeks after his first confrontation with Mr. Gage's spirit. Again, he felt a strong presence in the room with him, although he knew he was alone. This time he left the basement, climbed the stairs, and went out the door. He has not returned to the hotel since that night.

The rooms in the main building are furnished with antiques and are kept as authentic to the era in which they were built as possible. There are no television sets in the rooms. Many of the accommodations have been given names, such as Panther Junction, Persimmon Gap, Dagger Mesa, and Stillwell's Crossing. Furnishings are in simple ranch style, but there are some good antique beds and tables and some interesting Western and Native American artwork. Some rooms are Western in theme while others are Indian or south-of-the-border in their decor. All are comfortable and attractive!

Now, there's one room that has an added bit of ambience. That's room number 10. There are a couple of old violins hanging on the wall as part of the decor. Guests and staff members alike have reported hearing music playing in that room. It's hard to recognize the tune, but it's definitely music, and it's only heard in that one room. The evening we checked in, the desk clerk, Allen Russell, told us that several guests who have occupied number 10 have reported being awakened by a gentle tap on the arm, and they hear the soft voice of a woman reciting poetry.

Lobby, Gage Hotel, Marathon

Haunted guest room, Gage Hotel

As we checked out of the hotel after a restful night in beautiful surroundings, the morning desk clerks, Richard Lott and Gilda Martinez, mentioned that fairly recently a gentleman who stayed in room number 25 in the new Los Portales unit was awakened by someone tugging on his arm. He then plainly saw the figure of a young woman standing by his bed! She appeared to be in her early thirties and was rather misty in appearance. As the startled man stared at her, she slowly faded away.

Miss Martinez suggested I look up the grounds maintenance man, Jesus Tercero, whose nickname is Chuy. I did, and he told me a young woman also appeared to him one evening as he stood by the Coke machine in the Los Portales area. It was about 10 p.m. but he plainly saw her, as the unit is well illuminated at night. She was a youngish woman, somewhere in her thirties, had short brownish hair, and was wearing a white blouse and a dark skirt. He believed the skirt was a dark blue color. I asked him if it was long, and he said, no it was the modern street length women wear now. She just walked by him, but she looked sort of misty. He stared after her, and as she walked towards the court-yard where the swimming pool is located, she just slowly melted away, finally disappearing completely. He is positive she was a ghost!

Today, the Gage is just about the most attractive, inviting stopping-off place in that part of the state. The cuisine is as good as one might find in a fine restaurant in a major metropolitan area. The atmosphere of the place is outstanding; warm, comfortable, and charming. It has been faithfully restored to its original appearance. The public rooms with their high ceilings, transomed windows, and fine fireplaces and mantels have been lovingly restored.

Alfred Gage should be very happy with the way the hotel looks and operates these days. It certainly is a credit to him and his architect, and it's the perfect place to spend a peaceful night out in far West Texas!

For reservations or information call the Gage at (915) 386-4205.

The Scent of Magnolias

About fifty miles to the northeast of Lubbock is the small city of Floydada. Some 4,000 people make their homes in the community which boasts it's the pumpkin capital of the U.S.

Floyd County was named for a hero of early Texas, Dolphin Floyd, a man who gave his life at the Battle of the Alamo in 1836. Originally the county seat was called Floyd City, but when a post office was applied for, it was discovered there was already a Floyd City elsewhere in Texas. A prominent local citizen, a rancher named T.W. Price, suggested the name "Floydada," in which he combined the county's name with his own mother's Christian name, which was Ada. And it's remained Floydada to this day!

There's some mighty good ranch country around the community, and a popular stopping-off place for locals and visitors alike has long been the Lamplighter Inn, which was built in 1912 and opened for business in 1913. Three generations of the Daily family operated the hotel until about four years ago. In 1991 Evelyn Branch and her daughter, Roxanna Cummings, purchased it. They are restoring and redecorating the old hotel, bringing it back to its original ambience. Today they offer many services other than just bed and breakfast. They specialize in wedding receptions, luncheons, and special parties, and every day lunch is served to the public in the gracious old dining room.

Mother and daughter have enjoyed their four years as innkeepers at the Lamplighter, where they reside on the top floor. And by now they've also accepted the fact they must share their address with at least two ghosts. Who they are or why they hang around at the Inn is only a matter of supposition. When I spoke with Roxanna she said she has a

The Lamplighter as it appeared around 1920

few educated guesses as to who they might be. She still wonders why neither the former owners nor the real estate agent ever mentioned that they had either seen or heard anything out of the ordinary in all the years they had operated the hotel.

For starters, Roxanna said she knew there had been what she calls a "near murder" in the place back in the 1970s. The bizarre case concerned a local man who got wind of the fact his wife was carrying on a love affair behind his back. She and her paramour checked into the hotel for a lover's tryst. Her husband arrived at the hotel and demanded to know what room the two were occupying. He surprised the pair, and although he had gone up with the express purpose of confronting his rival, the other man got the best of him. In fact, the woman's husband was so severely beaten that there was blood splattered all over the room, and an ambulance had to be summoned to drive him to Lubbock to the nearest hospital. Unfortunately, he did not survive the severe beating.

Cummings told me that the wife's lover soon went to trial but got away scot-free because he managed to claim self-defense. The victim's widow soon married her lover. Both had children from their previous marriages, and they all settled cozily into a new his 'n hers family unit. But it wasn't long before both of them were killed in a tragic automobile accident, a grim ending to the whole sordid story!

Roxanna also told me that an elderly man who made his home at the hotel for a number of years passed away there. This was back when the place was still run by the Daily family. In those days, there weren't a lot of nursing homes, and often elderly people, especially old men, moved to a hotel or boarding house to live out their last days when their children or relatives did not step forth to look after them. This man, whose name was Mr. Cornelius, had been a local merchant at one time.

Whether the ghostly happenings at the hotel have anything to do with either of these deaths, no one knows. Roxanna believes there is both a male and a female spirit at the hotel. Recently a guest who spent the night there asked the two owners if they knew they had a spirit at the hotel. She told them, "She visited me last night. I felt her presence and smelled her perfume very distinctly." She went on to say that while she had not been particularly frightened, she did find it to be a rather strange and unsettling experience.

Cummings says there is often a cloyingly sweet fragrance that permeates the air, rather like magnolias blooming on a summer night. At other times they've caught a whiff of the unmistakable scent of Old Spice men's cologne.

Roxanna's mother, Evelyn Branch, used to say she absolutely did not believe in ghosts and there was a logical explanation for everything. Now, she's not so sure. Several times she has caught a glimpse of a man's feet and trouser-clad legs dashing up the stairs from her vantage point in the lobby. Usually this occurs after a large group has been there for a function. Once, the women ran upstairs to see if anyone was still there after having glimpsed the feet dashing up the stairs. A thorough check failed to turn up anything, or anybody, anywhere!

Recently some missionaries came to speak at the local Baptist church. They checked into the Lamplighter and almost immediately checked out again. When they turned in their room key and asked for a refund, they were asked the reason for their hasty departure. They mumbled something about the room being too small. Cummings told them a larger room could be readied for them, but they said, no, they'd already called their Baptist hosts and arrangements had been made for them to stay at another hotel. Later, the mysterious exodus was explained when a local woman had lunch one day at the Inn. She was talking to Roxanna, who mentioned her resident ghosts. "Oh! the woman said, "I know all about them. They scared the missionaries who visited our church." Roxanna pressed the woman to tell her what the pair had told her. She said they had just told her the room was haunted, and they wanted out of there fast!

Cummings and Branch used to have a dog that lived with them in their upstairs quarters. When they had to take him outside, he literally had to be dragged by the collar through the lobby. He didn't like to be in that part of the hotel at all.

Cummings revealed that sometimes the figure of a woman has been seen at an upstairs guest room window. She seems to be dressed in a style of the 1930s or '40s. The window shade, an accordion type that must be drawn, has been seen going up and down in the window when no one is occupying that room. At least one guest sensed the presence there, although she did not actually see the woman's figure.

Once, when Mrs. Branch was washing clothes in the downstairs utility room from which she had a clear view of the hotel dining room, she saw a woman clad in a purple dress walk into the empty dining room. She moved out of the laundry to see who the woman was and what she wanted, since the dining room was closed at that hour. The woman had literally disappeared, and neither Mrs. Branch nor her daughter have a clue as to who she might have been.

In one of the guest rooms where new drapes had recently been hung on rods well secured into the wood frame surrounding the window, the owners were stunned one day when they walked into the unoccupied room and found the draperies laid out carefully on the floor, straightened out on their rods, not crumpled or wrinkled, but looking as if they had been most carefully removed and rearranged on the floor. When employees were questioned no one could explain the strange occurrence.

A letter I received from Roxanna dated October 24, 1994, revealed that a recent occurrence really has the owners puzzled. To quote from her correspondence:

"After our last large group left a couple of weeks ago... after everyone had left we cleaned up the hotel and straightened up. The next morning (this was when there were no guests at all!) we awoke to find a table set in the dining room, not for breakfast, but for lunch, complete with china, napkins, cups, glasses, and silverware. No explanation. By the way, it was set up for two."

Then Roxanna went on to say that she believes they have at least two resident spirits, one male and one female, and because of where they hang out, they've given them the names "Floyd" and "Ada." Roxanna says these names will just have to do until they can ferret out the real identity of their supernatural star-boarders!

According to Roxanna, there are just lots of unexplained happenings at the hotel: sounds of footsteps, unusual noises, lights that switch on and off, doors that open and close all the time at all hours. The lady hoteliers often wonder if these haunting happenings are manifestations of the unfortunate husband still seeking out his two-timing wife and her lover, or could it be one, or both, of the star-crossed lovers themselves, slipping back to the place where their troubles began? And maybe Mr. Cornelius just misses his comfortable, friendly room at the Inn. No one knows.

Roxanna Cummings and her mother, Evelyn Branch, would welcome you for a visit, to spend the night, or just enjoy a good meal. All you need to do is pick up the phone and call them at (806) 983-3035. And just maybe you might smell the magnolias, too!

Turkey's Old Cowboy Ghost

I first met Jane and Scott Johnson in 1993 at a Historical Hotels Association meeting in San Antonio. The Johnsons told me that their hotel had a very interesting history, and a ghost for good measure! Then they proceeded to share a few interesting experiences they had had with me.

When I decided to write a book about West Texas hauntings, I recalled that chat and contacted Jane to see if she would enlarge on what she had told me that night. I was delighted to hear from her with quite a detailed accounting of her encounters with their cowboy-guest-ghost.

The Turkey Hotel, which the Johnsons describe as a country bed and breakfast, was built in 1927. Located at Third and Alexander in Turkey, it consists of fourteen rooms, and all but four of them have private bathrooms, complete with claw-footed bathtubs.

Turkey is a very small town. It got its first post office in 1893. In 1900 there was a population of around 500. But it didn't start to really prosper until the 1920s. Jane said the town was originally called Turkey Roost, after all the hundreds of wild turkeys that roosted in the trees along the creek running through town. But they just shortened the name to Turkey, and that is what has stuck all these years. The town was incorporated in the early 1920s, and Jane wrote that the railroad came to the community in 1927 and the entire town, as it now exists, was built in that year. The hotel opened on November 11, 1927, to provide lodgings for the salesmen, or "drummers," who came from Dallas and Fort Worth. It has never closed since the day it opened, although it has seen good and bad times and has had numerous owners.

Scott and Jane left a lovely home and an active social life amidst a wide circle of friends in the North Texas city of Denton, when they decided to move to Turkey. Scott knew the small town well, having attended many family reunions there. When he heard the old hotel was up for sale, he felt he and Jane could provide a real service to the community. The hotel had fallen on hard times. In great disrepair, the building was about to be sold for salvage and was already scheduled for demolition. Scott, who is the fourth generation in his family to live in Turkey, was sentimental about the building and wanted to save it. He and Jane now provide a special place where families can return for visits, family reunions, and funerals.

Also, the hotel, in its newly restored condition, doubtless does a great business during the annual Bob Wills Country Music Festival, which has been a featured event the last weekend in April for the past twenty-three years.

Hotel Turkey

The little farming hamlet, best known for its crops of peanuts and sweet "taters," really livens up during the festival. Wills, once considered the country's most successful bandleader, was born in East Texas, but he spent his boyhood and early adult life in Turkey. He used to play his fiddle in the Turkey Hotel's parlor, as well as at local dance halls.

Every year, devotees of country western swing music come to Turkey to pay homage to Wills, who died in 1975. There's a marble monument to him and a little museum filled with memorabilia and photographs.

A few of the members of Wills' band who are still around come back, too. They regroup and perform many of the songs that are considered country music classics, tunes like "Faded Love," "San Antonio Rose," "Deep Water," and "Cherokee Maiden." This must be the biggest weekend in the whole year for the folks up in Turkey!

Jane's interesting account of her experiences with the ghost who visits the hotel makes interesting reading. To quote from her letter:

When we took over the hotel, the lady told us, "All the rooms are locked because someone keeps getting upstairs somehow and sleeps in a bed." Evidently they never figured out is was a ghost!

During the first winter storm we had after moving into the hotel (just me there alone for the first nine months!) I was busy working and heard the old bell ring on the front desk. I stopped and went down to the lobby. No one was there. After looking all around and finding no one, I shrugged it off and went back to work. The next day I went into room number 20 and the bed was messed up in an odd way. The spread was not thrown back but there was a body form of where a person had lain on the bed, crossed his legs at the ankles, placed his hands under his head, arms out. The shape of one boot heel was on the bed. Then it struck me and I knew with certainty...an old cowboy ghost had spent the night. It was too bad and cold to sleep out.

From then on, when it was a bad night, I began to expect him. Sure enough, the bell would ring to let me know it was him. He would go upstairs to "his room" and never disturb anything. He only comes when it's either Scott or me alone, never when other people are at the hotel as he is a very private person and doesn't want to frighten anyone.

What is so strange, every old cowboy (those that are still living) that has come to spend the night in the hotel always asks for that same room, number 20. You see, it has two walls of windows, facing east and south, and it feels sort of like you are outside, only it's nice and warm.

My ghost kept me company on many a bad stormy night that first year. It was a comfort knowing I wasn't alone!

You might want to visit with the hospitable Johnsons and spend a night in their comfortable old hotel when you are up in the Turkey area. They even offer tours of the area. They have a horse named Gobbler that pulls a buggy for rides, and there's a pet llama on the property, too. For information and reservations, call them at (806) 423-1151.

The Haunted Hamilton

Down in Laredo, on the Rio Grande, there's a famous old and elegant hotel, the Hamilton. The place dates back to 1890 when it was built as a three-story structure. During renovations in 1928 a twelve-story tower was added.

Hamilton Hotel, Laredo

The hotel has 150 rooms and/or suites, and many of them are occupied by permanent guests. In its heyday it has been the home-away-from-home to some very interesting and important people. There have been a lot of recent ups and downs, and the current owners bought it from the Resolution Trust Corporation, which had it for about two years. It's now being renovated and is well on its way back to being the attractive landmark it once was.

At one time, in its prime, the hotel was the place to go for special gatherings of organizations and clubs, wedding receptions, and grand balls. It was a popular meeting place, too, for prominent businessmen, the "movers and shakers" who met there regularly to drink coffee and smoke fine cigars, while wheeling and dealing, discussing important business ventures and political campaigns that sometimes had long-reaching results across the country.

Tommy West wrote an article that ran in the March 14, 1993 edition of the *San Antonio Express News* magazine section which revealed an interesting fact about the hotel. He says it's haunted. And why not? It's sure seen a lot of living in its century of existence!

Workers who installed some equipment for a radio station located on the eleventh floor experienced strange incidents. When they left the hotel at the end of their work day, they put their equipment away, but on returning the next morning they found their tools and materials had been moved. Some of the sound equipment gave off odd and eerie vibrations as well.

Chaz Paz, a Laredo resident, owns a little shop half a block away from the Hamilton. He says that as the story goes, furniture moves from one place to another, lights go on and off, and the elevator runs erratically, just wherever and whenever it chooses to go. It often goes deliberately in the wrong direction!

Paz, who deals in incense and potions, herbs, and candles (but no black magic, he is quick to note), said the radio people came to him to buy some holy water to try to drive the spirits away.

There is a story told that a priest plunged to his death under strange circumstances. Chaz said the padre was supposedly pushed from one of the upper floor windows, but he could not recall the exact date.

Luciana Guajardo, head of the special collections section of the Laredo Public Library, is very interested in ghost stories. He says while they have not been thoroughly researched and therefore must be treated as rumors, he has heard that on one floor the lights do all sorts of crazy things. They will go on if you turn on a faucet! Guajardo said he had also heard the story about the priest. He said he believes the tragedy occurred in the 1960s or maybe a little before, and came about through a case of mistaken identity. There was some tie-in with racketeers, he recalls. Someone came and pushed the priest out of an open hall window, only to discover he'd gotten the wrong man. There's one consolation, I would have to suppose. Perhaps the padre, having led the good life, is residing peacefully in heavenly spheres. The gang's real target might not have fared as well!

Spirits at the Health Spa

Numerous people to whom I have spoken believe that the old Baker Hotel building, once a favorite health spa and social gathering place in Mineral Wells, is haunted. The building, which is mostly deserted, is a relic of the great days when people traveled hundreds of miles to drink and bathe in the "Crazy Waters" that burst forth from the ground around the town of Mineral Wells. These mineral waters were reputed to cure any and all maladies known to man!

The discovery of medicinal qualities in the waters around Mineral Wells in the 1880s made the town nationally famous. It was even said that the waters of the Crazy Well, discovered in 1885, could cure hysterical manias and all types of insanity! As a result of this discovery, health-seekers flocked to the town, and it became necessary to build accommodations for them. The first hotel built was the Crazy Water Hotel, a seven-story building. A nationally known broadcast went out over the networks for years from this hotel. Because this hotel was so successful, T.B. Baker, a Texan who was well known as both an entrepreneur and a hotelier, decided he would build another hotel in Mineral Wells. This one, named for its builder, was a fourteen-story structure with over 400 guest rooms. In addition to this hotel, Baker at one time owned the Texas in Fort Worth, the Baker in Dallas, the Menger and St. Anthony hotels in San Antonio, and the Galvez in Galveston. The Mineral Wells Baker enjoyed a great reputation as a resort that attracted wealthy and socially prominent guests from all over the country. It also owed quite a bit of its success to the proximity of Fort Wolters, located just east of Mineral Wells. This was an Infantry installation during World War II, and then it later became the home of the U.S. Army's primary helicopter school.

During its heyday, the Baker's grand ballroom on the twelfth floor was the scene of many a gala affair, and the tile-lined swimming pool in the basement was always filled with splashing bathers. Today, the lobby, which is sparsely furnished but still reflective of its grander days, is sometimes open for tours, and two people who sometimes conduct these nostalgia trips told me about some of their personal experiences at the old hotel.

Andrew Beneze, who is a producer and photojournalist for Channel 11 in Fort Worth, enjoys making frequent jaunts over to Mineral

Wells to show people around the Baker. He speaks as if he knows every nook and cranny. He said there are numerous areas where the old rooms are just standing empty, slowly deteriorating. Structurally, he feels the building is very sound, and the main problems are cosmetic ones that time, money, and fixing up could eradicate. But whether or not the Baker could ever attract the masses it once did is highly improbable.

The building is currently managed by Jane Catrett, a relative newcomer to Mineral Wells, who oversees the building for a friend who is the out-of-state owner of the property.

Beneze told me that Mr. Baker divested himself of most of his interests in the 1960s, leaving the property to a nephew. The Baker closed for a time in 1965. Then a group of wealthy citizens in Mineral Wells bought it and opened it for a time. There was a golf course and a lake that went with the property at the time they purchased it. The hotel finally closed in 1972. Beneze said he thought the final blow was the closure of Fort Wolters and all the trade the military installation had brought to the town.

Its competitor, the Crazy Hotel, has fared somewhat better. Today it is an attractive retirement center for senior citizens.

I first learned about the possibility of there being a ghost in the Baker from a Fort Worth acquaintance. She asked that I not use her name and I shall respect her wishes. She told me a strange and very tragic story about a young cousin of hers.

The event happened in 1948 when the hotel was still doing a brisk trade. Douglas Moore lived in Mineral Wells with his mother, who was single and trying to make ends meet. Her husband had deserted her and she was having difficulty supporting herself and her son. Douglas was about fifteen years old then but a big boy for his age. He felt obligated to get out and get a job to help his mother. He was delighted when the Baker Hotel hired him to be an elevator operator.

It wasn't very long before the teenager was making exceedingly good money. In short order, he began to flash big bankrolls! In fact, it wasn't long before he had enough money saved to buy himself a little red convertible, and then he had an addition put onto his mother's house to increase its size and comfort. Either his mother was extremely naive, or else she was so proud of her son's capabilities she never gave a thought to why such a young boy would suddenly have so much money!

Then a terrible blow fell. Douglas was laid off with no warning. He was utterly crestfallen and moped around the house for days. However, in a few weeks a call came to him from the hotel staff, asking him to come back to the Baker. They insisted he come back to the hotel that very evening, late, to pick up his elevator operator's uniform. He never dreamed he was being set up.

My friend told me the story that Douglas was just horsing around with a couple of his friends, fellow elevator operators, and one of them hit a starter button as Douglas started to board the elevator. The cage shot up and he was somehow caught between the elevator shaft and the closing door and was cut in half at the torso. The security people at the hotel called Mrs. Moore to tell her of her son's tragic accident. They explained to her he had somehow slipped and could not get all the way into the elevator and was caught, resulting in his being violently cut in two.

That was their explanation. But as Paul Harvey might say, "now, for the rest of the story." The real truth later came out. It seems the local sheriff about that time was operating a prostitution ring. His front men were closely aligned with the elevator operators and bellmen at the hotels. They supplied the ring with names and room numbers of single men who were hotel guests. Especially during World War II, there were many soldiers who came to the hotel looking for a good time. Since Fort Wolters remained in the area after the war, the ready source of income continued. The sheriff's boys were well paid for the information they supplied. This was the way young Douglas had received his sudden and bountiful windfall.

Even though he liked having all that ready cash, Douglas had been brought up by a loving and God-fearing mother who had taught him to be honest. And the more he saw and heard, the more he realized that he did not want to be involved in what was going on at the hotel. It was immoral and wrong. So he became an informer. Of course, he never dreamed that the very people to whom he was informing were connected to the racket!

The prostitution ring decided to get rid of Douglas. They apparently paid a couple of the boys to shove him into the elevator shaft, causing his heinous death.

My friend said she had been told that Douglas' restless spirit still roams the old hotel, especially around the elevators, and only the upper portion of his torso and head have been seen.

When I questioned Andrew Beneze and also Jane Catrett about this, they said they had not seen this ghostly apparition; however, both of them said they had strange feelings in the hotel. Catrett said she is especially uncomfortable in the old elevator! Both Beneze and Catrett said they would not be at all surprised if the story about Douglas' death was true because they knew the hotel had been used as a base for "high-class call girls" at one time.

Mrs. Catrett also told me about a secret room. This hidden room, which was obviously used as a guest room at one time because it still bears the marks of where a toilet and basin had been in the bathroom, is now just an empty room. It could only be reached by a freight elevator, and when it was reached that was the end of the line. Nothing else was up there. It is believed this is a room used by local residents for assignations, a place where they could go without being seen. Catrett said she first learned about the room from a friend who worked at the Mineral Wells Police Department.

Both Beneze and Catrett mentioned that they had heard the story that a very pretty young woman had died (was probably murdered) in the hotel. It was believed she was one of the prostitutes working there. No one could identify her, so the hotel management dressed her up and put her on display in the front window for a couple of days in hopes someone would come forth and identify her

Beneze told me that several times when he was in the building, either alone or with a companion or two, late at night, it was very spooky. He has an office in what was the old accounting office. When the sun goes down he gets the feeling that it is time to leave, that they don't want him there after dark. He feels this way all of the time, he said. He said once he and a friend, who was very psychic, went up to look around the old ballroom with flashlights because the electricity was cut off up there. His friend distinctly felt something was following them and became almost paranoid with fear. She claimed she felt that three spirits had followed them as they walked about the hotel, and she said there were two men and a woman who were very possessive of the building and wanted to know why they were there. She called them caretaker ghosts.

Another time Beneze was in the basement with a different friend and they heard footsteps following them as they walked around. There was a one-lane bowling alley in the basement during the hotel's active days. A strange triangular-shaped room is back in this area. This was the room where Beneze believes a janitor once stayed, a janitor who supposedly died there in the hotel. He said that particular night as they poked around in the old basement, they noticed a small bed, or cot, in the former janitor's room. The sheet was partially pulled back as they flashed a light around the dark room. They looked around a few minutes, and then for some reason, Beneze flashed his light across the bed again. They both saw it at the same time…the sheet had been pulled farther back, exposing the mattress! Beneze says he thinks they both exclaimed, "That thing just moved!" He's not sure. But of one thing he is very sure—it only took them a few seconds to get out of there!

Margaret Maxwell, who also serves as a guide at the Baker, told me she definitely believes in ghosts, because her own home is haunted. Although a medium once came to the Baker and could find no ghosts at the time of her visit, Margaret says she believes there are some around. At times she feels very uncomfortable and knows some presence is in the room with her. Once, she was alone about 10 p.m. when she suddenly realized she had not turned off the lights in the basement. When she went downstairs to switch them off, she was startled to hear a conversation going on. She knew she was all alone, yet she distinctly heard voices engaged in a lively discussion.

Maxwell said she had no details, but she recalls hearing that once a woman leaped off the roof, plunging from the roof garden area to the swimming pool in the patio fourteen stories below. She could not recall the date of that tragedy.

Mrs. Maxwell also said she believes that because the Baker played a part in so many lives, there is bound to be a lot of energy remaining. Some people came just to enjoy the spa and the social contacts they made. Others who were hopelessly ill came there in a last ditch effort to recover from their maladies. Some of those who waited too late died there while seeking a cure.

If you are ever up near Mineral Wells, you might enjoy a tour of the old building and a visit with manager Jane Catrett. She will probably tell you, as she recently wrote to me, "I can assure you there is a ghost at the Baker. I can't say who, what, or when…I only know that sometimes I simply will not go into certain areas."

The Ghost at the Texas Grill

Just about the most haunted place around Ballinger, Texas, is the old Texas Grill. In fact, it's so haunted that it has been the subject of numerous newspaper articles and television specials. The owners, genial Joyce and Larry Sikes, were kind enough to send me a long letter describing the antics of "Norton," their ghost, and a video tape of numerous TV shows that had featured the Grill. In the video, many people, both employees and customers, were interviewed. Each one had a special remark to make about the ghostly atmosphere at the restaurant, leaving little doubt that they think the place is haunted.

The old-fashioned, small-town cafe is located right in the middle of town. It sits on the main drag through town at 700 Hutchins Street. The building it occupies was constructed around 1901. It was first a saloon, but prohibition shut that operation down around 1913. Then it became a department store. Finally, it was converted into a restaurant in 1954. The Sikes have leased the building since 1989.

The Texas Grill, Ballinger

The upper floor of the building is presently unoccupied. Joyce Sikes told me that portion of the building was once where the saloon girls had their rooms. She thinks it is pretty spooky up there, and from the appearance of the place on one of the TV films, I would have to agree with her. She said she has only worked up the nerve to go upstairs two or three times since they have occupied the building.

The Sikes couple look like sensible, down-home, friendly folks that wouldn't be given to making up ghost stories. With a popular restaurant to run, they don't have time for tale-spinning. But lots of things continue to happen, convincing them that the Grill isn't just anybody's everyday restaurant!

Joyce wrote me a long letter. She said since 1991 they've had small items move around on their own. The first incident concerned a fork that was sitting in a glass on top of a microwave in the front dining area. About 5 a.m. the cook and a customer were sitting at a table about ten feet away when the fork just flew out of the glass and landed on the floor. They often have tostada baskets falling off the kitchen shelves. They've smelled men's cologne in the long hallway leading to the restrooms fully two hours after they have closed for the night. And Joyce said when just she and Larry have been in the front dining room at night after closing, they have heard the refrigerator doors closing in the kitchen when they knew full well they were all alone in the place.

Joyce said she has heard footsteps on the upper floor over the ladies' restroom at 5 a.m. And both Larry and Joyce have seen dark shadows walking by the back pass-through window leading from the back dining room into the kitchen on numerous occasions. When they turn to see who is there, they always find they are alone. In that same area, the salad bar girl has been pinched on the sitting portion of her anatomy. And when she turned to look, there was no one near her!

There have been customers asking about strange happenings in the back dining room. One man stated he was following a man down the long hallway, and when he looked off and then back the man had disappeared. One of the waitress's grandsons, a tot of three, came running out from the hallway one night telling them there was a man in the hall. They were closed at the time and knew they were the only people there!

According to Joyce, after so many strange unexplained things occurred, their daughter spoke with a psychic. The psychic felt like the spirit was a fugitive from justice who had lived on the land in a little shack prior to 1901 when the brick building was constructed. The law caught up with him, and they shot him right there on the spot. Joyce says for some reason they believe his name was Norton.

Well, if Norton was killed on that spot, he surely seems lively now! When the Sikes' had an employee Christmas party in the back dining room in 1991, they took some photos of the gathering. Norton showed up in the photo, as a white misty figure, but his face and broad-brimmed hat can be recognized.

The psychic told the Sikes that Norton seemed to be pulling little pranks because there was possibly someone working there whom he didn't like. They have a cook who came to work there in 1990. He was outside the building one night and a brick fell off the roof and landed right in front of him. That is the only incident that has occurred where someone almost got hurt.

Joyce and Larry were advised by the psychic that if they really wanted to get in touch with Norton they should light a candle in the back room, where many people seem to feel a presence, on the 4th, 5th, or 6th of July, 1993. They decided against doing this when the psychic warned them they could agitate the spirit and things might get worse. They just decided to leave well enough alone.

The Texas Grill is open Sunday through Wednesday from 5 a.m. to 11 p.m., and Thursday through Saturday it's open all night. They serve both American and Mexican food, and the food they were dishing up on one of the TV specials looked so good I was tempted to leap up from my comfy recliner and take off for Ballinger that very minute! I am sure Larry and Joyce Sikes would welcome you to the Grill, and who knows, you might even run into Norton!

The Spirit at Smokey Toes

I first learned about the ghost at Mike Leatherwood's Smokey Toes Island Grill from a Fort Worth acquaintance, writer Marsha Brown. The old building at 400 Main Street was built around 1902 and has served many purposes during its long years as a Fort Worth landmark. It was built to be the headquarters of the Northern Texas Traction Company, an interurban service. The main office as well as the ticket office for the commuter trains that once ran between Fort Worth and Dallas were located there. That business closed down in 1934, and the building has been used for numerous purposes since then, having served as a candy factory, a title company, a bookstore, and two different restaurants. It was known as the Deep Ellum Restaurant just prior to becoming the Caribbean-themed establishment it is today.

Now, it's not known just how long the spirit of a young woman hung around the building. Brown said she had heard it rumored that a murder took place in the building sometime back in the 1940s, but she has not been able to find the time to substantiate that story. The present manager of the Grill, Rick Scordo, to whom I spoke at length, says he has no doubt there has been a ghostly inhabitant of the building. Although he has never actually seen the apparition, he says he has felt numerous cold spots and a presence so strong that the hair has stood up on his arms and his skin has "crawled." He's also heard footsteps, like a woman walking in high-heeled slippers, walking across the upper wooden floors many times as he worked in his basement level office beneath the main dining room. He has often felt a chillingly cold presence in the basement level men's restroom. Several times a male employee heard the distinct cries of "Help me...oh, please help me!" coming from the next stall but found no one there.

A young woman employee, a waitress, said she once heard hysterical laughter in the ladies' powder room. She had gone into the restroom to change her clothes in one of the stalls. She heard no one come in, yet there were sounds of loud laughter coming from the other stall. She looked down, and saw no feet! She came out of her stall, and knocked on the other door. No answer. She pulled at the door and it opened, revealing an empty stall! Yet, she said the laughter she heard had been very loud and prolonged.

Another employee said she heard noises, like someone cleaning and moving things around on the upper floor. She decided to go upstairs to investigate. She saw no one around, on either the third floor or in the attic. Then she noticed a table at the upper stair level was covered with used light bulbs. The employees had just finished their annual job of changing all the light bulbs on that floor. Suddenly, as she stood there, the light bulbs started bouncing off the table, one at a time. She said she ran downstairs in a hurry when that started happening!

Scordo said all sorts of weird things continued to occur over the years. Lights have gone on and off or dimmed suddenly. The lever-operated frozen drink machines used to make daiquiris and margaritas would turn themselves on and off, with no human helper in sight.

Marsha Brown told me when Leatherwood first opened the Grill, the brother of the assistant manager took some photos of the old building. When he got home and had the pictures developed, a figure of a woman appeared in a window he knew had been empty and boarded up at the time the photo was taken. He told the people at the Grill about it on his next visit. When he got back home and searched for the photo he could not find it anywhere, and when he checked through the negatives he was astounded to find only one...that one...was blank!

When the Deep Ellum occupied the property, some of their employees actually saw the ghost and reported it was the apparition of a young woman. Rick Scordo said he is very disappointed that while he has heard the ghost, he has never seen her, although she was there for so long. Now he is afraid he will never get to see her.

It seems around Halloween of 1994 they decided to call a gifted psychic to come and hold a seance. A young woman who worked at a business next door to the Grill was recruited to be hypnotized so she might serve as the medium for the event. She was placed in a hypnotic trance and was very vocal in what she saw and heard in her entranced state. She plainly saw the image of a young woman. She appeared rather shy and would not speak very much. The medium got the impression the young woman was about ready to break her earth ties and was eager to "ascend to the light." The psychic called on St. Michael to assist her, and the medium said she saw the young woman ascending upward, surrounded by a halo of very intense white lights. Then she totally disappeared. The psychic said she believed the earth-bound spirit of the young woman had at last departed from the building she had clung to for so long, finding her way at last to a place of peace and light.

Scordo says he has not seen or heard anything since that night. There are no more cold spots. There is no strong feeling of a presence anywhere in the place. He admitted he was a bit sorry he never saw the image of the young woman, and while he and his staff were often irritated and sometimes frightened by the ghost, they sort of miss her now.

Frankly, I believe the spirit has departed. I would be very surprised if she ever returns to her former haunts. May she rest in peace.

A Ghost at the Landmark

Here's a story about a former hotel and a former cafe, located in Sterling City, a small town about thirty-five miles north of San Angelo on Highway 87, roughly halfway between Big Spring and San Angelo. There's a now-unoccupied two-story building on the main highway going through town. A Texas Historic plaque placed in 1982 proclaims it to be a landmark of considerable interest. And besides having an interesting history, the building was once said to be haunted as well!

A visit with some local residents who were dining and drinking coffee at the City Cafe, which is located in the next block down from the building, brought forth the information that it was a pretty well accepted fact the old building has a ghost story. Charlie Coleman, whom we met there, told us the upstairs portion of the place used to be a hotel, and he rented a room there for a time. He often felt a presence, as if some unseen being was there with him, and often he heard footsteps in the hallway outside his room. He said whenever he'd stick his head out of his door to look, there was never anyone there. The proprietors of the City Cafe, George and Maxine Turner, also said they believed the place used to be haunted. The Turners have their own resident spirit at their home, so they ought to know a ghost when they see or hear one! Since the old building is now closed up, it's hard to say if there are still any spirits hanging around.

My interest piqued, I decided to contact the present owners of the building, Pam and Hughbert Robinson, of San Angelo. Pam was happy to fill me in on the history of the corner building that covers around 14,000 square feet. Although the state historic plaque dates the building from 1910, Pam told me it was actually built in 1902 as the First State Bank of Sterling City and was the town's earliest financial institution. The second-floor area was called the State Hotel and had about ten comfortable rooms which were available for travelers. In 1926 the State Hotel and banking operation was acquired by the First National Bank.

The lower portion of the building also housed several businesses, according to Pam Robinson. A Dr. Swan maintained a long and successful practice for over fifty years in the ground-floor office he occupied. The city maintained offices in the building, a post office was once located there, and the first telephone company was also a tenant of the building. In addition, Mrs. Robinson said, a portion of the ground floor was leased out to E.B. and Hermine Butler who ran Butler's Drug Store from about 1926 to the mid-1960s. This was a very successful and prosperous establishment.

According to the historic marker, the site was associated with many of the most prominent early leaders of the community. The large hotel dining rooms (there were once at least four separate dining rooms) were popular meeting places for social gatherings and business conferences. Later, these dining rooms and the kitchen which served them became incorporated into the Landmark Cafe, which for a long time was a popular and well-known eating establishment.

For a time, after the hotel closed, a Mr. and Mrs. Horace Bates owned the building. Pam Robinson said they made the old hotel portion their home, living in most of the upstairs portion of the building. It was from the Bates that Pam and Hughbert bought the building in 1981. During some of the remodeling that took place then, the original old punched tin ceiling that had been in the bank was discovered under a newer ceiling that was torn out by the Robinsons. They also found a hidden room located just over the old former bank vault!

Pam said the Landmark Cafe operated in the building for a number of years. This was a popular gathering place, located as it was on the corner just across the busy highway from the county courthouse. The old cafe had the first telephone booth in town. It had been in the building for some time. Well, the telephone in the phone booth started ringing frequently, and when the busy waitresses would answer, an elderly lady would talk to them. She seemed to just want to chat. Finally, they were able to find out the identity of their frequent caller. She had been one of the early telephone operators who had worked in the building. And, she had been dead for a number of years! To stop the disturbing calls the management had to have the phone disconnected.

Robinson said that she and her husband had heard footsteps upstairs when they were downstairs, and they knew no one was on the upper floor. Then, they'd be upstairs when the building was empty late at night and would often hear the same footfalls, as the ghost paced the empty downstairs portion of the building. She believes the spirit was benevolent toward them and approved of the way they cared for the building, as they were never frightened by the sounds they heard. For a time the Robinsons had trouble with some managers whom they later found were stealing from them. These people had living quarters in an apartment upstairs which had been made from several of the former hotel rooms. At night they often heard the sounds of pots and pans in the kitchen being hurled around and the sounds of breaking china. Investigations brought forth no answers, because there was never anything out of place or broken. Robinson believes the ghost knew of the pilfering going on and was trying to frighten the dishonest managers away. This certainly seems plausible and in keeping with the behavioral patterns of benevolent spirits.

Mrs. Robinson said their young son found several interesting items in the hidden room located over the old bank vault while poking around as youngsters enjoy doing. There were mostly papers, deeds, and documents associated with Butler's Drug Store, such as tax statements, pages from ledgers, etc. They had most of these papers framed for safe-keeping. She told me one paper dating from the 1920s showed that Mrs. Hermine Butler had paid $8,000 in income tax that year, which would indicate the business had been very successful. It seems to me that at least one of the spirits in the place might have been connected with the drugstore, since these items were left at different times for the Robinsons to find. The son would find one or two items, and the next time he'd go back into the old deserted room, some new items would be there, just waiting for him to find them.

When workmen put in new flooring in the area where the Landmark Cafe had been after the restaurant was closed, they heard the paper towel rack in the restroom rattling and shaking and "just going crazy," according to Mrs. Robinson. They were extremely frightened as well as puzzled by this strange activity.

Right now the building is vacant. It has a wraparound porch around two sides on which a row of wooden drop seats from the old school auditorium are still arranged. The Robinsons believe with a little work and expense it could be restored and turned into a nice business, like a bed and breakfast inn, or maybe an arts and crafts center. The building is quite sound, and a peep inside the windows showed us it's in pretty good shape. No firm decisions have been made just yet, but I'll bet the old building and its proprietary ghost are just waiting for yet another new chapter to open in its long and interesting history.

CHAPTER 3

LINGERING SPIRITS OF SETTLERS, COWBOYS, AND INDIANS

THE BATTLE REPLAYED

In the light of a fading fall afternoon
Just before the rise of a full golden moon;
Out of the past, the fierce battle takes place
Repeated once more, o'er time and o'er space.
As warriors ride through the darkening night
And the wagon train circles, braced for a fight;
There'll be shouts and shrieks and wailing and crying
As settlers and warriors lie bloody and dying.
These are the souls that still can't find rest,
That's why they haunt those roads that lead West.

Docia Williams

Transported

Sometimes long ago events are thought to leave an imprint of energy somewhere, so that these events can reoccur and be seen for a fleeting instant by those who are sufficiently gifted with extrasensory perception. Energy can evidently be absorbed by the surrounding terrain. It's been explained to me to be rather like a tape recorder, where an image and sound can be recorded on tape. Under certain circumstances, long after an event took place, these images can reappear and their actions can be re-enacted.

My psychic friend, Sam Nesmith, told me that a true psychic imprint would be when the spirits, or reappearing images, do their own thing and do not digress from their activity or in any way react to the presence of a living person who is witness to the replay of the event.

Sam has experienced numerous psychic replays throughout his lifetime. One took place a number of years ago when he was near Ballinger in Runnels County searching a field for artifacts. He said it was near the site of the ruined old Spanish Mission of San Clemente, which was built over two hundred years ago. In those days Indian depredations were very common.

As Sam strolled along he suddenly was startled to see a young man, obviously a Spaniard, running across the ground in front of him! He was not dressed in a uniform, so if he was a Spanish soldier he was not on active duty. He appeared to be just a settler or farmer. He was clad in a white shirt and dark trousers, and his feet were bare. He was running as fast as he could, and in hot pursuit was an Indian wildly wielding a tomahawk. The young man soon reached a phantom tree and swung up into its branches, probably seeking whatever shelter he could. The Indian was able to grab him by the ankle and pulled him out of the tree. Then the savage struck him on the head with his tomahawk. Sam was frozen in horror as he witnessed the bloody scene. Then, just as suddenly as the action had taken place in front of him, the players in the strange drama, along with the tree, disappeared. The scene suddenly cut off as if it had never taken place, and Sam was once again alone in the field seeking arrowheads. It was long ago, but Sam has never forgotten the details of this startling experience!

Ghosts at the WIL S Ranch

My friend Mary Elizabeth Sue Goldman is the author of *A Trail Riders' Guide to Texas*. In this very interesting book she brought up the subject of ghosts.

The Caprock area in the Panhandle seems to abound in mysterious stories. Mary wrote about camping out on a dark and windy night with only her faithful little mare, Caroline, to keep her company. (Mary is a whole lot braver than I am!) Because of the atmosphere of the night, she turned her thoughts to a story some of her uncles had told as they sat around playing dominoes and visiting when she was a little girl. They spoke of just such a windy, dark night back in the days when there were still Indian raids taking place in far West Texas as the natives ran up against settlers who were slowly and steadily encroaching upon their hunting grounds. To quote Mary:

It was probably just such a windy night when Indians raided the log house that stood as headquarters of the WIL S Ranch and killed the women and children.

Years later, under a waning moon on a cold January night, a group of hunters took refuge from a storm there. Gathered around a small fire in the meager front room, they heard the sound of a baby crying coming from the cellar. Going to investigate, they held their lantern at the top of the cellar stairs. A ghost-like image of a woman stood at the bottom of the stairs holding the baby in her arms. It was then they heard a horse galloping towards the house and they turned and ran outside. No one was there.

When they returned to the stairs, the woman and child were also gone. Hands down, the hunters decided to camp outside that night in spite of the chilling winds.

Tossing bedrolls on the ground in the front yard just next to the family cemetery, they felt pretty comfortable now with the situation and started to chuckle about the apparition. Some joke, they must have thought! About then, a young girl appeared over one of the graves. Then they saw an old woman and a man appear, and the old woman spoke. "Leave," she demanded in a raspy voice. "LEAVE!"

It is not clear whether they rolled blankets and left or not. Mary said she knew what she would have done!

Today four little markers still designate the graves of the murdered family as they rest in the cemetery adjacent to the old abandoned cabin.

The Spirit of the Staked Plains

There is an interesting short account of a ghostly woman who is doomed to roam the Staked Plains area in Mary Elizabeth Sue Goldman's book *Trail Riders' Guide to Texas*. Mary writes:

A man at the QWIK Gas where I stopped late one afternoon was eager to enlighten me about this mysterious and colorful area of Texas. He told me about a pioneer lady that walks the fields every night in the summer. "Endless...on and on..." he says softly, "just keeps walking...not going anywhere...." A few years back, some farmers in the county got together and decided to put an end to the phantom once and for all.

They hid around the perimeter of the plowed field where she'd been seen by most everybody at one time or another. The moon was full so the night was real bright. Just as they hoped, she appeared, wearing a long dress and apron and a big bonnet that covered her face.

Drawing the circle smaller and smaller they closed in. Some could almost see her fleshless face, but before they could reach her they were staring into each other's eyes. She had vanished.

Over a cup of coffee, he told me she'd been following a covered wagon trail many years ago and had been "kilt" out there in the field. Most everybody out there in the plains accepted that her spirit was still trying to catch up with her family, but she was "sure nuff" trapped out there in the vastness of the Staked Plains.

The Phantom Indians

Back about eight or nine years ago, Charles Dennis of San Angelo used to deliver a paper route in the little community of Christoval in Tom Green County. He customarily left San Angelo around midnight and delivered the papers in Christoval in the wee hours of the morning so that his subscribers would have them first thing when they woke up.

One foggy night as he drove up a hill on his regular route he came to a large cedar-covered vacant lot, and there by the side of the road he saw a very strange sight! The headlights of his pickup highlighted the figure of an Indian brave mounted on a painted pony. The horse looked to be brown, black, and white, with the spotted markings of a paint as best he could make out. The Indian had long, loose, flowing hair, caught back with some sort of headband. He wore a breastplate and a breech clout and leggings. He wore a bracelet of some sort on his right arm and held a lance, or spear, in his left hand. Charles thinks there may have been a blanket on the horse.

Then, just as suddenly as the strange rider appeared, he disappeared! Naturally Charles wondered "Did I really see what I think I saw?" Then, about a week later as he traveled the same route, he saw the same Indian brave on the same horse. This time the rider followed right alongside the pickup Charles was driving for a short distance before completely disappearing.

For a long time, Charles didn't tell anybody but his wife about what he had seen in Christoval. Then, a couple of weeks later he was again there delivering his papers. It was about 2 a.m. as he drove up the hill in the early morning mist. The Indian again appeared. This time he held up his lance, like he was pointing at something. Charles looked in the direction where he was pointing. There was a woman, a little girl about eight or nine years old, and a little boy who looked to be five or six years old. They all shyly waved to Charles. Then the mounted warrior held his hand up again in sort of a waving motion, and all four of the Indians slowly faded off into the mist.

Although he was startled at first, Dennis said he never was really frightened. He was more puzzled than anything else. He did not have any feeling at any time of being in danger. When he saw the little family of the Indian brave, he said, he was happy he had seen them and felt a general feeling of well-being and acceptance.

Charles continued to throw the paper route in Christoval for several years, but he never saw the Indians again. He felt like he belonged there and that the spirits of the warrior and his family had come back briefly to welcome him to their old hunting grounds.

The Story of Mount Margaret

North of San Angelo there's a small mountain whose sharply pointed peak rises to an elevation of 2,282 feet above sea level. It is a well-known landmark in present-day Coke County near the small community of Tennyson. The peak is an especially impressive sight when viewed against a darkening sky.

Back in the 1850s the Butterfield Overland Stage route passed by the foot of the mountain as it wended its way westward into New Mexico on the way to California. Although there were often armed guards and outriders accompanying the stage, they were no match for the raiding parties of Indians that often waylaid them as they traversed the rugged, rocky, rutted roads that marked the stage route.

One stagecoach didn't make it. A party of marauding Comanches ambushed the coach, and all the passengers as well as the driver, save one, were killed and scalped. The lone survivor was a little girl named Margaret who was about six years of age at the time. The Indians took the terrified youngster to their encampment, intending to keep her and make her a part of the tribe. You can imagine the terror and fright the little girl must have felt as she relived, over and over again, the horrible massacre of her mother and father and the other occupants of the stagecoach. The memory of the bloodthirsty whoops of the warriors as they attached the bloody scalps of her loved ones to their lances and rode off from the scene of horrible carnage would not leave her.

The women of the tribe tried to befriend the captive child that the braves had brought to them, but all she could do was cry for her parents. She was naturally terrified of her captors and could not bear to have any of them come near her. She would take none of the food or drink that was offered. As the days slowly passed, she grew weaker and weaker as she retreated into a shell of shock and sorrow, refusing all nourishment. She continually sobbed and mourned. The Indians could not force her to eat or drink, and they just had to watch her slowly starve to death. They took her little body and wrapped it in blankets and laid her to rest high on the mountainside. Today the mountain bears her beautiful name and is known as Mount Margaret.

The people who live around Mount Margaret say the spirit of little Margaret has often been seen wandering there, and she sorrowfully sobs as she gazes out on the plains below as if still searching for the parents that were wrenched from her so suddenly and so tragically all those many years ago.

La Mujere Blanca

When Sam Nesmith was a young teenager living in Abilene, he had what he says was one of the most impressive and unusual experiences of his life. He had only begun to realize that he was a little bit different from his friends. He could see and feel things that others could not, and it was hard to explain this, even to his parents. It didn't happen all the time, of course, but there had been some times when he had been able to see what he knew were spirits, or ghosts, and he'd even been able to communicate with them. In other words, he was psychic. According to *Webster's New World Dictionary*, one of the definitions of psychic is one apparently sensitive to forces beyond the physical world.

Sam and his wife, Nancy, are very private people. They are also extremely well educated and very intelligent. They don't dwell on Sam's experiences or refer to them unless they are asked. They are very busy people too: involved in the community, dedicated historians, collectors of antiques and military memorabilia, and just all-round interesting and delightful people! That is why, when Sam, and to a lesser degree, Nancy, who also is somewhat psychic, speak, I listen. And knowing them and learning from them has helped a great deal in researching material for this book and in understanding what I research!

In sharing this experience, which he calls the "experience of the white lady, or mujere blanca," Sam told me this was his first really intense experience with an entity from the realm of the supernatural.

For quite some time the teenaged Sam had enjoyed the friendship of an elderly Hispanic man whose name was Jose Madera. Madera preferred to be called by the English translation of his name, and so Sam called him Joe Woods. Sam was about fourteen years old at that time, and he enjoyed visiting with his friend Joe, who told him stories about his days as a pistolero with Panco Villa's forces during the Mexican Revolution. Joe was a large, powerfully built man, appearing much younger than his seventy-odd years. He had suffered and survived four or five bullet wounds and was what one would describe as a pretty tough hombre. He enjoyed sharing his experiences with Sam and encouraged the youth in his pursuit of history. He also recognized Sam's rapidly developing psychic talents.

One afternoon Joe called Sam and asked him if he had anything planned that evening. He went on to explain that he had some friends that were being disturbed by what they'd described as "la mujere blanca," (a lady in white). The ghostly apparition was appearing more and more often to the family and causing great consternation in their lives. They had asked their friend Joe, who was considered to be somewhat psychic and whose abilities and judgement they trusted, if he would come over that evening. They hoped he could explain the meaning of the woman's strange nocturnal appearances in their home. Since it was the night of the full moon, Joe had agreed to go, and he asked Sam if he would like to accompany him.

The spirit appeared as the wraith of a young woman, and she had been coming on a fairly regular basis. Usually she came when the family was seated at the dinner table, and her appearances had spoiled many a meal for them. She habitually drifted through the rear wall of the house and floated across the room to the kitchen. The figure always appeared to be crying. The residents of the house, which was a very small, modest two-room tenant house built around the turn of the century, were at first hesitant to speak about the spirit. Sam could tell they were frightened. They spoke only in Spanish, but Sam could understand most of what they said, which centered around "la mujere blanca."

The family explained they had lived in the house for a couple of years, but the manifestations had only been occurring for a few months. Whenever the apparition came it was just about dark, and while she came at various times, she always came when there was a full moon. The family also told Joe and Sam that the neighbors had told them when they first moved in that the house was reputed to be haunted.

Sam said for some reason he was drawn to the backyard and decided to walk around outside for a while. At the back of the lot, about twenty-five or thirty yards from the house, there was a deep depression, partially filled with debris and bricks. As he walked up to the depression he began to feel strange vibrations. And then he began to both see and feel the presence of a young woman. She materialized in front of him as a grayish white figure clothed in a long gingham gown. The dress was all ragged and tattered. She was barefooted. From a fitted bodice, her full skirt fell to the tops of her feet. The sleeves of the dress were puffed, and Sam recalled one of them was torn. The face of the figure showed fine features, as if she had been very pretty at one time, but her skin was leathery looking, and her general appearance was that of someone who probably looked much older than her years. Her hair was wispy and unkempt and was light brown in color. Her eyes, which looked almost white…a cold, strange whiteness, could have been a light gray or a pale blue. Sam said it was hard to tell in the fast fading light.

The apparition was able to communicate with Sam, and she told him who she was and why she was there. She said her name was Amanda, and Sam can't recall but believes her last name was either Price or Page. He said he definitely got the impression the surname started with a P. She had come from back East, in Pennsylvania, in the 1870s, and she was traveling in a wagon train headed to California via the southern route. The wagon train was attacked by a raiding party of Comanches. Because she was young and pretty, the Indians did not kill and scalp her as they did the others. She was taken captive and enslaved by the Indians. Sometime later a group of men who were a mixed body of Anglos and Mexicans who called themselves Comancheros, because they traded with the Comanches, came to the encampment where Amanda was held captive. They were attracted by her beauty and bartered with the Indians to buy her. At first the Comanches didn't want to talk about trading her off, but the Comancheros made such a good offer they finally agreed to turn her over to the traders.

The Comancheros took her to their line camp near the location of present-day Abilene, which was not founded until 1881. They kept her in an underground cellar, and she was carefully watched. She was just as afraid of the Comancheros as she had been of the Indians. They were afraid she would try to run away, so they tied her ankles with rawhide hobbles and took away her shoes. They incarcerated her in a deep, dark root cellar. They told her they had to spend a lot of money for her, and they would like to get some of it back. She told them she had a sister back East, and if they would write to her she was sure that she would send them money to send her back home. Actually, they wanted to hold her for ransom but didn't tell her that at the time. They did write to her sister, telling her if she would send them the sum of $1,000, they would try to find her sister. Amanda's spirit told Sam that her family probably did not trust the sincerity of the Comanchero offer and decided not to answer the letter.

No money was ever sent for her release, and as her hopes of freedom faded, she gradually wasted away, forlorn, alone, and lonely. Finally she died there in the deep, dank, darkness of the cellar.

Amanda's figure seemed to be so forlorn and sad that Sam felt he must convince her to let go of the past and all the suffering she had endured. He told the spirit it was time to move on and cross over into the light.

Sam must have been convincing, because he said the image of the once beautiful young woman slowly started to fade away. Suddenly the atmosphere changed and he immediately felt the difference. A sudden light, airy feeling came over the little backyard. There was a general feeling of peace and tranquility. Sam believed there would be no more nocturnal visits from the "mujere blanca." Amanda had sought, and found, the way to the light.

Ghosts That Bring Messages

Sometimes spirits, or ghosts, are the bearers of messages. They bring both good and bad tidings. They warn of impending danger. They sometimes seek help. Over and over we read of them and always we are astounded. Intriguing indeed is the mysterious spirit world!

Dr. Kenneth Davis, retired professor of English at Texas Tech University in Lubbock and an active member of the Texas Folklore Society, shared a couple of West Texas messenger-ghost stories with me, which I will pass on to you.

During a heavy blizzard back around 1886 or '87, a cowboy's wife was expecting a baby. She had gone into labor and was having a terribly hard time of it. The poor young father didn't know what to do. There was a blinding snowstorm that night, but he put on his heavy coat and started off through the swirling snow to seek help from the ranch owner's wife up at the big house. Maybe his employer's wife would know what to do and come help deliver the baby, if only he could make it in time.

The storm was raging all around him, the wind blowing the snow into great drifts. The whiteness of the snow in the night was almost blinding. And somehow, he lost his way. He couldn't find the ranch house. Lost in the storm, he ended up in a snowdrift where he froze to death.

In the meantime, the rancher, his wife, and a few of the cowhands who had sought shelter from the storm in the comfort of the main house, heard a knock at the door. When the door was opened to the fury of the storm, a stranger stood at the door and told them of the plight of the cowboy's wife and pleaded for someone to please come right away. The rancher and his wife and one of the cowboys gathered their lanterns and what equipment they might need and hurried out into the night, to the place where the young woman lay wracked in pain awaiting the arrival of her baby. They were surprised that her husband was nowhere to be seen.

The next day, after the storm abated, the body of the cowboy was found, only a short distance from the ranch house where he had been headed. They all decided that the stranger who had arrived at the door was the spirit of the cowboy, lingering just long enough to summon help for his beloved wife.

Dr. Davis also told another story about a family who lived in a small community between San Angelo and Lampasas. They had a relative who had been very sick, and they figured they might get a death message at any time.

It had been raining all day, and the yard was all muddy. The wife had just scrubbed all the muddy footprints off of the front porch with lye soap and water and a mop.

Then, someone knocked on the door. There stood a stranger who they didn't recognize as anyone from around those parts. He said that the neighbors down the road sent him to tell them that their relative had just passed away. This was the news they had been dreading. After the man left, the woman commented she guessed the man would have left more muddy prints on her nice clean front porch and she would have to go out the next morning and do all that work over again.

The next morning, when they got up, she was astonished to find no muddy footprints on the porch at all! They dressed and walked down the road to their neighbor's house. The neighbors told them that no man had stopped at their place, and they knew nothing about the death of their relative. Sure enough, they soon learned that their relative had passed away, but they never could find out the identity of the mysterious messenger.

The Faithful Clock

Buffalo Gap is a small community near Abilene that has recently realized a rebirth of sorts. It offers a variety of restaurants, souvenir and gift shops, and a complex of historic restorations called the Buffalo Gap Historic Village.

The small settlement was once a gathering point on the old Dodge Cattle Trail. It was located at the site of a natural pass, or gap, in the Callahan Divide. For centuries, buffalo had traveled through the area until the buffalo hunters came in the 1870s and wiped out the great herds in order to profit from the sale of their hides. At one time the prairie grasses had grown waist high in the fertile land. Herds would sometimes run through, and the sounds of their approach would be like the rumbling of distant thunder. Sometimes they'd come at night, and in the morning no grass would remain after the great animals had feasted during the night.

Sam Nesmith, my psychically gifted friend who now lives in San Antonio, was brought up in Abilene. His father, Sam Nesmith Sr., grew up in Buffalo Gap. He used to tell Sam stories about events that took place at the Gap when he was a youngster living there. And when Sam asked his dad "Tell me a ghost story, Daddy," this was the story the elder Nesmith told him, a supposedly true story about a couple who once lived here when the grasses still grew high and the buffalo herds still came thundering through the gap.

John and Mabel had come to Texas from Tennessee after the Civil War, as many Southerners did. The war had left them without their home and without much hope. Like many another Tennessee family, they packed up their belongings on a covered wagon and headed west, hopeful of building a new life in a new land. At Buffalo Gap they found a nice little piece of land that John thought would do for farming. There was a good source of water, some shady oak trees, and the land looked to be good and fertile. Buttes and mesas surrounded the grassy valley they had chosen for their new homestead.

Among the meager possessions John and Mabel had brought from Tennessee was Mabel's most cherished treasure, an old family mantle clock. It found a new spot to chime away the hours on the mantle of the modest little log house John built for her. She loved its soft chimes and steady "tick-toc, tick-toc" sounds as it kept track of the passage of time. The clock kept her company through the long days when John was occupied in the surrounding fields.

Although they were fairly happy in their little cabin, John dreamed of a better life still. He didn't want to live in such modest circumstances forever, and he wanted to provide his beloved wife with some of the things they had been forced to leave behind in Tennessee.

So when the buffalo hunters came by to visit, John paid careful attention to their conversations. They told him if he would join up with them he'd be rich in no time. All he needed to do was be able to "shoot 'em and skin 'em." John didn't want to go off and leave Mabel in pursuit of buffalo, but he kept thinking about how she'd looked longingly at the catalogs, with the pretty things she'd like to have....

John decided he would join the buffalo hunters. Then he'd have the money to buy all those nice things for Mabel. So he went out and spent some of their savings on a second-hand 50-caliber Sharps rifle. It had a terrific sight and could shoot accurately from over 1,000 yards. He didn't want Mabel to know what he was doing, because he sort of figured she'd be upset if she found out he'd spent all that money on a rifle.

A few days after he purchased the weapon, he went 'way up on the hill behind the house to practice his marksmanship. It was a good distance to the house. He saw a red rag hanging out down near the clothesline and decided to use it for a target. He carefully aimed and fired. There was first a loud report and then a big cloud of smoke. Boy, he'd really bought a fine rifle! He dashed down the hill to see if he'd hit his target. As he came close, to his horror he saw it had not been a red rag that he'd singled out for a target. It was a red apron that Mabel was hanging on the clothesline, and Mabel, standing behind the bright "target," had been mortally wounded by the buffalo rifle. When John saw he had killed his wife, he just went crazy. First he set fire to their little cabin, and then he shot himself. All those dreams were over.

Now there is a big thicket growing where the little house once stood. It's where the old Buffalo Gap school was built later on, but that's gone now, too. Sam's daddy told him if you go up there where the little cabin once stood and listen real close, you'll hear it—the sound of a clock's constant "tick-toc, tick-toc...."

La Loma de la Cruz

I am indebted to the Val Verde County Historical Commission for some of the material in this charming and lovely story, which is fraught with both fact and legend.

There's a high hill, not quite a mountain, just outside of Del Rio, on the Texas side of the Rio Grande. Most people call it "La Loma de la Cruz," which translates into "the hill of the cross." It is a cone-shaped hill near the clay bluffs of Eagle Pass Hill. La Loma is a local landmark.

The hill can be seen quite plainly to the southwest of the point where the old Eagle Pass Highway, now U.S. Highway 277 South, goes over Eagle Pass Hill, if one is facing the west side of Del Rio. The hill has been called other names, as well. Some people call it Round Mountain, and others have nicknamed it Sugar Loaf Mountain. The most common name, La Loma de la Cruz, stems from the time the first cross was placed there in the early 1870s.

The mountain is on private property today, so one has to have special permission to go near it. It's just outside the south city limits of Del Rio, about a mile west of San Felipe's Brodbent Street, which was once a part of the old Eagle Pass highway. We viewed it from the old cemetery just off the highway.

There are lots of legends attached to the place. One local story is that the loma, or hill, is the location of the hidden treasures of Montezuma. At the time that the Spanish conquered the great Aztec empire, some of the treasures were taken out of Mexico and hidden, or so the story goes. Legend has it that once a year the mountain opens up for a short time and the wealth hidden within is exposed. Anyone nearby can run inside and take out whatever he can carry, but if a treasure hunter gets greedy or takes too long to gather up his riches, the mountain will close up and he will be entombed there.

With such stories around, there are naturally tales in abundance about ghosts hanging around the landmark. The people that live in the area don't like to go near the hill after dark. Since there's a cemetery there, that may be the reason. And of course, there are stories about the men who were killed near the hill during the last big Indian battle in the area. To pacify these wandering spirits, a cross was placed on the summit of the hill many years ago.

The Historical Commission sent me a history that was compiled by Mrs. Elizabeth S. Daughtery and Mrs. Thomas Henry Seale of how the hill got its name. To quote this information:

Dona Paula Losoya and her sister came to this area with their parents when they were children in 1862 or 1863. The family settled in the valley through which San Felipe Creek flows in its seven-mile journey from San Felipe Springs to the Rio Grande. Their farm was near the hill, a little farther down the creek where it flows to the east and then to the south of Qualia Drive. The family irrigated the farm with water from San Felipe Creek. The water flowed by gravity through the ditches they dug.

About eight years later, when Paula was a young lady, she married James H. Taylor. He was one of the four young men from Kinney and Uvalde counties who purchased over a thousand acres of land located from just south of San Felipe Springs along the San Felipe Creek for several miles to a point just past La Loma.

These men, along with all of their families and other kinfolks they could persuade, moved to this slightly settled area to form a new settlement. This was around 1868. The men intended to develop an irrigation system and place the whole area they had bought under cultivation, utilizing the water from San Felipe Creek.

James Taylor was single at the time, but he married Dona Paula Losoya very soon after he arrived. Their home was an adobe, which is now 100 Hudson Drive, and it is still in use as a residence.

This group of men formed the San Felipe Agricultural, Manufacturing, and Irrigation Company in 1871 and built the system of irrigation ditches and canals that are still being used for irrigation of many acres of land in the valley through which

San Felipe Creek flows for seven miles from San Felipe Springs to the Rio Grande. All of this waterflow is by gravity.

This irrigation system at one time furnished the water for 8,000 acres of cultivated land. Some of the original canals have been covered, and buildings are now where the canals were first made, but much of that same system of creeks, canals, and ditches are still being used. That is in a period of over 100 years!

At this time the settlement of San Felipe, which was sometimes called San Felipe Del Rio, and later still, just Del Rio, was very small. When the railroad was completed in 1883, a lot of people began to move here. Its population was only 300 in 1883 and by 1900 it had grown to 3,000. It was finally believed that it would become a permanent settlement. This had been doubtful before the railroad was completed. It was the first all-weather transcontinental railroad across the United States. There was one more railroad farther north, but in the winter months it was almost impassable.

James Taylor died April 4, 1876, so at that time Paula inherited the property they had. La Loma and the surrounding area was a part of that property.

Dona Paula married a young medic from Fort Clark very soon after her husband died, and she became Dona Paula Taylor Rivers.

At one time there was a fight between some of the Mexican inhabitants of San Felipe and some Mexican rebels who had come to this side of the Rio Grande to steal some horses. It is said that two Mexicans and three Mexican-Indian rebels were killed. They were buried near the spot where the fight occurred, close to the base of La Loma.

Dona Paula had a cross erected and placed on the hill to recognize the fact it was hallowed ground since people were buried there. From that day the hill has been locally known as "La Loma de la Cruz."

After these first few people were buried at the foot of the big hill, it came to Dona Paula's attention that other Mexican people were burying their dead either in their own yards or at the base of the hill since they knew other people had already been buried there after the battle. They were using these areas because they had no real designated graveyard or cemetery in which to bury their loved ones.

In order that these people would have a special place to bury their dead, Dona Paula, in 1884, gave 4.35 acres of her land to be used as a cemetery. The land which she gave them is just southeast of La Loma de la Cruz. Soon afterward, an Italian settler named Cassanelli gave a quarter of an acre for a little burial ground for the Italians who had just arrived to settle in the area. He bought the land adjoining the Mexican graveyard. Both areas are fenced and cared for as one cemetery today. This cemetery joins the south border of the Del Rio city limits, so it is located in Val Verde County. The local people lovingly tend it today, keeping the graves weeded and the shrubbery neatly trimmed.

La Loma de la Cruz, Del Rio

CHAPTER 4

GHOSTS OF THE GREAT BIG BEND

NIGHT OF THE COMANCHE MOON

The Comanche moon is glowing;
The light shines o'er the land,
As warriors come once more to cross
The muddy Rio Grande.
As we stand upon the cliffs of stone
That overlook the stream
Sometimes we see them once again,
Caught in the moonlight's gleam.
We hear the eerie chanting
Of the warriors dancing 'round,
To the cadence of their war-drums
As they beat a hollow sound;
We see the fiery redness
Of their campfires glowing bright
And feel their lingering presence
In the stillness of the night.

Docia Williams

The Ghostly Chisos

The high mountains that cluster around a natural basin in the Big Bend National Park are called the Chisos Mountains. How they got that name is a matter of speculation, but there are several explanations that bear repeating, since the name is generally accepted to mean "ghosts."

Dr. Robert T. Hill, a government surveyor working in the area in 1899, was the first to associate the name Chisos with the physical appearance of the mountains. Many people explain the name Chisos is a corruption of the Spanish name *hechizo* which means bewitched in the fearful sense and enchanting in the more complimentary sense. I might say I think they could take on both meanings! I've walked down the trails around the far "window" area of the basin in the moonlight. The mountains then are awesome...overwhelming...and sometimes frightening. When a night owl hoots and a coyote howls, as the clouds hang low, draped over the tall pinnacles, there is an eeriness in those mountains that long remains in one's memory.

Elton Miles, who wrote *Tales of the Big Bend*, published in 1976 by the Texas A&M University Press, related an interesting ghost story associated with the Chisos Mountains. According to Miles:

The legend of Agua Fria Cliff, as told by Isidoro Salgado of Alpine, deals with an Indian woman of the Chisos Mountains whose baby unfortunately was born at the foot of the cliff when the moon was full. The other women reminded her that everybody knew how a baby born under the ill omen of a full moon was sure to turn into some kind of animal, perhaps a coyote or a lizard.

To save her baby an ill fate and herself the shame, the mother carried it up to the edge of Agua Fria Cliff. In her arms the infant moved against her body as she listened to the water bubbling from the rocks below and as she noticed on the cliff the familiar paintings of deer and horses in red and brown. She held her squirming baby with two hands over the cliff, shut her eyes, let go, and closed her ears.

In 1954 Isidoro and his brother-in-law were working cattle near Agua Fria Cliff. "Here," he said, "at night the wind seems to be mysterious, because the running water is like singing, when an angel is going to heaven."

After supper one evening as the boys slept on the ground, a noise frightened the horses. Isidoro's kinsman told him, "The horses are scared of something, because all of the time I have been working here, they have acted like something was running after them."

Then Isidoro heard a cry in the darkness. It was the scream of a baby, as though it were falling down the cliff to its death. He told how he had heard this wailing at Agua Fria Cliff again and again. "His crying lasts for a few seconds," Isidoro Salgado concluded, "I did not believe in ghosts, but I was scared. Now that I have heard this cry, I am convinced that these legends that have been told are true."

Perhaps what Isidoro and his brother-in-law heard was just the cry of a panther...as there are big cats in the area. Or maybe it was the screech of an owl, or the howl of a lonesome coyote. Maybe it was just the wind whistling through the high mountains...or maybe, just maybe....

The Ghost of Alsate

Before the white men came, the land known today as the Big Bend area was the hunting grounds of the Apache; more specifically, the Mescaleros. Then the Texas Rangers came, and there were many altercations. Finally, the Indians moved over the Rio Bravo and made their camps in Mexico. Not wanted there either, things got uncomfortable for them and they once again moved over to the Texas side. There were also some renegade Mexicans who had fallen out of favor with the government and who had taken up with the Apaches. The Mexican government decided the whole lot should be exterminated, by whatever means available. For starters, they enlisted the aid of a turncoat named Lionecio Castillo who knew the Apache chieftains.

Now, for many years the greatest of the Apache chiefs was Alsate. So Castillo sent a message to the Apaches camped in the Chisos Mountains, to the effect that the Mexican government wanted to make a treaty with Alsate and his followers. They would be placed on a big reservation in Mexico and be well provided for there. Castillo told Alsate it was through his personal efforts that this was being accomplished, and he backed up the promises with fake papers, impressively signed, sealed, and beribboned to look official. The Apaches couldn't read the documents, but they looked legitimate to them and so they agreed to attend a meeting with the Mexican officials.

Alsate's chief lieutenant, who was named Colorado, went with a couple of other braves to San Carlos and met with the Mexican for a couple of days. Then they agreed upon a date where the whole tribe and their leaders would come for a big fiesta to celebrate the treaty, and there would be dancing, drinking, feasting, and gifts thrown in as a part of the bargain.

Well, it sounded good so far. Although doubtful about the whole thing, Alsate rounded up his followers and they duly arrived at San Carlos. Unknown to them, several companies of Mexican soldiers had encamped in a spot, under cover, away from the celebrations, and were ready to make their moves when ordered. After the Indians arrived, they were first showered with all manner of gifts, then much beef and mutton was barbecued over the open fires. Mescal, the fiery liquor, was passed out, and by nightfall nearly every Indian warrior was dead drunk. It had been quite a party! Even their lookouts had deserted their posts and had come to join in the celebrations.

During the night, while the Indians slept in drunken stupors, the Mexican soldiers sneaked into the town and captured and bound all the Indians. Before nightfall the next day, Alsate and his men had been shackled and marched to Chihuahua. When Alsate inquired where they were being taken, he was told they were being marched to Mexico City. Many of the group died along the way. Others died while in prison. Some few may have escaped. It was rumored Alsate was one of these. The rest were distributed to various wealthy Mexican families to serve as their slaves. All along the Rio Grande, and especially in the town of San Carlos where the ill-fated party had taken place, everyone rejoiced that the Apaches had been either captured, killed, or enslaved. The turncoat (they were called "rateros") Lionecio Castillo was especially pleased!

According to Virginia Madison, who wrote the book *The Big Bend Country*, this was not quite the last of Alsate. She wrote:

> Many moons later, a dark rumor began to creep along the frontier. The story was more venomous than the deadly rattler, because it struck fear into the hearts of the border people. The pastores and the vaqueros had seen the ghost of Alsate! People

in the vicinity became afraid to go out at night. Finally the Rurales were sent out to search the region to allay the fears of the people. They saw no ghost but they found a cave which showed signs of recent occupancy. After the search by the Rurales, the ghost appeared again and again, always in the vicinity of the cave.

Soon it became known as Alsate's Cave. Finally the ghost was accepted and seemed to worry no one except Leonecio Castillo, who became so nervous over the stories of the ghost that he left the country. After a long time he returned, and again there were reports of the ghostly appearances, and so Castillo disappeared again. Finally, the ghosts were seen no more, and the bravest and most curious decided to search the cave. There they found the remains of the great Chief Alsate near the ashes of a fire long dead. Alsate was the last of the Chisos Apaches.

The Deserted Mine Owner's House

The country out around the ghost town of Terlingua, on State Highway 170, is pretty desolate. The area, on the western fringe of Big Bend National Park, definitely isn't farmland. Nothing much will grow in the barren, rock-strewn soil but ocotillo, greasewood, lechuguillo, and prickly pear.

The name Terlingua comes from the Spanish, *tres linguas*, or three languages: Spanish, English, and Indian, spoken in the area. Now referred to most often as a ghost town, the tiny little community once enjoyed some shining hours. There were some really good years when briefly, like a candle glowing, the area lit up and shone brightly. Then it eventually sputtered and burned out.

The story of Terlingua's rise and fall makes mighty interesting reading!

There were Indians in the Big Bend area who used the red pigments they found in the rocky hills for their rock wall paintings and for their war paints. They didn't know the substance they used was called cinnabar.

The stories about how the valuable ore was discovered sometimes are in conflict. One popular tale credits a goat herder who stopped to rest on a rocky ledge along Terlingua Creek with the discovery. Seems he broke off a chunk of the rock with his staff, and the bright red of the freshly broken surface attracted his attention. He pocketed a small sample of the mineral, noting it was much heavier than the rocks which he often picked up as he went about the lonely task of herding. He didn't know if it was valuable or not, but he decided to take his sample to some educated friends who might know. This was in the year 1892. The herder's friends recognized it was cinnabar, from which comes quicksilver, or mercury. The end result was they contacted some promoters in New Mexico who bought up some of the land and developed it into the Marfa and Mariposa Mining Company.

Another story credits two cowboys, out rounding up strays in the area, with the discovery. Divine McKinney and Jess Parker were also attracted to the red mineral, did a little digging around, and decided the deposit might be valuable.

Whichever story is true, and both of them might well be, the land, in the most productive area, had fallen into the hands of a little Yankee businessman who had never even been to Texas! Howard E. Perry, who came from Portland, Maine, had come into possession of the land which was eventually to become the country's biggest quicksilver mine. There were several stories told about how he came to own the mineral-rich spread.

One story went around that Mr. Perry's father-in-law, who was in the shoe business, had accepted a couple of sections of land in payment of a debt. When Perry married, he came into possession of the land through his wife. Then there was the story that a local rancher, Ed Nevill, had seen Perry buy two sections of land at an auction in front of the Alpine courthouse, paying $150 cash for the property.

Then, according to *The Big Bend Country*, written in 1955 by West Texas resident Virginia Madison, Perry may have "gotten saved and gotten land" at one and the same time! Madison wrote:

Another report is that Mr. Perry was traveling through Kentucky about 1887 and happened to drop in on a revival meeting being conducted by General R.M. Gano, of Dallas, Texas. General Gano surveyed much of the land in the Big Bend in 1881-82 and acquired many of the original land certificates, which could be bought for less than a song, at first. The General was a former Confederate officer who had a predilection to preach the gospel and a couple of remunerative hobbies: cattle and land. Stuart McGregor, in his column in the

Dallas Morning News, reported that Gano's daily activities were recorded like this: "Saved thirty-two souls; sold sixteen sections of land." Perhaps Mr. Perry did buy the land from the general.

Perry was shrewd and very close-mouthed. Even people who knew him well did not seem to know the true story of how he came by the land. But he had it and he knew how to prosper from it. He owned more than just two sections, but two of the sections he did own formed the heart of the mine that made him his fortune. By making shrewd deals and buying up small claims, Perry was able to control the richest deposits of cinnabar ore in the area. He named his mining project the Chisos Mining Company.

Most of the workers in Perry's claims worked for a dollar a day, and the days ran from sunup to sundown. A hard taskmaster, the man controlled the lives of all who worked for him, and he wasn't the most loved character in the region, to be sure. It is said he wouldn't even let his miners, who were mostly Mexican laborers, off to go to church on Sunday. There were no siestas allowed. Only toil and low wages. But this was still better than no wages at all out in a country where jobs were hard to find.

The mines that produced quicksilver, or mercury, the end-product of the red cinnabar ore, peaked about the time of World War I. The Terlingua region produced 10,791 flasks, each weighing 76 pounds, in 1917. The ore had to be hauled by mule-drawn wagons to the railhead in Marathon, a trip that took several days to accomplish. Between 1900 and 1941 the Chisos Mining Company was the world's second largest quicksilver mine. Over 100,000 flasks of mercury were produced!

Most of the mining operations had ceased when World War II broke out. Then, there was an increased demand for quicksilver, as it is used in explosives and ammunition, as oxide for antifouling marine paint, in drugs and chemicals, and in certain instruments such as barometers and thermostats. Cinnabar, of course, is also used in cosmetics. (Today women use cinnabar rouge much as the Indians used it for their war paint.) So the mines revved up again and were active until 1944.

Perry controlled everything in the area while he had his mines. He owned the company stores, the schools (to make sure the only education local youngsters could get would be at the Terlingua school, thus ensuring their fathers wouldn't move elsewhere to work at other mines), and nobody ever crossed Mr. Perry. Even though he spent much of his time back in New England, he had managers to carry out all of his orders.

At the peak of production, as many as 2,000 people lived in Terlingua and the neighboring community of Study Butte. Most of the workers were of Mexican heritage, which can be plainly seen today when one looks at the markers in the old cemetery that lies to the left of the road leading into what is left of the village. The little adobe and stone houses that some of the miners lived in were carbon copies of what one might find just across the nearby Rio Grande. There are still some roofless walls standing, giving mute testimony to the town that Terlingua used to be.

On a high point, looking out over the mines and the homes of his workers, Perry built his mansion. According to Bill Ivey, longtime Terlingua resident and manager of the Trading Post there, the old house is haunted.

The old Perry Mansion, Terlingua

As previously stated, Howard Perry wasn't a particularly love-able character. He was tough and ruthless in his quest for riches and not very considerate of those who worked for him and helped to make him rich.

Strange to say, the man who could make grown men tremble in their boots wasn't able to call the shots with his own wife! She stayed in Maine when he initially went out to stake his mining claims and begin his mining operation. Almost immediately he set his laborers to work, building a large, comfortable house that he felt would be suitable for his wife to live in. According to Ivey, Mrs. Perry was a real "New England lady" and had absolutely no idea about what the country would be like where she was to make her new home. She must have become increasingly apprehensive as the train rolled over the tracks carrying her ever closer to her husband and her new home. She arrived in Marathon, a tiny town on the railroad line some fifty-seven miles distant from Terlingua. Perry sent a driver and wagon to Marathon to meet her and bring her over the dirt roads, crossing arid desert and mountain terrain to arrive at the little village of adobe houses and ocotillo jackals that was called Terlingua.

Although the house that had been readied for her arrival was spacious and fitted out as comfortably as possible for its new mistress, it is reported that just one night out there in the rock-strewn desert was quite enough for the lady from back East! When she awoke the next morning, she announced, "Howard, this place is just not for me. I'm going home." She summoned the mule-driver to take her back to Marathon where she boarded the first train east and never returned.

Although Perry spent a lot of time in Maine, on long visits, he was never able to persuade Mrs. Perry to come back to the home he had built for her. Although he was a short and stocky man and did not cut a particularly dashing figure, he did have an eye for the ladies. It was often rumored that a lot of Mr. Perry's lady friends came out for extended visits to the mansion. (Remember: he was very rich. That helped.)

After Perry closed down his mining operations, he left Terlingua. He died on a train headed to Florida in 1944. He was well into his eighties at the time of his death. Whatever may be said of the old gentleman, in the industrial world he is remembered as someone who triumphed over a rocky wilderness and developed the greatest quicksilver mine in the United States.

Today, Terlingua is but a shadow of its former self. Briefly, there is an annual revival when the International Chili Cook-off is held there.

And a few little businesses still hang on. There's Ivey's Trading Post, a few small shops, a restaurant, a Rio Grande float trip outfitter, and a newly restored theater. But it definitely isn't a metropolis! And the biggest house in town is still Mr. Perry's house, now deserted, high up there on the hill.

The old Perry Mansion, Terlingua

There are those who have, out of curiosity, wandered into the empty old building with its long galleried porch. Many a nocturnal visitor has been greeted by the ghostly wraith of a woman. She appears mostly in the upstairs area and just wanders from room to empty room. The apparition is misty in appearance.

Bill Ivey couldn't answer when I asked him who the figure might be. But I've done a lot of thinking. It could be Mrs. Perry, who, because she refused to come live in the house that her husband built for her, is now doomed to wander its empty halls and bedchambers in penance for not bending to her husband's wishes. Or, it might be a servant girl. Maybe she's afraid to leave on the off-chance Howard Perry might come back and find she'd deserted her post. After all, they say he was a very hard taskmaster! Then again, even though he didn't appear to be much of a romantic type, maybe the ghost of one of his former female visitors returns to the place where she and her married lover shared some romantic, illicit trysts together. Only those empty old rooms know for sure. And they aren't talking.

Light a Candle to the Dead

Out in Terlingua there's a good-sized cemetery. Most of those who are buried there are the Mexican laborers and their families who lived there during the days when the cinnabar mines were in full operation. Most of the graves are marked by crude wooden crosses, but some of them also have little altars on them where their relatives still come to place floral offerings.

Bill Ivey, who owns the Trading Post, told me that on November 2, 1993, he and his wife decided it would really be nice to observe All Saints Day (known as "the day of the dead" by the Mexican population) by putting a little candle on each grave. They got together a big box of Mason jars they'd had stored away and a lot of votive candles, and they went around to each grave and placed a jar containing a lit

Old cemetery, Terlingua

candle on it. Ivey said it was a very windy night and the candles were hard to light. His wife was also extremely nervous as after dark the place is really "spooky."

The Iveys got down to the very last candle and jar and realized they'd used up all their matches. The wind had kept blowing them out and it took far more to do the job than they had anticipated. As they reached down in the box for the very last jar, something fell out on the ground. It was a book of matches from a restaurant they had never heard of. The box of jars had been in their storeroom for a very long time, yet the matchbook looked new. What really seemed strange to them was what was printed on the back of the matchbook.

The words read, "Your hosts thank you."

Haunts at Lajitas

Right on the banks of the Rio Grande, there's a small settlement known as Lajitas. It is comprised mainly of the Badlands Hotel complex and the houses where the staff of the resort make their homes. One portion of the resort was built over the foundations of an old cavalry post which was used during the days when Pancho Villa and his men were running rampant all along the border. In fact, Villa is known to have made several sorties on the Texas side of the Rio Bravo. There's a boardwalk along which are located numerous shops, a drug-store and ice cream parlor, float ride outfitters, and the hotel lobby and registration desk on the lower level. The second story of the complex is given over to hotel rooms furnished in the style of the late 1800s. Another section of the large complex is devoted to quarters that dupli-cate the old two-storied officers' quarters at Fort Davis. The whole area is very popular, not only with tourists, but with film crews, and has often been used as the setting for Western films.

I have been out there many times as a tour operator. I conduct fre-quent trips to the Big Bend area, and Lajitas is a favorite spot to take my tour groups for good lodging and good eating. During a trip out to that country in May of 1994, I was told by one of the hotel staff that a small stone building adjacent to the bakery, which serves now as the accounting office, is haunted. The building has very thick walls of native stone and was once a dwelling consisting of a living room and three small bedrooms. Several of the people out there told me they didn't like to go around it at night, and "strange noises" had been heard there, but that's about all I could find out. The staff member said she had heard there had been a murder there a long time ago.

With little more than this to go on, I called Emily Moore, a long-time friend and manager of the Badlands Hotel. She referred me to Robert Salgado, another staff member. A call to Salgado verified that yes, he believed the place was haunted, but I had better talk to someone who had lived in those parts longer than he had. I finally reached a longtime resident of the area, Carolina White, who lives with her husband, Arturo, at nearby Terlingua.

Mrs. White said she vividly recalled the terrible murder that had taken place in the little stone house. She had visited the murder scene soon after it occurred, having been acquainted with the victim, one Matilde Hinojos. As best Mrs. White could recall, the crime took place in the early 1940s and was so heinous she said she wouldn't be surprised if the place was haunted forever afterwards! The young woman had a little boy, just a toddler, and was expecting another baby at the time she was killed. Neighbors heard the shouts of the couple as they had a terrible argument. Then the air was punctuated with screams as the man went about the gruesome act of killing his wife. Apparently, the man was extremely jealous of his wife, according to what

The haunted stone house, Lajitas

Mrs. White could recall, and he had a violent temper. Whether he had been drinking or not, she didn't know. But the murder was absolutely ghastly! The man had beaten his wife with a piece of iron; Mrs. White said it might have been a length of pipe. There was blood all over the room and bits of tissue and the woman's brains on the walls and ceiling! He had also apparently pulled some of her insides out and stuffed the body cavities with cotton and old rags. Altogether a gruesome sight!

Apparently Hinojos was caught right away and sent off to prison. Carolina White said she had heard he either died or was killed in prison soon afterward.

An elderly neighbor lady found the little boy, crawling around on the floor, playing in the blood of his own mother. She took the tot away from the bloody scene, and he was brought up by relatives of his mother.

Mrs. White said she and her husband were pretty sure that another resident of that same little stone house was killed there some years later. This time the victim was a man, and she believed he was either a Texas Ranger or a park ranger. She could recall no details.

Tom Moore, general manager of the properties at Lajitas, told me that several people on the staff have refused to go into the old building at night. This is where he now has his office, and he is not disturbed by anything there. However, he said Sheila McRae, a former restaurant manager, was especially leery of the place and felt enough presences there that she absolutely refused to enter the building.

The rest of the hotel complex is not haunted, however, and if you want to enjoy a wonderful West Texas experience in beautiful surroundings, you can do no better than to call and reserve your room at Lajitas. When you call Emily Moore at (915) 424-3471, send her my regards!

CHAPTER 5

MYSTERIOUS GHOST LIGHTS

The Mystery Lights of Marfa

They bob like giant fireflies,
Glittering in the starlit nights,
A mystery still unanswered,
That they call the "Marfa Lights."

Any book delving into ghosts…spirits…and unknowns in West Texas would be incomplete without including the phenomena of the mysterious Marfa Lights. What they are and why they are there have been unsolved mysteries for well over a century. Where they are is more easily answered.

The lights, which frequently appear in the foothills of the Chinati Mountains, have been seen by literally thousands of people. In fact, they've become enough of an attraction that there is a special Marfa Lights viewing area about nine miles east of Marfa on US 90. The site, near the old air base, is on the south side of the highway. There is a large turnout area on which stands a state historical marker, which reads:

MARFA LIGHTS

"The Marfa Lights, mysterious and unexplained lights that
have been reported in the area for over one hundred years, have
been the subject of many theories. The first recorded sighting
of the lights was by rancher Robert Ellison in 1883. Variously
explained as campfires, phosphorescent minerals, swamp gas,
static electricity, St. Elmo's fire, and "ghost lights," the lights
reportedly change colors, move about, and change in intensity.
Scholars have reported over seventy-five local folk tales dealing with the unexplained phenomenon."

The town of Marfa, about 125 miles northwest of the Big Bend National Park headquarters, is Texas' highest incorporated city, at an elevation of 4,688 feet. The small city of around 3,000 population is the county seat of Presidio County. The locale boasts of being the location for the famous movie *Giant*, and of having the best conditions in the world for soaring. The television series *Unsolved Mysteries* filmed the lights in July of 1989. The producer, film personality Robert Stack, described them as "ghostly gold" in color.

The lights have become so famous that the city celebrates each Labor Day weekend with a Marfa Lights Festival, which includes a parade, arts and crafts, food booths, street dancing, a rodeo, a golf tournament, and a panel discussion about, what else? The Marfa Lights, of course!

Since Robert Ellison's discovery, the lights have appeared frequently, unlike many ghost lights about the state that appear infrequently, such as the famous lights of Bailey's Prairie that appear only every seven years. Marfa's bright orbs appear regularly, although not at any particular time or season. They generally appear to be about the size of a basketball and can be startlingly bright and very white, or they can be red or yellow or blue. Sometimes they are said to shine with the intensity of a locomotive's headlight! They often appear to dance about in a wild, weird, nocturnal ballet!

At first people said they were just the headlights of automobiles driving over on Highway 67. But then, there were reports by pioneer settlers who saw the lights more than a hundred years ago, and of course there were no such things as automobiles then.

Pilots have flown over the area trying to pinpoint the exact locations of the lights, but they have been unsuccessful. Hikers and campers have searched the foothills of the mountains for them, but the closer they come, the more the dancing points of brilliance seem to elude their trackers.

For years articles have appeared in magazines and newspapers around the state. Each story seems to expound a different theory. There was one legend I recall reading way back in the January 7, 1965 edition of the *Amarillo Globe News* that stated, "it is a campfire kindled by the restless soul of a wayward Apache brave condemned to roam the Chinati Mountains forever."

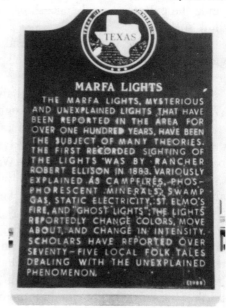

Ira Blanton, an English professor at Sul Ross University in Alpine, shared a similar story. A Chisos Apache chief, Alsate, is frequently credited as being the source of the Marfa Lights. He was betrayed and enslaved by the Mexican armies in San Carlos but later escaped to the Chinati Mountains near Marfa.

Alsate's spirit is said to be lighting his campfires every night in an attempt to summon his warriors back to assist him. Some people say that Alsate's wife is up in the mountains lighting her own fires as well!

The light, or lights, are visible on most nights. Then there will be nights when they make no appearance at all. Sometimes they will appear and go out and then reappear several hours later. Sometimes they will appear a few degrees to the left or right of previous sightings. Climatic conditions and temperatures, which vary greatly in summer and winter seasons, do not seem to affect the sightings at all.

Although some scientists say the lights are just reflections of the moonlight on a vein of mica, thorough searches of the Chinatis have revealed no veins of mica anywhere. And often the lights are seen on dark nights when there is no moonlight! Theories of "swamp gas" that might produce mysterious lights are pretty farfetched, as one would be hard pressed indeed to find a swamp in that part of West Texas! Some people have, fairly recently, latched onto the UFO theory. They think they are either spaceships or the landing lights put out (by whom?) to guide the extraterrestrial spaceships into their landing places. I don't think so!

Some people cling to the legends that the lights are the ghostly glow of Indian campfires where the spirits of long-dead braves dance in preparation for battle.

There was a good story about the lights, written by Rosemary Williams, which appeared in the August 1993 edition of *Texas Highways Magazine*. Also, you might like to read Wallace O. Chariton's detailed account titled, "The Best Mystery in Texas," included in the book *Unsolved Texas Mysteries*, by Wordware Publishing.

There was one story about the lights that might indicate they are actually "spirit" lights…of what, we know not. The late writer Ed Syres, in his fine book *Ghost Stories of Texas* (Texian Press), included a story called "The Mountain Light" in which he quotes Mrs. W.T. Giddens of Sundown. She told of an experience her late father had many years ago. Her dad was a rancher. He was up in the Chinati Mountains near Shafter rounding up some stray cattle when a blue norther blew in. He got caught in a howling, icy storm, with blasts of wind and snow that blew so hard his visibility was reduced to about zero. He tried to hurry so he could get to shelter before freezing to death. He soon found he was hopelessly lost in the blinding storm.

He came to an outcropping of rocks and tried to feel his way around them. Suddenly, from out of nowhere, a strong, mysterious light appeared. The man could never fully explain how they communicated, but somehow the light told him he was three miles south of Chinati Peak and was headed in the opposite direction from where he was supposed to be going. It also let him know he was very close to a dangerous precipice. The light advised him he'd better follow them to safety or he could die and led him to a small cave, where he was sheltered throughout the long night, and provided heat, light, and evidently some conversation as well! The light claimed it was a "spirit from elsewhere and long ago." It relayed to him that it meant no harm to him and wanted him to be safe from the storm. The next morning the man headed out, the storm having passed on through. He discovered he had indeed been off the trail and had been headed directly to the edge of a sheer cliff several hundred feet high. Had the light not headed him off, he most surely would have plunged to his death!

Mrs. Giddens said she believed her father. She recalls after that incident that lights often appeared in their pasture, and the family considered them friendly.

Having read and heard so much for so long about the strange lights, my husband, Roy, and I decided to go and see them for ourselves. On a clear spring night (April 11, 1995) we stopped at the Highway 90 drive-out, where a number of cars and campers were already situated. It was about 9:30 p.m. The moon was full, and the desert area was quite light. We got out of our car and for about an hour watched entranced as first one, then two, then finally as many as four lights danced and bobbed about, almost as if they were dancing in the moonlight, putting on a good show for their observers. The lights would dim and go out, then reappear, then brighten in intensity. Occasionally one light would separate into two or three segments. Mostly they appeared low, about at the foot of the far-off Chinati Mountains, but sometimes they would rise in elevation as they shifted positions. A couple of times all four went out and we thought it was all over for the night. Then, first one, then another, and yet another, would reappear. They are thoroughly fascinating, mystifying, and puzzling. We watched for over an hour, until the chill of the desert air drove us into our car and back to the warmth of our motel room in Alpine. When we retired, we believed in, but still wondered about, the Marfa Lights.

That the Marfa Lights exist, there's no doubt. Go see for yourself! But WHAT they are, and WHY they're there, remains a complete mystery, which is why they are still so fascinating!

The Lights of the Chisos

I have been an avid reader of...and subscriber to...*Texas Highways Magazine* for over twenty years. I save and catalog each issue and enjoy reading them again and again, never planning a trip without first heading to these useful sources of information!

I came across a brief mention of ghostly lights of the Chisos Mountains, as they appear now and again, in the October 1979 issue of the magazine. The writer, Elton Miles, who wrote the book *Tales of the Big Bend* in 1976, had this to say:

"Los Chisos Mountains are so called because of the spooky effect of the moonlight on their gray vegetation. Another reason is that on nights after a rain the mountains glow with phosphorescent light. Patches of light may be seen on a mountain slope, or sometimes an entire peak will glow as though illuminated from within. Bob Clanton of Fort Davis recalls that one night while on a camping and hunting trip he saw an entire valley light up. For an instant, as bright as day, every cactus and rock became distinct."

"Another kind of light reportedly moves across the highest peaks and ridges...a ghostly torch carried by the spirit of an Indian warrior stationed in the Chisos to guide other spirits to the Happy Hunting Ground...."

On a recent trip to the Big Bend area, my husband and I visited a small community on Highway 2627 near the Panther Junction entrance to the National Park. There is a store, called the Stillwell Store, and an RV park, several small houses, and the Hallie Stillwell Memorial Museum located there. It was our privilege to meet and visit with Mrs. Hallie Stillwell. She is one of the last of the pioneer settlers of the area, and at ninety-eight years young, she is still very alert and interested in all that is going on around her. She still enjoys talking about the place she has lived in for so many years. She is the author of *I'll Gather My Geese*, and co-author of *How Come It's Called That*, a collection of Big Bend area place names and the interesting stories connected to them.

When we dropped by the General Store, we also chatted with Hallie's sister, Glenn Harris. Mrs. Harris told us that ghost lights were pretty common out in this area, and that both she and her sister had seen them. Glenn recalled one night, many years ago—she believes it might have been back during the prohibition era—when she and her husband and Hallie were driving back to the ranch after a visit to Marathon. It was rather late, as she recalled. Suddenly, they saw a very bright, flashing light on top of a mountain across the road from the ranch. Glenn said she was very frightened because at first they thought it might be an outlaw gang, or maybe some bootleggers, but then they realized that no one could possibly get up those steep rocks. Glenn was too frightened to get out of the car and open the ranch gate for her husband to drive through. Hallie said she wasn't afraid (after all, this lady once shot a panther, at close range, right between the eyes!) so she did the honors. Hallie told her husband, Roy, about the lights and he shrugged them off as some sort of strange atmospheric condition.

Glenn told us many times she has seen strange, unexplainable lights at night around the trailer park where she lives. Sometimes they are just bright lights, twinkling somewhere out there in the mountains. Sometimes they flash on and off, and strangest of all, sometimes as she looks out of her window she's seen them suddenly whirling around like twin Ferris wheels turning in opposite directions. Both Glenn and Hallie have viewed the famous Marfa Lights as well. Both say the lights that shine in the Big Bend area are just "ghost lights," and that's the only explanation they have for them!

I too have seen lights at night in the mountains, lights where none should be. They appear where there are no roads or campgrounds. Perhaps they belong to a late night hiker, though anyone with any sense at all wouldn't wander far afield after dark in that high country. (There have been sightings of both bears and panthers in those mountains!) Maybe I saw moonlight reflected on mica-flecked boulders. I know they were eerie sights. I was glad to retire to the comfort and safety of my warm bed at the Chisos Basin Lodge and reflect on those things I still do not quite understand about the Chisos....

The Lights of the Lost Padre Mine

Dr. John West, an English professor at the University of Texas at El Paso, kindly provided me with some interesting stories from that far West Texas community. Two of his students, Sheila Stopani and Harriet Sturgeon, did a term paper which was submitted to him on December 11, 1975. He sent me a copy of the paper, which included a story about the Lost Padre Mine. There actually were several mines, found both in the Franklin Mountains near El Paso and the Hueco Mountains some miles to the east. It seems that early Spanish Jesuits found a very rich vein of silver in the mountains. At the bottom of the deep shaft they hid 300 burro loads of silver bullion when they suddenly had to leave the country in 1680 during the Pueblo Rebellion. They ordered their Indian laborers to fill up the tunnel to keep the treasure hidden. One version of the story told by Jim Moore of El Paso, himself of American Indian descent, stated that the Indians who had buried the treasure for the priests were then killed to protect the secrecy of the location. And it is said that the wails of these dead Indians can still be heard emanating from the entrance to the mine!

There are numerous versions of the story, but they all center around the mountains, lost mines, and lots of still undiscovered treasure!

A brilliant light used to guard the hidden mine, according to an article that ran in the *El Paso Times*, April 18, 1965:

> The ghost, which takes the form of a spectacular ball of brilliant light, is said to be the composite of spirits of long-dead Indians, which forever guard the locations of the Padre Mine against rediscovery by the hated white-eyes.

> Its last known appearance was back in 1939. The reporter was a man named Henry Gardiner, who was in company with the Boy Scout Troop 11, led by Scoutmaster H.R. Miller, who were all camped in the canyon.

> Shortly after dark the canyon was suddenly lit bright as day by a dazzling fireball that bobbed slowly up and down like a demented yo-yo as it moved ponderously towards the canyon wall, then disappeared.

The Amarillo Lights

There are a number of famous ghost lights in Texas. Especially notable are the famous Marfa Lights, which I have already mentioned. The lights of Bailey's Prairie, near Angleton, and the Saratoga Lights in the Big Thicket, which I wrote about in an earlier book, are also well known. And not to be ignored are the ghost lights of Amarillo!

George Turner, a staff writer for the *Amarillo Globe News*, wrote about some unusual lights sighted around Amarillo in the May 31, 1971 issue of the paper:

One winter's night in 1946 two of us were driving north towards Tascosa in my prewar sedan when, about 7 miles northwest of Amarillo, we saw a phosphorescent object hovering over the road several hundred yards ahead. We slowed the car so as to better observe the object and realized it was moving toward us at approximately the same speed as we were traveling. It was about 5 feet in the air.

Its size could not be determined exactly because it was surrounded by a shimmering glow. As it came within the range of our headlights it veered sharply to the west side of the road, over a barrow pit, and moved along beside the car, having reversed its direction.

Suddenly, with incredible speed, it rushed towards the car until it was against the window, then flew upward and out of sight. We searched the area for some time without finding a trace of it.

We made the mistake of telling a few friends and were variously laughed at, accused of drunkenness or given explanations that seemed logical to anyone who wasn't there. We decided to keep our own counsel.

Imagine our delight, when, shortly after, reports of similar sightings began to appear. Floating phosphorescent blobs were seen at many points between Amarillo and Tascosa on both sides of the Canadian by numerous residents.

Lest the reader ascribe these reports to "flying saucer hysteria," please remember that the flying saucer was not at that time a part of our nomenclature. And as for that "swamp gas" explanation: surely not in winter in an area where swamps are as scarce as frog hairs.

Lights Over a Lonesome Grave

The Lonesome Grave

A pile of white rocks on a hillside so bare
Shows us where someone lies buried up there.
As the big herd moved onward 'neath a stormy gray sky
One of the drovers in pain, had to die....
Now his soul wanders lonely, o'er the hillside where deep
'Neath the shelter of rocks he was laid down to sleep.
Sometimes he searches for those who went on,
Wondering why they up and left him alone.
If you look close you might see his little white light
Flickering and glowing in the dark of the night.

Oh sleep ghostly figure, for now they also have gone.
You'll find them in Glory, for they all have moved on,
And we who are left will come pray you'll find rest
And peace as you sleep on your hillside out west.

Docia Williams

Writer-historian Winona Rinehart, of Spur, says maybe they just have stars in their eyes. But teenagers out for an evening of romancing, and other teens just out cruising, swear they have seen strange, ghostly lights flickering at night, bobbing up and down like giant fireflies up on the slopes of Negro Hill outside of Spur.

The story, according to Rinehart, is that a cattle drive was in progress, taking the route across an area lying to the west side of Dickens County and the east side of Crosby County. This was probably sometime in the very late 1800s when cattle still had to be driven north to the railroads in Kansas. About dusk, the herd and its drovers reached a hill which was an outcropping on the Caprock. They decided to make camp for the night at the bottom of the hill. Today there's a dirt tank about where the drovers camped, according to Mrs. Rinehart.

A black man, one of the drovers, took seriously ill that night. By morning he was dead. No one could explain of what malady he had died, but the cowboys delayed their usual early departure to carry their dead companion up on the side of the rocky hill to bury him where predators could not reach the body. Since that time, the place has been called Negro Hill.

Mrs. Rinehart told me around 1920 her mother, whose maiden name was Georgia Martin, and her mother's brother Forrest had traveled some distance to help another brother, Ricky, move to Crosbyton. They had worked hard and were late getting started home. When they got to the hill they decided to camp there for the night. Early the next morning, Georgia, who was then about eighteen years old, went up on the hill to see if she could find any traces of the grave they had all heard about. Sure enough, she found it. It looked as if someone had tampered with it, and there was one very old decaying man's brogan shoe laying beside it. She later told Winona about the incident.

Since those early times the hill has retained the name Negro Hill. A local group of Crosbyton Boy Scouts put up a marker commemorating the early cattle drives and honoring the unknown black man who lies where he was laid to rest by his friends, high on the side of a rocky hill.

A Grisly New Year's Eve

The Fort Concho Museum archivist sent me this account of a strange, bizarre New Year's Eve celebration.

It seems a man from the small community of Bangs, Texas, whose name was "Bones" Wilson, told the story. Bangs, incidentally, is located just south of Coleman.

According to Wilson, back in 1940 a Bangs man shot and killed his wife on New Years' Eve. Then he evidently regretted his actions and proceeded to hang himself. On the next morning, which was New Year's Day, some friends of the couple decided to drop in on them to wish them a Happy New Year. Imagine their shock to make the grisly discovery of the dead bodies, the woman with a bullet in her lifeless form, while her husband still swung from the rafters.

When the couple's son, who lived back East somewhere, according to Wilson, was informed of the tragedy, he didn't make any effort to rush out to Bangs to take care of the funeral arrangements. He wrote the Justice of the Peace and requested that arrangements be made to auction off the couple's household furnishings. The man said as soon as he was able to get away he would travel to Bangs to look over the land and house and decide what disposition he wanted made of them. Doesn't sound like a very loving son, does he?

A full year went by after the tragic murder-suicide had taken place. Wilson, who was in his fifties at the time, said on New Years' Eve in 1941 he passed by the house where the tragedy had occurred. He recalled it was around 11:30 p.m. Suddenly he heard a shot! He turned towards the house and glimpsed a light glowing from within. He thought this was strange since he knew the house had been unoccupied since the deaths of its owners. Then, through the front window he saw the shadowy form of a body. It was hanging from what must have been a rafter! Bones said he stared at the window and the gruesome sight of the body for a long time, as he just couldn't believe what he was seeing. Then, suddenly the light disappeared.

Wilson was thoroughly unnerved and frightened by what he had seen. He had never had such a strange experience before and didn't know what to think of it. He ran to the house of some people who lived nearby, and they returned with him. They found nothing out of the ordinary; just an old, deserted house.

There are still a few old-timers in Bangs who knew Bones Wilson and remember the strange story he told. And there are also those who still report seeing unidentified lights in the old house from time to time.

The Flickering Lantern

Woodie Howell, a sheriff's deputy who lives in Coahoma, near Big Spring, told me this story, which is both sad and mysterious.

There are some vast salt marsh lake flats just west of Big Spring. The area is pretty spread out over a great distance and is pocketed with a number of quicksand deposits.

The story goes that around the 1880s a little girl wandered off from her mother as the family crossed the area by covered wagon. Frantically, the woman searched for the child, but she was never found. Nor was a body ever located, which led to the belief that the youngster had perished in the quicksand. The mother, crazed with grief, spent the rest of her life out there, roaming the area, still searching for her little daughter. She even went out in the darkness, carrying a lantern as she searched the vast salt flats, calling out in the emptiness for her lost child.

Some folks in the Big Spring area swear they've been out there on still nights and have seen the light of the lantern bobbing up and down far out over the salt flats as the mourning spirit of the mother still seeks a reunion with her lost child. And while they say it might just be the dry West Texas winds blowing over the sands, they think it sounds more like the wailing, moaning cries of a broken-hearted mother.

This story, so often told, has taken on the aspects of a legend. It is, in some ways, related to some of the La Llorona (weeping woman) stories so prevalent in many of Texas' Hispanic communities.

The Blue Flame

This story came to me from Dr. John West, professor of English at the University of Texas at El Paso, from his files of folklore material. Two of his students, Sheila Stopani and Harriet Sturgeon, included this story in a paper submitted to West in December 1975. An elderly resident of El Paso, who asked not to be named, related the story to them:

This story is not very old, and the people it happened to are still living and are my friends here in town. However, they keep the story very hush-hush and do not want it to be known, therefore I am not able to give you their names or address. Otherwise I will tell you the story just as they told it to me.

They had just moved into one of the houses in Anthony when one night they awoke and saw a blue flame burning in the corner of their bedroom. It would disappear when they went near it. They also heard many different noises coming from the roof and the rest of the house. They called in a priest to exorcise the house. While he was there he came into communication with the spirit. The spirit told the priest to leave a quill and a bottle of ink in the corner where the blue flame had been. This was done. The spirit wrote where to dig, how far to dig, and what they would find. They did this and found a box of gold coins which they sold on the black market. However, the noises failed to stop, so again they left the quill, ink, and pad near the blue flame. This time the spirit wrote where to dig, how deep, what they would find, and what they must do when they found it. They found the body of a man! They had him properly buried and a Catholic mass said for him to permit his soul to rest. After doing this the noises stopped and the blue flame was never seen again. These people are now very wealthy and have moved to a much larger house.

Big Country Cemetery Lights

Cemeteries naturally seem to attract ghost hunters and ghost stories. The old Baird Cemetery, which is about a mile north of the town of Baird on U.S. Highway 283, is said to be the habitat of a woman ghost who stays there to protect her husband's grave. I first learned of the story while reading a feature in the *Abilene Reporter News* which ran on October 30, 1985. The writer, Kathy Sanders, had collected a lot of good tales for a special Halloween feature.

The story goes that this woman's husband died. She didn't want anyone to come near him, even in death, so she guarded his grave every night. She would carry a shotgun and a lantern with her as she assumed her duties. If anyone came anywhere near the grave, she would run them off. Then, after she died, her spirit still came back to take care of her beloved husband's final resting place. Many people over the years have reported seeing the lantern, or a light that resembled a lantern, in the vicinity of the grave.

There's another cemetery in that area called the Big Country. Out at Anson Cemetery there's a light said to sometimes remain in one place, and sometimes to just float about. Some people have said when they entered the cemetery at night the light would rush towards them and then suddenly back away. Some skeptics have argued that car headlights from U.S. Highway 277 cast reflections that cause the appearances of lights in the cemetery. However, some people have driven out on the highway and attempted to create the strange lights in the cemetery, to no avail.

Seems like to me it would be a good idea to just stay away from all cemeteries at night!

The Strange Blue Light

The little town of Winters, located not far from Ballinger, is the locale for at least one good ghost story. The *Abilene Reporter News* issue of October 29, 1985, had an article by Kathy Sanders, Assistant Regional Editor, which told about a family that used to be troubled by poltergeists. Armed with the information from the article, I telephoned Mrs. Nadine Bedford, in whose home the poltergeists were said to hang out, to see if I could obtain some additional information since the Sanders article was written ten years ago.

John and Nadine Bedford and their four children moved into the house in 1966. Perry Marvin, the youngest child, was about eighteen months old at the time. The house was old. It was built around 1907 and a lot of people had lived there throughout the years. The Bedfords had bought it from a Mr. Holloway.

It wasn't long before the Bedfords noticed some strange things about their house. It just seemed different. The couple had their own four children and then they kept foster children as well. They don't do this anymore, and their own children are all grown, but Mrs. Bedford does run a day-care center in her home, so there are still lots of youngsters about.

Soon after they settled in, the children noticed a strange blue light shining on an upstairs wall. Mrs. Bedford first thought it was the reflections of automobile headlights or maybe faulty electrical wiring in the house that caused the strange glow. Finally, they had the house rewired, but the light still continued to glow at night.

Mrs. Bedford told me that sometime in the 1970s a Mrs. Vick came to see her one afternoon. The lady had once lived in the house, was in Winters visiting a daughter, and decided to pay a call upon the occupants of her former home. She seemed very agitated and told Mrs. Bedford they really should move out of the house. She recalled how in the mid-1950s she had moved into the house with an infant and a four-year-old son. Her husband was winding up business affairs and had not yet been transferred to Winters, so Mrs. Vick was there alone for a time with the children. She soon noticed her little boy was always very tired, with big circles under his eyes, and he looked like he was not well. He was always drowsy. The youngster occupied a bedroom next to his mother's and she began to hear him talking to someone late at night.

She told him if he didn't quit talking and staying up at night she'd spank him. The little boy started to cry and told his mother that "they" wouldn't let him sleep. "They" came at night and forced him to play with them all night. The women moved the youngster into her room after that. But that, and other things, convinced her they should not stay in the house, and so they left within about three months. She urged Mrs. Bedford to leave the house as soon as possible! Bedford said the woman was clearly frightened of the house.

Mrs. Bedford told me she couldn't recall for sure, but she believed the woman may have told her the poltergeists included a family of four, a man, woman, and two small children, who had forced the little boy to stay up and play with them.

For a number of years, while the Bedford youngsters were growing up, and while a succession of foster children came and went, strange things continued to happen. Lights went on and off. The radio turned itself on and off at will. Sometimes when the children went to bed, covers pulled up under their chins and the lights all turned out, they'd awaken in the middle of the night to find all the covers pulled off of them and the lights all turned on. And the blue light continued to shine at night.

Then, when all the Bedford children left home, and Mr. and Mrs. Bedford ceased to keep foster children, the activity finally ceased. Mrs. Bedford thinks maybe the little foster children, who were often very troubled, may have attracted the poltergeists. Children do often attract them. The Bedfords said, strangely enough, they were never frightened, as Mrs. Vick had been. Sometimes they were puzzled, and sometimes they found the tricks annoying. She believes the spirits finally decided the Bedfords were there to stay for the long run and they weren't going to run them off by their antics, and so they just settled down and cut out their pranks. Even now sometimes, especially when she's in her kitchen, Mrs. Bedford says she has a distinct feeling that someone is right behind her. Of course, no one is ever there.

CHAPTER 6

PROPRIETARY PHANTOMS IN PUBLIC PLACES

The Haunted Monastery

Out near Big Spring and in some of the small ranching communities nearby, there are some pretty good ghost stories! Whether they are all factual or the oft-told tales that just spring from overworked imaginations, they've been around for a good long while. One interesting article from the October 3, 1993, edition of the *Big Spring Herald* by staff writer Janet Ausbury referred to a local personality, Sheriff's Deputy Woodie Howell, as a "resident who knows some of the area's best creepy legends and places."

Armed with this information, I decided to telephone Mr. Howell and see what I could learn from him. The friendly deputy, who is a Coahoma resident and president of the Lions Club of that community, was a wellspring of local stories, some of which Ausbury had referred to in her article.

Howell told me about an old graveyard out in Garden City that contains a grave that is said to glow in the dark. He said because there had been so many curiosity seekers, they had finally made the place off-limits after dark and a deputy is stationed there to see that no trespassers enter the area after the sun goes down. He was unable to tell me much more than that.

He was very interested in talking about an old, empty building in the town of Stanton. He said even if it weren't haunted (and residents say it is!) it would make a dandy movie set for a West Texas version of *Dracula*. He said the building was constructed in the 1880s by the Catholic Church. Its purpose was to be a large monastery and school serving the Catholic settlers in that area. The town, which was established in 1881 as a section on the Texas and Pacific Railroad, was first named Grelton. Catholic settlers, however, petitioned the railroad to rename the town, calling it Mariensfeld, which meant "field of Mary." In 1882 the Carmelite Monastery opened and maintained a boarding school for elementary and middle school-aged children.

By 1890 Protestant settlers outnumbered the Catholics, and the name of the town was changed to a more acceptable name to that particular group. It was given the name Stanton, honoring Edwin McMasters Stanton, Secretary of War under President Abraham Lincoln.

Today the Kelly home is the only structure that remains of the old school once called the convent and Academy of Our Lady of Mercy. It was the only Catholic facility between Fort Worth and El Paso for many years.

According to Howell, there are several stories—and he doesn't know if any of them are actually true—concerning the long deserted monastery in Stanton. His understanding is the town just sort of dried up and the Catholic religion didn't take with the newcomers to the area very well. Then around the time of World War I the great Spanish influenza epidemic that killed thousands of people across the nation did not spare the good brothers at the monastery. A number of the monks died, and the monastery finally closed its doors, abandoning the great buildings to the elements.

Many people used to report seeing figures moving around behind the open windows. Some were even seen in broad daylight. They might be vagrants, although Stanton isn't on the hobo trail or the homeless route. Today the Gothic arched windows have been boarded over.

We drove to Stanton to see the place. The monastery is behind a wrought iron fence with a padlocked gate. A very small portion of the wall of the church of St. Joseph still remains next to the boarded-up dormitory.

The old monastery, Stanton

A Texas historic marker at the location states:

> With the purpose of founding a monastery and a German Catholic community, Carmelite monks in 1881 began the first Catholic church between Fort Worth and El Paso. The adobe and brick monastery was completed in 1884 and St. Josephs Church in 1885.
>
> Sisters of Divine Providence opened a short-lived school in 1887. It closed and was reopened by Sisters of Mercy. In 1897 Carmelite monks disbanded and sold the property to the Sisters of Mercy who operated a convent and academy until abandonment after the tornado of June 11, 1938. All that remains are a dormitory, ruins of other buildings, and a cemetery.

The Ghost at the
Reeves County Courthouse

Pecos is a real old-time Western town situated not far from the New Mexico border. It was established in 1881 as a stop on the Texas and Pacific Railroad and fast drew fame as a hangout for rowdy cowboys, gunslingers, and the lawmen who had to know how to draw fast, shoot first, and ask questions afterwards! One of the nation's oldest rodeo events began here in 1883 and is still staged annually.

And there's at least one ghost story attached to the old Reeves County Courthouse in Pecos. I had a long talk with Steve Balog, former Deputy U.S. Marshal. Now he has taken on a second career, that of the court security officer at the courthouse.

Back in the early 1970s ('72-'74 to be exact) Balog occupied an office on the second floor of the courthouse. The courtrooms and library were on the third floor of the old building, just above Balog's office. He said there was an accordion type metal gate that was used to close the staircase that led to the upper floors. This was secured with a padlock, and it was customary for anyone who planned to work late at night to unlock the gate, then lock it behind him as they left to go to their offices. This assured them that someone who didn't belong there would be unable to get access to the upper floors.

Balog said that they've always handled a lot of illegal alien cases there in Pecos, and often after he had been out in the district all day in his capacity as Deputy U.S. Marshal, it would be very late, sometimes 8 or 9 p.m., when he finally got back to his office in Pecos. Then he would have a lot of paperwork to do, which was part of handling each alien's case. Sometimes he said they had as many as a hundred aliens a week to process, and the paperwork on each one ran anywhere from three to five pages. Often Balog would be at his desk at the courthouse until the wee hours of the morning, just trying to stay caught up with the workload.

Soon after going to work there, Balog began to hear the sound of footsteps up on the third floor, in the area right above his office.

He judged they were men's footsteps and said the person would have been a rather large man, at least 175 pounds in size. The sounds were very clearly those of someone walking down the long hallway. Balog often went up the stairs, looking thoroughly all over the vacant third floor, calling out, "Who's there? Come on out, I hear you!" There was nothing ever; but by the time he could get downstairs and back to his second floor office, the steps above him would start up all over again.

Finally Balog asked a friend of his, J.E. Travland, who was then Superintendent of Mails, and later became the U.S. Postmaster, if he would come and spend a few late hours with him. He had told Travland about hearing the untraceable footsteps, as they had become quite annoying when Balog was trying to get his work done. Both of the men heard the footfalls during Travland's visits to Balog's office. The steps seemed to move from the east to the west corridor. Sometimes they seemed to come from the old library which was located directly over Balog's office.

On several nights Balog's wife came down to the courthouse to keep him company. She also heard the phantom footsteps. Finally the couple brought a three-pound sack of flour to the building and went up to the third floor and sprinkled it all over the floor of the library, the courtrooms, and the corridor. About 1:30 or 2 a.m. the footsteps began. They were all over the place! After listening to them for some time, the Balogs went upstairs to check, and there was not a single footprint to be seen where they had sprinkled all that flour!

Finally, after months of hearing the disturbing footfalls, Balog said they suddenly began to be heard descending the stairs to the second floor. He said he believes now, looking back, the spirit, or ghost, was getting friendlier, and maybe it might have eventually materialized to him, as he had begun to see a shadowy form moving within his peripheral vision. About this time these occurrences were mentioned to a young woman clerk who worked in the courthouse and she said, "I knew it! I knew it!" She had also heard footsteps and had seen something passing her office when she worked there at night. After a couple of such disturbing evenings she elected not to work at all after regular hours.

Balog began to talk to the ghost so that it knew he recognized its presence. This seems to be what most ghosts want: to be heard or recognized. And often, in frustration, he would yell upstairs, "Knock it off, or else come down and help we with my work!"

Just as the ghost began to start coming downstairs, an extensive renovation and restoration project began at the courthouse, which was to last about eleven months. Now anyone who knows much about ghostly behavioral patterns knows they hate change, becoming very agitated and confused at times. This is just what happened to Balog's friendly ghost! The steps seemed to come from way in the back of the jury room, and there would be four or five steps in one direction, then they'd turn and come back, three or four steps, back and forth. They no longer came out in the corridor or to the library over Balog's office or down the stairs as previously. Now since Balog's job has changed; he is seldom in the building at night, so he has not heard the foot-steps lately.

Because he earnestly believes that someone from another time comes back as this walking spirit, Steve has done a bit of checking into the building's past. He said he heard that one of the construction work-ers who worked on the building when it was first built fell from the third floor or attic level to the ground and was killed. He also heard that back in the 1930s an illegal alien might have hanged himself in the building, but he isn't sure about this story, whether it was fact or fiction.

In speaking with Balog about "his" ghost, I ventured to offer my own theory. I believe the footfalls are those of the spirit of someone who spent a great deal of time in the old courthouse and was somehow locked there in time…not necessarily a person who had died there. It may have been a law officer, an attorney, a bailiff, a judge…someone whose working hours were spent on the third floor of the old Reeves County Courthouse. Maybe the man did not complete a job he had wanted to complete. Maybe he felt he had been derelict in his duties and had let somebody down. Maybe he was an attorney whose innocent client was adjudged guilty because he had not presented the case strongly enough. Maybe he was a judge who felt he had made a mistake in judgement. Who knows? The maybes are endless!

Balog is pretty sure the spirit is still there, just as it has been for a long, long time: caught in time, in space, in the dark of night, in the old Reeves County Courthouse, walking... walking... walking....

The Haunted Asylum

Doy Terry, a resident of Wichita Falls, owns an old, boarded-up building locally known as "the asylum." He believes it is haunted. It certainly looks as if it might be!

Located at the corner of California and Olen roads, it was once a private sanitarium. A Dr. White built it around 1926 as a private institution for his mental patients, desiring a more pleasant place for their treatment than the old State Hospital. It spite of its run-down appearance today, one can see that at one time the cream-colored stucco building with red tile roofing built in the Spanish style of architecture

Old asylum, Wichita Falls

must have been a peaceful place for the treatment of, and recovery from, various types of mental illnesses.

After some years the doctor sold his institution, and the building was eventually converted into an apartment house. Now it's just deserted, standing amid numerous trees and shrubs on a large corner lot. Terry hasn't decided what he is going to do with the building. It obviously needs a lot of work and "T.L.C." before it can be put to a new use.

Terry and a friend, Gerry Wilkinson, decided to spend a night out there one time just to see what might happen, as they had heard rumors that the old place was haunted. They set up comfortable reclining chairs in the lower level of the building. Finally, after several hours of conversation, they both dropped off to sleep. Around midnight both men were awakened by the sound of footsteps shuffling across the cement floor. Then, they heard sloshing sounds coming from the basement level beneath them. At that time, there was about six inches of water in the basement. Then, coming from outside the building, both Doy and Gerry heard the plaintive cry of a woman as she called over and over again, "Susan…Susan…Soooosan!" A thorough check revealed nothing, either inside or outside of the building.

As they discussed the strange sounds they'd just heard, probably to settle his nerves, Gerry lit up a cigarette. Doy asked him to put it out, explaining if there was something or someone around, they'd see the glow of the cigarette in the dark. So Gerry tossed it onto the cement floor, but the light kept glowing, and glowing, and glowing, all through the building. It bobbed up and down at different levels as if someone had caught it in mid-air and carried the burning cigarette off with them into the depths of the deserted building. It was a strange night, indeed!

At first, Doy reasoned that maybe he and his friend had been tricked by prankster teenagers, so he went back to his building, alone, a couple of weeks later. But once again he heard the footsteps and the voice of the unseen woman as she called for "Susan." He hasn't repeated his evening vigil since that time!

From a *Wichita Falls Magazine* article written by columnist Peggy Cline (date not available, but Doy thinks it was around 1976) the writer made this interesting observation:

Famed British ghost writer Elliott O'Donnell says old mental hospitals are always likely places to find ghosts, especially if any of the patients died on the premises. Although no records seem to be available about Dr. White's patients, youths bent on terrorizing themselves don't worry about the lack of documentation. They have a healthy respect for what they consider our own version of bedlam.

Relatively isolated, abandoned, and rundown, the old asylum is alive with rumors about blood on the plaster, handcuffs affixed to the basement walls with chains, and the wails of tortured souls.

Having looked it over, I would have to say the building surely looks like the sort of place a ghost might like to take over. Doy firmly thinks it is haunted. But by whom, or for what reason, only the ghosts can say. And they aren't very good at communicating.

The Fragrance of Lilacs

In 1950 the city of Fort Worth received a gift of several log cabins that once dotted the prairies of Parker County. They were moved to the city and made into a museum complex that accurately depicts life in the Lone Star State in the late 1800s. The name Log Cabin Village was selected by the parks department as a name for the new addition to the city's park system. In 1966 Bettie Regester, then the registrar of the Fort Worth Children's Museum (now known as the Fort Worth Museum of Science and History), was chosen to get the village on its feet. Charles Campbell, then director of the city parks department, made the selection.

Regester began to research the history of the individual cabins and collected donations of period furnishings. She also sought other buildings to be added to the exhibit. She and her volunteer docents, many of whom later became employees, turned the cabins from static exhibits into a working museum of how life was lived on the Texas plains back in the 1880s.

In the early 1970s Regester and her staff transformed one cabin, the Shaw cabin, into a working mill, and they obtained the Harold Foster cabin as an interesting addition to the growing complex of cabins and buildings. This cabin, which had been located on the banks of the Brazos down near the cotton producing town of Calvert, in Milam County, was quite large. Built in the late 1830s or early 1840s, it had undoubtedly seen a lot of life in the early Republic of Texas. It had actually been located in a now totally vanished community that had been called Port Sullivan. Except for two small cemeteries, there is no evidence whatsoever of a settlement ever having been there.

The large two-story house, which is about fifty-two feet long, was completely disassembled, moved to Fort Worth, and put back together again, just as it had been before. Bettie Regester is convinced that at least one of its former residents moved to Fort Worth with it!

She explained to me that the place had been built by Harry A. Foster for his family soon after they moved to Texas from Mississippi around 1852. The family included Martha Foster, Harry's wife, two or three daughters, and two sons, William Henry and Joseph Ancell. Foster named his new home Lucky Ridge.

According to Regester, Mrs. Foster died in 1870. United States census records of 1880 listed Mr. Foster, who was then quite an elderly man. Included in his household was one Mrs. Jane Holt and her small son of about six years of age. Evidently Mrs. Holt, the widow of a physician, was highly thought of by the Foster family, as one of the Foster boys, Joseph, named his own son Joseph Holt Foster. In those days it was rather a common practice for respectable widows who had no one to provide for them and limited means to become tutors, nursemaids, or housekeepers. It is believed Jane Holt was housekeeper to the aging Mr. Foster.

Bettie Regester remained as historical curator at the Log Cabin Village for twenty-eight years, retiring in 1994. She said over the years she and her staff had many unusual encounters with what they believed was the spirit of either Mrs. Foster or Jane Holt. The female spirit seemed to spend most of her time in one upstairs corner bedroom. There would be a heavy, overpowering "presence" when the spirit came around, and it was almost always accompanied by the very fragrant, cloyingly sweet scent of lilacs. At the same time, there would be a definite drop in the room temperature, as a sudden coldness would grip the atmosphere.

There was apparently a static electric field in the room as well. There was one place, Regester recalls, when one walked through it, the hair would visibly rise on the arms and back of the neck. When this happened to her, Bettie always knew without a shadow of a doubt that the ghost was close by. She even called in some parapsychologists to check the place out. They said there was a definite "hot spot," as they called it, in that upstairs corner bedroom.

The apparition of a woman has been seen in the house several times by various staff members. She appears to be about thirty to forty years of age and is very attractive, with long dark hair. The times she was seen she was clad in a long black skirt and a mauve-colored, high-collared blouse with wide-shouldered leg o' mutton sleeves. This was the type of outfit commonly worn by most pioneer Texas women. Most of the time the specter appears to visitors on the upper floor, but she has been known to venture downstairs where she has made at least two appearances.

Several visitors were visibly shaken by experiences they had upstairs in the old cabin, so the city has closed the upstairs portion to the public, making that area into an office for the staff. Regester said while she was working there, "I wouldn't have thought of her for months, but then I'd have to go up into the attic for something, and at the base of the stairs I would suddenly feel her presence. I knew she was up there, waiting for me. Three times that happened, and each time I just couldn't do it. I turned around and didn't continue up the stairs."

After researching all the former residents of the house, Regester and her staff concluded, although the spirit might be Martha Foster, they think it more than likely is that of Jane Holt. Of course, both women had close ties with the house, were probably quite happy there, and it would be the natural thing for either of them to return to the scenes of contentment and joy. As for the lilacs, they often were grown outside old settlers' homes. I recall they grew in the yard of my great-grandmother's house in Fannin County. Perhaps the first location of Lucky Ridge was ringed with lilacs. I wouldn't be surprised.

The Phantom of the Plaza Theater

In the days before television and sophisticated motion picture productions, there wasn't much in the way of entertainment for the average middle class American. Of course, there was the theater, the opera, and symphonic productions, but many could not afford these forms of entertainment. And back in the 1920s and '30s there was much unemployment, confusion, disappointment, and poverty among the middle classes. It was called the Great Depression.

But there was one bright spot. The motion picture had come along! Not yet developed to its full potential, the fledgling industry gave the weary and forlorn a few moments of pleasant diversion. There were the rib-tickling antics of slapstick comedians such as Charlie Chaplin and the Marx Brothers, and the heart stopping adventures of the "Perils of Pauline," to say nothing of the pantingly romantic scenes between such screen lovers as Rudolph Valentino and Pola Negri. And of course, there was the vampish Theda Bara and everybody's sweetheart, Mary Pickford. To properly showcase the talents of Hollywood's darlings, the most magnificent theaters possible were constructed. There were plush velvet seats, soaring balconies, elegantly appointed boxes, and all sorts of other amenities. Many movie houses had twinkling lights installed in the ceilings to emulate starlit nights.

One of the first such palaces was erected in 1929 in El Paso, Texas. Named the Plaza, it opened on September 30, 1930, amid much pomp and ceremony. It hosted the most famous vaudeville players of the day and also presented the best of the new motion pictures. Elegantly and lavishly decorated to depict a Spanish courtyard, the theater seated 2,300 patrons and drew its enthusiastic clientele from both sides of the Rio Grande. Its decor, in fact, was very similar to another Texas theater built about the same time, the beautiful Majestic, located in San Antonio.

Unfortunately, the grand old Plaza has fallen on less prosperous times. Not presently open, it awaits a complete restoration to its former grandeur. This project is slowly moving towards fruition, thanks to the dedicated efforts of the El Paso Community Foundation.

The venerable old theater is interesting enough for its history and its decor. But it's also rumored to be haunted, which adds another dimension, making the place even more intriguing.

I first learned of the existence of the Plaza, and of its possible hauntings, from an article that ran in the *El Paso Times* on Tuesday, October 31, 1978. It was written by *Kaleidoscope* staff writer Ed Kimble.

Kimble said there may be more than one ghost at the theater. First he told about a house that once existed on the site where the theater now stands. It was built by a wealthy and influential Spaniard for his beautiful young wife. The high-ranking official was very jealous of her, so he moved to a place that was rather isolated from the center of population, which, in those days, was mostly on the Mexican side of the

Rio Grande. Although she gave him absolutely no reason to distrust her, he did. The poor young woman spent most of her lonely hours tending a garden filled with flowers that surrounded her house.

Her husband must have lacked self-confidence because he is supposed to have flown into one of his jealous rages, accused her of having an affair, and, in this unreasonable state, choked her to death. When he realized he had killed his beautiful young wife, the object of his affections, he was so filled with remorse he set fire to the house and left, never to return.

It is said that the spirit of the poor young wife comes back to the theater (which is really the site of her beloved flower garden) and has been seen watering the artificial flowers that adorned the tiers in the auditorium. She thinks, no doubt, she is still in the garden where she spent so many lonely hours.

Another spirit that is rumored to still hang around the theater, according to Kimble, is the ghost of a man who was stricken with a heart attack when he went to look for a drinking fountain on the mez-zanine level. Several patrons and employees reported seeing his ghost roaming the theater, probably still searching for the water fountain.

A telephone conversation with Dolores Gross of the El Paso Community Foundation brought forth more interesting information.

Gross told me that the Foundation has made an offer to the city of El Paso. If the city pays for the physical restoration of the old building, the Foundation would fund ten years of management and operation to get the building "on its feet," so to speak. Further, it would continue to raise money so that another one and a half million dollars in endow-ment funds would be held to hand over at the end of the first decade of operation to help perpetuate the project. The Foundation raised one and a half million dollars to save the building from demolition, purchased it from the owners, and donated it to the city.

As Ms. Gross pointed out, not only is the building beautiful and historically significant, but it holds a sentimental soft spot in the hearts of many El Paso residents. So many "firsts" for so many people; the first date, the first moving picture, and in many instances, the first jobs for many young people of the community. The theater employed them as ushers and workers in the concession stands.

About a year and a half ago, Dolores Gross and two gentlemen went into the old building to look around the stage area to see what needed to be done in the way of repairs and restoration. The building had been closed up since 1976, and there was no electricity. They plugged in a halogen lamp to a very long cord that ran to the building next door. Gross estimated that the cord was several hundred feet long. It ran through the large lobby area, down the center aisle to the stage where the big lamp was located. Suddenly, the cord began to swing violently from side to side of the aisle, like a gigantic black whip snake. No one was near it to manipulate it and cause it to swing. At the same time, a large frame to which stage lights were attached in the orchestra pit moved forward at least five feet, of its own volition, as no one was near it to propel it. Gross believes it was one of the resident spirits of the theater. She and the men with her were not frightened, just terribly startled. She said she thought, "Wow! Would you look at that!" She thinks the spirit of whoever is there is elated over the possibility of the building being restored, and it worked up enough energy to sway the electric cord and move the light frame, much like a dog might wag its tail to show joy and happiness!

Gross told a slightly different version of the water fountain story which I had read in the *El Paso Times*. She heard that a young man of about eighteen years of age was out on a date and at intermission went to a water fountain in the basement level to get a drink of water, and he mysteriously keeled over dead! She said she had heard tales that icy cold drafts had been felt at that location, and often the fountain used to turn itself on and off when no one was around to operate it.

Gross said she'd heard another story that concerned a ghostly apparition that was sometimes seen in the lofty upper balcony. It only appeared when someone lit up a cigarette. I'll bet the Surgeon General would like that ghost!

Is Isaiah Still There?

Ballinger resident Martha Beimer bought a small flower shop in 1970. In 1972 she moved her business across the street into an old building that had been occupied by various businesses over the years. The previous occupant had operated a small dress shop at the location. She told Martha that sometimes strange things happened there. Dresses that were placed in the back room to be held in layaway would end up hanging back on the store racks the next morning. Packages that had been beautifully giftwrapped ready for pickup the next day would be found unwrapped, their contents scattered about, when the owner would open up the next morning. Yet no one had a key to the place but the owner, and there were never any signs of forced entry.

The first time Martha experienced anything strange was during one evening when a large number of young people and several women were in the building with her. They were working late at night on corsages and decorations for an upcoming school prom. One of the boys who was working in the back room said he heard the front door bell, and he asked Martha if she had locked the door. Martha and the boy went to the front of the shop and found the keys still in the dead bolt lock, but they were swinging in their key ring!

There was a staircase up to a storage area behind a partition. Suddenly they all heard heavy footsteps on the stairs. Two of the older boys went with Martha to investigate. They took a flashlight to shine around the storage area where boxes and cartons were stored. They even said, "Come out...we hear you, and we are going to call the police." However, a thorough search revealed nothing or no one in the area.

The group went back to their tasks in the workroom until they were again interrupted by the sound of three heavy footfalls on the stair landing and then a "thump!" sound as if something heavy (it sounded like someone jumping) hit the concrete floor from the stair landing about six feet above it! Right after this sound was heard, the back door closed as if the unseen noisemaker had exited the building.

Martha kept her floral business for a time and then decided to sell out to a friend named Linda. Her youngsters were growing up and needed more attention at home than she could give them while running a full-time business. Later on, she did go back to work part-time for her friend in the same building.

Martha had become acquainted with an elderly gentleman who was a friend of the lady who had bought the shop. The man, who had been a store owner in Ballinger for fifty or sixty years, told Martha that a man had been killed in the building where her flower shop was located, back in the days when the property was a saloon. Although he could not recall a surname, the old gentleman said he was pretty sure the victim's name had been Isaiah. From then on, whenever the resident spirit made one of his periodic disturbances, Martha and her friend referred to him by name, feeling reasonably sure Isaiah was the troublesome spirit.

Isaiah never did anything really bad that Martha could recall, except for one time. Then, he actually struck a lady! A woman, who was a customer and friend of Martha's and the new owner, was in the shop when the subject of Isaiah came up. The woman said she absolutely did not believe in ghosts, and there was just no such thing. She went on to say she thought Martha and Linda were just plain stupid to believe in such an entity as Isaiah. She walked over to a large plant holder that was standing on the floor. It held various hanging baskets and potted plants, and as she reached down to pick up a potted plant off the floor one of the suspended baskets fell at her feet, barely missing her head. It quite clearly was purposely dropped! Linda, Martha's friend who owned the shop, pointed her finger at the customer and said, "There, I told you!" At that moment the woman jumped as if she'd been shot and announced someone had just slapped her! Although there were four or five people in the shop, no one was near enough to have struck her. Still, the woman accused Linda of striking her, even though there was no way she could have, or would have. Yet the woman repeated that she'd been struck, hard. All Linda could do was tell her that Isaiah was real, he was there, and he was perplexed the woman had made fun of him and ridiculed those who believed in him. This was the only time to Martha's knowledge that the spirit ever touched anyone in the building.

Today the building is home to the Rheem Air Conditioning Company. Ghosts like cold spots. We all know that. So we imagine that Isaiah is right at home with the folks who make a profession out of keeping cool.

The Haunted Hattery

I first learned of Peters Bros. Hats in Fort Worth from an article that ran in the *Fort Worth Star Telegram* on October 31, 1993. A haunted hattery! That ought to be worth a trip to Fort Worth just to learn more about the establishment at 909 Houston Street.

Going back to beginnings: The Peters brothers were Greek immigrants who changed their names soon after their arrival at Ellis Island. Somehow, they worked their way down to Texas and established a shoeshine parlor in Fort Worth. At one time the huge business employed as many as thirty-six shoeshine men! The Peters boys branched out, making and selling hats. The shoeshine business gradually faded out, but the hat shop, which was begun in 1911, is still going strong!

Today there are two Peters men, father and son, Joe Sr. and Joe Jr., who are running the store along with numerous staff members. There are hats everywhere! And they say, sometimes, unaided by human hands they just drop off the long display hooks on the walls for no apparent reason. Then, the two Joes just knowingly nod and say, "That's Granddad again."

Several years back the store was able to expand its floor space. This was when Eli's Pizza next door closed, and the Peters family bought the additional space in order to have more room for their popular hattery. It seems that the pizzeria was haunted by a spirit named Jack Martin.

Martin had been a dishwasher and odd-job man about the restaurant. He worked there over ten years, and according to the *Fort Worth Star Telegram* article, his ghost started coming back to the restaurant soon after he died. Just about 4:15 p.m. every afternoon the door to the restaurant would pop open, then gently close with a sigh, as the spirit of Jack would depart the building. This happened over and over again. It seems when a new man was hired to take Jack's place his spirit didn't like that idea at all. He just naturally felt obligated to keep an eye on things.

It is said when a new employee would stroll past the dishwasher it would turn on by itself and spray the man with water. It happened even though the machine had several safety features, and the door had to be closed and the start-up button had to be held down before the machine could begin its cycle. It got to be a regular occurrence. Anytime a new employee came, he received just such a "welcome" from Jack Martin's dishwasher! It was almost as if the machine had taken on the spirit of its former operator!

In addition to the spirit of Jack Martin, it is also known that one of the early Peters Bros. shoeshine men fell down the basement steps and was killed. Perhaps the ghost of this former employee is also there.

And then, of course, there was the founder of the business, Tom Peters. When he died in 1991, he was just a little shy of his 101st birthday. And he had been a fixture at the shop for many of those years. So when hats move around on the walls or other objects are moved or if something turns up missing for a time, Joe Senior thinks it's just because Granddad wants them to know he's still interested in the business!

"I feel that the spirit of my grandfather is here. But I don't feel haunted. I feel blessed," Joe Senior said.

The Peters make beautiful hats, all styles, but in Fort Worth, most of their customers just naturally go for the Western styles. Their most famous hat is the Shady Oaks, a plush 100 X of soft, beaver fur felt that looks just like what it is, a rich man's chapeau. These hats are decorated with a little solid gold oak tree emblem caught into the hatband, and the handsome number that Joe Senior was wearing costs around $800. This was the type of headgear that the late Amon Carter, publisher of the *Fort Worth Star Telegram*, used to order.

My husband, Roy, didn't order the Shady Oaks, but he couldn't resist one of the good-looking Stetsons the Peters had in stock. While he wrote his check, I interviewed the owners. Interviews can be expensive!

Peters Bros. Hats, Fort Worth

The Literary Spirit

For the literary minded, Barber's Bookstore at 215 West Eighth Street has long been a Fort Worth institution. Brian Perkins has been the owner of the business for many years, having purchased it from Mrs. Irene Evans in 1955. Evans sold the popular business because her husband was terminally ill and needed her constant attention. Later, after Mr. Evans passed away, she began skydiving at the age of fifty-three. Unfortunately, the spunky lady was involved in a tragic accident soon after she took up this new sport when her parachute failed to open during a jump.

When I questioned him about the ghosts at his shop (having heard of them from several sources) Perkins said he believes he has at least three separate entities that call Barber's their "hauntquarters." The first ghostly presence seems to be very quiet. It doesn't do much but turn the pages of books. On Sundays, sometimes when Perkins is restocking the store or doing paperwork, he quite clearly hears the pages of books being turned. He said he has cut back on his hours now and isn't in the store much during those quiet times. So he is not sure the "Sunday spirit" is still around. As we discussed the page-turning ghost, we agreed it might possibly be the spirit of Mrs. Evans, still keeping an eye on her old bookstore. Perkins also theorized it might be the spirit of a compulsive book-browser.

There is a stairway leading upstairs that is located in one corner of the shop. It was not always visible in the shop, however, until Perkins cut a door through a wall. The old building, erected in 1908, had once been a walk-up hotel. Perkins said there were numerous rooms on the second floor, and there had been stairs at both ends of the building. He said when he cut the opening the door didn't fit the frame, and light shines though the sides. The light comes from a skylight high above the staircase.

About two years ago, on a quiet Sunday, Perkins heard a noise upstairs. Then he saw shadows pass by the light that was coming through the crack at the side of the door frame as if something, or someone, had suddenly passed by. It frightened him, as he felt sure no one could have gotten in there because he had a very good alarm system.

Since he had heard noises and had seen shadows, Perkins went to the door of his shop, turned the alarm on, and left, locking the door behind him. He went out to a telephone booth and called his son to come down to the shop. He told him to bring a gun. He thought sure the burglar alarm would go off any minute, but it didn't. A man working at the business next door on that Sunday went with Perkins back into the bookstore. They turned off the alarm and then cautiously went up the stairs. They searched the entire upper portion of the building and found absolutely nothing that could have made any noise or created any shadows.

Often Perkins has heard someone (or something) run up the stairs, but they never seem to run up the entire length of the staircase. The footsteps seem to hit seven or eight steps, then the sounds cease. Most often the steps are heard when Perkins is there working late at night, either alone or with an employee. He has the distinct feeling that something may have happened to someone on those stairs sometime in the past.

About a year ago, on a Sunday morning in May, Perkins' son came to the shop very early. He is a writer, and he enjoys working in solitude early in the mornings. As he sat at his desk, he suddenly heard footsteps outside the open door. First there were three very light, soft footsteps. Then he heard heavier footsteps following. He looked up just in time to see a man wearing blue jeans and a t-shirt pass by the open doorway. The figure was no further than eight feet away from where young Perkins sat. He grabbed his gun and searched the building. He went all over the store and found no one. He believes he most certainly saw a ghost!

The owner feels his spirit-guests are benevolent except for one. On another Sunday when he was alone in a back room doing some paperwork, Perkins suddenly felt the chilling presence of something "evil and frightening." He leapt up "ready to fight," he said, but there was nothing there at all. This negative source of energy has only manifested itself that one time.

Mr. Perkins was a very interesting person to interview. I am sure his store, long a popular Fort Worth landmark, certainly warrants a visit from those of you who are avid readers, or like Mrs. Evans' ghost, just like to stand around riffling through the pages!

CHAPTER 7

HAUNTED HALLS OF
HIGHER LEARNING

HAUNTED HALLS
OF HIGHER LEARNING

Oh, the spirits still are yearning
For those hallowed halls of learning
Where they spent so many hours
In the lost lost days of yore.
They come in wraithlike forms
To haunt familiar dorms,
And walk the halls to classrooms
As they often did before.

Docia Williams

Learning Institutions Attract Ghosts

For some reason, institutions of higher learning often attract ghosts. An academic atmosphere has a certain mystique about it and often compels its former students to return. That's why Homecomings are so popular! Partly, it's to see former classmates whom one has not seen or heard from in years. Obviously many of those friendships were only temporary, not lasting enough to survive the years after graduation. Often we go on to life after college and seldom think of former college friends. Then, again, there are those friendships that last forever, because a special bonding was made on campus many years ago. Frankly, I have always enjoyed just returning to see the old buildings, to visit old dorms, to walk old pathways. It's the special feeling of nostalgia one receives while recalling the experiences, both good and bad, that so colored and influenced our young lives, that make Homecomings so special.

Here in this chapter there are some good stories connected with high school and college campuses. They tell of former students and faculty members who could never quite let go, and of the current campus residents who have experienced their supernatural appearances. It isn't surprising to me that ghosts would like to hang around campuses. So much life, energy, emotion, and ambition exists where young minds are being molded and taught to unravel all the great mysteries of life! Where energy levels are high, and overly active student imaginations work at top speed, ghost stories often become a part of the campus experience.

The Ghost at Fletcher Hall

I first learned that Fletcher Hall, a coed dormitory at Sul Ross University in Alpine, was haunted, from a newspaper article sent to me by a friend. The story, penned by Sul Ross student writer Lisa Kay Hart, was titled "Hitchhikers and Dead Janitors Haunt Alpine Area."

Hart's mention of the old dormitory, once known as Morelock Hall, stated:

Sul Ross has its own phantoms lurking in the woodwork. These ghosts range from dead janitors to students who have taken their own lives. The most notable of the campus ghosts is the one living in the old Morelock Hall. This ghost is a man who died in Morelock when it was an all-male dormitory. Residents have felt his hand on their shoulders while sleeping and have awakened to find no one around.

After the hall became coed, one female resident felt his hands on her shoulders so often, she moved out of the dorm. A friend of hers who did not know she had left asked her at lunch one day why she didn't answer her door the night before. When she had explained to her friend that she had moved out a couple of weeks ago and that the room was empty, her friend seemed confused, for she had heard the shower in the room running and drawers opening and closing.

There are several variations to the Morelock Ghost stories as well as other area apparitions.

Although the Hart article stated the ghost of former Morelock Hall was a man, very reliable sources have revealed that there is also a female spirit there, one who has revealed herself to a number of residents of the dormitory.

Joshua Rangel, a San Antonio student attending the university, told me he's heard a lot of people say they have seen the ghost at Fletcher. He went on to say that a friend described seeing her standing at a window at the end of a hallway. As the young man approached, the apparition just disappeared. Another student told Rangel that the ghost once wrote something with toothpaste on a mirror in her old dorm room, but Rangel could not recall what words she had written. He said the figure was always described as rather misty in appearance but definitely a young woman with long hair and without a doubt, a ghost!

A visit with Sul Ross English professor Ira Blanton proved very fruitful. Professor Blanton questioned numerous students and located one who had actually seen the ghost and was willing to talk to me about his unnerving experience. John Klingemann, a junior student who serves as a Spanish language tutor at the writing lab, lived in Fletcher Hall up until the end of his sophomore year. Then he moved off campus where he now resides.

Klingemann told me he lived in a room which was right next door to the room that the Fletcher spirit occupied in life, number 308. Her name was Beverly, and she supposedly died sometime in the 1970s while residing in the dormitory. Klingemann said the stories he had heard about Beverly's death were told differently, by different people. One version is she committed suicide there in her dorm room, and the other is that it was a murder made to look like a suicide. At any rate, it seems to be a known fact that there was a death in that room, number 308, at Fletcher Hall.

Of one thing John Klingemann is absolutely certain. Beverly came to visit him one night about a year ago! It was in the wee small hours of the morning, about 2 or 3 a.m. when she appeared. John had stayed up very late, studying for an exam he was to take the next day. He had barely drifted off to sleep, when he awoke with a start to see the figure of a young woman standing at the foot of his bed. While he could clearly make out she had long brown hair and was clad in an orange sweater and blue jeans, he said the wraith was rather foggy or misty in appearance, and it definitely looked ghostly. She just stood there a few seconds, staring at John, and then she turned and sort of drifted out of the room.

John said he didn't get any sleep that night, as the sudden appearance of the ghost was just too disturbing to him. In fact, he made arrangements right away to vacate the room at the end of the semester. He told the residential assistant about seeing the strange nocturnal apparition. After he described her appearance, the R.A. told John that other students had also reported such visits, and his description of the spirit exactly matched theirs.

John Klingemann absolutely knows the spirit of Beverly visited his dorm room. He understands she is still making periodic appearances in old Fletcher Hall. Why she keeps coming back, John can't explain. But he knows he doesn't want to see her again.

The Singing Spirit

It seems only fitting. Wayland Baptist University, a small private institution of higher learning located in the West Texas town of Plainview, has a ghost! At least, that's what they say.

You see, once upon a time Wayland was one of only two institutions in the country that conducted parapsychology research projects. The other one was Duke University. And to make it all even more bizarre, would you believe the conductor of such research was a doctor of philosophy named Dr. North East West? He passed away a number of years ago. Then Assistant Professor Mark Pair occupied West's old lab for about six and a half years, using the space for his music studio after the third floor of Gates Hall had been turned over to the music department.

Pair firmly believes his former studio, which had been West's old lab, is haunted. At least it was when Pair occupied the place. The music department moved out of the old red brick building in the spring of 1973.

Today, the third floor of the old campus landmark has become more or less a storage area, and there are no classrooms there. Pair says he has heard no recent tales of ghostly noises or other strange happenings in the building. But it surely used to be a spooky place!

Ghost tales have been tossed around the campus for many years. The story most often told by the students was that a young female voice student there at Wayland was killed in an automobile accident, and she would come back to sing in her old practice room. Pair told me late one night he heard her, singing very loudly, when he was practicing for a piano concert in his studio. He knew he was alone on the third floor. Later, when he got to thinking about it, he decided it must have been a friend of his, one of the voice teachers he knew. When he asked her about it, he found she had been out of town that evening. He could not find anyone who had been on the third floor of the building with him that night.

Another version of the vocal student story comes from an article in the Plainview *Daily Herald* that ran March 12, 1993. The writer was Phillip L. Hamilton. He had interviewed Dr. Estelle Owens, well known as a Wayland historian. She believed the ghost was that of a music major who came to her juries and failed. She was so distraught that she jumped off a balcony (or maybe the roof) to her death. At any rate, all the stories seem to point toward a female music major who died while a student at Wayland. Pair thinks she was a voice major. Dr. Owens stated, "It's always told that she's a music major, but there's a debate over whether she played the piano, was majoring in voice, or was a flutist."

Hamilton's article quoted Bobby Hall, a University spokesman, as saying he had heard that the founder of the university comes back to check up on us. Hamilton said Hall had told him that tale wasn't as popular as some of the others. Then Hall went on to say that there was one story that a male student was murdered up on the third floor of

Gates Hall and still roams around up there. But Hall did add, "There is no evidence that there was ever a murder or suicide on the third floor."

Speaking of the ghost, Alumni director Joe Provence, who was a student in the 1960s and then returned later to work for the university in 1967, said, "No one has ever seen it." Tales of the ghost date back at least fifty years, as Provence has heard alumni who returned to the campus for their fiftieth reunions talk about the haunting spirit. When the class of 1941 got together a couple of years ago, some class members got to talking about the night they put a cow in the president's office. Provence said they swore they were chased off by the ghost of Gates Hall!

Vice president for denominational relations Dr. Charles Bassett said the old building can be one of the spookiest places in the world at night if you happen to be alone there. He said you can hear doors slamming, and the whole building sort of creaks and groans. But, he also said he had never seen a ghost.

When I spoke with Pair, still a professor of music at the university, he said he is still convinced that there was a ghost in Gates Hall when he had his studio there. Besides hearing the singing of the phantom student, he also cited another strange experience he had one night when he and a security guard were out in the hall talking and suddenly "something" went by. Pair said it was like a really cold breeze, and it was a black thing. Both of the men got out of there, fast!

There were other incidents, also. According to Hamilton's news story, Pair had numerous strange brushes with the unknown. He admitted sometimes the mysterious happenings sort of "put him on edge." And numerous students spoke of seeing something in the window of Pair's studio long after he had vacated the building for the night.

Pair spoke of Wayland in a very prideful manner. He said the small university of around 8,000 students has a student body that takes great pride in their alma mater. They have a lot of school spirit and enjoy the academic environment of the wholesome liberal arts university. And, of course, there's the Baptist School of Theology there, too, which trains ministerial students. Pair said when his mother was a little girl, she lived in a small town west of Plainview. One time her parents gave her permission to ride up to Plainview with a school teacher friend of the family. She said that Plainview was such a small town at the time that she recalled seeing Gates Hall out in the open plains, looking to her for all the world just like a real storybook castle!

According to Pair, Gates Hall served for a time as a hospital. And during the Depression when times were really hard everywhere, it's said even though they couldn't afford to pay the professors, many elected to stay on and teach without pay. So much has gone on in the old building, which was erected back in 1906, that Pair said he could often feel the tiredness and dedication, the struggle and sadness, as if it had permeated the very walls. Perhaps some of that has just endured and hung on, causing people to feel the building is haunted.

With or without a ghost, Gates Hall, by Pair's description, is a venerable old building of orange-red brick, a very sturdily built structure. A lot of steel beams were used in its construction. It even has a basement which has often been used as a tornado shelter when storm warnings come to the West Texas plains.

Whether the tales of ghosts are born of students' vivid imaginations, or if they are really true and old Gates Hall is haunted, I think they must be good spirits, just there to keep an eye on the beloved old landmark.

Who Was "Georgia"?

Theaters seem to have a natural affinity for ghosts. Maybe theatrical people can't resist coming back for a final curtain call! At any rate, I've managed to uncover quite a few stories of hauntings connected with theaters and auditoriums across the state.

I learned there might be a ghost story connected to the Fine Arts Building Theater at Texas Wesleyan University in Fort Worth in a roundabout way. Some Fort Worth visitors to San Antonio chanced to mention that they had heard that the theater on the campus of TWU was haunted. This was all I needed to be off and running to the nearest telephone! I called the university operator, and she connected me to the Alumni office, where I talked with Mr. Quentin McGown, the director. He said he had heard lots of stories about the ghost at the theater and would try to get some information together for me. As good as his word, McGown sent a copy of a tape-recorded interview made on March 24, 1987, that described the ghost of the theater. The interview was conducted by Fort Worth resident Terry Smith with the late Mason Johnson. Johnson, who passed away in 1989, was then professor emeritus of theater arts and speech, and he granted an interview to

Smith, who describes himself and his partner, Mark Jean, as ghost stalkers. The two men met in the empty theater to discuss Johnson's many encounters with Georgia, the specter of the theater during his tenure at the university.

Now, I had been in Fort Worth in October of 1994 to publicize one of my books and had been interviewed by Terry Smith on public television. So when I called him to tell him Mr. McGown had sent me the tape of his interview with Mason Johnson, it was basically renewing an old acquaintance. Smith offered to send me some more material related to the haunting, as well as a typed copy of the interview, which certainly made my job much easier!

Mason Johnson directed many of the musicals at the university, then known as Texas Wesleyan College during his years there. He had first served for a number of years as stage manager for the Dallas Summer Musicals during the early 1950s. Soon after he came to Texas Wesleyan he had his first encounter with the ghost at the campus theater, during a rehearsal of *Brigadoon*. In the conversation on tape with Smith he said:

It was late one evening, I'd say about 10:30 or 11:00, and we were rehearsing for *Brigadoon* in the auditorium here. I was sitting about midway in the auditorium, taking notes. Something kept bothering me. I kept thinking someone was back of me all of the time, and on several occasions I turned around, but I saw no students. If I was having a final dress rehearsal or was getting near the opening of a show, I never let anybody sit in the house. Everybody is backstage except for those in the light booth on the second floor. There was never an audience. Then, I saw this distinguishable (sic) woman sitting, not on the same row as I was, but slightly forward of me and over on the right, in one of the aisle seats. I thought, "How rude of her to just come in like that." Dr. Bullard, the Fine Arts Chairman, didn't mention to me he had a guest because we would always tell each other if we had a guest. There was a regular list and you'd have to check it. So I thought, how rude of her to come in and just stare at the stage. So I went ahead doing what I was doing, watching the stage, and thought the very next possibility I am going to go and ask the person to leave or go down front and see what the problem is and ask him (Dr. Bullard) if she's supposed to be here. So the next time I got up and started down the aisle to where she was, she just disappeared! I thought, I'm having hallucinations and I need a rest.

Johnson went on to say that this was the first big show at Wesleyan for me, that is, both directing and choreographing. I asked Dr. Bullard, who was sitting in the orchestra pit at the piano, if he had ever seen an apparition or anything like that in the auditorium. He said, "Oh, well, it's probably the ghost. She's around all the time. Don't pay any attention to her." I said, "You've got to be kidding. This has unnerved me terribly." Well, I just went back and sat in my same seat, and there she was again, so I just turned around and stared at her awhile. The figure never moved, and so I got up and started down the aisle again, and it just dissolved.

Smith asked Mr. Johnson when this all took place and he said it was in 1955. Then Johnson went on to tell Terry about all the times he had seen the figure during the many years he spent at Wesleyan. He gave a detailed description of how she looked as well:

It's sort of a mist, if anything, a grayish misty look, but it has a definite outline, features and body size…. When Smith asked Johnson how she was dressed, he said, it seems like it has on some sort of homespun dress, by that it's a loose-like fabric that falls to the floor. I've seen it standing also, and would say it's Victorian or 1890s style. It's a slightly puffed sleeve, but not a big leg o' mutton thing or Gibson Girl type, not that bouffant. It has a real simple bodice, and a little brooch and a collar that comes up and I think a shawl, but I'm not sure about that. Sometimes from the back and the side I have the idea it has a shawl on, but then from the front it could be something down the front of the dress like a little dickie or applique, something maybe with ruffles. It's frilly and very feminine.

When questioned about the age of the figure, Johnson replied, "about sixty, certainly fifty-five to sixty-five, in that area; she's not old, and I would not say at all decrepit as she walks marvelously all over the place." He went on to say she was about five feet to five feet two inches in height. Her hair was grayish, parted in the middle and pulled back into a big bun at the back of her neck.

Johnson said he had seen her many, many times; a very conservative guess would be a dozen or more times during his years at the university. Sometimes during rehearsals she was just heard as she would walk back and forth up in the balcony. Although he said he felt foolish doing it, sometimes he would just stop the rehearsals and tell the students that Georgia, a name Johnson gave the spirit, was up there in the balcony making noise, and if she would kindly stop they could proceed! When Terry Smith asked Johnson why he called the spirit Georgia, he said he had no earthly idea why he called her that; it was just a name he suddenly made up, for no particular reason.

Johnson said he has seen it from the audience, in the audience, and he had been on stage many times and looked out and saw it from the stage. Many of the students also saw it from the stage. Johnson said, "I've seen it and have come down the aisle and walked up to see it, and it just goes away. I have said, 'Wait, can I communicate with you?' and, 'Do you want to leave a message... is there anybody here you want to communicate with?' And, I have said, 'Wait, who are you; why are you here?'" Johnson told Smith he knew it made him sound ridiculous but he assured Smith he was not insane.

Johnson went on to tell Terry Smith he believes the ghost really liked theater because she always appeared during rehearsals, and he could recall her being around for *South Pacific*, *Kiss Me Kate*, *Carousel*, *Cabaret*, *Gypsy*, *Oliver*, and *Fiddler on the Roof*. It seems she was most often seen during the dancing sections in the rehearsals when lively music was being played. Johnson said several student assistants have actually encountered her. One young man, who has since married and moved to Oklahoma, actually had the wraith touch him on the shoulder as he went down the aisle. It upset him so much he quit his job and would not return to the theater!

One of the strangest occurrences took place during a rehearsal of *Cabaret*. Johnson described it as one of his most dramatic moments with the ghost. He told Smith, "I was leaving and turned off the lights; it was about 12:00 midnight when I walked up to the stage right side. Now, I always look back to see if she might be out there, for one thing, because it's become sort of like a friend; I just want to see if she's there. I wanted to say 'Hi.' Well, that night she was there, plain as day. The students had just gone out and were still not all the way to the parking lot at the back. I went to the backstage door and yelled out for the students to return, saying, 'Come back! Come back! She's here and you can see it very clearly. Now promise me, everybody, do not scream and yell and tear the back door down. Be calm and adult grown people, please, and you can see, it…it's very clear…and if you'll just, everybody be adult and calm. Most of them managed it. Not all, but several just went berserk and said they didn't believe in ghosts; it was against their religion, and they were just really upset about this. But they all saw it. We walked right back out there on the stage and there it was."

Johnson went on to say it just stayed there, looking straight ahead at the stage, but nothing else happened. He said like always, her face was completely expressionless, no movements of her head or face. It was just staring straight ahead. It was an unnerving ending to a good rehearsal, and the students never forgot it!

When Terry Smith asked Mason Johnson how long the appearances were, he had to stop and think. Then he answered the sightings usually lasted for a couple of minutes, or maybe a little longer when it would be walking around up in the balcony. Johnson added, "She didn't really walk. Move would be a better term; like a slide or a glide."

When further questioned about the ghostly visitor to the auditorium and the possibilities of whom she might have been in life, the fact that the Fine Arts Theater is built over the site of where an old church had stood, and that there also had been a cemetery there, was most interesting! It seems that the university was founded in 1891 as Polytechnic College. There was a little piece of land nearby that Dr. W.C. Dobkins, the first doctor at Polytechnic, had purchased sometime early in the 1890s to be used as a family burial plot. When he bought the land, there already were a few graves located there. Over the years other members of the Dobkins family were buried there. Then a man named Lowe bought the land and got permission to move the bodies to other gravesites. Dr. Dobkins didn't like the idea of moving his kinfolk, so the bodies of his sister Sarah and two children were left there. Early in the 1900s Dr. Dobkins had a little fence built around the three plots. Sarah, who was crippled and who never married, was buried there in 1896. A small son, whose age was unknown and who was named Joe, was interred in 1897, and an infant who died just a day after birth, was laid to rest in 1898. Although there are no tombstones, it's believed that Sarah must be the sister who was buried there, since Dr. Dobkins' three other sisters all had married and would more than likely have been buried with their families. In all, Dobkins had three wives and twenty-two children!

Now this is my own far-fetched theory, but it could hold some water. If Sarah Dobkins is indeed the body buried in the old Dobkins plot near the theater, could she possibly be the wraith that often appeared during Mason Johnson's tenure as speech professor there? She would, after all, have had a close connection to the college, since her brother had been its first physician. She might even have attended services at the church that once stood on the site of the Fine Arts Building. A cripple, never married, her life must have been far from exciting. Now suddenly…a theater! Lights! Music! Lots of activity and young people around! What a place to enjoy and make up for lost time that she didn't have while she was alive! Certainly the mode of attire that Mason Johnson described would fit into the 1897 time period.

Just before Terry Smith concluded his interview with Mr. Johnson, the late professor told Terry that he finally got over being unnerved by the appearances of the ghost and started looking upon her visits as a good luck omen. Whenever she appeared, they always had a tremendous hit!

Smith asked Mr. Johnson when he last saw the specter, and he said he believed it was around 1982. Since that time there have been numerous remodeling projects in the auditorium, including a number of windows being blocked off so a better "black out" could be achieved. Ghosts often don't like change, and maybe the remodeling turned her off. Johnson left the university faculty in 1985, and he had not seen her for a couple of years before he left. Maybe she'd seen all the musicals she wanted to see and didn't care for any reruns!

The Ghostly Tower of Loretta

Loretta Academy, a girl's school in El Paso, is home to a supernatural resident who is said to occupy the Academy's tower. Dr. John West, an English professor at the University of Texas at El Paso, provided me with this interesting story as reported by two of his students, Sheila Stopani and Harriet Sturgeon, in a term paper in which they collaborated, back in 1975. These young ladies had interviewed a young woman named Becki Pemberton, who was nineteen years old at the time. Pemberton told them:

While in my early childhood I lived over by a place called Loretta Academy, a school for girls which was run by nuns.

This school is both old and beautiful, and it is notorious for its tower. Let me tell you about the legend of Loretta Tower.

The family that lived next door, a very religious Catholic family, told me this story. One night as they were driving past the Academy they glanced up at the high tower. They saw a shadow of white mist float slowly out from it. They stopped to watch it drift slowly down towards them. The night was lit by a full moon. They were scared because they didn't know what it was, and they started to drive home. The white shapeless mist was seemingly following behind their automobile. They drove up their driveway and looked for their follower. It was gone, and they were relieved and were laughing at how foolish they had been, scared at the thought of a ghost following them.

They went into their house and sat around the fireplace. Slowly an air of uneasiness filled the room. Each member of the family looked towards the fireplace. Their shapeless white mist was drifting down through the fireplace into the room and was soon formed into the shape of a woman. She looked at each person and began to speak: "They locked me in the tower because I was bad, and they left me there without food or water. I called and called for help but no one could hear me. Now I live there because my soul cannot rest until I find the nuns who left me."

She looked once more around the room and drifted up the chimney and was gone. This family has never seen this ghost again, but many people in the vicinity have gone through similar experiences with the legendary ghost of Loretta Academy.

The two ladies also interviewed another El Pasoan, who was a graduate student at the university at the time of their research project. The man, whose name was Raul Carillo, told them: "I have lived in El Paso all of my life and have lived in the same house most of that time. My house is about two blocks from Loretta Academy. Loretta has a very high tower, and I have heard from my parents and others who lived around me that it has a very old legend concerning a young nun who became pregnant while teaching there. Because of the disgrace, the nuns of the school locked her in the tower and left her there without food or water. She died, and now her soul cannot find rest. I myself have never seen her, but many of my friends have seen her come out of the tower and float down, looking for rest.''

Herkie Haunts the High School

There's an oft-repeated tale about a ghost of a man named "Herkie" that's supposed to haunt the auditorium of the high school in Plainview. Several people mentioned him to me, but the whole story came off very piecemeal and vague, but interesting, nonetheless.

Kids just love ghost stories, and like the old game of "gossip" that can change constantly as it moves from one player to the next, some of these ghost stories change as each new generation takes hold and molds them to fit their own set of circumstances.

I first heard a little about "Herkie" from Cindy Hawkins, a former student of Plainview High. She now resides in Amarillo, where she works as librarian for the *Amarillo Globe News*. She said she had a few strange experiences at Plainview High herself, and as far as she knows the rumor still persists that there's a ghost there. But oh, the versions of the story I was to encounter!

Hawkins said she thought the ghost might be that of a man who hanged himself in the high school auditorium, a workman, she thought. She said the clock used to spin around for no reason anyone could explain, and a large lighting board used to light the stage would suddenly start to "misbehave." The lights went on and off at will around the stage area. Hawkins suggested I call a drama teacher or someone currently connected with the school to see what was going on now.

A call to a teacher, Jo Ann Bowers, didn't net that much information. She referred me to retired band director O.T. Ryan, who spent many years at the school and most of them around the auditorium stage. Mr. Ryan said he thinks "Herkie" is just a made-up name that some long-ago students must have invented. He did say he recalled that a big spotlight had been given to the school by the Lions Club, and its huge lens would cause some strange reflections at times when it caught the light just a certain way. O.T. said it could look very "eerie." He also mentioned, as had Hawkins, that the stage lights would blink and the lighting board would flicker and dim at times, but he said he attributed that to the lighting board being old and worn out.

Ryan just thinks Herkie is a friendly spirit, sort of like a mascot, invented by the overactive minds of students.

After sort of getting nowhere fast, I tried one more time. This time I called on Mark Pair, the music professor at Wayland Baptist University in Plainview. Now Pair said he had heard of Herkie, too. He thought maybe there had been a man named Herkemer or something similar who had owned the land the school was built on at one time. He didn't want the high school built on that lot. Now this is WILD! He got so upset he is supposed to have bricked himself into the walls of the auditorium where he died. Pair said that during drama rehearsals and performances, sets will come rolling down, lights go on and off at will, etc.

With all these stories, told enthusiastically by numerous people, I have come to one conclusion. I think Herkie of Plainview must be a lot like "John Isom" in Garland. Unless you had gone to Garland High School, in Garland, Texas, as I did, you wouldn't have a clue as to who John Isom is, or was. None of us did, either. But regularly, John Isom's name would be on the ballots for class president, or best all-around boy, or class favorite, or most handsome boy, or some such. Many times he won by a landslide! Then, of course, there would have to be another election. Isom was just an imaginary school hero, but real enough to us. Perhaps Herkie is just a kindred spirit!

The Friendly Professor

In the 1920s Texas Tech, in Lubbock, was still a rather small institution. There was a real rapport between professors and students back then when classes were smaller and people seemed to have more time for one another.

At that time there was a very popular professor in the chemistry department who got along extremely well with all his students. He often spent his off-duty hours tutoring those who were having a difficult time, in what to many must have been a very difficult subject.

His students were therefore deeply saddened when the professor died of a rather mysterious illness. According to Dr. Kenneth Davis, retired professor of English at the university, who told me this story, the chemistry prof was sadly missed by his students.

But evidently he couldn't stay away from the subject and the university students he loved. It seems a slightly built, elderly gentleman, who sports a neatly trimmed gray beard and wears rather antiquated-looking clothing, not of today's style, has been seen entering fraternity and sorority study halls, where he offers to help the students who are having trouble with their chemistry studies.

Many students, and former students, say this has really, truly happened, and they have reported that even mediocre students have suddenly started to make excellent grades after they've had a tutoring session or two with the ghostly professor!

The Phantom in the Faculty House

San Antonio friends Steve and Bonnie Gallant told me about a relative of theirs who used to live in a haunted house in Lubbock. They put me in touch with Roy Roberts, who now resides in Granite Shoals.

Mr. Roberts, a retired therapist, was most cooperative and willing to talk about the house in Lubbock in which he had lived between September of 1980 and September 1990. Located on Eighteenth Street, the old brick dwelling was one of several houses that were built in 1921 to house Texas Tech faculty members. Roberts purchased the place after the original owner, a professor's widow, died. He asked me not to use the woman's name since some of her relatives are still living. The woman passed away in the house when she was about seventy-four years of age.

The house, Roberts said, is located in what is now a rather "artsy-craftsy" part of Lubbock, just a few blocks from the Tech campus. As a former faculty residence, it is now listed on the National Historic Register. Of old red Chicago brick, it is uniquely decorated with blond brick trim on the corners of the house and beneath the eaves. The light-colored bricks are arranged in double Ts, the initials of the nearby university.

In January 1995, Roberts sold the house, after having used it for the previous four years as a part-time summer home.

Mr. Roberts said almost from the beginning he felt the house was different. At first he felt cold spots in several rooms, and he had the strange, uneasy feeling that a presence was there with him. Roberts, who is single, resided alone in the house but often had visitors who also reported feeling an unearthly presence in the place. Roy said many nights he would suddenly awaken in the middle of the night just knowing she was in the hallway outside his room looking at him, and sure enough, there would be the glowing, hazy figure of a woman outside his bedroom door. He never saw her completely, looking like a real person as some ghosts appear, but he could always make out her shape and some of her features. She looked to be elderly, an old, wrinkled woman, and always appeared in the same fog-like haze. He is sure it is the spirit of the professor's widow, who died in the house.

When Roberts purchased the house it was pretty run down, and he did quite a bit of work on it, replacing old wiring, repainting, and remodeling. During this process the spirit was quite agitated and became very active. This is quite common with most ghosts. They just don't like change!

The spirit would often create problems for the new homeowner to let her displeasure be known. Roberts said she once took several potted plants that were sitting on the windowsills and threw them into the middle of the living room floor, breaking the clay pots and scattering plants and potting soil all over the rug. Another time the cooking pots and pans were all removed from their regular storage places and thrown into the middle of the kitchen floor. Roberts said since he lived alone, and no one was visiting him at those times, it just had to have been the ghost who did these things.

During remodeling, when one of the walls was opened up, two bundles were revealed: one of papers, photos, and clippings, about seventy or eighty pieces in all, and another bundle of a dozen or so old letters tied up with an old, dusty rose-colored ribbon. There were several visitors there when these papers were discovered. Roy and his friends took them into the kitchen and spread them out on the table, so they could look them over. He said a casual glance showed most of the news clippings to have 1920s and 1930s dates.

It was late at night when these things were discovered. Roy and his friends soon became tired and decided to just leave the papers and letters on the kitchen table until morning, when they planned to read and sort them.

The next morning, when they awakened and returned to the kitchen, the table was bare! Not a scrap of paper, photo, or letter was to be found! Roy never saw any of them again and can only surmise the ghostly resident must have removed them while he slept.

After several years, Roberts said the ghost seemed to settle down, accepting his presence in her former home. He often spoke to her, which probably helped, since most ghosts make disturbances in order to be noticed. He would say, "Please be nice and leave me alone," or, "You are welcome to stay if you'll just not disturb me." She quit appearing so frequently, and he didn't feel her unseen presence as much as he previously had. When she did come it was usually in the late afternoon or at night.

Roberts leased the place to some friends in mid-1994, and his friend and her daughter called him to tell him they had seen the ghost since they had moved in and were quite unnerved by the experience. Roberts explained that things would settle down after the spirit got used to having new owners in what previously was her exclusive domain. They will just have to get used to knowing that, along with a National Register plaque, their new residence comes complete with a live-in ghost!

The Jealous Mother

While in Houston on a visit, I chanced upon an interesting article in the public library files there. It ran in the *Houston Chronicle* on November 28, 1984. It concerned a group of people in Laredo who are interested in the supernatural and have formed a club, of sorts, to investigate some of the local stories. I was able to get in touch with Luciana Guajardo at the public library in Laredo. Guajardo often lectures at different events, telling stories that pertain to the supernatural.

The *Chronicle* article cited one story that I questioned Mr. Guajardo about. It concerned the Laredo Independent School District's Azios Building, which today houses LISD Title I workers. The lovely building, once a private residence, was very plush and elegant in its day, with a beautiful courtyard, stables, and gardens. As sometimes happens with old landmarks, the families who had owned it either married and moved away, or died. Finally, the Salesian Sisters bought the house, named it Mary Help of Christians, and established a Catholic school there.

Later the sisters moved their school to Del Mar, and the house again became vacant. This time a man rented the lower portion of the building and turned it into a used clothing store. He hired several young women to work for him. That's when the problems started. The young women began to notice an old woman who would come in and then just disappear when she reached the back of the store. When it came time to close, they would go back to tell her she had to leave, but no one could ever find her. But they had never seen her leave the building! This happened many times, and finally the girls told their supervisor about this. He knew Guajardo and his group and asked them if they would look into these incidents.

Guajardo said they checked into the history and background of the house and determined that the old lady was the spirit of a former owner. She was a doting, jealous mother and had always been afraid that her only son would marry some young lady and leave her to fend for herself in her old age.

The poor mixed-up spirit was trying to frighten the young women away, because she wanted to keep them from attracting her young dead son. After the group was able to determine who the spirit was, through one member who is a medium, they were able to contact the woman and let her know the girls were in the building strictly to work and not to steal her son away from her.

Guajardo said the woman never reappeared after that to frighten the young women. Everything was peaceful in the used clothing store.

Then, several years later the Laredo Independent School District purchased the property and converted the former residence and school into an office building. And of course, young, attractive teachers and secretaries were assigned office space there. The story goes that the old lady, who had been a dormant spirit for some time, rose to the occasion!

Back she came, turning lights out when the secretaries were working late at night, in order to frighten them. She also disturbs their paperwork and hides things from them. It looks like she's just a part of the property, and they've all more or less come to accept her presence.

CHAPTER 8

STORIES OF
HAUNTED HOUSES

THE HAUNTED HOMESTEAD

Not much of the old-time homestead remains
Decaying now on the windswept plains…
The windmill's arms lie broken and still
As its tower stands at the foot of a hill.
But the spirits of those who lived long ago
Come back sometimes when the dry winds blow;
They roam o'er the prairie, surveying the sky,
Watching the windstorms that often blow by.
If you'll listen you'll hear them on dark summer eves
When not even a breeze comes to rustle the leaves.
Even yet they return, though long years have gone by,
To haunt their old homestead, as darkness draws nigh.

Docia Williams

The Mysterious Mansion on the Plains

Why Hollywood hasn't discovered this story and cashed in on the mystery and intrigue attached to it is beyond me. The story of the old Weldon Ostrander house, sitting out on the prairie near the small community of Paint Rock, is fascinating. There have been many articles and stories printed about the place over the years, and many of them are in direct conflict with one another! What is fact and what is fiction still remains, like a snarled up skein of yarn, waiting to be untangled. And, in so many cases where there is a very old, deserted house, mysterious rumors, and an eccentric cast of characters, tales of hauntings seem to fit in with the package!

Weldon Bens Ostrander and John Loomis, believed to have been half-brothers, were wealthy men who came to West Texas from Syracuse, New York. Loomis spent his early years living in the lap of luxury, traveling in Europe, living for a time in Paris, and seeing much of this continent as well. He visited Colorado in 1879 and became fascinated with ranching. He traveled to Austin and San Antonio in 1881 and finally was lured to the area between Paint Rock and Fort Concho, where land was cheap. There was a good water supply on the Kickapoo Creek. Loomis' half-brother, Weldon, came to join him in the venture, and together they formed the Loomis-Ostrander Cattle Company. Some stories place the size of their ranch at 100,000 acres. Other accounts say is was no larger than 70,000 acres in size. It was big, but no one seems to agree to just how large the spread really was.

The magnificent house that Ostrander had built around 1882 for his wife, Sarah, and their two daughters was a huge edifice constructed by a work crew of Irish craftsmen who came to the ranch from New York. The building stone was blue limestone rock quarried on the property. The wooden beams and rafters were of Spanish oak. The house, large even by today's standards, really stood out in the days when most settlers were living in crude log cabins, scratching out a living as best they could on the dry, dusty plains while still fighting parties of Indian raiders. There was bound to have been some jealousy among the neighboring ranch families.

There were nine very large rooms on the two floors, plus a twenty-by-thirty-foot dirt-floored basement, and an attic. In addition to a large and (for those days) very modern kitchen, the ground floor also consisted of a twenty-five-foot-long living room, a twenty-foot-long dining room, and a very large bedroom. On the second floor were five bedrooms, all at least twenty feet long by fifteen feet in width and heated by individual fireplaces. A dumbwaiter operated between the kitchen and the basement, where the ranch hands were often fed.

The fine English Gothic type house, with its broad front porch, was considered one of the finest houses in all of West Texas. Ostrander brought furniture from New York, fine hardwood pieces. There were imported carpets, priceless paintings and tapestries to adorn the walls, stained glass windows and hand-carved woodwork imported from Europe. The stairwell with built-in cabinets and woodwork of hand crafted Spanish oak was very impressive. In addition, indoor plumbing, practically an unknown in that part of the state, complete with built-in bathtub and hot and cold running water was installed. There was even a plant to make ice located on the property!

Another extremely innovative feature of the mansion was the fact that opening any one of the many gates leading onto the ranch property would trigger a warning signal in the house. The signals indicated an approach was being made and from which gate, even gates as far as two miles away from the house.

The old Ostrander mansion

Ostrander named his fabulous home Thornfield, because there were so many thorny agarita plants in the area. His half-brother, John Loomis, built his house about twenty miles from the Ostrander mansion. Just about as grand, he christened his homestead, Silver Cliff. It was reported that Loomis often entertained large parties of guests, serving meals in courses and conducting activities around his place as though he might be the lord of a great manor on Long Island. He even tried, with little success, to get his cowboys to take up Eastern ways, insisting they dress up for the evening meals. One might imagine this did not set too well with the cowhands!

The brothers successfully ranched for several years. It was rumored they were actually being backed by British investors to whom they sold stock in their ranching operations and much of the money poured into the ranch was not their own funds. The Easterners were not really cut out to be Texas ranchers. One account stated when they entered the livestock business around 1885 they owned nearly 45,000 acres of land, 3,000 sheep, 500 horses, 60 head of cattle, and 3 thoroughbred stallions. Another account, totally different, that I found, stated that they had as many of 2,500 fine brood mares and a number of prize jacks from Missouri and they planned to raise the first Missouri mules to be bred in Texas.

Whatever the size of their livestock holdings, their venture suffered greatly after the hard winter of 1885-86 followed by a very hot, dry summer in 1886. They had to sell off some of their livestock. They especially took a beating on the horses, since Texans wanted cowponies and work horses, not thoroughbreds.

Now here's where the mystery starts to enter the picture.

The Ostranders lived in high style in their mansion for several years. They didn't mix much with the locals. Mr. Ostrander got out and about some, since he was in the livestock business. Sarah Ostrander and the girls lived a very reclusive life in their big mansion, having little to do with any of the people in the area. It is said Mrs. Ostrander never liked living the isolated life of a rancher's wife. She certainly must have missed the cultural life she had known back East in Syracuse. Some people said she vowed she would never set foot on the soil of the ranch, and in order to keep her vow, whenever she went out, she got in and out of her carriage from the high steps of her front porch!

A story that ran in *Coronet Magazine* in the December 1956 issue, penned by Oren Arnold, states that a cowboy named Demps Tucker was riding through the country around Paint Rock in 1889. It was shortly after noon, and he rode right up to the front gate of the imposing homestead and shouted a loud "hello!" When no one answered, he dismounted, went up on the wide veranda, and knocked on the front door. Again, there was no response. Trying the door and finding it unlocked, he stepped inside. He was shocked to find the great mahogany table in the dining room was set for noon "dinner" with silver, fine china, and platters of untouched food. Demps waited around a bit, and when no one came, he helped himself to some of the victuals, wrote a note of thanks, which he left on the table, and headed on down towards the Concho River. Ten days later, he stopped off again. As on his last visit, there was no one in sight. A knock on the door brought no response. And then, when he again went inside, he was really disturbed when he found his thank-you note right where he had left it, there on the table with the now dried-up and decaying food. Tucker rode away fast to spread the alarm that all was not right at Thornfield!

Neighboring ranchers rapidly gathered at the mansion to investigate what might have happened to the Ostrander family. There was the untouched food on the table. Items of clothing were strewn about the bedrooms as if the occupants had carelessly and hastily departed, taking very little with them. Only the most expensive clothing items, several exquisite fur pieces, and Mrs. Ostranders' precious jewelry were missing, indicating the family had probably left of their own accord and had not been kidnapped.

As the neighbors who had gathered were standing around the yard talking and guessing what might have happened to the eccentric family, a woman burst out of the house, screaming. She'd been up in the attic, where she found blood all over the floor, under a rope hanging from a rafter. She just knew the Ostranders had been murdered! That set everybody to looking for bodies and graves until John Loomis rode up. He explained that his brother had always hung newly killed beef up in the attic, away from flies. He'd had a fresh kill not long before. The onlookers were relieved that what they'd found was only steer blood.

The fact the family suddenly left their noon meal still uneaten, gave rise to the "Paint Rock Mystery" stories that became the main topic of every dinner party, every campfire gathering, every saloon drinking session, and every church meeting for months after the family disappeared.

The *Coronet* story put forth one good theory. The writer more or less reenacted that last day in 1889 when the family left in a hurry. It must have been around 11 a.m. since most ranch folks ate early. They were probably just ready to eat when a man on horseback rode up to the ranch to shout that the Alien Land Law was about to be passed in the State Legislature. That meant their British investors, already in bad repute because of alleged exploitation practices, could no longer own Texas land. Ostrander was told the Texas Rangers would be coming and he'd better get going. The rancher would be stripped of power, and Ostrander, already unpopular in those parts for his high and mighty ways, would lose prestige and possibly could face actual physical danger. He must have panicked, sending his wife and daughters to gather up a few valuable personal belongings while he hitched up the carriage, let out the livestock, and prepared for a hasty departure. At least that's one version of what might have happened to the family.

I read another account that stated the family must have headed south, because anybody coming by rail to the ranch would have come from the north and Ostrander would not have wanted to meet up with his pursuers as he fled.

John Loomis is said to have told the authorities that the family left the ranch because Sarah had become bored with Western life and insisted on moving back East. He must not have been fearful of any one coming to close down the ranching operation, as he never tried to leave. The hasty departure of the family would not indicate that they left because Sarah was unhappy at the ranch. It seems like that would have been a planned departure, with the family taking the time to pack their clothing, and certainly, they would not have left an untouched meal on the table.

Loomis is supposed to have stayed on, living on his portion of the ranch until his death in 1949, according to an article by Ross McSwain that appeared in the *San Angelo Standard Times* on March 5, 1984. Another article that ran in the *Times* on December 6, 1964, written by Judy Denney, stated that the house was occupied at that time by a Mr. and Mrs. Elma White and their college age daughter, Charlotte. The Whites had lived there for about fifteen years, since 1949, and had made many improvements on the spread, which by then had been reduced to only about 11,500 acres.

The first inkling that the house might be haunted, as had been rumored for years, came from Denney's article:

Mrs. White admits she was scared to move in, and she tells the story of the time she and Mr. White heard mysterious music in the house.

"It was one night right after we first moved in," Mrs. White said. "We were in bed but we weren't asleep. I heard music coming from somewhere and I asked my husband if he heard it. He said he heard it too, and I asked him just what he heard. He said he heard "O, Susanna." I heard the same song, too."

Mrs. White said they checked through the house, even to an old, unused phonograph on the second floor, but found nothing. A few dusty records lie in the phonograph cabinet in the bedroom that is not used, and has never been cleaned up since the Whites moved in.

"O, Susanna" was not among those records, Mrs. White said. There wasn't even a radio playing.

"I don't know whether someone was playing a trick or not," she said, "but it must have been intuition that we'd both think we heard the same song." (Later, the couple decided the sounds they had heard might have been the wind coming down the chimney.)

One accounting I read stated that Ostrander came back for a short visit some years later, to sell off any household goods that had not been stolen by that time. A man from Scotland, T.K. Wilson, bought the ranch in 1889. For a long time he did not live in the house, preferring to occupy the bunkhouse with his ranch hands. He later moved into the mansion. In 1915 Wilson sold the property to John N. Simpson, who left it to his son, Sloan, who once was the postmaster in Dallas. Sloan Simpson sold the inherited property to Jim and Albert Smith in the early 1920s. According to an article in *Frontier Times* (March 1952) the place was divided into a number of smaller acreages and many of them became valuable farms.

An article from the *Denton Record Chronicle* (February 25, 1974) about the mysterious house added another strange twist to the bizarre story. It mentioned that a Texas couple who had known about the old mansion at Paint Rock spent their vacation in New England a few years prior to the writing of the article. They made one stopover in Syracuse, New York. They just happened to pick up a local newspaper and found an article on the obituary page that caught their attention. The story told about the death of a very wealthy woman who had lived in a beautiful home on the outskirts of Syracuse. The surname of the woman was Ostrander, and the article stated she had never married. Was this aged spinster one of the two Ostrander daughters who once lived in the great house known as Thornfield, in far-off Paint Rock, Texas?

Another article I found ran in the October 1984 issue of *San Angelo Magazine*. It mentioned that the house had been occupied by numerous owners and at present was empty and in very poor condition, which had given rise to rumors of ghosts and murders.

A longtime resident of the Paint Rock area, Helen Mathiesen, with whom I have both spoken and corresponded, says that now the house is a hunting lodge for the current ranch owners and is being well kept up, although it is no longer furnished in the elegant style of its colorful past. Helen says she doesn't think the house is haunted, if indeed it ever was. She sent me a fine collection of articles and photographs from a book titled *The Texas Ranchman*, which are the memoirs of John A. Loomis.

There may not be any ghosts about, but there still is an aura of mystery surrounding the great Gothic mansion that was so hastily deserted by its owners over a hundred years ago.

The Sounds of Rushing Water

Maria and Cres Delagarza were married in 1966. They built their own house on a large lot in the small town of Mereta, which is about twenty miles east of San Angelo. A tiny little community today, it does not even appear on many Texas highway maps. Maria says there are a few houses, a cotton gin, a gas station, and a post office still remaining, but there are not even any grocery stores in the town. She estimated that around 125 people live in the community today.

Maria said the house, which was begun in 1966, was ready for occupancy in 1967. They built the dwelling of old wood, on the site of a former community schoolhouse. She said there was also a burial site on the grounds, somewhere between the Delagarza yard and the neighbors' backyard. She was told that a little boy died and was buried there sometime in the 1930s or '40s. The story she had heard was that the youngster was a son of a family of migrant farm laborers who were in the vicinity looking for work. The child, which the Delagarzas believe was named Manuel, took sick and died during a torrential rainstorm. The land was literally inundated with water, and the roads were impassable. The family had no means to take his remains to the cemetery for burial. Cres Delagarza, Maria's former husband, told me he understood the burial took place in the dirt floor of the tent in which the farm workers were camping. That is why the child was buried in an unconsecrated site in the back portion of Delagarza's lot. Whether or not a priest presided over the rites is apparently unknown to anyone in Mereta.

During the first several years that Maria and Cres lived in the house, nothing unusual seemed to happen. They were busy starting their family, and within about five years, Diana, Alma, and Norma had arrive to brighten their lives and keep them very, very busy!

Then, suddenly, about the time Norma was born, "strange things" started happening, and they continued to occur from time to time between 1972 and 1986.

For starters, the family often heard the gurgling, rushing sound of water flowing beneath the house as if there might have been a river or stream located there. It was the kind of sound one might hear while

The Delagarza house at Mereta

standing on a low bridge over a swiftly running stream. Frequent examinations under the house revealed no trace of any water at all.

Then the Delagarzas often heard scratching noises, like someone scratching on a screen window. Again, searches revealed nothing. They also sometimes heard noises up around the ceiling, like a raccoon or squirrel might have gotten up under the eaves between ceiling and roof. Careful searches revealed no animals or rodents of any kind, and yet the noises persisted for a long while.

In the room assigned to Diana and Alma, the Delagarzas had built a large, doorless, cupboard-like closet, which extended from one wall to the other. It had a lot of clothes-hanging space. For some unexplainable reason, the clothes would slide back and forth on their hangers from one end of the clothes rod to the other. This did not happen every day, but it happened often enough to be disturbing since there was no logical explanation for the movements.

Often little running footsteps were heard in the hallway of the house. They decided if they had a spirit, it was rather playful, like the ghost of a youngster, perhaps. Norma, who was the youngest daughter, felt someone, or something, sit down on the side of her bed, and once it even stroked her face.

One night in their room, Diana and Alma started to feel small objects pelting their heads. It felt like someone was throwing small pebbles, and some of the blows were quite painful. Diana firmly told Alma to stop it, and she added, "it hurts!" Alma replied that she hadn't thrown anything at all, and she had felt the rain of pebbles, too. In fact, she had thought Diana was throwing things at her! The two little girls became so frightened they huddled down in their bed and pulled the covers up over their heads, too terrified to venture out of their bed all night!

In view of the fact so many unusual things kept happening, the girls came to accept the presence of some other entity in the household. Diana even named their spirit Simon. Maria said there was really no reason for the name, but they all soon started referring to their "unknown" as Simon.

For fifteen years the family lived in their house. Then baby Menna Marie, whom they nicknamed Moe, arrived in 1983. Maria said things seemed to accelerate then, and the spirit or spirits started to get wilder and more frightening. Unexplained noises and feelings the family had long just accepted became more frequent and more upsetting. Maria said she often felt cold chills, especially after they remodeled the house and made some additions to it. She had sudden weird feelings as if something had grabbed at the back of her neck, and this always brought on a real feeling of fear, especially when she was in the master bedroom, near Cres' closet. She always tried to keep the closet door closed!

Then, suddenly, into the already slightly turbulent scene, entered one old-woman ghost. Maria first saw her when she decided to give the kitchen a complete cleanup after they had repainted the house. The kitchen stove had been moved out into the backyard for a thorough cleanup job. She said she recalled it was late in the afternoon, probably about five-thirty, and it was just starting to get dark. She recalled it was quite chilly, so she thinks it was probably in late October. Hastening to finish her task before darkness fell, she just happened to look up and out into the backyard for a moment. She was startled to see, at the far back of the yard, the figure of an old woman wearing a long skirt, with a shawl or rebozo pulled over her head. She was walking towards the garage. Maria called out to her, but she did not look up and acknowledge Maria's call. When the woman came to the far corner of the house she disappeared from sight, so Maria dashed over to see who she was and where she might be going. She said it only took seconds to reach the corner of the house, but when she got there, the woman was nowhere to be seen. She had literally disappeared!

Later on the family went to visit relatives in Mexico. A cousin of Cres', named Raymond, who also lived in Mereta, told Maria that while they were away he had seen "an old lady sitting in a chair under a tree," in their backyard. Raymond, who has since passed away, said he called out to the woman to see what she was doing in the Delagarza's yard, but the figure just stared straight ahead and did not acknowledge his greeting at all.

Once when little Marie was about three years old (her mother told me this was around 1986) the toddler was headed out of the kitchen into the hallway to the den where she wanted to watch TV. It was during the Christmas holiday season and they had promised the tot she could watch a special Disney production. Suddenly they heard a scream, and little Marie ran back into the kitchen, obviously terrified. She had seen "something" going into the bathroom and it scared her. Maria and Armando, her father, who was there visiting them, calmed the child down and took her on into the den to watch television. Maria checked the bathroom and found nothing unusual there. Then Maria's father confided to her that the child had not imagined things, because earlier he had seen a dark figure in a long skirt walk into the bathroom. She had gone right through the door. He had not told his daughter or the children for fear of frightening them.

That same evening Cres was working his shift as a deputy sheriff. He had been out near Eden, some forty-four miles east of San Angelo. About 1 or 2 a.m. he arrived home and dashed into the house. The first thing he asked was, "What happened? Has something happened to Marie?" This was the same evening, of course, that the toddler had been badly frightened by the dark figure in the hallway that her grandfather had also seen. Cres, some forty-four miles away, had such premonition of something frightening taking place at home, that he had asked to be relieved of duty and hastened home to see if anything had happened.

The family was so disturbed by all of this, they packed up their pillows and blankets and headed off in the cold night to Cres' family's house. Cres' father and Armando, Maria's dad, talked about the ghost situation for what few hours remained of the night.

The next day, which was a Monday, Maria drove into San Angelo to the Catholic church of St. Mary's, which she attended. After mass she asked the priest if he would spare her a moment. She told him about the events of the night before, and of some other things that had happened at the house, and pleaded with him to come and bless the house. The cleric told her that he would tell her something that she could do herself. If, after she had followed his instructions, things did not settle down, then he said he would try to prevail upon the Archbishop to give him permission to come out and take care of things. He did not use the word "exorcise," Maria said, but she presumed that is what he meant to do if necessary.

Armed with a vial of holy water the priest had given her, Maria sprinkled the water in each room of the house while reciting the rosary for five days. Then, on the fifth and final day, she did just what the priest had told her to do. When she came to the last room, after sprinkling the holy water and reciting the rosary, she firmly, forcefully, and loudly, told whatever it was to go away, right now!

Maria carried out the priest's instructions to the letter. And after that, for a period of about four or five months, things seemed to get better. Then, slowly and insidiously, little things began to start up again.

For one thing, the marriage that had produced four beautiful young daughters seemed to be crumbling. There were frequent disagreements and arguments. After one particularly bad argument, as Maria and Cres stood in their bedroom, a box suddenly came flying out of the closet for no reason! It could not have just fallen off the shelf, because it had been stacked in between two other boxes. And the box fell open to reveal a Ouija board! That certainly stopped that particular argument.

The Delagarzas had always managed to get by, but now there were serious financial problems as well. Finally, the couple separated, going their independent ways. The bank was forced to foreclose on their property and their home was put up for sale. Maria and the girls moved to San Antonio, and Cres stayed in West Texas where he now resides in San Angelo.

Maria recalls that the final days she spent in the house were very unsettling. She felt a frightening presence in it that, to her, was "evil and scary." She said it evidently affected the girls as well. One of the girls, Norma, who was about fifteen at the time, experienced something sitting down on her bed, and then she felt "it" lean over and press down against her body. Little Marie, still just a tot, started to have frequent conversations with "somebody." She also had frequent nightmares, where she said she saw ugly little faces flying at her! Of course, she was too little to tell her mother who it was she was speaking to, but she was definitely seeing something and talking to it as well. Looking back, Maria attributes many of the family problems to the presence of the spirit that seemed to permeate the house in Mereta. A friend of mine here in San Antonio has described this sort of manifestation as that of a "negative spirit." They are not as evil as a poltergeist, but they certainly are not among the desirables of ghostdom if one must live in a haunted house!

Maria learned that the people who purchased the house from the bank only stayed there about three months. They left because they said it was haunted. The next owners remodeled the place, spending quite a lot of money on the project. Yet they, too, left shortly thereafter. Maria was told they left because they constantly heard water running under the house. It was more than their nerves could stand, since they knew there was no water there. Maria hasn't heard lately what has happened to her former home. A conversation with Cres brought forth the information that the place changed hands a couple of times, and now it is used mostly for storage.

During our talk, Maria kept asking me if I could supply her with any explanation for all the things that happened in the house. I couldn't give her an answer then. Later on, I began to think. I do not pretend to possess psychic abilities. Neither am I a ghost-buster, nor have I made a thorough study of the supernatural. But having interviewed scores of people in the course of writing several books on the subject, and having read a number of works on the topic by other writers, I have sorted out several possible, fairly plausible explanations for the hauntings:

The youngster, whose name may have been Manuel, who died there on the property, passed away during a heavy rainy season. That is why he had to be buried there instead of in the consecrated ground of a cemetery. Could the sounds, so often heard, of running water under the house be connected to that time of flooding, when the child died? And the mischievous acts the Delagarza children experienced, such as the pebbles dropping on the girls' heads, the sounds of little running feet in the hallway, the scratching sounds—couldn't that be the little boy spirit reaching out to other children to come and play with him? And what about the figure of the old woman? Could she have been Manuel's mother, or even his *abuela*, or grandmother, who had returned to watch over the grave of her lost little one? Could she have been resentful that the Delagarza house was filled with healthy, happy children growing up normally, while her little one was denied that privilege and left to the confines of a dark, cold grave at the back of the property? Was this the reason her dark spirit took up residence with the Delagarzas?

Maria asked me if I thought a spirit would follow people after they moved from a haunted house. She went on to say one of her daughters, Norma, who is now a single parent living in San Antonio with her own two young daughters, has lately been troubled by water running from the faucets, which turn themselves on and off at will. And other strange things seem to happen at Norma's house. I tried to assure Maria that generally, spirits seem to attach themselves to places more than people, and if the spirits are still active in Mereta, they are still probably hanging around the Delagarza's former home. But the running water and various other strange things that are happening in Norma's San Antonio home might possibly be another spirit, completely different and apart from the Mereta ghost. I am afraid this is small consolation, indeed!

Gussie's House

When Fort Worth resident Jim Lane first saw the house, he just knew he had to have it. He liked the location, tucked away, as it was, sort of back in a corner as the street curved around, up high on the bluff overlooking the Trinity River. In fact, the multiterraced yard was an added attraction. Although the old place needed quite a bit of work, it had such charm and potential, Jim was anxious to accept the challenge of bringing it back to its original appearance. When he consulted a decorator to find out the colors most often used in the post-Victorian era the house was constructed in 1906, they came up with, of all things, pink and blue! Jim said it really is a "woman's house," even though he, a bachelor, planned to live there. It was originally built for Gussie Armstrong, and Lane wanted Gussie's house to be a place that she would have been proud to claim. Gussie lived and died in the house. And Jim says that Gussie's spirit is still very much a part of the house. He says he feels like he's just the custodian of "Gussie's house."

Lane, a prominent attorney and a member of the Fort Worth city council, took time off from his busy schedule to take us to see his lovely home, which is filled with antiques and memorabilia. He showed us an old album with a photo of Gussie Armstrong taken at about the time the house was built, and he told us the poignant story of her sacrifice and dedication to her father and her siblings that prompted her to live in the house.

W.L. Armstrong, whose portrait hangs in the front parlor of the house, was a Confederate war veteran. He later lived with his wife and children in the small town of Rising Star. Mrs. Armstrong died young, of tuberculosis, leaving the widower with six children. Gussie was the oldest child. She was around twenty at the time her mother passed away.

Gussie was young, pretty, and very much in love. In fact, she was engaged to be married. But her father asked her to make a terrific sacrifice. He told her he would build her a lovely big house if she would break her engagement, move with him and the younger children to Fort Worth, and take over as housekeeper, hostess, and surrogate mother to the five younger Armstrong children. And that is exactly what she did. She never married, devoting the rest of her life to her father and siblings. By the time that Armstrong died, in 1923, Gussie was left alone in the house. The other children were grown and had moved away. As she grew older, climbing the stairs became too difficult for her, and a small kitchen convenient to her room was installed upstairs. She seldom left home until she died, sometime in the 1940s, a greatly loved and respected member of the Armstrong family, who had sacrificed her own personal happiness for theirs.

Almost from the time Lane, a good looking bachelor, moved into the former Armstrong house, Gussie began to make her presence known. Although she was getting on in years at the time of her death, the spirit that returns is a young and attractive Gussie, who looks just like the portrait Jim showed us upon our arrival at the house. He has seen Gussie's apparition numerous times. His mother and father have also seen the specter. Jim's mother, who went with us to see the house, told us one day she and her husband walked up on the big front porch and glimpsed a young woman standing in the dining room as they stood before the glass paneled front door. As soon as they entered the house, the woman was nowhere to be seen. They first thought she might be a friend of Jim's who was visiting, but after comparing notes with Jim as to Gussie's appearance, they are convinced they saw the ghost.

Gussie's house, Fort Worth

The very first time Jim saw Gussie was one evening when he had retired early to read. She came to the doorway of his upstairs bedroom as he sat up in bed, reading. His dog, Higby, was at his side. Gussie had her right hand up against the door frame. She was young and pretty, with long dark hair, and she had beautiful big brown eyes. She was wearing a diaphanous white garment. Lane said she gave him quite a provocative look and then just slowly faded away.

Gussie has appeared at the same place several other times. The last time Jim mentioned was just a few weeks prior to this writing (October 1994). Jim says he thinks maybe Gussie finds him attractive, as she always stares in a rather flirtatious "come hither" manner before fading away. Having met Jim Lane, I would say Gussie has good taste!

Sometimes the figure of the young woman has been seen from the outside of the house as she stands in one of the front upstairs windows looking out, as if she might be watching for the children to come home after school.

Although Lane is not at all afraid of Gussie, he said others don't always feel like he does about her being there. When he went to Europe on a trip, two police officer friends moved in to house-sit. He could never get the officers to tell him exactly what happened, but they must have had one terrifying experience! One officer left in the middle of the night, clad only in his underwear! He even refused to return to the house the next morning to retrieve his clothes. The officer who stayed did not want to talk about the incident and asked not to be named.

Jim keeps the house, which is filled with all sorts of lovely antiques, artwork, plants, and photographs, in immaculate condition. He thinks Gussie appears to him ever so often just to let him know she is proud of how the house looks and is appreciative of the care he takes of it. Lane thinks his color schemes are probably brighter and more cheerful than the way it might have been when Gussie lived in the house. Her life was bound to have been stressful and tiring, with five young children to watch over, and an aging father to look after as well. And when she grew old, she was left all alone, with no one there to share her home. It must be pretty nice for her now. No more work or worry; a cheerful, pretty house with lots of roses growing outside in the well-manicured yard, and the company of a handsome bachelor thrown in for good measure!

Spirits at the Old Schoonover Mansion

They say it's haunted. The old Schoonover house at Eighth and Pennsylvania streets in Fort Worth is no longer a residence. Built by a prominent jeweler as a family dwelling in 1907, the Victorian style buff-colored brick mansion is located very close to the Harris Hospital in what was once referred to as the "silk stocking district." It has led many lives since it was a beautiful residence.

An interesting article that ran in the *Fort Worth Star Telegram* on October 31, 1993, a Halloween special, no doubt, stated that some of the odd occurrences in the old house might be brought on by the women who lived, and later died, in the house. Ann Maurine Schoonover Packard, who lives in Birmingham, Alabama, grew up there. She recalled her grandmother, Velma Simmons, had died in the house. Her father's office secretary, Lorene DeLipsy, also passed away there. DeLipsy had no family and had a crippled hip. They found out she was dying of Hodgkin's disease and brought her there to live out her days. DeLipsy died in a little upstairs back bedroom. That same room was also once occupied by Elsie Scaman, an English nanny employed by the family. Packard also recalled that at one time the room had served as a schoolroom where the children were tutored by their mother until Ann was ready to enter the sixth grade.

The large basement once housed a coal bin, laundry, and canning closet. It also had a storage place where houseplants were kept during the winter months. There was a large room under the dining room where the housekeepers lived. Two couples served as housekeepers at different times. First there was Mamie and John Henry Jones, and later, Frances and Grady White. But no one ever died in the basement.

Although Mrs. Packard did admit some puzzling things happened as she helped her parents move from the house, she never thought about any ghosts being there.

Fred Cauble, an architect, and his partners, Larry Hoskins, John Esch, and Toby Harrah, purchased the house from the estate in 1981 and set up their offices there. They were to find out soon enough that they weren't the only occupants of the old house.

Cauble said one night soon after they had purchased the house, he went down into the basement, which at the time smelled very musty like a house does when it's been closed up a long time. When he reached for a light switch he felt cold fingers clutching at his shoulder. When he turned around, there was no one there, but he knew he had not imagined this. Later real estate agent Trish Bowen had a similar encounter in the basement. She was out of there in short order!

Although Cauble did not have the same encounter again, he still experienced some strange happenings during the years he occupied the building. However, he said he wasn't afraid. He thought the ghost was either inquisitive or maybe trying to be helpful. Once the ghost opened a door for him when he was having trouble moving a big box into a room at the head of the stairs. The door was closed. As he bent to put the heavy box on the floor so he could open the door, it suddenly opened for him! He said sometimes when he would search for plans and couldn't find what he was looking for, he'd come to the office the next morning and they would be on his desk. It wasn't just a coincidence, he is sure of that!

Cauble even heard the sounds of piano music drifting up the stairs to his second-floor office. He'd pause to listen but never bothered checking it out. He just accepted the fact that his building was "different." One of his friends and fellow architects, the late Bill Pruett, recalled a day in 1981 when he had a strange experience in the attic. According to the news write-up in the *Star Telegram*, Pruett said while they were working on the renovation of the building on a cloudy, cool, wet day, he saw a ball of light about the size of a softball. It just seemed to zoom from one side of the attic to the other. While Pruett said he wasn't a believer in ghosts, it surely was strange and he couldn't explain it. The ball of light just danced around from one place to another and seemed to be all over the place, all at once.

Cauble said the occurrences grew less and less noticeable, until by the time the building changed hands again in 1990, there had been no encounters for over a year. That is probably because the ghost had accepted the architects and trusted them to take care of the house.

Then, with new owners came new manifestations. This, of course, is not unusual. Ghosts seem to get active whenever the status quo changes, be it ownership of the property, or renovation. They really don't like things changing around in their old bailiwicks.

Currently, Dr. Roger Harman's offices occupy the main, or first floor, of the old mansion, while the basement level is occupied by the advertising firm of Marketing Relations, Inc., partnered by Denis Russell and Jerry Gladys. A recent visit to Fort Worth to see the house and visit with the two advertising executives revealed they still are having encounters with the unknown occupants of the house. Gladys said the evening of the first day the firm occupied their new quarters he worked late at his desk. He recalled it was around 10:30 p.m. when he suddenly started hearing strange, loud clanking sounds, metallic sounds coming from an air duct high in the wall behind his desk. The noise continued for quite a long while. There was no one else in the building at that hour. Gladys knew he was all alone. Finally, having been alerted to the presence of a ghost in the house, he told the spirit, "Look, I've got to get all this work done and I just don't have time to fool with you." It must have worked, because the noises stopped.

Russell, an Emmy award winner for the work he did some twenty years ago in optical effects for the TV series *Star Trek*, had another unnerving experience. One afternoon he was alone in the offices painting the walls. A door that he knew was locked suddenly opened, slammed shut, and then came to rest, slightly ajar.

A continuing irritant exists in the offices. The temperature is impossible to regulate. The partners will turn the air conditioning thermostat to about 70 degrees, since they both like it cold. Soon the

The Schoonover house, Fort Worth

place will be hot, and the thermostat will be up to 80 degrees or above. They'll reset the thermostat and soon the temperature goes down, but it won't be long till it's up again! They've even put heavy tape over the setting and arrived the next day to find the tape has been removed and the temperature control has again been set at 80 degrees. This happens when they are positive that no one was there during the night. This is a constant irritation to both partners.

After our visit with Gladys and Russell in their attractive offices, we climbed the stairs to enter the offices of Dr. Harman on the first, or ground, floor. We chatted with Bobette Vroon, Harman's medical assistant, and Kimberly Bradley, the office manager. Both young ladies openly admitted there was something "different" about the office space they occupy.

Vroon made the same observations about the temperature of the offices and said they also had placed duct tape over the thermostat control, but it would always be peeled off in the morning, with the control set way up, leaving the temperature much warmer than they wanted it to be.

There is a kitchen down in the lower level of the building. Both young ladies said they had often heard water running when they worked late at night. They knew they didn't turn it on, and they could never find anyone else who would own up to doing it.

The big chandelier in the main reception room often turns itself on and off, as do some of the other light fixtures in the place.

Bradley said she once heard the sounds of something, "like a ton of bricks," falling upstairs, but a thorough search revealed nothing out of place. Vroon said she'd heard stacks of books and magazines falling in the office area, but again, nothing could be found to explain the disturbing noises. (Note; this is evidently a common denominator with many ghostly encounters. People often report hearing sounds of things breaking and falling and then when they search, there is never any sign of anything being out of place.)

Both of the women said that on numerous occasions they would search and search for a patient's chart and would be unable to find it anywhere. But on arrival at the offices the next morning, the first thing they would see would be the missing chart, either on top of the manager's desk, or atop the file cabinet where it was ordinarily kept.

The front doorbell frequently rings. But many times no one is there. The door sometimes opens by itself. From a small office to the left of the main entrance in a room which was formerly the Schoonover breakfast, or morning, room, Bradley has frequently heard the doorbell ring and then has seen the front door slowly inch open. From her vantage point she can plainly see through the beveled glass front door, and if anyone were to ring the doorbell she would be able to see the person standing there.

The ladies told me that the receptionist, who was not there during my visit, has often mentioned that she felt someone was walking up behind her, but there's never anyone there. Both Vroon and Bradley also said often they encounter strange smells that suddenly permeate the reception and examination rooms. Sometimes they are pleasantly floral, and other times a very offensive "rotten egg gas" sort of smell is in evidence. They have absolutely no explanation for any of this.

Creaking footsteps on the winding stairs leading up to the second-floor level are frequently heard. There used to be a beauty salon on that level, but after constantly having her bottles of shampoo, skin treatments, and nail polish fall off the shelves, the beautician decided she'd had enough, so she isn't in the building any longer.

Both of the women I talked with said one of the strangest things they have experienced is how the plants get watered. They said they hardly ever water any of the beautiful house plants which decorate the reception area, in what was once the big Schoonover parlor. The plants aren't just damp, either. Sometimes they are almost overflowing with water. None of them have watered the plants, and they can't explain who has. Maybe one of the former residents was an avid gardener.

There's an old-fashioned radio in the reception room. They always turn it off when they go home. For a while, when they arrived in the morning, they would be greeted by loud Mexican music coming from the radio! For some reason this finally ceased.

Both ladies said they and several others had seen a dark shadow drift past one of the side windows. This has happened a number of times. All anyone can make out is the shape of a man in a dark suit going past the window. He always looks the same to everyone who sees him. However, thorough searches, inside and out of the building, have revealed no such person is anywhere around.

There is no creepy feeling about the building. It is light, airy, and pleasant, with the ambiance of an old, venerable building that's there to stay. Evidently its ghost is also there for the long haul!

The Spirit of the Musical Mistress

The first time Fort Worth resident Barbara Doop ever saw her future home, she already knew it was "different." Barbara and George had been seeing each other for some time. Then, he invited her over to see his home, a gracious old pinkish-beige brick dwelling trimmed in white, in the Mediterranean style. She said as soon as she stepped into the spacious living room, she exclaimed, "What a lovely room!" and then (she doesn't know to this day what suddenly possessed her to say it), "That's where the baby grand piano used to be." She said she just saw it in her mind's eye.

And she was probably right! The house, which was begun in 1913 and completed in 1916, was built by a wealthy oilman for his mistress. The lady was a gifted musician. The gentleman was a staunch Catholic, and although he was separated from his wife, he refused to divorce her in order to marry his paramour. Apparently the romance finally went sour, and the story went around that the woman moved out of the house and spent the rest of her days as a music teacher. The house was obviously built for music, as it is acoustically perfect with its eighteen-foot ceiling in the huge (thirty feet by twenty-two feet) drawing room.

After the musician moved out, the man sold the house to a family named Carshon who lived there for about twenty-five years, and the house has sort of held on to the title, "the old Carshon house." Their daughter married a Jewish rabbi in a beautiful wedding ceremony in front of the magnificent fireplace in the spacious drawing room.

Soon after her first visit to George Doop's house, Barbara was back one evening visiting with her fiance. They were sitting in the original breakfast room, which was divided from the dining room by closed glass French doors. Barbara happened to glance up, and she saw a figure of a woman standing on the other side of the glass doors. She seemed to be listening to Barbara and George's conversation. Barbara asked George, "Who's that?" He looked up and told Barbara, "I don't see anyone." He got up and went over and turned on the lights in the dining room area and said, "See, there's no one there." But Barbara knows that she saw a woman standing there. She described her as attractive, fair-skinned with light, probably blue, eyes. She wore her light brown hair swept up in a high pompadour a la the Gibson Girl fashion. She was clothed in a dark brown skirt, and her white blouse had wide shouldered leg o' mutton sleeves. The high collared neckline was caught with some sort of brooch.

Barbara said after she and George were married and she came to the house to live, various strange things happened to convince her that the house was haunted. Lights went on and off, and doors opened and closed, the sort of things that are associated with the presence of ghosts. One theory might be that the first mistress of the house, whose romance didn't culminate in marriage as she had probably hoped, was frustrated and sad that her life didn't turn out as she had wished. So her spirit returns to a place where at least for a time she had been contented, and in love, with high hopes for a "happy ever after" ending to her affair.

The Doops even gave the ghost a nickname. They called her "Mattie." She evidently left quite an impression on the family cat, too. Barbara said many times the cat would suddenly bristle and then take off running through the house howling bloody murder and acting as if it were pursued by the devil himself! Other times, the animal would be dozing as Barbara and George watched television. Then, suddenly, without preamble, the cat would leap "four feet up in the air," according to Barbara. Its tail would stand straight up and its hair bristled as if it had been electrically shocked! It looked as if it were having some sort of terrible seizure, and it seemed absolutely terrified of whatever it had seen, heard, or just sensed.

All sorts of things kept occurring to indicate the Doops had a resident spirit. Then, for some reason, after they thoroughly cleaned out the butler's pantry and straightened everything up, the manifestations seemed to slow down. Apparently the ghost felt the house was being properly cared for, and she finally accepted Barbara in her role as the new mistress of the house.

The Doops remained in the house for the first ten years of their marriage. Then George had a heart attack. They decided to move to a smaller place with no large grounds to keep.

When they started making preparations to sell the house and move away, strange things started happening. Appliances that were in good working condition started breaking down in rapid succession. First the trash compactor hung up and refused to function. Then the dishwasher came apart, the bottom dropped out, and it began to leak like a sieve. The hot water heater was the next item to malfunction. It started acting up and water ran all over the floor. It was quite obvious that "Mattie" was not at all pleased the Doops were moving out of her house! Finally,

Barbara told her, "Lay off, Mattie. We're moving, and that's final!" They were supposed to be out before midnight on their last day and they really rushed to make the deadline. Barbara felt something awful might happen to them if they weren't out by the time the clock struck midnight!

A young couple with a twelve-year-old daughter moved into the house. Barbara told them not to leave the child alone in the house; to have someone there for her when she got home from school. They reported some pretty unsettling occurrences and were not there for very long. The couple got a divorce, and they all moved out. Next came a young doctor and his wife. They started to do some remodeling, decided it was just too big an undertaking, and did not ever move in. Next, a woman whom Barbara described as very strong willed moved in. Barbara said she just knew that Mattie wouldn't like having her around! During this time, much remodeling took place as well. Two ceilings were dropped, a skylight was added in one room, a powder room was put into what once was a huge closet, and a door into a hall-way was closed off. All this remodeling probably had a negative effect on Mattie, as ghosts never seem to like change, especially if they loved a place as it was when they lived there.

The remodeling owner did not stay. Mattie must have run her off pretty quickly! Now, according to Barbara, a nice young couple owns the house and is taking excellent care of it. They have mentioned feel-ing a "presence" there, but they do not appear to be frightened. Barbara, who had come to accept Mattie as a part of the household, hopes the current owners are as kind and tolerant of her as she and George were.

It's a shame that Barbara and George didn't buy a piano while they were there. I'll just bet they might have been treated to some pretty good nocturnal concerts!

The Humming Ghost

Two young men who call themselves "ghost stalkers" live in Fort Worth. Although they are not psychics, they do believe in the super-natural, and they try to capture spirits on film or tape-record their voices. Terry Smith and Mark Jean have a great number of good stories to share about their adventures, and one of them concerns a Mistletoe

Heights home. The two men have interviewed numerous former residents of the home, and at least three of them came up with remarkably similar descriptions of the ghostly resident of the house. The wraith is a woman, and more than likely she was a former resident who either lived or died in the house. She is described as wearing an ivory-colored blouse, a long skirt, and she has a placid smile on her face. Often she sings! The melody is not recognizable, and sometimes it sounds more like a hum, or even a moan.

Although they have heard her refrains, Smith and Jean have not seen the spirit. Once, with the owners' permission, they spent five nights in the house. Twice they also enlisted the help of a psychic, Elaine Gibbs, to conduct seances in the residence. On the night of July 11, 1987, a woman's voice was heard by all three, Smith, Jean, and Gibbs. Smith stated "Although we could not locate the whereabouts of the voice, the three of us heard it coming from three different directions." However the video and audio equipment they had brought picked up no sounds whatsoever!

One former resident of the Mistletoe Heights house told Smith the specter liked the pantry, the basement, and the stairwell going up to the pantry from the basement. The woman reported she awoke one night to find the apparition standing next to her bed. The spirit was apparently upset that some food was missing from the pantry. The woman replaced the food and the ghost disappeared!

The Haunted Mineral Wells Mansion

Margaret Maxwell lives in a stately old house in Mineral Wells. She says there's no doubt in her mind that her twenty-room mansion is haunted. She was told the house was built by a family who had two sons. One of the sons died of pneumonia when he was about twenty-one years old. Both the apparition of this young man and the spirit of an older man have been seen in the house. It is presumed the older specter may be the spirit of the other brother.

Margaret told me the young man's apparition tried at first to run her family off by frightening and harassing them. He virtually leapt out in front of her, appearing as a dark, shadowy form, having no feet or hands. She once saw him reflected as she looked in her mirror. He appeared as a dark form standing just behind her. She says he had even walked on the headboard of her bed, and once he sat down on her bed!

Margaret's family is not the first to have been disturbed by the active ghost. Since 1979 several families who have occupied the house have reported strange happenings. No one stayed very long. In fact, the house once stood vacant for about six months.

Maxwell told me that she finally came to terms with her live-in supernatural guest. She told him she'd try not to disturb his room. She told him she was quite willing to share her house with him if he would not harass or frighten her family anymore, explaining to the spirit it would be better for everybody if they could just "get along," co-habiting in the old house. Although he still appears from time to time and is often heard, the spirit has settled down considerably since Margaret talked to him and made her wishes known.

The Misty White Form

Leslie "Joe" Moore Sr., lives in a house that used to be haunted. Why it was haunted for a number of years, but isn't now, remains a mystery to the genial Wichita Falls resident.

Moore, who is now retired, lives alone in the small but comfortable house on Jacqueline Street. He has seen a misty white apparition of what appears to be a human form (he thinks it is a female) on a number of occasions. His late wife, Wilma, and the maid also saw it. Even the pet beagle dog seems to have sensed a presence, as at numerous times it would bristle and then growl when there was nothing around to explain such behavior. Moore says several times when the dog would be napping in front of the television set, she would suddenly awaken. Her hair would bristle along the neck and then she would growl and get up and walk over to the doorway. There she would look around, and then she'd growl some more.

Usually the strange phenomena took place about 9 o'clock at night. The misty form always took the same route, going from the bathroom down the hall to the master bedroom. When I questioned him, Moore says he has never felt a cold spot in the hallway, which is often the case in hauntings. He said neither he nor his wife had been particularly afraid of the apparition, but they were definitely puzzled as to who, or what, it might be. The house was not old. There had been no deaths or violence there. It was not near a cemetery, nor was there any old wood or building materials in the house. Moore says it's about a mile from the Wichita River, and all he can think is perhaps a party of pioneers once passed that way and camped near the site. And what if one of them had taken sick and died and was buried in an unmarked grave where the house now stands? Many a pioneer traveling over the country in those hardship days met with such a fate. It's all the explanation Moore can think of. Have you a better one?

The Grant Street Ghost

There's an old house in Wichita Falls that used to be haunted. I'm saying "used to be" because we can't get in touch with the present owner, who seems to be away a lot, so we don't know if the ghost is still around or not.

A January 1983 edition of the *Wichita Falls Times Record-News* ran a story written by Louise Gregg, a staff writer, concerning a one-story, rather ramshackle old house on Grant Street. I decided to follow up on the Gregg story by contacting the person whose experience was narrated. His name is Dale Terry. I found Mr. Terry to be a very personable and cooperative individual.

Terry is the district public affairs officer for the Texas Department of Highways and Public Transportation. As a sideline, he sometimes organizes and conducts estate sales.

Some years ago he was called by neighborhood friends whom he had known for many years to come help sort through the personal belongings of their mother, who had passed away in the house. It had been her home for about sixty years and was crammed with her personal effects, including many letters, photographs, and papers. Terry said that at each estate sale he conducts, he feels almost as if he knows the deceased, as he sorts through their belongings, personal papers, clothing, etc. Since this time he had actually known the lady, the task of sorting through her memorabilia was a very poignant experience.

Because family members are still living, Terry asked me not to use real names. So for their benefit, I'll refer to the lady as "Sarah Jones."

Terry said the first night he began the project of sorting, he was in the dining room of the house. This was the night that Terry, a total skeptic until then, began to believe in ghosts!

The old house, built around 1916, had no air-conditioning. The summer night when Terry set about his task was exceptionally hot. The daytime temperatures had hovered around 110 degrees. Since the house had been closed up following the death of Mrs. Jones, it was like a roasting oven. Terry said he removed his shirt, placed a damp towel around his neck, and placed a sweat-band around his forehead to keep the moisture from dripping into his eyes. He said he couldn't remember when he had ever been so hot!

Then, suddenly, for no explainable reason, the room turned icy cold. It was the most agonizing, penetrating, all-encompassing cold he had ever felt! It permeated the room and literally engulfed Terry. He first thought, "My God, I'm having a heart attack, or a stroke." Then, he thought of any other reason why he could suddenly be so cold. He thought, maybe I'm taking pneumonia. Nothing made sense. Finally, he got up and left the room. When he entered the living room, it was as hot as a furnace. The same temperatures existed in the hallway and the kitchen. He went back to the dining room, and again it was excruciatingly cold. He decided to leave all the items he had been sorting on the dining room table and get out of there. He went home for the night.

At first Dale didn't tell anybody about the strange temperature changes in the house. His wife guessed something was wrong. She said he was as white as a sheet and looked like he'd seen a ghost! Not understanding the strange coldness that had gripped him that night, and why it was just centered in the dining room, he finally consulted a university professor whose judgment he trusted. The scholar was not at all surprised or shocked at Terry's disclosure. He told Terry he believed in ghosts and had even seen them. He told him that cold spots were common with hauntings. He also told Terry that when he thought of people he had known who were now deceased, sometimes they would actually appear to him. At least Terry felt better, having heard an explanation for the intense cold from a man he knew was neither ignorant nor superstitious.

Dale Terry told me that several people who had lived in the house had passed away there. And while he did not actually die in the house, one previous owner, Mrs. Jones' first husband, had been badly burned in an accident in the backyard which resulted in his death a couple of days later. He had been using a machine to recycle motor oil. The blow-off valves were the wrong size. The apparatus blew up and the man was so badly burned he didn't survive the explosion.

Then, another woman, the mother of Mrs. Jones, had died in the house. She was a very interesting old lady and quite eccentric in her manner of dress. She was tall and slender, wore a lot of heavy makeup, and preferred wearing black and white ensembles. She had once occupied the back bedroom.

Then Mrs. Jones married a second time after her first husband's tragic death. The second husband didn't live too long, either, dying a very painful death of cancer in the house.

The circumstances surrounding Sarah Jones' death were eerie, to say the least. It seems she had been up in Canada for an extended visit with a son and his family. Suddenly, without preamble, she announced, "I'm going home to Texas." She was shortly on her way back to Wichita Falls. Concerned about his mother, her son called Dale Terry, who arranged to go to the airport to meet her flight. For some reason, she changed her plans, arrived on an earlier flight, and Terry failed to find her at the airport. When he got back to Grant Street, he found the elderly woman had arrived by taxi and was sitting on the couch in her living room.

The house had been closed up for a very long time and was stiflingly hot. Terry told her he would call the electric company and get the power turned on so they could plug in some fans to cool the place off. She didn't have much to say and seemed rather upset that anyone even knew she had returned to Texas.

In short order, Terry got the electricity connected and placed some fans around the room to cool the place off. It was unbearably hot, "like a blast furnace," in Terry's words.

Mrs. Jones had arrived home on a Saturday afternoon. Terry didn't see her the next day but presumed some of her family and friends were in touch with her. When he drove to work on Monday, he heard on his special car radio that there was an ambulance call to Grant Street. For some reason, he said he was not surprised. He just knew something terrible had happened to his old friend and neighbor. Sure enough, Mrs. Jones' body had been found in the back bedroom, the room which once had been occupied by her mother. Although the room was extremely hot, Sarah Jones was found clad in her heavy wool coat, lying in bed. Since she was clad in that fashion, Terry could only surmise that the coldness which gripped him later on in the dining room as he sorted through her effects had caused her to don her winter coat on that hot summer day.

After Terry had the dining room experience, he was glad when his estate sale assignment was over. Fortunately, he very quickly found a buyer for the house, a young man in his early twenties. The man had fallen in love with the old house and saw a lot of possibilities for it. He planned to restore and repaint the house, bringing it back to its original appearance. He intended to have his living quarters on one side of the hallway that split the house from front to back and use the other side for an antiques business!

Soon after the purchase, the new owner called painters in to work on the house. Terry said he was out watering his lawn when he looked across the street at the old house and saw the painter there do a very strange thing. He threw his ladders and paint cans out in the yard, gathered everything up, tossed them in his truck, and drove off in a hurry! He apparently never came back. Later on, more painters showed up to work on the place. To Terry's amazement, these men also threw their equipment into the yard and departed as well. Finally, the new owner had to wade in and finish the job himself.

When the new owner told his fiancee about the place and how it would soon be ready for them to move into, naturally, the young woman was very anxious to see her future home. When they arrived at the place, in the company of another couple, one of the women said, "Something's just not right with this house. I'm getting out of here." She went outside to the car and could not be persuaded to come back into the house. The young man's fiancee went through the house, examining every room. She seemed fine until she reached the back bedroom. Then, she suddenly screamed and ran out of the house as fast as she could!

After the young woman calmed down, she told the others she had seen a woman in the back bedroom. She was tall, slender, and gray haired. She was clad in dark clothing from head to toe and wore unusually heavy makeup. When the young woman had walked into the room the wraith waved her hands and made motions as if to shoo her out of the room. The girl said she just knew she had encountered a ghost! And, of course, her description matched that of the mother of the late Sarah Jones, a woman who had been dead for over twenty years!

The would-be antique dealer never occupied the house. He decided then and there he wouldn't move into the place after all, and promptly put it up for sale.

Dale Terry no longer lives in the old Grant Street neighborhood. He has heard the old house has changed hands several times. He doesn't know if anyone else has experienced the chilling cold or seen any ghostly figures. But nothing will ever convince him that the old house isn't haunted!

The Blood Speckled Shirt

This unusual story was sent to me from the librarian at the Fort Concho Museum in San Angelo. The story was told by James Baker of Ballinger to Marylou Collard, who recorded it, as follows:

For as long as James can remember, he has known of a haunted house that is south of Ballinger on a farm-to-market road. When he was a senior in high school, he and eight other boys went out to the fabled haunted house one night. They'd heard an old lady had lived there many years before, and because she was afraid of thunder and lightening, whenever there was a storm, it was her custom to go down into the cellar and wait it out. One especially stormy night she went down to her sheltered place. She must have thought she heard someone prowling around upstairs, because, armed with an ax, she started up the stairs to investigate. Unfortunately, she slipped on the stairs and fell upon her ax. She died as a result of the accident.

When James and his friends approached the house, a light suddenly appeared in an upstairs window. At first it was just a tiny glow, but it got very large and then went out. Naturally, this frightened the boys. Three of them decided they would go inside the house, while the rest of the group "stood guard" on the outside. James was one of the group that went inside the deserted old house. He said they just walked around downstairs for a few minutes. A board overhead squeaked. The boys froze in their tracks to listen. Then, one of the boys felt something wet hit his shirt. The creaking noises continued, and the teenagers decided they'd had enough. They decided to leave the house and join the others who were outside. As they were getting into the car to leave, a boy who had waited outside pointed to one of his friends. The friend was the boy who had felt something wet hit his shirt while he was in the house. Everyone looked and saw that the boy's shirt was spotted with blood! According to James, the boy still has that shirt. He never washed it or tried to get the blood out. He also is reported never to have returned to the old haunted house!

The White Lady

I have had several conversations with Martha Beimer, a resident of the small town of Ballinger. From my talks with her, I judge her to be a devout Christian who lives her religion by serving others. She also seems to be more than a little bit clairvoyant, because at numerous times in her life she had just "known" when certain things were about to happen. Her batting average up to now seems amazingly accurate.

Martha told me that in 1966 she and a young man she was dating and some other friends had discussed going for a ride in the country after attending an afternoon wedding. I believe the young people call it "cruising" today, when they just ride around. Suddenly, Martha changed her mind and said she really didn't want to go. However, the others succeeded in cajoling her to join them, and only reluctantly did she climb into the car with her friends. It was just a few minutes later that the group was involved in a terrible automobile accident. Martha was thrown from the car and then the car that had hit them ran over her. Miraculously she was thrown into a ditch. As she regained consciousness, through great pain and confusion, she recalls telling God that if He would spare her life, she would try to dedicate her life to helping others as much as possible. She says many times she has been called, sometimes in actuality and sometimes subconsciously, to come when someone is dying, to pray with them, and stay with them, until they pass away. Most recently she said she felt a sudden urge to go to the hospital to be with a friend whose mother was terminally ill. She went into the hospital room with her friend's mother, took her hand and prayed with her, and said the Lord's Prayer. She told the woman to quit suffering and go and seek the light that God had prepared for her to follow. In a short time the woman quietly slipped away. Martha said her friend, the woman's daughter, told her that she could never have let go of her mother had Martha not come to help.

Having had numerous experiences with helping the dying to peacefully pass away, Martha says some of her friends there in Ballinger refer to her as "the Angel of Death." Recently (August of 1994) a sixteen-year-old boy, whom she knew through her church, was involved in a tragic automobile accident. Although he lingered for several months, he was badly brain damaged and was sustained only through various life support systems. Martha visited him regularly, praying and reciting "Jesus Loves Me" and the Lord's Prayer to him, hoping to somehow reach him through his subconscious. Gradually as hope faded completely for him to ever recover, all the support systems were closed down and only water was given to him.

The night the teenager died, Martha visited him just a few hours before he breathed his last. She went to the bedside and told him that God loved him very much and needed him to come and live in heaven. She told him he needed to be a brave Ballinger Bearcat (he had been on the football team, the Ballinger Bearcats). Martha told him to move towards heaven with his head held high. She said she closed her eyes as she prayed and asked God to come to Ballinger and lead this boy home to live with Him. When she opened her eyes, the young man looked so peaceful, "just beautiful," she said. His bedclothes glowed with a white intensity, the shadows had a bluish cast, and the highlights showed a rosy pink glow. She said all she could do was gaze at the beauty and serenity of the scene before her, unlike anything she had ever before experienced. She said, "Thank you, Lord." Her young friend quietly slipped peacefully from this mortal life into eternity just a short time later.

Then, Martha shared the story of her home, how and when they moved into it, and why she believes there is a spirit there.

Martha and her husband, Daniel, used to live out in the country, a short distance from Ballinger. Martha was absolutely terrified one day to discover a big black bullsnake in her bedroom. She was ready to move to town!

Now, Martha had often admired a "barny-boxy" old house on Eighth Street. She was therefore delighted, when driving past one day, to see a moving van in front of the place. Its occupants were moving away! She stopped to inquire about the soon-to-be-vacated dwelling, and the lady who was moving out offered to rent it to the Beimer family. It didn't take Martha long to convince Dan to lease the house!

The Beimers soon moved their two youngsters, Melissa, who was about five, and Anthony, a toddler of two, into their new "town" house. Prior to their signing the lease, the owner had a strange warning for Martha. She said "Under no circumstances must you let your little son stay in this bedroom." She was referring to a middle bedroom, with an outside entry door and airy wide windows that afforded a pleasant view of the shady yard. Martha didn't ask why, but she did heed the unusual warning and assigned that room to Melissa instead of Anthony.

Shortly after the Beimers moved to their new address, the owners decided they really wanted to sell, rather than rent, and offered Martha and Dan the first option. They were delighted to have the opportunity to purchase the place in which they had already become very much at home.

It wasn't too long after they'd settled into the house that young Melissa came to her mother one morning and told her, "There's a white lady who comes out of my closet and goes to the door and out into the hall." Martha told the child she had probably just seen a light from the street outside shining through the windows. "No mommy. It was a white lady," the child repeated. Now, Martha explained to me that she had never mentioned or talked about ghosts, or spooks, or goblins, to the children, nor had they ever had any special observances of Halloween, so the child was not frightened as much as puzzled by the sudden appearance of the "white lady" in her room.

The next night Melissa came to her mother and told her, "The white lady is back." Martha went to the child's room with her, turned on the lights, looked around, and assured Melissa no one was there before tucking her back into bed.

The lady continued to appear from time to time, and Martha, who first thought the appearances might have been just an imaginary playmate that Melissa had concocted, began to wonder just what might be going on. Finally, one night Melissa, plainly terrified, came to her mother's room, and said, "Mommy, the white lady came out of the closet and just stood and looked at me. Mommy, she scares me."

Martha decided it might not just be a figment of the child's imagination. She started to wonder. And to investigate. She discovered that the first family to live in the house had built the place in the early 1920s. They had a son and a lovely young daughter. The girl became very ill and apparently died in the house. Since the middle bedroom had wide, spacious windows, a lovely view of the big yard, and an outside door, it would have made an ideal room for someone who was ill and needed a cheerful, sunny room. Martha was almost sure that Melissa's "white lady" must have been the spirit of the girl who had died in her late teen years. The parents of the girl and her brother had continued to make their home there for many years. The girls' mother died while the family still resided in the house, although Martha was told she died in the hospital and not in the house. This was sometime around 1975.

Up in the attic Martha found some very old boxes and items that had probably been in the house for some time and had gone unnoticed, or were unwanted, by the previous owners. Among the memorabilia was a memory book, which contained photos and clippings from school events back in the 1920s. There was a photograph of an attractive young girl dressed completely in white; white dress, white shoes and stockings. She was even holding a white handkerchief in her hand. Her name was in the book. I shall call her "Laura," although this is not her real name. Martha said there are still some family members living in Ballinger. The photograph looked like a graduation or special party photo. There were stacks and stacks of magazines in the attic as well. Most of them were issues of a publication called *Fate*, a magazine dealing with the occult and the supernatural, and the issues dated from the 1930s up to the 1960s. Martha thinks maybe the grieving mother of the dead girl read and studied the magazines with the hopes of communicating with her daughter, or at least keeping her spirit close at hand.

Now that Martha had tentatively identified the spirit and little Melissa had identified the girl in the photograph as looking just like her "white lady," the family started to call her by name. And to calm young Melissa, Martha went to the room late one night and said, "Now Laura, this is my little daughter, Melissa Ann Beimer. This is her room now. She is a nice, sweet little girl. She believes in Jesus, and she and I believe that God loves her, and we believe He loves you, too. Please don't frighten Melissa anymore. She really is sweet, and we are sure you were a sweet little girl, too. She promises to take good care of her room, just like you did, and we just want to ask you not to frighten her anymore."

After this plea was made, Melissa's "white lady" did not come on a regular basis. But the family still knew that she was around!

As Melissa grew up, "Laura" would appear from time to time, especially as Melissa grew into her teen years and then prepared to go off to college. Then, when she prepared to enter the adult world as a bride, the most astounding thing happened! The wedding photographer took some candid shots of the bride and her five bridesmaids and Daniel, her father, as they entered a long corridor that leads to the sanctuary of the United Methodist Church where she was to be married. A glass wall divides the corridor from the sanctuary. When the photographs were developed, a single figure in white standing slightly aside from the bride and her attendants was seen reflected in the glass window. Melissa had a very simple explanation for the unexplainable figure. "Why, Mother, Laura came to my wedding."

Martha told me when she is often occupied with one of her many hobbies (she is a weaver, but she also does needlework and sews) she will catch a sudden movement in the room, a glimpse out of her peripheral vision, and at the same time strongly sense a presence in the room. Most especially does she feel there is someone with her whenever she is in Melissa's old room.

Melissa is now a young woman of twenty-eight. When she comes home to visit she occupies her old bedroom with her husband. One time when Melissa was brushing her hair in front of her dressing table she caught a flash of white moving behind her. She turned and said, "Well hi, Laura." The image vanished.

Martha says she knows the spirit of the young girl, who never got to grow up, go to college, or be a bride, is still there. Perhaps she is enjoying, vicariously, through Melissa, the experiences she was denied the chance to enjoy.

It's Still Jack's House

The process of researching for a book of this nature is long and tedious. A lot of people have ghosts but don't want to talk about them. And sorting out "made up" versus "really-truly" stories is sometimes hard to do, too.

I fired off a volley of letters to editors of newspapers all over West Texas, hopeful their files would reveal some good information, and also hopeful they might appeal to their readers to send me their own personal stories of brushes with the supernatural.

One such lady from the town of Hereford up in the Panhandle area was good enough to do just that. But she did not want to let her identity be known, for whatever reason, and therefore she just signed her letter, "name withheld, Hereford." Her story rings true; I don't think she would have gone to the trouble to write to me otherwise. She's just a little bit shy and perhaps afraid her neighbors might laugh at her. I have shortened and edited her story just a trifle, but basically, it is just as she sent it to me:

I am a 42-year-old housewife, and I've lived here in Hereford all of my life. The house I grew up in was, and is, haunted. One of the ghosts' names is "Jack." I have investigated the history of the house, finding that it was built in the late 1800s. It first was located on the Terra Blanca draw between Hereford and Dimmitt before being relocated to Hereford and somewhat remodeled. Today it is a large two-story dwelling.

The west bedroom was mine when I was a child. Late at night while I was lying in bed I could faintly hear a harpsichord playing. When I'd raise up in bed, the music stopped. I told my parents about it but they laughed and added that it must be the music coming from a nearby drive-in movie. Later when I left to go away to college, my parents took over that bedroom and soon found out how right I was, as the drive-in had closed and had been completely torn down.

As the years have passed, there have been more and more strange things happening at the house. Nobody at the house smokes, yet somedays as my mother irons on what we call the "back porch" a cigar can be smelled quite strongly. When it gets too strong, Mom sometimes just gets in the car and leaves for a while. Sometimes you can faintly hear people talking, too. You cannot make out what they say, however. One Saturday afternoon around 2 p.m. we were both in that part of the house, and we did make out the word "Jack." It seemed to be two men talking, so now we all ask about "Jack" when we came back home to visit.

I studied parapsychology at Texas Tech and wanted to do a study on the house with sensors and recorders, but my mother would not hear of it. She's still that way about it and so we just have had to leave things alone.

Once I was home visiting from college for the weekend. I arrived about 7 or 8 in the morning. No doors were open, and as my Mom usually sleeps late, I started backing out of the driveway. I had decided to go for coffee, allowing her a little extra time for sleep. The front door window curtain parted, so I pulled back up into the driveway and walked up on the porch, thinking my mother was awake and had seen me. Well, she hadn't. I had to wake her up. It had not been her parting the curtains. We both just laughed about it and decided it must have been "Jack."

Every now and then when we walk across the backyard we catch a glimpse of someone standing in the door (we think), but we never quite catch it. The two family dogs go running to the door some days and look quite silly when they decide no one is there! We wonder, what could they be seeing, or sensing?

Because of our faith and religion we actually enjoy the excitement and think nothing about it. It has never scared any of us, as we were raised with such happenings. I just thought you might enjoy reading about my little ghost, "Jack," who still lives in my mother's house.

The Ghost of the Friendly Farmer

The El Paso Herald Post edition of Thursday, August 3, 1978, carried an interesting story about an El Paso ghost. Staff writer Kathy Satterfield interviewed a lady who asked her identity not be made known. For that reason Satterfield called her "Carol" in her story.

As of the date of the article, Carol's other-worldly houseguest had been a part of the family household for about twenty-four years. "Joe," as the family has named the ghost, first appeared one night when Carol was reading a book in her bedroom. It was her custom to read in bed prior to dropping off to sleep. She felt that someone might be staring at her. It was such a strong feeling that it broke her concentration on the book she had before her. She turned around and was startled to see the figure of a man, just standing, looking at her. He was a tall, slender, Anglo man, with reddish-brown hair. He wore khaki work clothes, and Carol said he was quite nice looking. As she gazed at him, he suddenly disappeared. She searched the house, at first thinking he was a burglar or intruder. Then it came to her. The figure she had seen was a ghost!

The visits continued. Strangely enough, no man in the family ever sees him. He is only visible to women. Carol named him "Joe" and also refers to him as "little Joe, my gremlin."

At first perplexed over the appearances, Carol consulted a priest. He came to bless the house, not once, but twice. He told Carol to ask the apparition, "In the name of God, what do you want?" She did, but Joe didn't answer. He just disappeared.

For the most part Joe is silent, but he has been known to call out to the children in the family. Often he slams doors and turns on the water in the shower, and sometimes he flushes the commode.

Sometimes when Carol is busily involved in her kitchen Joe starts slamming doors to draw her attention. She has to go out in the hallway and tell him she doesn't have time to play now.

At night Joe has been known to lift up the corner of her mattress. She asks him to go away so she can sleep, and he obediently leaves.

Carol says that maids are not too receptive to ghosts. Once when the family went off to Cloudcroft on a short trip, they left a new maid in the place to house-sit. Carol had neglected to tell the maid about Joe. The maid became so unnerved she called Carol's son to come, because she was terrified when Joe started turning on the shower and slamming the doors. Carol said it was hard to convince the girl that although it may be unnerving to see or hear Joe, he is really quite harmless, a "good ghost."

The family wonders who Joe might have been in life. As the handsome man in work clothes stands in her doorway and stares at her, Carol wonders if he once owned the land on which her house now stands. Did he work in the fields of cotton that once covered the site? Was he murdered, or was he killed in a farming accident? Or did he just love the land so much he wants to come back and visit with the present owners? For whatever reason, the last we heard he's still around, an accepted member of Carol's family circle!

The Adobe House by the River

In his book *Memory Fever, Journey Beyond El Paso Del Norte,* Ray Gonzalez tells a story about his graduate student days in El Paso. He shared a small, very old four-room adobe house with a roommate named Gary.

The house was located at the back of a big parking lot adjacent to a popular Mexican restaurant called La Hacienda. About twenty yards from the house there ran an irrigation ditch which more or less paralleled the Rio Grande. The little house was situated about a hundred yards or so from the Mexican border crossing point. Old Fort Bliss is just down the street from the location. The former old cavalry outpost is now used for low-income housing.

The young men lived in the house for two years while working part-time and attending graduate school. They enjoyed their life of study, partying, and companionship. They both liked to write poetry, and they enjoyed sitting on the front porch in the evening. It was a good life. But almost from the beginning of their occupancy, Ray sensed there was something different about the house they rented.

For one thing, Gary's female collie, Carita, barked at one corner of the living room, often long and loud. And she would gaze at the empty corner where two walls met. Although the young men looked at the area, there was nothing there to make the dog react in that manner. There was a dark spot on the ceiling just above that corner of the room. It was a round, brown spot and looked as if it had splashed onto the ceiling. They explained it away as either a rain spot, or as dirt, since the place was very old.

There were bars on the windows, and the heavy wooden front door was thick and had two rows of braces that wooden beams could be placed across. The locale was in a high risk crime area, so the young men always closed the door using the cross beams on the sturdy door. There were huge nails or bolts that they slipped down the braces, locking the beams into place. They had to remove the bolts with a hammer every morning. It was a nuisance to fool with, but they slept more peacefully because of taking this extra precaution.

Then one night they both heard "it." They had been in their separate rooms when both men were awakened by the scraping of the bolts as they rose off the braces. They went to the door but found the bolts still in the braces. Carita barked and barked at the door. Both men agreed they'd heard something. Without saying it, both of them knew the bolts had been lifted off the braces, as they were used to the sound of the scraping metal. They both agreed someone (or something) had pulled on them, but they were now back in place. Uneasily, they both went back to bed, but neither of them slept very well that night.

Then a few weeks later a friend of Ray's who was a fellow substitute teacher in the El Paso school system dropped by. They went over to La Hacienda for lunch. During the meal, Ray told his friend about the strange incident concerning the door bolts. The man didn't seem a bit surprised, which surprised Ray! When asked why, he told Ray the story of "the woman in the trees." It seemed about thirty years before, a relative of Ray's friend had worked at the restaurant. He told about three waiters who were walking under the cottonwood trees near the place when they glimpsed a woman in black clothing crossing the restaurant parking lot. They thought she looked lost or confused, because she stopped, hesitated, then walked in circles around the lot. Wanting to help her, they came out of the grove of trees to speak to her and offer assistance. When they emerged from the trees, she suddenly vanished! When Ray asked his friend how that could happen, his friend said she'd just totally disappeared when she got to "the marker over there." He indicated a stone monument connected to the historic Fort Bliss grounds.

It scared the young men, and two of them quit working at La Hacienda. They thought the woman's appearance, then disappearance, might have somehow been connected to the "killing." Not quite prepared for another surprise, Ray nonetheless asked his friend "what killing?" Ray was astounded because he had never heard of a killing taking place anywhere around there.

His luncheon companion told him, "A man was killed in that house. It happened a few years back before the woman ever appeared in the trees. He was a Mexican gateman." He went on to explain that the adobe had been a sort of living quarters and utility shed for the canal gateman who had controlled the irrigation water from the river. The river was always deep and full in those days before Elephant Butte Dam was built.

Somebody, Ray's friend couldn't say who, had killed the gatekeeper. More terrible still, his body had been cut up into small pieces. Many body parts were found in the canal, but there were also lots of gory remains left in the adobe house. Ray had to wonder if the body parts were found in the front room near the spot where Carita always barked. And the dark brown spot on the ceiling...could it have been blood from the gruesome butchering?

Soon after hearing these frightening facts about the place, the young men moved out of the adobe house.

Upon returning to El Paso for a visit a few years later, Ray said he discovered the old house had been torn down. There was just a pile of rubble with weeds and bushes growing through piles of brick out behind the restaurant. It was hard to recognize the remains of the place where he and Gary had shared some happy times.

One might wonder. Did the ghostly resident move on, or is it still clinging to the crumbling remains of the old adobe?

Spirits in Sunset Heights

In Ray Gonzalez' fine book *Memory Fever*, one of his friends shared a ghost story with the author. This friend had taught as a substitute teacher with Gonzalez in the El Paso Public Schools. One day, over a pleasant lunch, the conversation turned to the subject of ghosts.

Gonzalez' friend had lived in a very old neighborhood in El Paso known as Sunset Heights. The area is full of two- and three-story mansions, many of which have been designated as historical land-marks. When Ray's friend was just a little boy of about six years old his family had bought one of these old houses and began to re-store it. But things started happening soon after the family took up residence there.

Once, when the family was upstairs watching television, they heard a tremendous crash downstairs. It sounded like breaking glass, like the china cabinet in the dining room might have fallen over. They dashed downstairs, but a thorough investigation showed nothing at all was broken or disturbed. The china cabinet was in its customary place, with the glasses and dishes unscathed, and nothing else was out of place, anywhere. There was no explanation for the noise, which was repeated several times that same evening.

Maids in the house didn't stay very long, either. They refused to sleep in the maid's room, which was located in the basement. Several of the girls claimed they tried to sleep, but they were disturbed by something pulling at their feet and hair. This was not conducive to a peaceful night's repose.

Ray's friend said his parents actually saw the figure of an old man standing at the top of the stairs several times. Sometimes family members felt a sudden nudge on the chin as they walked around the house. It felt like a very cold finger pushing at their chins.

Finally, when Ray's friends' parents were sleeping one night, the bedroom turned icy cold, and it caused them to wake up. When they turned on the light they both saw the marks of a weight pushing down on the deep piled carpet. The marks of the silent walker moved slowly towards their bed as they watched in fascinated horror. Then the steps ceased just before reaching the terrified couple.

About two months later the family decided they'd had enough. They moved to a peaceful address in another part of town.

Ray said his friend told him that his mother had decided to go downtown to the City and County Building to look up some old city records. In researching the area where they had lived, she discovered that the whole block of houses where they'd lived had once been a part of the old Fort Bliss cemetery!

Grandfather's Ghost

El Paso resident Debbie Koortz told her story to Sheila Stopani and Harriet Sturgeon, who were preparing a special report for an English course at the University of Texas at El Paso. The report, dated December 11, 1975, was titled "Strange Things in the Night" and was sent to me by Dr. John West, professor of English, at the University of Texas, El Paso, and a noted authority on Texas folklore.

In 1975 Debbie was twenty-four years old. The story she told Sturgeon and Stopani concerns a house the family had lived in for many years. The place would be about ninety-five years old now. Debbie had this to say:

> The house is on Robinson Avenue. I had lived in that house for twenty-one years. My father's parents, Mary and Ben Koortz, had lived there before my mother and father moved in (David and Holdie Koortz). About seven years ago (this would have made Debbie about seventeen years old at the time) I

went into the kitchen for breakfast, and my older sister, Leah, came in. Before I could say anything, Leah told our maid and me that she had seen our grandfather in the form of a ghost. After Leah told her story, I said I had seen the same ghost, and then our maid said she had seen him, also. We were all frightened, and each of us believed the other.

After this experience I would hear voices coming from the attic as well as see the ghost flashing by quickly in my mother and father's room. The most frightening experience I had was one day when I had just returned home from a church convention in Dallas. My father woke me up at 6:00 in the morning and told me that my mother was ill and that she was in a Dallas hospital. He said he would be back to take me to lunch. When I went into the house I stepped into the den from the dining room and saw my grandfather sitting in my dad's chair. He said, "Come over here and kiss me, Debbie." I felt like I was in a trance. I dug my nails into my hands, so I would know I wasn't in a dream. I went over to him slowly, it was so real, and I kissed him, and he disappeared! He was dressed in his usual attire: brown pants and suit coat, and a white shirt and tie. I ran out of the house, screaming, and stayed at the neighbor's across the street. I looked at my hands where I had dug my nails into them, and my hands were bleeding.

That was not the last time I saw grandfather. I saw him frequently, walking from my father and mother's bedroom and back to the closet. He was always dressed the same way, but he never talked to me again. We moved out of the house in 1973.

Grandmother's Sweet Spirit

This story also comes from the report "Strange Things in the Night," submitted by Harriet Sturgeon and Sheila Stopani as a project for Dr. John West, Department of English, University of Texas at El Paso. The report, dated December 11, 1975, relates a true experience that Harriet Sturgeon recalled:

As a child I was very close to my grandmother because my mother worked all day and therefore my grandmother took care of me since I was a small child. When I was about sixteen years old my grandmother died. I remember being very lonely and heartbroken that she had to leave this world.

About three years later when I was nineteen I got married. Being students, we moved in with my parents in an apartment behind their house. I am a very particular person with my possessions and keep each in one place, in order to find them quicker. However, one day I came home to find that some of my cosmetics and knick-knacks had been moved. Everything was locked, and no one had been in the apartment. I just shrugged it off, until it happened again. This time there was also some cream missing from its jar. A little while later I was alone in the apartment when I felt someone watching me. I looked up and saw a dark shadow move across the room. I felt very sick at my stomach and queasy all over my body.

This same event continued to occur over the next two years. Then, two years later my husband and I moved to a new apartment nearer to college. I had been there about a week, when my sister's friend told me that she had seen a ghost of an old woman in my previous apartment. The ghost had asked her where I had gone and at that moment, had disappeared. At about the same time, I was again alone in our new apartment when I felt this same presence and again looked up to see the dark shadow moving across the room. As before, I would come home to find personal items missing or moved. I spoke to my parents about these happenings. My father then told me to think about what was moved and what was missing and find something that related to all of them. I gave it some thought and before I knew it, it dawned on me who the ghost was. It was my grandmother, because all of the items missing or moved had been things my grandmother and I played with or a cosmetic she had used. From that day forward I never was afraid of the shadow, for it was like a guardian angel to me and I knew that it would never harm me. I have since continued to see the shadow in different places where I have lived.

The Happily Haunted House

This story came to me from Janet Bonner, now the United States attorney in Midland. A few years ago, she and her daughter Heather Melton, lived in Alpine, in a house she says was haunted. Heather, who now attends Texas Tech University in Lubbock, agrees with her mother.

Located in a nice section of town, a pretty residential area near the Alpine Country Club, the house is built of cinder blocks covered over with stucco. It is crowned by a Spanish style red tile roof. There is a low retaining wall around the house, which has arched Spanish style doorways. Heather said the house, which was built sometime in the 1930s, has a lot of character, and she would really love to own it someday!

The house has wooden floors, and there is a small basement located beneath the kitchen and breakfast room portion of the building. Perhaps it was intended to serve as a storm cellar.

Bonner said the original builders were an old West Texas family whose surname was Kokernot. They were prominent ranchers in the area. She said a Beulah Kokernot had built a smaller, newer house at the rear of the lot, and she often stayed there on visits to Alpine.

Bonner told me that she had heard that a relative, maybe a mother-in-law, of one of the Kokernots had died in the house, but she did not know any details as to dates or cause of death. Heather added that she had also heard a youngster, a little boy, had also passed away while living there.

Janet said she knew from almost day one, when they moved into the house, it was "different." They lived there from March 1990 to March 1992. While they were never really frightened, there were certain occurrences that were puzzling and which led both mother and daughter to believe the house was haunted.

Doors opened and closed at will, even when there were no drafts or wind to cause them to do so. Lights turned on and off, and cabinets opened and closed. This was especially noticeable during the time they were moving into the house. I explained to Janet this is fairly common among the ghost population. They don't like change, and they mistrust new tenants coming into "their" domains.

Heather told me, she believes her room might have been the room which had belonged to the little boy. She feels it was the most haunted section of the house. She vividly recalls waking one night from a sound sleep and seeing a little boy sitting on the floor beside her bed. He was playing with something; blocks, or a ball, perhaps. The figure she saw was transparent, as if he were caught up in a mist, but she could definitely tell it was a youngster. There was a certain glow about him. Although startled, she was not particularly frightened. Several times she heard childish laughter in the room, but she only saw the figure that one time.

Once, after wearing a favorite silver charm bracelet, Heather placed it on her dresser. The next morning it was in four evenly spaced separate pieces, but still right where she had left it. She is sure no one was in her room during the night, at least no mortal being!

The house had old-fashioned latch-hook type locks on the doors. Heather's bedroom had two exit doors. One led to the hallway and the other to a bathroom. Both closed with the same type latches. One day as she left her room she heard a distinct clicking sound. When she tried the door, it was firmly locked. Oh, well, she thought, I'll get back in through the bathroom. But no, that door was locked as well. She was completely locked out of her room! She said she was glad she had some clothes down in the laundry room, because she was locked out for about twenty-four hours. She finally went back to her room and tried to jiggle the doors hard, to see if she could dislodge the latches. Still locked out, she just sort of threw up her hands and walked away. Suddenly, she heard a distinct "click!" from within her room, and then, ever so slowly, the door knob started to turn, and the door into the room slowly started opening! Astounded, she walked inside and found her room just as she had left it the day before! Heather and I agreed that this was just the sort of trick a little boy ghost would have enjoyed pulling off!

Heather said over the years the family lived in the house, she was visited four or five times by the apparition of a woman. She usually came late at night and Heather always saw her standing at the foot of her bed. Heather would be sleeping, then suddenly wake up with a start, to see a woman's figure, bathed in a glowing light, just standing there as if she were looking after her. She appeared to be about forty years old, neither very young nor old. Her hair was brown and pulled up on top of her head in an old-fashioned bun, or chignon. The dress she wore was rather nondescript, either a light brown or gray, and seemed to be of floor length. She felt the woman was very protective and so she was never frightened by her appearances.

In the rear portion of the house there was a small bedroom which might possibly have been used as a maid's room. In this room the owners had stored some personal possessions in the closet and in a chest of drawers. Heather said, out of curiosity, she once opened one of the drawers, and a lot of old photographs were in the drawer. One of the photos was an exact likeness of her nocturnal visitor! When she later showed the picture to one of the Kokernot family members, Brian, he identified it as the likeness of a relative of his who had once lived in the house. Heather is sure this was the lady she had seen, and she was just coming back to check up on things.

Heather also mentioned that the antique bed in which she had slept had come with the house. She wondered if her sleeping in the bed which might have belonged to the phantom lady had anything to do with her appearances. Who knows? Ghosts are hard to figure out sometimes.

Janet told me that her daughter seemed to be blessed with a certain amount of extrasensory perception and that's why the ghosts appeared to Heather, rather than to Janet. She said Heather had the uncanny ability to be able to look at a photograph and tell if that person was living or dead. She once looked at a group photo of her grandmother's graduating class and was able to identify every single person who had passed away. When asked how in the world she could do this, she replied, "It's the eyes. Eyes look different when they are dead."

As Janet and I discussed the house in Alpine, we wondered if the ghosts still come around. If they do, I'll bet they are hard pressed to find anyone who likes their house as much as Janet and Heather did!

CHAPTER 9

STRANGE UNEXPLAINED THINGS

The Ghost at McDow Hole

To this day, there are those who say they've seen the wraith of a woman carrying a baby around the deep blue hole on the Green Creek up in Erath County, known as McDow Hole. Who she is, and why she's there, is a fascinating story. It goes way back to the early 1870s when Charlie and Jenny Papworth and their infant son, Temple, came to Texas from Georgia to escape the malaria that was plaguing Georgia that year. They chose to build their log cabin a couple of hundred yards from a deep blue pond that was a part of Green Creek.

For several years they worked hard. They were happy. Jenny gave birth to a second baby when little Temple was about four years old. Then Charlie received the word his parents had died back in Georgia and he needed to go as far as Texarkana to pick up some household goods they had left him in their wills. Little did he know when he told Jenny goodbye before he left on the long journey that he would never see his beloved wife and baby again.

When Papworth returned, he found that Jenny and the baby were missing. The furniture was in disarray. Chairs and tables were turned over. There was blood all around the cabin. He just knew he would never see them again. Little Temple was there, unhurt, but terribly confused and frightened by what he had witnessed. He was able, however, to tell his daddy that the man who had come and hurt his mother spoke English, which ruled out the possibility of an Indian attack.

A shady character, a man named W.P. Brownlow, whom everyone categorized as a carpetbagger, was in the vicinity. For a time he was suspected of being the perpetrator of the crime. To cover up, he made a big show of rounding up a posse to go look for the Indians who had carried Jenny Papworth and her baby away.

The Abilene Reporter News ran an interesting article about the hauntings and the disappearance of Jenny Papworth in the October 29, 1978 edition. Arts Editor Danny Goddard wrote that account, and later the paper ran another feature in more or less the same vein which appeared on October 28, 1983. This article was penned by Kathy Sanders. Both writers mention that Brownlow had feared Papworth would decide he'd killed his wife and would come gunning for him. So he started circulating the rumor that Papworth was a horse thief. This was a hanging crime in those days. Brownlow persuaded a group of vigilantes to string up Papworth and several other men. The place they chose was a big pecan tree on the banks of McDow Hole. Papworth's young son, Temple, watched the hanging and managed to cut his father down before he expired. Then, fearful for their lives, the Papworths left the country, fleeing to the Oklahoma territory.

Soon after the father and son departed, a man named Keith and his thirteen-year-old son decided to spend a night in the abandoned cabin. They'd been working hard hauling water from McDow Hole and were tired. Soon after they retired, they felt an eerie sense of foreboding, and the room grew penetratingly cold. It was a summer night, but even the quilts they'd found in the cabin could not warm them. Then, there was a knock on the door of the little house. Keith went to the door and saw the figure of a woman, holding a small infant in her arms. Then, as suddenly as they had appeared, they disappeared into the swirling mist that surrounded the area by the creek. The rest of the night Mr. Keith had fitful dreams about the woman and her baby.

The pair decided to spend another night at the cabin. This time they barred the door and the only window. Soon after they went to bed they saw a woman carrying a baby walk across the room and then disappear. Determined to get to the bottom of these strange appearances, the Keiths stayed yet another night. On this third night another knock came at the door. Both father and son answered the knock and both saw the woman standing in the doorway, holding her child in her arms. Keith recognized Jenny Papworth, whom he had known. He called out to her and was answered by the most awful, hideous, blood-curdling scream he had ever heard. Both father and son took off running and didn't stop until they'd reached their own home some four miles away!

A man named Charlie Atchinson, a coffin maker by trade, came to the area around 1880 and moved into the little cabin. He lived there about a year and never saw a ghost. The late Mrs. Mary Joe Fitzgerald Clendinin, a local lady who wrote a little pamphlet about the hauntings called "The Ghost of McDow Hole," said her father and brother used to visit Atchinson and listen to the fine fiddle music he played. Then, early one morning, a group of farmers who lived in the area were out rounding up livestock when they dropped by Atchinson's cabin. They found the front door and the only window shut tight. When no one answered their knock, the worried farmers decided to break in. There, lying on the floor, they found a very dead Charlie Atchinson, his lifeless eyes staring at the ceiling. He had a look of stark terror on his face.

Before W.P. Brownlow died, the old, sick man woke up one night moaning and crying, "That woman...blood. No! Get away from me...away. How did you?" Then, more distinctly he was heard to say, "That woman! Don't let her touch me. Look at the blood on my hands. So warm between my fingers. For God's sake, get if off! Look!" Mrs. Clendinin's father had been sitting up with the sick man. He turned and looked, and there, at the foot of Brownlow's bed stood a woman, holding a baby in her arms. Brownlow died the next day, but not before he had confessed that he had killed Jenny and her baby because she had caught him talking to some cattle rustlers, and her testimony could have gotten him hanged.

Mary Joe Clendinin had one brush with the ghost herself. When she and a cousin were youngsters, they had gone to the blue hole in the creek to fish when they saw the ghost appear in the water and then slowly rise up into the night and float away. She and her cousin ran all the way home. Some ten days later, her cousin died of an apparent brain hemorrhage.

Buck and Penny Henson live about a mile northwest of McDow Hole. They were told by neighbors that a log cabin used to sit about where their house is now located. They were also told that neighbors used to see a light dancing around inside the deserted cabin. Then it would take off across the pasture and end up at McDow Hole. They tried to get their dogs to go chasing after the light, but the frightened animals refused to give chase. The Hensons have never seen the ghost but they've talked to people who claim they have seen her, mostly on foggy nights walking in the mist.

The railroad used to run close by Green Creek. But after several days in a row when a railroad engineer saw a woman and baby on the tracks, pulled the train to a stop, only to find no one there at all, the other engineers decided they didn't want to pull that run. Finally, being unable to get engineers to drive by that locale, the railroad rerouted its trains and the tracks were abandoned.

If you're ever down in Erath County, near the town of Alexander, you might want to take a look at McDow Hole. Maybe some of the old-timers can give you directions. And who knows? You might just pick a time when Jenny and her baby decide to reappear!

The Shootout at Hord's Creek

Back in the late 1930s and early '40s it was rumored around Coleman, especially among the local teenagers, that the old Abilene Highway bridge that spanned Hord's Creek just outside Coleman was haunted. Nobody knows for sure, but there's a good story that goes with the rumors.

Charlyne Mills Griffith, a friend of mine who resides in Coleman, is the daughter of the late Frank Mills, who served as sheriff of Coleman County from 1928 to 1937. Mills began and ended his law enforcement career as a Texas Ranger. Charlyne lived with her father, mother, older brother, Billy, and younger sister, Jackie, in the first-floor living quarters of the old limestone jail which still takes up a corner of the Coleman County courthouse square.

There had been a trio of brothers, Dave, Luke, and Starkweather, better known as "Doc," Trammell, who had plagued that part of the state with their habitual robberies, car thefts, kidnappings, and general hell raising. This was during the Depression, and the brothers would go on a rampage and rob somebody and steal their car. When the gas tank ran dry, they'd abandon that car and start all over, stealing another car, terrorizing another victim, on and on. The people in Coleman County

Bridge abuttment, Hord's Creek, Coleman

were terrified of the brothers. In June of 1933 Luke shot and killed John Lampkin, a nightwatchman, in the small town of Blackwell. The boys were on the run, and Sheriff Mills and his deputies were after them.

On July 7, 1933 Sheriff Mills was notified by a local rural mail carrier named Ralph Stubblefield that he'd seen the Trammell boys down near Hord's Creek Crossing. Mills and his deputy, George Robey, and a friend who just happened to be in the sheriff's office, visiting, named Leon Shield, got ready to go after them. Stubblefield asked if he could go along, and the sheriff gave him a gun to carry.

As soon as the sheriff and the others arrived at the bridge they spotted Doc and Luke Trammell in the brushy area along the creek bank. When they yelled to them to come out, the brothers started shooting. The final result of the shootout was Sheriff Mills got young Doc Trammell right in the hatband. The bullet went through his brain and he fell on the spot, right under a big pecan tree. His brother Luke surrendered.

Charlyne said she was only about five years old at the time but vividly remembers sitting with her mother and Billy, her brother, who was about seven, on the back stoop of their living quarters, waiting for her daddy to come home. They heard the sound of the ambulance siren in the distance just about the time Sheriff Mills, Robey, Stubblefield, and Shield drove up. She said her father told them, "It's all right. We got them, don't worry." Luke, who was handcuffed, was led up the steps to the jail and locked up.

Later on, Luke was convicted of the killing of the nightwatchman and was summarily executed at the penitentiary in Huntsville. When Doc Trammell was shot by Sheriff Mills he was only eighteen years, ten months, and seven days old according to the *Coleman Democrat Voice* that mentioned his funeral arrangements in the July 13, 1933 issue.

Charlyne said after that incident, for years the local high school kids would go out to the old bridge. They would look out to the banks along the creek where Doc Trammell had fallen and would say they'd seen a ghost walking those banks. Charlyne introduced us to several of her friends while we were in Coleman on a recent visit with her, and they all verified they'd heard the area was haunted. They just sort of grew up hearing the story.

The owner of the land on which the shootout occurred, Herman Burrow, took us out over the rutted ranch road in his pickup to see the place. It was a bumpy but intriguing trip! Burrow showed us where the big pecan tree had stood. He called it a "three-meat pecan," an unusual species that had three nut meats in each kernel instead of the usual two. Burrow said his late father had always said that a tree under which a man has died will live no more than three years and then it too will die. That is exactly what happened to the big, healthy pecan tree under which Doc Trammell fell.

The old Abilene highway was replaced by a newer, wider road, and during the 1940s the U.S. Army came out and blew up the old bridge over Hord's Creek in a demolition exercise. Only the abutments remain to mark the place where a brave sheriff and his friends shot it out with the outlaw Trammell boys back in 1933.

The Bloody Butcher of Erath County

Every Halloween this story seems to be bandied around Stephenville and the surrounding area in Erath County, as the bloody Snow murders are again discussed. One of the murders took place at Cedar Point Mountain, according to an account in the *Abilene Reporter News*, October 31, 1985. The writer, Kathy Sanders, told the gruesome tale of F.M. Snow's marriage to Maggie Poston. They lived in a little house in the Indian Creek community which is about eight miles southeast of Stephenville.

When Snow married Maggie, her mother, Mrs. S.A. Olds, and Maggie's nineteen-year-old son by a previous marriage, Bernie Connally, came along with the package. At first Mrs. Olds and Bernie just lived in a covered wagon on the property, but it wasn't long until they moved into the house with the newlyweds. This was in November of 1925.

Snow must have been a vicious man with an uncontrollable temper, because on November 25, 1925, he came home in the morning and started arguing with his wife in the front yard of their house because she hadn't chased a cow out of their field. The angry man grabbed a piece of firewood and chased after his wife, beating her until she collapsed and died. Then he decided he'd take care of her mother, too. He took his double-bladed ax and went after the poor old lady, who was nearly blind and almost deaf. He crept up behind her chair, and with a single blow of the ax almost decapitated her.

Snow cleaned up the mess he'd made and pulled up some floor-boards, hastily hiding the bodies of the two women beneath the floor of the house. Then he decided to go after his stepson. He found the young man in Stephenville and told him that his mother was ill and he needed to come home. As soon as Snow got the young man back to the house, he pulled out his gun and planted two bullets in the boy's head and neck.

After it got dark, Snow took the body of young Bernie Connally up to Cedar Point Mountain and chopped the head off. He threw the naked body over a fence and then took the head, which he'd put in a sack, to a cellar near an abandoned house about seven miles from where he'd left the body.

The next night, according to Sanders' story, Snow took the bodies of his wife and mother-in-law out of their hiding place beneath the floor and chopped them up in pieces with his ax. He built up a big fire in the fireplace and began to cremate the remains. He carried out the ashes daily for several days, believing he had destroyed all the evidence. However, his eyesight wasn't too good, and small pieces of flesh and bones remained in the ashes. These were later discovered by lawmen.

Snow thought he'd gotten rid of Connally's head, too. He didn't count on a stray dog locating it in the cellar where he had hidden it. The head was taken to B.I. Trewitt's Funeral Home in Stephenville. It was embalmed and discreetly put on display for identification purposes. When Snow made a trip to town he discovered the head had been found. To throw off any suspicion, he went along to the funeral home to view the head, hopeful it had darkened and become disfigured, but it had not. Connally's head looked very lifelike. Mrs. Ned Gristy iden-tified Bernie Connally, and the lawmen came to talk to Snow who swore that he had taken his wife, mother-in-law, and stepson to Iredell the night before to catch a train to Waco.

His alibi fell apart and he finally owned up to what he had done, taking the lawmen to see where he had discarded Connally's body. The sheriff's men had already found the grisly remains of Snow's wife and her mother in the ashes that had been thrown out.

Snow was electrocuted in Huntsville in 1927 and buried near the penitentiary.

For years before Snow's house was finally destroyed, visitors to the abandoned house of carnage often maintained they could plainly see the two women's faces etched in the back of the fireplace wall.

A Study of Spirits

It was Big Spring resident Clarice Rountree's ambition to write a book about ghosts. For years she had collected stories from her students at Big Spring High School, where she taught English and Spanish. And, she'd compiled quite a collection from other sources, too. These stories were mostly about haunted houses and supernatural experiences, which fascinated Clarice.

According to Tom Rountree, Clarice died in 1990, after a long bout with cancer. She was never able to realize her dream of publishing a book. Mr. Rountree was kind enough to tell me I might quote a few paragraphs from her work that was sent to me from the librarian at Fort Concho Museum in San Angelo.

In one work she titled "A Study of Ghosts," Rountree wrote:

From research I have done on ghosts and ghost stories, I have come to the conclusion that nearly all ghosts appear with a birth, a death, a marriage, or a new home. These ghosts are always friendly, unless they have returned for revenge on one person. They appear in many forms and can do nearly anything that can be thought of. Most people say they do not believe in ghosts, but when questioned extensively or if caught off guard, they are really not too sure what they believe. I suspect that each and every one of us has at least a little superstition in our thoughts.

Then Rountree went on to explain that the stories she was collecting had been shared with her by various individuals who firmly believed in ghosts and were happy to share their experiences with others who were also interested in the "division of folklore" called ghost stories. These people, said Rountree, don't consider their accounts to be "stories," because they are truths to them as they happened.

I believe Mrs. Rountree felt more or less that the ghost stories she collected were "folklore," while I believe most of them are unique, one-of-a-kind experiences that actually happened to the people who shared them with me. Folklore, to me, is more the definition given in *Websters New World Dictionary*, "the traditional legends, or beliefs of a people." There certainly are some stories that fit that definition, and those are the old oft-told legends I will touch upon in the last chapter.

One story in Clarice Rountree's collection concerned a spirit that was contacted through the use of a Ouija board. This is most unusual. I do not advocate the use of Ouija boards, as I have heard of so much negative energy being unleashed by them. In this case, however, the opposite seemed to take place, as the spirit which came forth was very benevolent.

According to Rountree, Jim is a Chinese man who, according to his own admission, has been dead for nine hundred years. He resides in a home on the outskirts of Lubbock. Mr. and Mrs. Leland Bouldin told Rountree he began to inhabit their home when their youngest son was born. They have a grown son and one who is fifteen years old. (Note: these ages are the ages the boys were at the time Clarice Rountree wrote her story in 1974.) To quote Rountree:

Jim watches over the boys and can be counted upon to "go out and find them" if need be. Jim is contacted through a Ouija board on a glass topped table. A glass of water is placed on the table, and when Jim is ready to "talk" he moves the glass; sometimes he moves it in a circle and sometimes in a figure eight movement. Jim has told them he likes to watch television. He is said to have a definite personality and is very likeable. When a seance takes place, Jim prefers to generate the energy needed for contact. Usually four people sit in a seance, and one of them takes notes. They use letters and he spells out yes, no, and other more complicated words. I am told, incidentally, that he is not too good in spelling but gets his message across.

When the children are gone, this couple calls on Jim to seek them [the children] out and return with information about them. One example of Jim seeking out one of the sons occurred during a seance concerning the whereabouts of their older son. He had left to drive to Dallas. They asked Jim to check on him and let them know if he arrived there all right. Jim returned and reported he had not gone to Dallas. He spelled out "Austin" on the board. When asked why their son had gone to Austin, Jim spelled out "girl." Jim also told them they could not contact him then because he was "between nightclubs." They could contact him a little later. When asked where, Jim gave them the name of a motel and a room number. Later, in the presence of these other people at the seance, they called this motel in Austin and asked for the specific room which Jim had given them, and their son answered the phone. The guests were quite mystified about what they had witnessed, but they left with no doubt in their minds that there really is a ghost named "Jim."

A friend of mine [Clarice Rountree's friend], Mrs. Lois Fields of Sonora, was visiting in the Bouldin home and participated in a seance. She seems quite sure that the above story must be true because of the experience of seeing Jim tell things at the seance she attended. Lois attended one seance in which Jim would not answer many of the questions. When asked why he hesitated to answer, he told them someone else was there with him. Mr. Bouldin asked him who it was and Jim spelled out "Myr." Bouldin asked if anyone at the table had someone who had been close to them who had passed away. Lois said her mother was dead and her name was Myrtle. After this disclosure by Lois, the ghost left and did not return. Mrs. Fields says that other people have seen these phenomena and can attest to what occurred.

Charlie, the Friendly Ghost

Most ghosts are said to cling to places, not people. But here's a story that contradicts that common belief. Leona Billington of Petrolia, a small community near Wichita Falls, tells a story about a ghost who has been following her around from place to place for at least thirty-five years!

Leona first told the story to Gene Mathews, librarian at the Kemp Public Library in Wichita Falls. Gene relayed the information to me, and I then had a lengthy conversation with Leona in order to hear all the facts:

Thirty-five years ago Leona and her three children were living in Gladewater. She was separated from her first husband, and the little family rented a small frame house that was then about twenty or thirty years old.

At first, life was fairly calm in the household, but it wasn't long until strange things began to happen. For a while, Leona thought someone might be trying to break into the house. And then there were noises, like giant footsteps, on the roof over the master bedroom most evenings, around 10 p.m. Sometimes strange singing would be heard, and the piano would play a few notes all by itself, just a "plink, plunk" sound, no recognizable tune.

Leona and the youngsters, who were twelve, thirteen, and fourteen at the time, became so frightened they'd barricade themselves in the front room. Leona got a gun and sat up most nights to guard her little brood, and then she would try to catch some sleep during the daylight hours when the children were in school.

Leona said there were times when she knew she had turned the lights out, but upon returning to the house, they'd all be burning brilliantly in all the rooms! Several times when she'd be lying in bed, just about to go to sleep, the covers would rise up and fly off of her. Then she would smell gas and dash into the kitchen to discover the pilot light off and the gas turned up high. She could not figure out how this happened. She gradually began to realize the house really was haunted. At the time she moved in, there were rumors around town that the house was haunted. Now she believed there was something to the stories she had brushed aside as figments of someone's overly active imagination. She also began to sense there might be two entities in the house: a bad spirit and a good one. The bad spirit turned the gas on; the good spirit woke her up to warn her of the danger by pulling her covers off.

Leona told me she knew that a former resident of the house who had suffered from cancer had died there. The room where the woman had died always seemed to be cold and could never be heated properly. Leona was told the woman suffered great pain in her last months and may even have died of an overdose of pain medications, but she is not at all positive about this.

Billington is positive the good spirit is male and that he has permanently attached himself to her as her protector, sort of like a guardian angel. After she'd been in the Gladewater house awhile, the shadowy spirit appeared as a dark, tall, thin man in Western clothes. He looked misty and shadowy, but she could definitely make out it was a man. For some unexplainable reason, she started to call him "Charlie." She told me she would really like to know who he was in life and why he has attached himself to her and her family.

Today Leona doesn't live in Gladewater. First, she moved to California and lived for a time in both Los Angeles and Sacramento. Then the family moved back to Texas and settled in Petrolia, just outside of Wichita Falls. Charlie went along on all the moves! Unlike most ghosts, it wasn't the place but the people to whom he attached himself. Now that the children are all grown and gone and Leona has remarried, Charlie doesn't appear as often as he once did. But he still resides in her household. Tex, her husband, at first was very dubious about the entity the family all referred to as Charlie. In fact, he outright scoffed at the idea! So one night, after they'd gone to bed, Leona said, "Charlie, Tex doesn't believe in you. Let him know you're really here." No sooner said, than done! Charlie began to pull on Tex's toes so hard the bed shook! And he did it the next night, too, just for good measure! Now Tex accepts Charlie's presence just as the rest of the family does.

Leona says sometimes she wonders if Charlie might be somebody she knew at some point in her life, or maybe in another life, if there is such a thing as reincarnation. Sometimes when she's about to fall asleep, she feels someone gently smoothing back her hair, or gently caressing or rubbing her face. This began in Gladewater and has continued for all these years. At first this frightened her, but she came to feel that these were gentle manifestations of a reassuring presence, and she felt as if she had a protector around her. It gave her a sense of security and she was never frightened.

Charlie is felt more than seen, but he has made a number of appearances. He has been seen sitting at the table, as well as in various rooms. He has even appeared in Leona's daughter's house in Oklahoma, and in her brother's home in Wichita Falls. Once her brother missed his pillow and then sighted it floating above his head! He reached up and snatched it, saying, "Alright, Charlie, quit hiding my pillow." It seems when there's a family reunion, wherever it is, Charlie comes right along. Sometimes he's very playful. Once, when Leona's daughter was about eighteen, they were having a party. The teenager bent over to get something out of a kitchen cabinet and there was a loud "whack!" as something, or someone, whacked her across the derriere in a playful spank. Several people were present and heard the whack and saw Leona's daughter jump! But no one was anywhere near her when it happened (except Charlie, of course!).

While over the years Charlie has calmed down considerably, he is still there. His last appearance was in the spring of 1994. He still materializes as a tall, slim fellow in Western clothes. Sometimes he walks through walls, appears in the hallway, or sits down at the family dining table. When Leona is happy and things are running smoothly, he seems to stay dormant, making no appearances. But when she is sad, depressed, or disturbed, like she recently was when her young grandson died, Charlie appears to her, a caring and sympathetic presence, like a friend coming by to extend his sympathy.

Tex and Leona and the whole family accept Charlie. He is a part of their family now, and they all agree that life just wouldn't be the same without him!

The Landfill Murder

Sheriff's Deputy Woodie Howell, who lives in Coahoma, near Big Spring, told me an interesting story about a much publicized murder case that took place in that area a couple of years ago. Woodie participated in the investigation. He told me there was a married couple who lived out in the country near the Big Spring landfill. The man, who was in his late 30s, worked at the landfill. One morning about 3 a.m., after he and his wife, whose name was Betty, had argued all night, he'd had enough. He shot her in the head, dragged her body out to the landfill, and covered her up, knowing the next day some sixteen feet of refuse would be dumped on top of her. Then he waited a couple of days.

Finally, he called the sheriff's department to report his wife missing. (Enter: Woodie Howell.) The man, whose name was Donald, didn't appear to be too upset, leaving the general impression that his wife often "ran off to cool off after an argument." Howell decided to follow up on the case, and he went out to the landfill to visit the couple's home. The man seemed to be extremely nervous. Woodie asked if he could look around the house a bit. He noticed all the woman's clothes and underwear seemed to be there, or at least so much was there that she couldn't have taken much with her. Howell told me his experience through many such cases indicated that women who really wanted to leave usually took most, or all, of their clothing with them when they left.

Howell said he started watching the man and playing "mind games" with him. He finally figured that maybe he could catch him in a lie. Then Donald told the authorities that he'd gotten a postcard from his wife with a New Mexico postmark, probably to get the persistently inquisitive Howell off the case. Howell didn't believe Donald and told him that he believed he had actually driven to New Mexico one night, mailed a postcard to himself from a truck stop, and then told the deputy his wife was probably somewhere in New Mexico. The man's story just didn't ring true to the wise deputy, and he told the man as much. Finally, the man broke down and told Howell he had come home from work at the landfill and found his wife dead. Afraid he would be accused, he took her out and buried her in the landfill. When Howell also refused to accept that story and continued to badger him, Donald finally confessed to killing his wife. He took Howell to the approximate location in the landfill where he had dumped her body. Howell said it took a crew of men all day, working in 106 degree temperatures, to locate the badly decomposed remains.

Later, searches into the house turned up some unusual and interesting items. There were all sorts of books and pamphlets on demons and Satanic worship. Howell believes maybe the couple had been delving into these practices.

The perceptive deputy has been told, since the bizarre murder and subsequent trial, that there seems to be "something creepy going on out there." No one wants to live in the house where the murder took place. Howell thinks it might possibly be haunted.

The murderer is now serving a seventy-year sentence for throwing his wife out with the trash.

She Had a Grandma After All!

On a trip to Wichita Falls, I met a very attractive brunette named Bonnie Lane. She and her husband and daughter attended a book review I gave at the Kemp Public Library there. After my talk, she came up and told me she had an interesting experience with the spirit world when she was just a small child, and it was still as vivid to her as it had been then. I was very pleased she chose to share her very special story with me.

As a little girl, Bonnie had been extremely sheltered by a loving but strict mother. She was never told anything about ghosts, or goblins, or any of the scary tales kids hear around Halloween. Her mother didn't want her to be afraid of those things, so they were never mentioned. She really didn't know a thing about ghosts at all. She said she was always "overly protected."

At the time of her experience, she was probably no more than six or seven years old. It was a hot summer day, and her mother always made her take naps in the summertime. It really wasn't what she wanted to do, but she had no choice in the matter. This particular summer day, her mother came and lay down on the big bed beside her, just to make sure she really would go to sleep! Soon, her mother rolled over on her side, with her back toward Bonnie, and fell sound asleep. Bonnie was restless, not at all sleepy, and rather sad that day. She'd heard some of her little playmates talking about getting ready to go visit their grandmas and what fun they anticipated in going to see their grandparents. Bonnie had no grandmother. It made her sad to think she would never experience the joy of visiting a grandmother like her friends.

As she lay awake thinking about this, she suddenly looked up and saw the figure of a lovely lady looking down at her. She looked to be floating, not on the floor, but a little higher up. She had on a long, pale-blue and white "floaty" sort of gown, rather like a peignoir, and although the figure was rather misty in appearance, Bonnie could still make out the features. She had big blue eyes, very straight, even teeth, and a loving, sweet smile. Her hair was dark and curly, and she appeared to be of middle age. Her arms were in front of her, her hands loosely clasped together. Bonnie just stared at her. She wasn't frightened at all, because the lady was so pretty and was smiling at her. She called to her mother to wake up and "look at the pretty lady." Her mother just shushed her and told her to be quiet and go to sleep. She didn't turn around to look, or perhaps she would have seen the apparition, too.

In just a few moments the figure seemed to waiver and ripple, with a shimmering motion, and then was completely gone. Bonnie was just sure this lovely lady had to be her grandma!

When her mother finally woke up, Bonnie told her what she had seen, and at first her mother didn't believe her. But finally, after hearing such an exact description of her own mother, she agreed to go and look up some old photographs she had put away in a trunk. She found one of her mother, taken just a short time before she passed away. She was forty-five years old at the time. As she gazed at the photo, Bonnie said there were the same big blue eyes, the wavy, dark hair, and the straight, even teeth. She later learned her grandmother had worn dentures, so of course her teeth would have been perfectly even. And her mother told

Bonnie later that her grandmother had been laid to rest in a lovely pale-blue and white peignoir and gown set. And of course, her arms had been folded in front of her.

Bonnie says she can vividly recall the figure she saw that day. It was as if it came to say, "I am the spirit of your grandmother. Don't be sad, Bonnie. You do have a grandmother who loves you and will always be near you in spirit."

Bonnie also revealed that, according to her mother, her grandmother had been a very psychic individual. She held seances, read cards and tea leaves, and believed in spirituality. And somehow, for just a few fleeting moments, she was able to "visit" with her little granddaughter and convey her love to her.

The Haunted Teddy Bear

When I visited Wichita Falls in the fall of 1994 to review one of my books, I met some wonderful people. The librarian, Gene Mathews, as part of a Halloween project, had asked some of her "regulars" to call and give any ghostly experiences that they might have had to her. She knew I was contemplating doing a book about West Texas and thought this might be of help to me. It was!

Mathews herself even admitted she'd had an experience with the supernatural. When her grandmother was terminally ill, she kept saying she needed to go upstairs. But there was only one floor in the house! She had, however, once lived in a two-story house. Shortly after the lady died, at least nine people heard her footsteps, which were easily identified, because she had to wear a special shoe, on the roof of the house. The family thinks she was looking for the second story of her old home.

A Mrs. Helms, who lives in Jack County, northwest of Fort Worth, called to say that her father had told her that somewhere in Jack County a rancher shot and killed a man whom he thought was a threat to his family. Evidently, the rancher was eating his dinner when the man rode up, just seeking directions. Shooting first, before thinking, the rancher killed the man, and for years afterwards, the ghost of the rider kept coming to the ranch shouting out "Hello! Hello!" trying to raise up the family so he could find a place to spend the night!

Perhaps the strangest story Mathews collected for me was called in by Melinda Rails, who resides in Archer City, a small town south of Wichita Falls. She had moved into her mother's house to live with her mother who was very ill at the time. The house evidently had several resident spirits, because Melinda said when her young daughter invited a friend to sleep over one night, the young visitor was actually physically moved to the other side of the bed!

Then there was the time Melinda's sister came for a visit in 1965. She actually saw the ghost of a woman with long silvery-blonde hair in the house.

And stranger still, a teddy bear in the house was haunted, too. At night in the darkness, its eyes would suddenly start flashing like coals of fire!

CHAPTER 10

FOUR-LEGGED PHANTOMS

A Word About Phantom Animals

Some say animals have no souls,
So when they are dead they are gone.
And then there are stories we've been told
That say they still live on.

Most people say that animals have no souls, and therefore it would be impossible for them to come back in phantom form. I don't know. How can anyone know this for sure? I know there are those of us who hope they have souls, because when we lose a beloved, devoted pet, it is hard enough. But to think that is it…the end, finis, is even harder to bear. And so there are those of us who wonder, what does happen after death to our animal friends?

The fact that many ghost stories have been told, over the years, about animals—dogs, cats, cattle, horses, etc.—by numerous people, indicates that someone, somewhere, believes that there are such things as animal ghosts and hauntings.

I saw something one night, soon after the death of my beloved little terrier, whose name was Lady, that I still can't explain. I may have been dreaming, but it was so realistic, I don't think I was. I believe I was awakened by her rearing up on the side of my bed as she often did, to be petted. Her eyes, as dogs eyes do, glowed in the dark, and I saw her very plainly. This was just for a few moments, but it was so disturbing I did not sleep again that night. After having that experience, which I cannot explain, I don't doubt experiences concerning animals that have been shared with me.

Lois McCullough, who lives in the Big Bend area, near Terlingua, wrote to tell me she had seen ghosts of rabbits when she lived in Tuscon, Arizona. She said the family raised angoras, and it seemed always near kindling (birthing) time she would see them. She said they varied in size, then added, considering that animals are mammals, maybe the idea is not too absurd.

The Story of Stampede Mesa

It's never taken a whole lot to spook cattle—lightening…a sudden yell…a clap of thunder. Even a tumbleweed tossing and blowing over the prairies can stir the animals into a frenzy. They are creatures easily agitated.

Long ago, when the great cattle drives spread over the western part of the state as they headed towards the railheads in Kansas, a legend was born. You see, there's this mesa up in Crosby County that is special. An extension of the Caprock, it gradually leads down to good water across a small neck of land. Or climbing, the slope broadens to green grassland, good grazing that runs right to the edge of a sheer cliff.

I first learned of the legendary mesa in a story written by the late Ed Syres for his book *Ghost Stories of Texas*. A friend of mine, Mary Elizabeth Sue Goldman, also mentions the mesa in her book *A Trail Rider's Guide to Texas*. Located somewhere out there on private ranch property today, it's not far from Kalgary, on a county road that runs to Post, southeast of Crosbyton. The mesa is near the canyon of the White River, or Blanco Canyon, but it's hard to find, as so many low hills and mesas seem to run together.

The story goes that late in the last century a group of drovers were herding their cattle up the trails to market. They stopped for the night on the grassy mesa. Just before they settled in for the night a "nester," or farmer, approached the cattlemen. He was driving a few pitifully poor-looking steers. He drove his motley herd right into the big herd, which seemed pretty strange to the trail boss of the big outfit. He figured the nester hoped to add to his herd a few head of cattle from the big herd that was bedding down for the night. The trail boss told the newcomer he could stay the night, bedding his cows down with the larger herd, and they'd help him cut out his livestock come morning light. This wasn't what the nester wanted, of course. He wanted to keep on moving, with a few extra cattle picked up as he crossed through the larger herd.

During the night a terrible blind stampede came from out of nowhere! The cattle made frenzied dashes toward the edge of the cliff and many dropped into the blackness of the waiting abyss. Two of the drovers and their mounts met that terrible fate as well. One cowhand told the trail boss that he thought he'd seen their visitor waving and

shouting to stir up the cattle, thus causing the stampede with its resulting loss of life to man and beast alike. So angered was he at hearing
this, the trail boss ran the nester down, had him tied to his saddle, blind-
folded his horse, and drove the terrified animal and his cargo over the
cliff onto the jagged rocks below.

Shortly after this tragic incident, strange sightings began.

Gina Augustini, state editor of the *Lubbock Avalanche Journal*,
wrote a feature story that ran on Sunday, October 30, 1994. She described the strange events up in Crosby County that led to the strange
mesa being christened Stampede Mesa. Augustini had this to say:

> Folks around Crosby County don't seem to share the tale
> over campfires anymore. But a time once existed when the
> mere mention of Stampede Mesa brought a chill to the tired
> bones of cowpokes, young and old, camped around a blazing
> fire on a murky night.
>
> Herdsmen in the area claimed their cattle would spook
> without reason and stampede in the direction of the mesa's
> edge. They also reported seeing a phantom horseman, who
> looked as if he'd been gagged and tied to his horse, floating
> among a herd of cattle spirits.

It's a story that has passed down through several generations of
cowboys. Of course, by the early 1900s the cattle drives north were
over, as the railroads had reached West Texas by then. Now it's largely
a story told at Halloween to the little cowpokes as they gather around a
campfire to roast weiners and marshmallows. It always brings forth that
sudden little shiver that only a good ghost story can produce.

The Sacred White Buffalo

I was interested recently to read in the paper, and to see on television, that a rare white buffalo calf had been born, and that many native
American tribes were very elated over this unusual event. You see, to
many, the white buffalo is considered a sacred animal.

In a short story written for the *Amarillo Globe News* on May 31,
1971, staff writer George Turner wrote:

> A beautiful basin on the Tule Ranch, between Tulia and
> Silverton, was long held in superstitious veneration by the

Plains tribes. No Kiowa or Comanche would venture near the place for fear of being trampled to death by a herd of ghostly horses.

The herd, consisting of about 1,450 horses and mules, was slaughtered at the site on September 29, 1874, by order of General Ranald S. Mackenzie of the 4th U.S. Cavalry. They had been captured on the previous day from Kiowa-Comanche forces in the Battle of Palo Duro Canyon. Mackenzie deemed the drastic action necessary to prevent the Indians from night-stampeding and recapturing them.

For many years the long western slope of the basin was piled deep with bleached bones. Eventually they were carted away by a fertilizer company. Today nothing is visible on the surface, but a bit of scratching will uncover teeth and small bones.

About twenty-two years ago I was there during a light spring rain and was astonished to observe that, as the surface silt washed away, the hill seemed almost to glow with an eerie whiteness. Teeth and osseous fragments were so numerous as to change completely the appearance of the area.

That night I slept on the ground near the old ranch head-quarters at the foot of the slope. At dawn I dreamed of the fabled ghost herd and imagined the rumble of horses' hooves. The sound increased in fury and I awoke...and realized that a herd of horses was thundering past only a few feet from where I lay.

When the mind is fogged by sleep it will accept almost anything, even the most fantastic of superstitions, as fact. My feelings, before realization came that the ranch horses had just been run out to pasture, can only be imagined.

And then, Turner continues:

If the Indians were horrified by the slaughter of their beloved horses, they were outraged by the even more wanton destruction of the bison herds by the white men.

Kiowa legends insist that the spirits of millions of buffalo reside in a vast cave within the Caprock and that there will be a day of reckoning when the white populace will be crushed beneath their hooves. Leading them, according to the medicine men of a hundred years ago, will be a giant white bison bull.

Stone Calf, a leading war chief of the Kiowa, believed that he would live to see the return of the gigantic herd. Before his death, however, the sacred white bison had become lost in the bowels of the earth and the white men had escaped their just punishment.

The Phantom Deer

Woodie Howell, a sheriff's deputy and a resident of the small town of Coahoma, has some interesting stories to tell about things that go "bump in the night" in that part of the state. He says many of his rancher friends out in the county that is his territory have had some pretty strange experiences.

There's a man who swore Howell to secrecy, so Woodie wouldn't divulge the man's name to me, but he did tell me the story that the man had told him. He said the man was a friend, someone he could trust to tell the truth, and so he believed him. He'd had the same strange experience for three different years in a row. He told Howell he just had to tell somebody what he'd seen, because it was bothering him so much.

It seems that the fellow had been out in the country when he'd seen this great big white-tailed buck, with a real trophy rack, just standing there like a sitting duck, in a field. The animal had eyes that seemed to glow like big red hot coals burning, and when the man shot it (and this happened three different times) it did not die.

Either this was a dandy decoy set up by the game wardens to catch poachers (I've heard they do such things) or as Woodie's acquaintance seems to think, it's a genuine "ghost deer" that continues, year after year, to look after his territory!

Tales of Two Stallions

The Black Stallion

This story comes from the collection of the late Clarice Rountree of Big Spring, who tells about a legendary haunted ranch a short distance from Wichita Falls. Rountree had this to say:

Diana Mitchell, a young drama major at Midwestern University in Wichita Falls, knows about a ranch that belongs to a young man who is a friend of hers. He asked her not to use his name. It seems every male in line to inherit this ranch has died a violent death. The first recording of a violent death was the young man's grandfather on his father's side of the family. He died in a barn fire, and no cause for the fire was ever found. The ghost of the grandfather resides in an upstairs bedroom, where the man died and was "laid out after death." Today the ghost is said to stay mainly in this one room. The door to the room is always locked; the family has the key to the door but it will not open it. The only time the door opens is when the ghost comes out of the room. The lights come on at night in this room, and from the hall you can see the shadow of a rocking chair moving next to the window. When everyone leaves, the ghost turns on all the lights in the house. They say that all the doors are locked, but still the lights are all turned on.

During a seance which Diana attended, a number of unusual things occurred. There were sounds from the kitchen and no one was there. One of the participants at the seance tried to open a closet door, and the knob turned itself in his hand. During the seance a wind blew out the candles, although all doors and windows were closed. A few moments after the candles were extinguished, the lights came on, and the boy found a note by his hand, signed by "Susan," telling him to leave the house before it was too late. No one knew who Susan was, but they decided she was apparently a relative from the "beyond." The handwriting was compared to the handwriting of each person present, and it matched none of the samples. During this seance the grandfather's voice was heard telling the young man to leave before it was too late. The door to the "death room" opened, but when the young man and a friend ran upstairs to see why the door opened, they saw the door close. It closed itself and was again locked to outsiders.

The second actual recording of a violent death of the heir was the young man's father. He was thrown by his favorite horse, which he rode every evening. First he was thrown, then the black stallion turned on the man, fatally injuring him. Again there was no apparent reason, for the horse had always been the man's friend. The ghost of the father is believed to inhabit the barn now.

Many mysterious events are connected with the horse and the saddle which was being used by the man at the time of his death. The horse, locked in a stall which is padlocked every night, disappears during the night and returns the next morning, lathered and hot and with the bridle on. Sometimes the horse has been found locked in the stall in this condition. It has been speculated that during his nightly disappearances he visits the grave of his owner, which is on the ranch property.

There is mystery surrounding the special show saddle that was used on the horse when his owner rode him. This saddle is kept locked in the tack room. Nearly every morning the saddle is gone from this locked room and can always be found in the same exact spot where the man was thrown and killed. No one knows how this saddle can be removed from this room.

Today, the young man has moved from the ranch and lives in Wichita Falls. He still has the black stallion, and it is exercised in a small corral and returned to the stall each day. The ranch hands make no attempt to catch or ride this animal as he has "gone crazy" and will let no one close to him, not even the men who have worked there for years.

Rountree concluded her story thusly:

Everyone who has ever had any connection with this family and the seances believes in these ghosts and fears for the young man's life if he should ever move back to the ranch.

Now, isn't that some story? I don't know in what year Mrs. Rountree wrote it, but I know it must have been at least a decade ago. I wonder if the black stallion is still alive, or if he is now grazing in the green pastures of eternity.

The White Stallion

Dr. Kenneth Davis, retired professor of English at Texas Tech University, shared this delightful story with me. He says according to legend, some seventy or eighty years ago a man who owned a big ranch out between Benjamin and Knox City, which is about 120 miles east of Lubbock, possessed a fine saddle horse, a white stallion he valued highly. During his final illness he requested the horse be brought to his funeral. Then afterwards, it was to be turned out to pasture and was never to be bridled or saddled again. Soon after the requests were made, the man died, and his orders were carried out to the letter.

Many young people, who seem to gravitate toward an area where there's a country road and a big cotton field today, a favorite "lover's lane" area, have reported seeing a ghostly white horse, cavorting and running over the moonlit fields, in the very place where he was given his freedom so many years ago by a loving and thoughtful master!

CHAPTER 11

LEGENDS THAT LINGER

Legends That Will Not Die

Along with many documented stories included in this book there are a few well-known legends that should be included. They are largely regional, known just around a certain town, or county, or section of West Texas. Others are more generally known, such as the first story in this chapter, the story of La Llorona, who is known all over Texas, Mexico, and New Mexico.

Since legends are largely stories that are handed down by word of mouth, generation to generation, some of them have subtle changes as they are altered in the telling. Yet, because of central themes, they are recognizable to the reader.

It seems many of these legends are especially well-known and often repeated within the Hispanic communities of our state. Whether it is because this group is more sensitive to such things or whether they just enjoy good stories of strange things, I cannot say. But some of these stories, which will be revealed in this chapter, are what makes Texas unique. Ours is a very diverse culture. Many ethnic groups came together in the settling and development of our state. It is no small wonder that even our ghost stories would be more interesting because of this diversification!

As defined in *Webster's New World Dictionary*, a legend is "a story or body of stories handed down for generations and popularly believed to have a historical basis." As you read the stories which I have painstakingly collected for you over the length and breadth of far West Texas, it is up to you to decide whether they are based in historical fact or just the figment of some very active imaginations!

La Llorona

No collection of Texas ghost legends would be complete without at least a brief mention of La Llorona, the "weeping woman." In another of my books, *Ghosts Along the Texas Coast*, I gave her a lot of coverage, noting her many appearances in the Rio Grande valley, in Laredo, Goliad, and San Antonio. She evidently gets around, because lots of stories have come to me from El Paso, Wichita Falls, and numerous other places in West Texas. They know all about her in the neighboring state of New Mexico, too!

The legendary spirit seems to be most often seen or heard by Hispanics, and most of them believe she truly exists. I have spoken with several very credible people who claim they have actually seen her.

My favorite account of who La Llorona is came via a story I read in the October 1983 edition of *Texas Highways Magazine*. The author, Jane Simon Ammeson, is a Corpus Christi psychologist. She described La Llorona thusly:

> Stories of beautiful women who have been wronged are many. Supposedly, their ghosts walk at night, searching for justice. La Llorona, the Weeping Woman, can be seen walking along several Texas rivers. She is the ghost of Luisa, a beautiful peasant girl who was courted by the wealthy, aristocratic Don Muno Montes Claro. When his family refused to allow him to marry Luisa, Don Muno bought her a little house. For six years he lived a "double life," spending his days tending his estates and family business and his nights with Luisa. They had three children and were happy, until one evening Don Muno didn't come to the little house.
>
> Luisa waited that night and many more before summoning up the courage to walk to the big mansion where Don Muno lived. She begged to see Don Muno, but a servant told her it was impossible. Don Muno was getting married to a wealthy woman of his own class. Luisa ran from the house, but not before seeing her lover and his new wife as they made their way from the church. In a frenzy, she rushed home and murdered her children, throwing their bodies into the river.
>
> She was taken to jail and died there, crazed, calling for the little ones she had killed. On the day she died, Don Muno, in his fancy house with his new wife, mysteriously died also.
>
> Some say that Luisa was freed from jail after killing her children and that she lived a carefree and abandoned life (instead of dying in jail). When she died and went to heaven, Saint Peter asked her where her children were. Shamefaced, she looked away from him. Her children were in the river, she replied, so Saint Peter sent her back to search, endlessly, for her lost little ones. Even now, people warn their children to stay

away from the river because La Llorona may be there, just waiting to drag them under, sending them to the same fate she sent her own offspring.

Marc Simmons, a columnist with the *El Paso Times*, wrote an interesting article about La Llorona in a story he called "Ghostly Woman Described," which ran on June 10, 1979. Simmons stated that he had heard many sober-minded adults, both of Anglo and Hispanic backgrounds, tell about actual personal encounters they had had with the legendary lady. He went on to say:

> Many scholars believe the origins of the Wailing Woman can be traced back to the Aztecs. Those Indians had a goddess named Tonantzin who snatched babies from their cradles and then roamed through the streets of the Aztec town, shrieking and weeping.
>
> But the fact is, the peasants of Spain, far back in the Middle Ages, knew all about La Llorona, so she was a figure in Spanish mythology long before contact was made with the Aztecs. There's even a similar character in Japanese folklore. So it is evident that the tale of a sorrowing mother who haunts the streets is known to many people of the world.

A well-known Texas folklore authority, Dr. John O. West, a professor of English at the University of Texas at El Paso, sent me a report that two former students of his submitted in December 1975 that contains some accounts of sightings of La Llorona in El Paso. The writers, Sheila Stopani and Harriet Sturgeon, interviewed an elderly woman who was then living in Anthony, Texas. She was about seventy-eight years old at that time. The woman had this to say:

> One time when I was walking along the river at Anthony, I heard her. She was dressed in a white transparent gown and was floating across the water. Her cry was like a thin wail. I was frightened; therefore I began to run and have not seen her since that time, but I have heard many of my friends who have seen her and heard her. They describe her the same as I do.

The same two students also interviewed a young lady, a student at the university, who was nineteen years old at the time of the interview. She related what an uncle had told her:

My uncle works for the city, surveying land in different areas of El Paso, and it so happens that on a particular early morning in August, he was working in the southern part of El Paso called the second ward, when he experienced an unbelievable phenomenon. He was strolling by the canal or ditch that runs through the second ward and through the housing areas. It was 4:30 a.m. He heard someone sobbing. He recognized the voice to be that of a woman. He couldn't find her but just heard her cry and plead for the children. He heard her words asking for her babies, saying, "Where are my babies... I want my babies!" He cried out, "Where are you? Can I help you?"

Afterwards, he gave up and met his fellow workmen. He explained to them about the incident, and they stared at him in disbelief. One of the workmen said that according to a factual story, a woman's ghost or spirit is said to be walking the edge of the ditch or canal. She walks by and cries for her children whom she killed by drowning them. Afterwards, she committed suicide. She was seen by other people wearing a black Spanish dress with a mantilla. She is called La Llorona, the "crying woman."

The Tuesday, October 31, 1978, edition of the *El Paso Times* featured a number of stories in honor of Halloween. The writer, Ed Kimble, had a similar story to tell, about a young woman down in Chihuahua City:

When the Hotel Victoria in Chihuahua City was new, there was a certain cleaning woman employed there who was particularly pretty and especially polite. Because she was so charming she made lots of money in tips.

A few years after she began working there, a distinguished gentleman from Mexico City came on business to Chihuahua City and stayed at the Victoria Hotel. His family had come from Spain and he was supposed to have noble blood.

From the very first moment he saw the pretty chambermaid, he was in love with her. He courted her affections and soon persuaded her to live with him in his suite, promising to marry her when the right time came.

The right time seemed to never come, and finally the gentleman moved back to Mexico City, supposedly to take care of business. By that time the young woman was pregnant, and so the businessman wrote her letters frequently and enclosed money with every one.

She worked at the Victoria until she had to stop to have her baby. Having to care for her child, she could no longer work, and she was more dependent than ever on the money her lover sent her, and more anxious than ever for his return. But a few months after the child was born, the letters and the money stopped.

Destitute, she made the trip to Mexico City and went to the house where the man lived. There she discovered that he was already married and had seven children. Enraged, she returned to Chihuahua City and murdered the little baby.

She confessed her crime to her priest, telling him at the time she killed the infant she had been glad, and had not just repented.

Soon after, she went insane and began wandering the streets of Chihuahua, calling "Niño, niño, venga a su mama" ... "Baby, baby, come to your mother."

Finally, the woman, now haggard and filthy, was found dead on a side street. But the crying in the night continued, and some claim to hear it to this very day. Sometimes it is heard on the roof of the Victoria Hotel, where the lovers used to meet in secret.

This version of La Llorona closely resembles the first story I quoted, with the central theme being an illicit love affair with the participants being of widely diverse social castes. And the conclusion was more or less the same ... rejection, tragedy, and finally, repentance for her deeds.

In Wichita Falls La Llorona is known as well. The Spanish-speaking people there, according to some acquaintances in that city, believe her to be the ghost of a young woman who drowned her children for love of a soldier who rejected her. Then she drowned herself. She is said to have made numerous appearances at the old Burnett Street bridge in Wichita Falls.

The wraith seems to appear differently at different times to different people! Sometimes she is dressed all in white flowing robes and is very beautiful. Then, she has been reported to be garbed all in black and her face has been variously described as skeletal, hag-like, or sometimes resembling a donkey or a horse. Her fingernails have been described as long and shining, like silvery knives. Just thinking about her is enough to cause little children to have bad dreams!

Whether La Llorona actually exists or is a figment of many overworked, vivid imaginations, she is very much a part of Texas folklore. And if nothing else, her legend teaches a lesson to those who would listen: "Women: Don't be exploited by men of wealth." And to mothers, "Don't be cruel to your children or you will live to regret it." And to the little children, "Stay near your mama. Don't go near the water."

> *From the depths of the river, the sad mournful cry*
> *Of La Llorona is heard, to those who pass by.*
> *But no one can save her, forever she's there,*
> *Luring her victims, her sorrow to share.*
> *Keep your children away from the rivers and streams*
> *Don't let them be lured by her sorrowful screams.*
> *She's waiting to claim your child for her own...*
> *So hurry away. Leave La Llorona alone!*

The Lady of the Lake

Abilene boasts a legendary female ghost that is said to hang out on, or near, Lake Fort Phantom Hill. There are several versions of why she's there and who she might be. They can't all be true, of course, so Abilene residents have a choice of what they choose to believe. Whatever brought the phantom lady here, most all who claim to have seen the wraith agree she is young and beautiful and is capable of walking over the waters of the lake. She sort of floats, or glides, along the surface of the lake and is surrounded by a faintly glowing mist. Some say the color of this mist is blue, while others who have seen her say she appears in a glow of red. Many people who claim to have seen the strange phantom say she's wearing a white dress, or robe, and is carrying some kind of lantern in her hand.

One popular tale says the Lady of the Lake is a young woman drowned in the lake by her lover after a terrible quarrel. She's spending her time searching for her murderer among the couples who park along the banks of the lake to make out, and she has frightened the living daylights out of quite a few of them!

Another oft-told story says the young woman was sent into eternal shock because she was left at the altar by a bridegroom who didn't show. A search was launched for the errant groom and he was found lying in a boat in the middle of the lake, wearing his wedding tuxedo. He was dead, his eyes staring out with a contorted expression of horror covering his countenance. The phantom bride, still dressed in her wedding gown, is searching the lake for her lost sweetheart.

There's another story around that goes way back to when the lake wasn't even there. Near the vicinity of where the lake now is, there was a couple living on a small plot of land they were homesteading. This was during the days of Indian raids. The settler told his wife when he was away from the house out working in the fields she was never, never to let anybody in unless they knew the agreed-upon secret password. Well, the man went out to gather firewood and was attacked by Indians. He broke and ran for the house, frantically beating on the door for his wife to let him in. In his haste to escape the pursuing savages he forget to call out the password. His wife thought he was an Indian and shot him as he forced the door open. She went into shock over her terrible mistake and now must wander the area forever, searching for the soul of her lost husband.

Some Abilene people think it might be interesting to try to call up the phantom woman, and they say it can actually be done. One must go out to the old Fort Phantom Hill cemetery, which is located near the lake and not very far from the ruins of old Fort Phantom Hill. You must go there on three consecutive nights. On the third night, you must remain silent for exactly sixty-two minutes. At that moment the ghost is supposed to appear and walk among the tombstones. She often carries a lantern. She is also said to have been seen walking around the ruins of Fort Phantom Hill.

Lake Fort Phantom Hill is a very beautiful recreational area. But I wouldn't want to go swimming there. You see, they say the phantom is a vengeful spirit. When there's a drowning at the lake, she is often blamed for causing the mishap, and the Abilene natives often say, "Well, the Lady has taken another one."

Phantom Hill Cemetery

The Legend of San Felipe

There is a delightful legend well known in the area around Del Rio. Although there are several versions, the one most often told is this especially lovely version which appeared in the 1921-22 edition of the Del Rio High School yearbook, the *Guajia*. It was authored by Lee Woods, Class of 1922, and sent to me by Val Verde County librarian Barbara Hamby:

There was a time when no white man had seen this part of Texas, and the only settlers were the primitive Mexican Indian peoples, who inhabited a small thatch-roofed pueblo near the hill known to us as Round Mountain.

On this hill up to the nineteenth century stood a large wooden cross, probably planted there by the Franciscan friar from far Quertero. Tradition says that at the placing of this cross, happy brown-skinned maidens of that far-off time gathered to scatter the wild flowers of their clime at its foot, and the hill became known among their people as "La Loma de la Cruz." Standing aloof, as if fearing to reveal its many untold secrets, La Loma de la Cruz ever watches Del Rio by night and by day while the silent stream at its side glides slowly down from the springs in the hillside to the slopes beyond.

Such were the nights, when evening after evening found Felipe and Dolores wending their way from the pueblo of La Loma de la Cruz among the shadows of the stream to keep their lovers' tryst at the distant springs.

Thus, the days drifted into weeks, and the weeks into months. Felipe and Dolores continued meeting and going to the spring on the nights when the moon was at its best.

On a bewitching July night at the full of the moon, Dolores went to the usual place to meet Felipe for their accustomed walk to the spring. Felipe was not there. The stars twinkled brightly in the sky; an occasional flutter announced the presence of birds gone to roost, the cool air was intoxicating, and Dolores was happy, for surely Felipe would come!

Time passed. Dolores grew impatient and started on towards the spring, for surely, she thought, Felipe must be there! An entrancing night it was, and the moon shone in all its glory. But Dolores was restless and hurried on. As she walked, it seemed the stream, the trees, and the hushed wind were keeping something from her. The deep silence was unbearable, and her anxiety for Felipe increased more and more. Many times had she traveled that distance before, but never had the way appeared so long.

At last Dolores reached the spring, and as she neared the low bank she was conscious of a feeling of dreaded calamity. The surface of the deep and naturally quiet spring appeared disturbed. Intently she gazed into the blue depths before her, and there, as she looked, she saw Felipe, her lover, slowly but surely sink from sight. She saw him carried away by the silent underground stream of the mystic, fathomless spring.

Heartbroken, Dolores returned to her home. The story of Felipe's tragic death was never known, yet it was whispered down the years how each eve a brown-skinned maiden on La Loma de la Cruz bowed in prayer and longed for her lover.

How a bent old woman there beneath the cross called "Felipe, O Felipe!" And whispered, too, in the hush of nightfall is the rumor that on every July night of the full moon, when nature displays all of her charms most vividly and pleasingly, when the wind sighs in the trees in mellow sadness, when the stream puts forth its best efforts in scarcely heard semimusical tones that swell and die on the night air, the sorrowful spirit of Dolores walks about the deep spring, crying always, "Felipe, O Felipe!"

The lifelong passionate prayers of Dolores were answered. Felipe's name was listed among the saints; and the springs, the stream, and the little pueblo near La Loma de la Cruz were christened San Felipe.

In time, as the town of San Felipe grew and reached the dignity of a post office, it became known as San Felipe Del Rio, which was finally abbreviated to Del Rio, because of another and earlier recognized Texas town bearing the name of San Felipe. Yet, in the old town, in the springs, and in the stream, the name San Felipe still lives, and with it the memory of one of the prettiest legends known.

San Felipe Springs, Del Rio

Francesca, Where Are You?

The late J. Frank Dobie edited a book, *Legends of Texas*, a publication of the Texas Folklore Society, in 1964. In that publication I first read the story of Francesca. Then later on, while visiting in Fort Stockton, I also had occasion to hear the story verbally from some old-time Hispanic residents. The gist of the story, which is often related by ranchers and members of the Hispanic community, is there was once a beautiful young woman named Francesca, who lived near the old fort. She was young and very lovely. Many eligible men sought to win her affections, but her heart was set on only one, a man named Ferenor. He was the nephew of the parish priest who served the small community of settlers and soldiers. He'd already begun to study for the priesthood himself and had taken his initial vows.

But the beauty of the lovely Francesca was just too much of a temptation for Ferenor to bear, and so he announced to his uncle, the priest, that he wished to leave the priesthood and marry her. One night he took the girl to visit his uncle, and the couple announced they wanted him to marry them. The old padre refused, of course, since it is impossible and totally illegal in the eyes of the Catholic Church for a priest to marry. Although they begged and pleaded with him, he adamantly refused and finally ordered them to leave his house. There was a fierce storm blowing, and the hour was very late. En route to Francesca's home the couple got lost in the blinding storm, and they wandered for hours in the darkness and freezing cold.

Finally Francesca became so exhausted she could no longer move. At least, that's how the story goes. She dropped to the ground, totally spent. About that time, Ferenor saw a light in the far distance. He told her to stay right there. He would follow the light and summon help.

Although he started walking in the direction of the light, he could seem to get no closer. The light seemed to always be moving farther and farther away from him. He too was exhausted and numb with cold. Finally, he turned back, going to where he thought he had left Francesca. He could not find her, and as he wandered, searching for her, he fell in the darkness, hitting his head on a rock. He was knocked unconscious and did not awaken until nearly dawn, when he again began to search for the girl. Although he searched and searched and called out for her, he never found his sweetheart. It was later rumored that Indians had found her and taken her captive.

It is said that at certain times of the year on very stormy nights, the winds still call out "Francesca...oh, Francesssssca" as the spirit of Ferenor comes once again to seek his lost love. Folks around Fort Stockton say if a lover hears the sounds, it means either he, or his betrothed, is in grave danger. This might be a good reason to remain indoors on stormy cold West Texas nights!

Disappearing Hitchhikers

Legends of hitchhiker ghosts seem to be pretty prevalent all over the country, and West Texas has its share of them.

According to the *Sul Ross Skyline*, October 27, 1994, edition, writer Lisa Kay Hart says there are at least two varieties of hitchhiker ghosts known to exist in the Alpine area. There's the "woman in white" story. This young woman appears in a white or very light pastel dress and always disappears when approached.

An old man said to be wearing a large Mexican sombrero and a serape flung over his shoulder has been observed by the roadside by many people. He frequents the areas just outside the towns of Alpine, Marathon, and Sanderson along Highway 90. No one has ever seen his face, and when they turn their car around after passing him as he stands by the roadside, he disappears. He is usually seen at the outskirts of towns, and who, or what, he is, is not known.

An acquaintance from Balmorhea, Patty Towler, said she'd heard stories of a "red-eyed woman who is supposed to jump in the back seat of your car as it travels through a certain area around Saragosa," but that's about all she could tell me. That was enough! I plan to stay away from that area in the future!

I was told a most unusual story by Maria Nunez, of Midland, about her uncle and aunt, who live in Fort Stockton. I was able to talk to her uncle, and the elderly gentleman, described by his niece as "an honorable man, much respected as a church leader, and certainly not a person to exaggerate or make up stories," filled me in on the details. He did ask that I not use his real name, and I agreed.

The man told me that several years ago his wife had undergone surgery in Odessa, and he had been at the hospital in that city all day, visiting her. After dark, he left to drive back home to Fort Stockton, traveling by way of Highway 1053. He was driving along through flat country in his pickup truck when he came to the big bridge that crosses the Pecos just north of the town of Imperial. Suddenly he felt the most penetrating cold in the truck, and at the same time was overcome by an almost overwhelming fear. He felt the presence of someone, or something, on the truck seat beside him. He could see nothing in the darkness but said he felt so much fear he didn't know whether to speed up or just take his chances and jump out of the truck! He said nothing before, or since, has ever caused him to be so frightened.

He finally drove into the small town of Imperial and pulled over to the side of the road where there were bright street lights. Convinced he was alone in the truck, he settled down and gained the courage to continue on his journey back to Fort Stockton. But as soon as he reached the outskirts of Imperial, where the road was again plunged into darkness, he once again felt the bone-chilling cold and the same unexplainable fear as he once more felt a strange presence in the vehicle with him. He finally arrived home and, after he gained the sanctuary of his dwelling, was able to calm down. He said he left all the lights on in the house, but even then was unable to sleep very much that night. He said he prayed most of the night, as he felt the presence might have been some evil thing. Why else would he have been so terrified?

When he went out to check his truck the next morning, the strange presence he had felt was no longer there.

The gentleman's wife told me that over the years there have been many stories told about the figure of a lady being seen beside the highway at just about the spot where her husband first felt the fearful presence. Drivers reported seeing her, but when they turned around to go back and offer her a ride, she disappeared. Also, a number of bad accidents have occurred in that vicinity, with cars running off the road for no explainable reason. Some people say it is the spirit of a young woman who was killed along that highway. Others have said that a pioneer woman is buried near the river crossing, and it is her spirit that roams the highway.

The Legend of the Witch's Gate

People who have lived around Wichita Falls for very long know all about the Witch's Gate. Actually, it's just a piece of isolated land out between Wichita Falls and the tiny community of Jolly. There have been frightening tales associated with the area for years, and they always seem to surface around Halloween. The former owner, a not-too-loveable woman, is said to still hang around the land, even though she has been dead a long while. She is supposed to lie in wait for trespassers, tracking them down with a pack of vicious bloodhounds!

Now if that isn't enough to make one's blood curdle, it's said that people that drive down the narrow road often have a sudden change of heart and want to get away. As they turn around and get near the entrance, they find a mysterious gate has appeared out of nowhere and now blocks their way, trapping them!

Now, doesn't that make a great little story for All Hallow's Eve? The forbidding gate is supposedly an optical illusion. And in spite of the fact nobody can come forth and actually say they've seen the witch and her hounds, it still holds a lot of fascination, especially for the teen-aged crowd. A different version surfaces every once in a while. One story concerns a headless apparition who drives around on a tractor (which is suitable for that farm country) and has a horrible fate in store for the unwary traveler.

Witch's Gate sounds a little like "snipe hunting" to me. When I was a teenager, some poor "nerd" type would be led out on a dark night to a dense, gloomy wooded area, or a cemetery or such and be told to hold the sack while others beat the bushes and scared this wonderful, exotic bird called a snipe into running into the bag. It was supposed to be a big honor for the unsuspecting victim. Of course, the others would make a big noise and then run off, leaving the poor unfortunate out in the darkness to find his way home the best way he could. I wonder if anybody ever got left behind around the Witch's Gate? If they did, they might have ended up in Dr. White's sanitarium, the insane asylum conveniently located in nearby Wichita Falls.

The Ghosts at Buie Park

Up in the Big Country area, near Abilene, there's a small town named Stamford. Near that community, there's a brushy, overgrown park on Farm to Market Road 1226 about five miles south of the town, which is known as Buie Park. The old park harbors two well-known ghosts of the area, and the legendary spirits are known as the Hatchet Lady and May's Mother. Whether they haunt the wooded park area simultaneously, or whether they take turns, I'm not certain. But according to an article by Kathy Sanders that ran in the *Abilene Reporter News* on October 30, 1985, they are well known around Stamford.

The Hatchet Lady's story is, years ago, when the park was still a well-kept beautiful spot, a young woman from Stamford was engaged to be married. Shortly before the wedding was to take place, her fiance took her out to Buie Park, and there in that remote setting he broke the news to her that he really didn't want to get married after all. The young woman was shocked...hurt...crushed by this disclosure. In her distraught state she refused to accept her fiance's decision, and in a moment of unreasonable rage and heartbreak she killed him with a hatchet. (No one has been able to explain how a young woman, supposedly out for a tryst, could have so conveniently been supplied with such a deadly weapon!)

Anyhow, the story goes that, hatchet in hand, the spirit of the young woman still returns to stalk the park, preying on amorous couples. I guess she figures if she couldn't be happy, why should anyone else be? She is a vindictive spirit, apparently.

The other ghost that roams Buie Park is the pathetic spirit of a broken-hearted mother. Years ago, according to the legend, a woman had a little girl, about ten years old, named May, who had been playing in the park by the riverside when she disappeared. She was never seen again. Everyone believed she drowned in the river. The grieving mother looked and looked for her daughter until she finally lost her mind. Now dead herself, she still is said to return, wandering all over the park crying for her lost child. Many people claim they have heard her sad and mournful cries... "May, oh May...May...May...."

Strange Spirits at Christoval

John Boon, who is editor of the *Toenail Tribune* at Christoval, a small community of around 520 people in Tom Green County, says there are a number of ghost legends known in that area. When I asked John how the town got that unusual name, he said he believed it was a name formed from the name of an early settler, Christopher Columbus Doty, using the first two syllables of his given name, Christopher, and then adding the first part of the Spanish name for valley, "valle." And some people say it was just named Christ's Valley.

There are a number of ghost stories connected with the place. John told me there's a hill near the town that is called "five mile hill." It has been the scene of many accidents over the years. A slash was cut through the hill for the highway to go through, and a number of people have reported seeing a family consisting of a man, his wife, and two children, a boy and a girl, dressed in old-fashioned settler's clothing, walking along the side of the road. When motorists slow down, the whole group always disappears! This is the town, also, where Charles Dennis saw the Indian family as he delivered his paper route, which I wrote about in Chapter Three.

According to John, several people have also claimed to have seen the ghostly figure of an Indian standing up on the hill. Then he suddenly disappears. This is probably the same warrior that Dennis told me about.

Boon told me there are also legends that seem to circulate in that vicinity about a ghost lady whose children drowned in a flood of the South Concho River. She always wears white and has been seen searching and crying along the banks of the river. I believe she may be yet another version of La Llorona.

The Booger Man

Now here's one for the books! This is a great fright legend to tell the children when you are trying to get them settled down for the night. I will guarantee you won't hear a peep out of them all night!

English professor Ira Blanton at Sul Ross University in Alpine sent me this story from his files. The old booger man of the Booger Y Ranch over in the Monahans sandhill area is a well-known personality. The ranch hands and workers have all reported seeing him at one time or another, and he's apparently a pretty awesome sight. The booger man is often seen, or so they say, by cowboys as he goes about quenching his thirst.

Now, the booger man doesn't drink his milk from a bottle. No siree. He's been seen drinking milk straight from the cows on the range—no mean feat, since cows have been known to kick! And they say he needs a lot of milk to survive, because once somebody slit his throat from ear to ear and most of the milk he consumes escapes from the gaping wound, along with a lot of his own blood. He must be a terribly hideous sight, with all that bloody milk oozing from his open throat!

The milk-drinking ghoul is said to lean forward in a completely horizontal position so his head would be facing straight up. Now each time a cowboy would ride in and try to rope him, he'd jump a seven-foot fence and run off like a whitetail buck, heading for the sandhills! They say he can outrun any pursuer. Nobody has been able to get a lariat around him yet. If you have a thirty-foot rope, he'll stay thirty-one feet ahead of you; if your rope is twenty-five feet long, he'll outdistance you by twenty-six feet, etc. They say it's an awesome sight, chasing that old booger man with his head lolling back between his shoulders and looking upside down at you, square in the eye every step of the way!

Well, that's the legend. All those cowboys in the Monahans area know it well. Personally, I think the cowboys who tell that tale have been drinking something a whole lot stronger than milk!

The Devilish Dancer

In numerous places in the state there are legends that have become accepted as fact. Many are variations on the same theme. I have heard several versions of a story centering around a devilishly handsome stranger. Either the stranger moved around a lot, slightly changing his modus operandi as he shifted location, or else there are some very active imaginations here in the state of Texas. Since I first heard the story in San Antonio where I reside, I have heard the same theme, with variations, all over West Texas. I wasn't surprised to find another version from out El Paso way, which placed the man in a Juarez bar, just across the Rio Grande. Now, just recently, an acquaintance in Balmorhea sent me a story of what REALLY happened in that far West

Texas community! Each story centers around a handsome stranger who could really dance, giving all the young ladies reason enough to want to attract his attention.

Twice the *San Antonio Express News* ran stories about an event that is supposed to have taken place at the old El Camaroncito Night Club located at 411 Old Highway 90 West. The place is now closed. But on that night, Halloween of 1975, there was a big dance going on.

A big crowd had gathered that night. Lots of couples were out to enjoy life and have a party. There were a lot of pretty ladies there and the place was really jumping. The band played some mighty rhythmic conjunto music, rancheritas, polkas, and one good cumbia after another. Everybody was having a ball!

Then, in walked a stranger. He was a handsome Latino wearing a white vested suit, complete with lots of gold jewelry, and a black shirt, worn "open chested" style. He was plenty "macho," as the ladies later described him. One of the women who supposedly was there that night was quoted in the *Express* article as saying "He was the most handsome man I have ever seen. I noticed him right away. He was just the type of man you can't take your eyes off of...." The woman, whose name is Rosa Garcia, said, "And could he dance! He never got tired. He danced with several of the women. And it's funny, you know, because I don't remember him ever sitting down at a table. He wasn't with a woman...he was just everywhere." And did Rosa Garcia dance with him? "Oh yes, indeed I did, and I wish I could have danced with him all night long. We danced a couple of cumbias and he danced circles around me. Now and then he would grab the hem of my chiffon dress and swing his arm with it. Just his touching my dress was like he was touching me. I can still remember the chills going up and down my back," she said. "He had some kind of power."

Finally he asked a young beauty who was rather aloof if she would like to dance. Soon he had her on her feet and they began to sway to the music. She soon became almost entranced as they moved over the floor. The unsuspecting woman rested her cheek on his shoulder. They swayed...their feet were still.

Then, something really strange happened. For a moment the enchanted woman broke out of her almost hypnotic trance and she glanced to the floor. "Your feet...your feet!" she screamed, and tore herself from the tight embrace of her partner. Dancers on the floor stood frozen as she shouted and struggled to free herself from the man's clutches.

Then, the other women began to scream, too, and some started mumbling prayers. Two ladies actually fainted! Then, the men, less frightened but still not wishing to approach the man, grabbed their partners and retreated to their tables or backed up against the walls.

But their eyes never left the well-dressed man's feet, which had been dancing away in fashionable Stacy Adams shoes. Now, in horror, they watched the shoes disappear, and four long-nailed stubs stuck out from each of his trouser cuffs.

They were chicken feet! This was a sure sign of the devil!

After the commotion subsided, the shoeless stranger ambled off towards the men's room. Rogebo Cruz and three of his friends chased after the man. But Cruz remembers that only a cloud of smoke and the strong smell of sulfur remained in the men's room. The window was shattered where the stranger had made a hasty exit. (Everyone knows the devil prefers the smell of sulfur to the fragrance of Old Spice!)

The devilish stranger never came back to El Camaroncito, but the story goes that he also made a surprise visit to the Rockin' M Club over in Lockhart back in the 1970s.

In El Paso a similar story is told about a handsome stranger who liked to frequent the bars in Juarez just across the Rio Grande. It seems at one time the bars there were required to close very early, which didn't please either the bar owners or their patrons.

According to an article by staff writer Ed Kimble, that ran in the October 31, 1978, edition of the *El Paso Times*, the devil himself paid a visit to one of those bars!

One night, as one of the bar owners was visiting with some patrons, he told the men who were drinking there not to leave at regular closing time. He said if the police came, he would take care of everything. Well, suddenly, the music stopped, the lights went out, and strange and horrible noises were heard. Everybody was frightened! Then, through all the confusion a man started to dance upon the bar!

Now, just about everybody there was drunk. Some were so drunk they couldn't get up from their chairs and so they just stayed there, rooted to the spot. Those who could run, did. They got out of there, fast!

Those who were left started to sober up pretty fast. The man was really horrible to see because he had "fire eyes." He began to motion to the bar owner to come closer, but at first the frightened barkeep could not even move.

The dancing man continued to beckon him over to the bar, indicating that he had something to tell him. At last the owner moved over towards the man, and the dancer told him that if he would give him his soul he could have anything in the world that he wanted.

And that is when the bar owner sold his soul to the devil. Since that time, the bars close much later, and nobody knows the real reason why. The other bar owners bought licenses, but this man never bothered. He was never afraid to be caught by the police for not having a license.

The story goes that the bar owner didn't stay in Juarez long after that. He went down to Mexico City to get away from the questions that people asked him.

Dr. John O. West, professor of English at the University of Texas at El Paso, sent me a term paper that one of his students had submitted. West, who is a well-known authority on Texas folklore, thought I might enjoy a couple of El Paso based stories about the handsome dancer, with slight variations on the theme. The paper, written by Mary Scott in December of 1964 states:

> Another interest area of the folklore in El Paso is the story of the girl who dances with the devil. About thirty years ago the following story was told among the Mexicans in El Paso. (Note: this would have been around 1934.)

> "I was in grammar school, probably, when I heard this. Down on Alameda there was a nightclub where they had dances on the second floor of a building. There was this girl...she loved to dance. This night her mother said she couldn't go. Then, this girl, who was mad at her mother, went anyway. At the dance she said, "Not even the devil takes me to dance!""

> "Then a guy, a real handsome one, came in and asked her to dance. He asked her to go out to the car and talk. He might ask her for a date or something. She said she would go."

> "When they got out there the guy scratched her! (The informant showed with her hands that the girl had been horribly scratched on the face.) When they were out there she looked down at his feet. They had turned to rooster feet, and his hands, too! And she had said that about the devil, and he

scratched her. They found her like that...her face was
scratched. They say he was the devil, but I don't know."

Scott went on to say that she had heard a similar thing happened at
the Carousel Night Club in El Paso the early 1960s. A few details were
different. The girl didn't go outside with the man, but the lights in the
club went off suddenly, and while they were off the devil scratched her.
She died a day later.

Mary Scott wrote, in the report she submitted to Dr. West, "In none
of the other stories I heard about did the dancing girl die. In all the tales
but one the girl was scratched. In one story the man's feet turned to
horse's hooves. In another, centered around Pyote, a disobedient girl
was kidnapped by the dancing devil and was never seen again."

Some information sent to me by Pat Towler of Balmorhea indicates
there was some excitement in that place not too many years ago, at a
street dance. It was fiesta time and everybody in town was there dancing and having a good time. The mariachis played louder and louder
with each dance. As the pace increased, some of the younger people
there started begging the musicians to play "La Murca" while the older
people shouted, "No!" The old folks didn't like La Murca very much
because it has suggestive lyrics, and people dancing to the piece seem
to get a bit carried away with its furious beat.

But the young folks prevailed, and soon the musicians were playing the tune, not once, but over and over again.

Just when things were really jumping, a tall, dark, very handsome
stranger suddenly appeared in the middle of the dance floor. He was so
good-looking every young woman was enthralled.

He didn't just have good looks, either. He was a terrific dancer, and
every single one of the young ladies took her turn as his partner, each
one enamored by the handsome stranger.

Now, all the people had gathered around the dance floor. Some
were standing and some were sitting on wooden benches around the
perimeter of the floor. Most of them were shouting and clapping their
hands if they weren't actually dancing. Only a few old diehards sat and
frowned, refusing to get caught up in the frenzy of excitement the
music had inspired.

One woman was watching the dancers. Her little boy kept tugging
at her skirt to get her attention. Impatient, she told him to lie down
under the bench and go to sleep. He tried to do so, but the music was

so loud, and there was so much excitement, he couldn't possibly sleep. So, wide-eyed, from his vantage point beneath the bench, he watched the feet of the dancers.

And that is when he saw them. He screamed. And screamed again!

His mother became alarmed and dragged her little boy out from under the bench and hugged him. The child kept screaming, pointing at the handsome stranger. Then the music stopped. The dancers stopped their whirling around the dance floor.

Then everybody looked. And everybody saw. The stranger's feet had become the clawed talons of a giant rooster!

There was silence! Then the handsome stranger looked all around him, threw up his arms, turned into a blazing ball of fire, and disappeared!

Now we understand that the tune, "La Murca," hasn't been requested at any dances over in Balmorhea since that night.

The devilishly talented dancer with the handsome face and rooster feet is said to have been seen in numerous other Southwestern locales. My advice to all the young ladies would be:

"Beware the devil when you meet...
With handsome face, and rooster feet!"

The Ghosts of Transmountain Highway

In October of 1978 *El Paso Times* writer Ed Kimble did a series of stories in the Kaleidoscope section of that paper to commemorate Halloween. One of the most intriguing was the story of the ghosts who guard the Transmountain Highway that Kimble compiled from information given by Dr. Karen Ramirez, associate professor of linguistics at the University of Texas at El Paso, and a section of a 1971 term paper by Alan V. Embry for Dr. John O. West, a UTEP English professor who specializes in folklore.

The ghosts of the highway are considered to be the most dangerous ones around El Paso. That is because they seem to appear out of nowhere in the middle of the highway. There is usually just a man and his dog. Many a motorist has been caused to swerve off the dangerous stretch of road to avoid hitting them. At least, that's what they say!

There are two versions about the origin of the ghosts, which sort of places the whole tale in the realm of "legends."

One version states the Franciscan priests who built the Guadalupe Mission in Juarez in the mid-1600s also operated a gold mine somewhere in the Franklin Mountains. When the Manso Indians revolted near the end of the century, the Franciscans left, leaving only a single priest and his faithful dog behind to guard the mine.

Prior to the building of the Transmountain Highway, gold seekers out looking for the legendary mine reported that when they came close to the site of where the treasure is reputed to be located a large dog would come running after them ready to attack. Other miners reported seeing the figure of the priest himself!

Soon after the highway was opened in the late 1960s, several drivers were involved in automobile accidents on the curved, four-lane highway because they said they had swerved to miss a man in a long, flowing robe and his dog, who were standing right in the middle of the road.

The other version that has been bandied about for a while says the ghost is the spirit of a Texas Ranger who chased a group of outlaws into the mountains and was killed by them. He often chased bandits into a particular canyon, and once trapping them, was able to force them to surrender. But one time he didn't succeed, and now he is re-enacting his unsuccessful chase, much to the chagrin of unwary motorists!

The Ghost Who Loved the Ladies

According to a story that ran in the *Kaleidoscope* family section of the *El Paso Times* on October 31, 1978, there's a legendary ghost in the El Paso area that's a real ladies' man. The story, by Ed Kimble, a *Times* staff writer, is credited to Dr. Charles Sonnichson's article, "Mexican Spooks from El Paso," which was published in 1937 by the Texas Folklore Society in a collection which they titled *Straight Texas*.

The amorous ghost is said to hang out in the little town of San Elizario just south of El Paso on the banks of the Rio Grande. He inhabits a large, old, rambling adobe house, which according to Sonnichson, has pretty well gone to wrack and ruin. The adobe walls are crumbling and no paint has been added to the place in years.

Once the house, situated near a Catholic church, was considered quite a mansion. It was owned by Mauro Lujon, a local civic leader, who was considered quite a character even back in those early days. (Now, we know there was a Mauro Lujon who lived in San Elizario at one time. A census of the Valley area for the year 1841 lists a Mauro Lujon, then two years of age. We have to presume it is the same man who owned the adobe.)

The place was often the scene of much political activity. Meetings took place there between plotting politicians. It was a house of intrigue, and during the bloody disturbance known as the "Salt War," in 1877 the place became headquarters for the mob of rebels.

After Don Mauro died, the house was inhabited by numerous families. His ghost appeared to one couple, Alejo and Maria de Ramirez, who were renting the place. To them, the spirit revealed the location of a cache of money. The spirit asked the couple to use the funds to have masses said for his soul. They found the coins but did not carry out Don Mauro's wishes. The greedy pair took the money and moved across the Rio Grande to the Mexican side and set up a grocery business with the money. They got their just desserts for not keeping their promise to Don Mauro's spirit. Their grocery store was not a success and Maria soon died.

Then an elderly couple named Mr. and Mrs. Maciel moved into the house. They knew little or nothing about the original owner, Don Mauro. Antonio Maciel had a job that kept him working till very late at night, so his wife, Bonifacia, had to retire each night alone. Finally the elderly woman went to see her friend, Dona Tomasa Giron, and told her a very strange story.

"Every night," she said, "I go to bed by myself, because my husband is working and comes home late. And every night the ghost of an old man with a long, white beard comes and gets into bed with me. When my husband comes home and wishes to go to sleep, he has to say 'con su permiso' (with your permission) before the old man will let him get into bed."

"Hmmm," said Dona Tomasa, "does he get out of bed when your husband gets in?"

"Oh, no! He just moves over."

"It sounds like Don Mauro," remarked Dona Thomasa, thoughtfully, as her mind traveled back over Don Mauro's record. "He used to be fond of the ladies," she added, "era muy enamorado."

"Y todavia es," said Bonifacia de Maciel, looking very wise. "Y todavia es. Me hace carinos." (He still is. He caresses me.)

If the old house is now deserted and crumbling into ruin, as Dr. Sonnichson's article indicated, Don Mauro's ghost must be pretty frustrated, with nobody left there with whom he can climb into bed!

The Empty Room

Dr. John O. West compiled and edited a fascinating anthology of Mexican-American folklore stories as a part of the *American Folklore Series*. One of the stories the UTEP professor situates in the El Paso area was most fascinating to me.

This story, which circulates largely in the El Paso area, concerns the Bishop of Durango, Mexico, when he was a very young priest. It seems that late one night three men came to his door and knocked. He was asked to come quickly, for a young woman lay dying and had need of the services of a priest. They gave him good directions and went on their way. He quickly dressed and assembled the equipment for the rites he needed to minister to the woman, and hastened to the house, which he found at the end of a long and winding road. No one came to meet him as he came up on the porch, so he opened the unlocked door and went on into the house. There was a long hall, with a dim light at the end, and he made his way in that direction. There he found a girl on the bed, writhing in pain and crying out for a priest. He calmed her as best he could, heard her confession, gave her absolution, administered the last rites, and tried to comfort her. He promised he would return to see her the next morning.

When dawn came he once again made the trip to the home of the girl. He couldn't believe what he saw! The yard was overgrown with weeds, the house was just about to fall down, and when he stepped up on the porch he nearly fell through the rotting floorboards. He pushed the door open and walked into a place that looked as if it had been deserted for many years. He went to the end of the hallway he had entered the night before. The room where the girl had been was still there, but only a rusty bed with bare springs was in the room. There was no sign of his, or anyone else, having been there just the night before. He was thoroughly puzzled. He went to a neighboring house and asked the people for some information about their neighbors, but nobody knew a thing, until a very old lady came into the room. She told the priest about a young girl who had died in that house, calling in vain for a priest to come to her. But, the lady said, that was over fifty years ago!

Who, the priest wondered, were the three men who had come to summon him in the night? Were they ghosts, too? For surely the young woman was a ghost. Somehow, some way, her unanswered cries for help had finally been answered by that young priest. We hope her soul is finally at peace.

Epilogue

Even as this manuscript goes to the publisher, the stories keep coming in. No doubt, I have missed some good ones. I do believe that many interesting, well-documented accounts of hauntings have been presented in this work. A few good legends were also included in the final chapter. I hope that you've experienced a few good shivers while reading the stories included in this collection!

THEY ARE THERE

If you look for them, you'll find them
In the darkening of the night.
If you listen, you will hear them,
Even though they're out of sight.
If you stand still, you will feel them
For they bring forth a sudden chill.
In all their poignant stories
You can feel their presence still.

Docia Schultz Williams

Sources

NEWSPAPERS
Abilene Reporter News
Oct. 9, 1969; Oct. 29, 1978; Oct. 28, 1983; Oct. 29, 1983;
Oct. 29, 1985; Oct. 31, 1985; Oct. 3, 1993
Amarillo Globe News
Jan. 7, 1965; May 31, 1971
Big Spring Herald
Oct. 31, 1993
El Paso Herald Post
Aug. 3, 1978
El Paso Times
Oct. 31, 1978; June 10, 1979
Fort Worth Star Telegram
Oct. 29, 1989
Lubbock Avalanche Journal
Oct. 30, 1994
Plainview Daily Herald
March 12, 1993
San Angelo Standard Times
May 3, 1968; Jan. 20, 1980; June 8, 1989; Oct. 29, 1989
San Antonio Express News
March 14, 1993
Sul Ross Skyline
Oct. 27, 1994
Wichita Falls Times Record-News
Jan. 9, 1983

MAGAZINES AND PAMPHLETS
Abilenean Magazine
Vol. 4, No. 2, Summer 1974
San Angelo Magazine
October 1984

257

Texas Highways
Oct. 1979; March 1985; May 1993
Manual for Museum Guides
Resource Manual 1985, Fort Concho National Historic Landmark
Guidepost Magazine
Nov. 1994

STORIES

"The Legend of San Felipe," Lee Woods, from the 1921-22 edition of
The Guajia, Del Rio High School Yearbook
"Legends and Historical Facts about Round Mountain," Mrs.
Elizabeth S. Daughtery and Mrs. Thomas H. Seale, for Val Verde
Historical Commission
"A Rainbow Thread," by Mary Scott, December 1964
"Strange Things in the Night," by Sheila Stopani and Harriet Sturgeon,
December 1975
"A Study of Spirits," by Clarice Rountree
"The Black Stallion," by Clarice Rountree
"Mexican Spooks from El Paso" by Dr. Charles Sonnichson

BOOKS

Ghost Stories of Texas, by the late Ed Syres, Texian Press, Waco, 1981
How Come It's Called That? Place Names in the Big Bend Country, by
Virginia Madison and Hallie Stillwell, Revised edition, self published,
1988
Ghosts Along the Texas Coast, by Docia Schultz Williams, Republic of
Texas Press, 1995
The Big Bend Country of Texas, by Virginia Madison, Revised edition,
October House, Inc., New York, 1968
A Trail Rider's Guide to Texas, by Mary Elizabeth Sue Goldman,
Republic of Texas Press, 1993
Unsolved Texas Mysteries, by Wallace O. Chariton, C.F. Eckhardt, and
Kevin R. Young, Wordware Publishing, Inc., 1991
Castle Gap and the Pecos Frontier, by Patrick Dearen, Texas Christian
University Press, 1988
Mexican American Folklore, by Dr. John O. West, August House, Little
Rock, 1988
Memory Fever, a Journey Beyond El Paso Del Norte, by Ray Gonzalez,
Broken Moon Press, Seattle, 1993

Legends of Texas, edited by J. Frank Dobie, Publication of Texas Folklore Society, 1964

Straight Texas, edited by J. Frank Dobie, Publication of the Texas Folklore Society, Number XIII, 1937

PERSONAL INTERVIEWS

I wish to especially thank the following individuals who shared information in the form of personal and telephone interviews and through correspondence:

Steve Balog, former Deputy U.S. Marshal, Pecos
Martha Beimer, Ballinger
Andrew Beneze, Channel 11, Fort Worth
Leona Billington, Petrolia
Ira Blanton, Professor of English, Sul Ross University, Alpine
Janet Bonner, U.S. Attorney, Midland
John Boon, Editor, *Toenail Tribune*, Christoval
Jo Ann Bowers, Plainview
Kimberly Bradley, Fort Forth
Marsha Brown, Fort Worth
Jayne Catrett, Manager, Baker Property, Mineral Wells
Charlie Coleman, Sterling City
Marylou Collard, Bangs
Pete and Georgia Cook, Fort Clark Springs
Roxanna Cummings, Owner, Lamplighter Inn, Floydada
Dr. Kenneth Davis, retired Professor of English, Texas Tech, Lubbock
Cres Delagarza, San Angelo
Maria Delagarza, San Antonio
Charles Dennis, San Angelo
Barbara Doop, Fort Worth
Vivano Garcia, Ranger-guide, Fort Leaton State Historical Park
Jerry Gladys, Fort Worth
Dolores Gross, El Paso Community Foundation, El Paso
Luciana Guajardo, Special Collection, Laredo Public Library
Mark Hancock, Owner, "Miss Molly's," Fort Worth
Mrs. Glenn Harris, Stillwell Ranch, Marathon
Barbara Harrison, Ballinger
Phil Hamilton, Writer, *Plainview Daily Herald*
Cindy Hawkins, Librarian, *Amarillo Globe News*
Woodie Howell, Deputy Sheriff, Coahoma

Bill Ivey, Owner, Trading Post, Terlingua
Mason Johnson, (deceased) taped interview with Terry Smith, Professor Emeritus, Texas Wesleyan University, Fort Worth
John Klingemann, student, Sul Ross University, Alpine
Jim Lane, Attorney, City Councilman, Fort Worth
Richard Lott, Staff, Gage Hotel, Marathon
Helen Matthieson, Paint Rock
Margaret Maxwell, Mineral Wells
Heather Melton, Lubbock
Leslie "Joe" Moore Sr., Wichita Falls
Lois McCullough, Terlingua
Barbara Niemann, San Antonio
Sam and Nancy Nesmith, San Antonio
Mark Pair, Professor of Music, Wayland Baptist University, Plainview
Brian Perkins, Owner, Barber's Bookstore, Fort Worth
Joe Peters Sr., and Joe Peters Jr., Peters Bros. Hattery, Fort Worth
Joshua Rangel, student, Sul Ross University, Alpine
Betty Regester, former Curator, Log Cabin Village, Fort Worth
Winona Rinehart, Spur
Roy Roberts, Granite Shoals
Pam Robinson, San Angelo
Allen Russell, Staff, Gage Hotel, Marathon
Denis Russell, Fort Worth
O.T. Ryan, Plainview
Robert Salgado, Lajitas
Rick Scordo, Manager, Smokey Toes Island Grill, Fort Worth
Joyce Sikes, Owner, Texas Grill, Ballinger
Terry Smith, El Dorado Productions, Fort Worth
Hallie Stillwell, Stillwell Ranch, Marathon
Bill Stephens, General Manager, Gage Hotel, Marathon
Jesus "Chuy" Tercero, Staff, Gage Hotel, Marathon
Dale Terry, Wichita Falls
Doy Terry, Wichita Falls
Velma Turner, Sterling City
Maxine and George Turner, Sterling City
Bobette Vroon, Fort Worth
Carolina and Arturo White, Terlingua
Russell and Joy Williams, Fort Clark Springs

LEADS
I am also extremely grateful to the following individuals who referred me to persons willing to share their ghost stories with me:

Billie Mae Avis, Henrietta; Helen Dieker, Fort Worth; Steve and Bonnie Gallant, San Antonio; Peggy Garrett, Abilene; Floyd "Twister" Geery, Fort Bliss Museum, El Paso; Lois McCullough, Terlingua; Mitzi McKinney, San Angelo; Leon C. Metz, El Paso; Peggy Montgomery, Henrietta; Maria Nunez, Midland; Melinda Rails, Archer City; Jamison Reed, San Antonio (formerly of Midland); Richard T. Room, Historic Fort Stockton; Gus Sanchez, Big Bend National Park; Bernie and Susie Shaffer, San Angelo; Rick Smith, Columnist, *San Angelo Standard Times*; Vickie Stone, Fort Stockton; Pat Towler, Balmorhea; Mrs. Warren Walker, Lubbock; Mrs. Morton Ware, Fort Worth

PHOTOGRAPHS
All photographs taken by Roy and Docia Williams with the exception of the Ostrander House ("Mysterious Mansion on the Plains"), courtesy of the *Abilene Reporter News*, Glenn Dromgoole, editor; and the photographs of the Lamplighter Inn, Floydada, and the Hotel Turkey, Turkey, supplied through the courtesy of the hotel owners.

Index